Wavecrossed

by Andrea Colt

Tiffany,
Never give up
on your dreams!
♥ Andrea Colt

Other books by Andrea Colt:

Torched

Wavecrossed

Summary: To Cassandra Kelleher, trust is a dirty word. A teenage selkie who grew up on land, all she wants is to save her family from the man who stole their sealskins. Battling broken friendships and alarming romantic entanglements, she finds that trust may be the key to winning her family's freedom ... or losing her own.

ISBN 978-1-939108-03-6

First Edition

For Winston

Chapter 1

Midnight is the perfect time to eat a turtle.

Submerged in an icy river, I focused briefly on the thought, then let it go. My brother should be close enough to hear, and it would make him come running, so to speak. Mentally, I grinned.

My lungs craved air, so I flicked my hind flippers to propel me upwards. As my head broke the surface, I spun to scan both sides of the forested shore. No human faces peered back in the moonlight, but I pivoted in the water to check again as I sucked in a breath. Not that a nighttime fisherman would see anything odder than a seal poking her nose out of a coastal Maine river—which wasn't a totally crazy sight, though most seals kept to saltwater—but it wasn't random humans I was worried about. It was the other kind, the kind who knew what I was. The lying-in-wait kind.

But if anyone lurked in the shadows, I couldn't see them. Or, I noted as I drew another breath, smell them. So I was safe. Probably.

Letting my muscles relax, I lifted my nose further into the

air so the crisp breeze could ruffle my whiskers. I spun in the water again, this time for fun. Despite the danger, I loved these nights, these escapes. For a while I could lose myself in motion and instinct, forget the problems waiting for me ashore. Here, I didn't have to pretend to be a normal teenage girl, didn't have to smother my anger and growing desperation. Here, weightless in the river, the world felt *right.* For a moment, at least.

The water around me shifted, and my brother surfaced two feet away. The seal version of my twin was darker than my dappled cloud coloring; he was gunmetal spotted with shadow, his eyes round wells of midnight as he huffed out a breath.

Cass, you can't eat turtles. Outrage tinged Brennan's thought. *What would Nicky say?*

Nicky was the snapping turtle Brennan had found injured in a pond when we were in middle school. He'd taken him home and kept him in the basement bathtub for a week until his leg healed. Now whenever we met a snapping turtle, Brennan claimed it was Nicky's uncle, or grandmother, or sister-in-law.

Nicky can't talk, so he wouldn't say anything. I dove, abandoning the moonlit surface. Water pressed against my fur and skin; from below came the faint clicks and rustlings of crayfish scuttling over rocks. The bottom of the river beckoned, a fascinating murky dark, and as always a part of me wanted to paint it. But if I tried, the result would look like a squid threw up on canvas—oils could never capture the life and motion of an inky midnight river.

In any case, I didn't paint anymore. Not even in human

form. I'd won schoolwide awards for it freshman year, but now I wouldn't touch a brush for all the fish in the sea.

Brennan fell in beside me as I swam upstream.

Maybe turtles ***can*** *talk. Like we do.*

Mind-speaking reptiles? I snorted, bubbles betraying my mirth. I started to tell Brennan how ridiculous that was, then paused. Three years ago, when I thought I was just an ordinary high school freshman, I'd have called the idea of creatures like us ridiculous too.

They can't talk to ***us****,* I pointed out instead.

Brennan swam above me, a shadow against the pale surface, then butted my shoulder with his snout.

Well, in any case, selkies don't eat turtles. Weaving through the water, he sped on ahead.

I frowned. *Says who?* Not our parents, for sure. Trapped on land, they found the ways of our people too painful to talk about. And in the two and a half years since Brennan and I discovered the truth about ourselves, we'd never met another selkie.

Without opposable thumbs, how would they get through the shell? Brennan's logic floated back to me as he somersaulted through the water.

They could eat them while in human form. Turtle soup is a delicacy in France, right?

Gross. Brennan paused to nose under a submerged log. I surfaced for another breath, then ducked safely down before continuing upriver. My whiskers caught vibrations through the water: I sensed fish milling about below, tasty swimming morsels, but they'd get a pass tonight. It was late.

After another thirty seconds, I realized my brother had fallen behind. I twisted in the water, but moonlight only penetrated a few inches; I couldn't see him in the darkness. The river's weak current tugged at me, the flow undisturbed by another seal-sized body nearby.

I sent a thought out like a beacon: *Come on, Brennan, let's go home. Tomorrow's shift is going to suck even more if we don't get any sleep.* We were scheduled to work the Sunday brunch rush at The Golden Fish, our older brother Declan's restaurant. I'd rather roll in needles, but skipping wasn't an option.

In my mind, I heard a monumental sigh. Then, hardly more than a shudder of a thought:

What if we just left, tonight?

My stomach clenched. Whirling, I swam upstream without answering. Maybe Brennan hadn't meant me to hear, and didn't realize I had—sometimes the line between musing and directed thought was thin. Usually we laughed at apparent non sequiturs from stray thoughts, but this one wasn't funny.

Selkies belonged at sea. I knew that. And it wasn't that I didn't want to bid Granite Harbor, Maine, a thoroughly unfond farewell. Frankly, staying on land blew chunks. Big, slimy ones. It meant rules and bargains and danger, and being forced not to spit in faces that desperately deserved it.

But selkies couldn't become their true selves without their sealskins, and my parents and older brother were trapped apart from theirs, forced to stay ashore in human form. Until two-

and-a-half years ago Brennan and I had been trapped too; we hadn't even known of our true natures then, so we'd grown up like normal kids, or near enough.

Now that we knew the truth, and had our sealskins — a gift with a price I hated to think about — we should be at sea. It was unnatural for selkies to stay on land. But though Brennan and I were free, the rest of our family wasn't. I couldn't leave them behind, not without a fight, and despite his possibly-unintentional comment, I knew Brennan wouldn't either. If I looked back, he'd be following.

He'd better be following.

When I reached the stretch of bank where we'd left our clothes I finally turned to check, but no torpedo-shaped shadow darkened the water.

Brennan? I called mentally, but there was no response. My heart seized. ***Brennan?*** For an agonized second I thought he'd left us behind after all, but then there came a faint snap, as if of teeth.

Just let me eat this catfish, will you?

At my brother's happy distracted tone, relief surged in like the tide. Brennan was my twin, and my best friend. My only friend, if you wanted to split hairs; we couldn't trust any of our classmates with the truth about ourselves. Brennan still went to parties, but I found it next to impossible to socialize with classmates when my paranoid side branded the word THREAT invisibly on their foreheads. If any of them found out what we really were ... Disaster. So if Brennan ever did leave, I'd be alone in my fight.

But he was still here, and I exhaled a bit, bubbles trickling from my nose up to the surface. I let Brennan enjoy his fish; I'd make sure the shore was safe.

Edging toward the bank, I raised my head from the water and scanned the woods carefully. This was always the most dangerous part of our nighttime swims. What if someone had come across our haul-out spot while we were downstream? What if they'd found our clothes? What if they were waiting for Brennan and me to emerge and *change* back into human form so they could snatch our sealskins?

It wasn't so far-fetched a notion: after all, that's what happened to our parents.

I inhaled deeply, my nose sorting scents: tangy pine needles, rotting fall leaves, a faint trace of fox scat. Nothing human besides our own belongings. I counted silently to thirty, but heard nothing beyond the normal rustling of small birds. As far as I could tell, we were alone. Time to trudge back to my landlubber life.

Bracing myself, I started the *change*.

Bone-deep hurt stabbed everywhere, stretching and cracking and reshaping my limbs and flesh. When I was ten I'd broken an arm, and it felt like that—except all my bones at once, while sandpaper raked my skin. I kept going, and after an agonizing eleven seconds—Brennan and I had timed each other once—my form solidified into one with legs and arms and breasts and hair.

And, thank God, thumbs. I used my lovely thumbs and fingers to grasp my sealskin, now floating like a cape beside me. Still underwater, I wrapped it around my torso before kicking my legs to take me to shore. The shallows here were little more than a two-foot-wide submerged ledge between the deeper part of the river and the earthen bank. I pulled myself up onto the ledge and crouched on the slick rock, water lapping at my shoulders. Steadying myself with one hand on an adjacent boulder, I stood.

Heavy. That first moment out of the water always felt like being saddled with a backpack of granite. Though the thigh-deep water would turn a normal human's toes blue in twenty seconds—it was October, after all, and winter showed up early on Maine's doorstep—I stayed stock still. My gaze raked the shadowed underbrush for dangers I might have missed from the water, and my ears strained for the sound of a footstep. My muscles tensed, ready to hurl me back into the river, but the night remained quiet. All clear.

Bending over, I found two smooth river stones and rapped them four times against each other underwater—the signal to let Brennan know it was safe. Our mind-speech only worked in seal form. As I clambered onto the dirt bank, Brennan surfaced mid-river, whiskers gleaming white. Waving, I slipped behind a thick, squat fir tree and found my backpack, nestled among the branches close to the trunk. I pulled out my clothes, then reluctantly unwrapped myself.

Once I was dressed, my fingers lingered on my damp sealskin, this strange key to my secret self. Growing up, my sealskin—and I—had been another's possession, but it was mine now. *I* was mine now.

I'd never give that up again, not for anything.

To the untutored eye my sealskin looked like a dark, misshapen towel. The skin side was rough but supple, the reverse sleek and padded with guard hairs. There were no claws or a face or anything creepy like that, just an amorphous shape roughly twice as long as it was wide.

Home, I thought. My sealskin was home to me, more so than my bedroom in my parents' house, or even the ocean. Contact with my sealskin made me feel strong. Cleared my thoughts. I'd been anxious and tightly wound this afternoon, in a mood Brennan classily termed *megabitch*, but now that I'd had a good swim I felt steadier.

I folded my sealskin, smoothing down the guard hairs possessively. My whole freedom was tied up in this thing. It killed me to part from it, to stow it in one of a dozen hiding places we'd found in the area, but we couldn't take our sealskins back to the house. It wasn't safe.

Slipping my sealskin into my backpack, I returned to the riverbank. Was Brennan getting dressed? I heard nothing from behind the holly bush where he'd hidden his backpack of clothes, and the dirt beside the water was dry except for my damp footprints.

I peered into the depths just beyond the ledge.

"Come on, Brennan." The water would distort my voice, but Brennan would hear. How long did a catfish take to devour, anyway?

I inhaled, but my nose now caught only the overwhelming scent of pine. My senses were always sharper in seal form, except perhaps for touch. My human skin, without the guard hairs that covered my other self, was definitely more sensitive. And delicate—I'd nicked myself on a thorny bramble earlier, and I stretched out my hand to inspect it. The pad of my thumb, which had sported the wound, was pristine again. *Changing* healed little injuries, though it didn't, sadly, maintain things like manicures. I hadn't bothered to paint my nails in over a year.

A shadow in the river caught my eye. Finally. Brennan was … coming up too fast.

"Wait," I yelped, but before I could move Brennan exploded out of the river, leaping into the air right beside the ledge and flopping down again. The wave of wet hit me nearly full-on. Sputtering, I shrieked a curse as Brennan disappeared underwater. Surprise cannonballs had been my brother's signature move at the public pool when we were younger—his and every other boy's.

My twin surfaced ten feet offshore for my reaction. My jeans were drenched, my sweater half-soaked. Not that it really mattered—my long dark hair dripped down my back anyways—but getting mad was part of the fun. I stamped my foot and cupped my hands around my mouth.

"That's it—I'm making turtle soup out of Nicky's cousins!"

Brennan blew out his breath in what amounted to a seal laugh, then submerged. I hastily backed up, but when Brennan reappeared he only pulled himself onto the ledge. I settled on a tree stump to wring out my hair, averting my eyes while Brennan shifted forms and wrapped his sealskin around him.

"You wouldn't dare," Brennan said, out of breath from the *change*. It had only taken him seven seconds; I wasn't sure why he was faster than me. I rolled my eyes as he pushed himself upright. In human form my brother stood two inches taller than my five-foot-eight frame, his driftwood-colored hair lighter than my dark brown waves. But we shared the same blue eyes, and our mother's narrow nose. And, of course, our selkie genes.

Still grinning about his prank, Brennan jumped up onto the bank and headed for his holly bush to swap his sealskin for his clothes.

As I finished wringing out my hair, my thoughts returned to our trapped family. They were admittedly never far from my mind, but although swimming cleared my head and calmed my nerves, it always brought home exactly what our parents and older brother were being denied. We'd been trying for two years to get their sealskins back, but so far we'd failed. Sometimes it felt hopeless.

"What are we going to do, Brennan?" I said, my humor gone.

"About what?"

"About our parents." As if I could mean anything else.

"We're doing everything we can." His muffled voice was not nearly as urgent as I'd have liked.

"It's not enough." An understatement. Last week our latest

attempt to find the sealskins had gone belly up, just like all the rest. The fresh failure cut at me like the icy night breeze.

I heard a sigh. "Give it a rest, will you?"

My mouth went flat. A rest. That's all Brennan said lately. Remembering his possibly private thought, I wondered if he'd given up entirely, if he was just biding his time until I gave up too. Anger twined through my voice.

"They'll die here if we don't free them."

Brennan stepped out of the shadows and shouldered his backpack.

"Melodrama alert." Seeing my face, he hesitated. "Let's sleep on it, okay?"

I wanted to tear into him, but getting into an argument now wouldn't do any good. Taking a deep breath, I stood and twisted my hair into a bun, securing it with what looked like innocent hair sticks—knives, after all, weren't allowed in school.

"Okay." I jerked my lips into a smile and picked up my backpack. "There are sandwiches in the truck, right?" *Changing* took a boatload of energy, so we were always ravenous once we returned to land. Peanut butter was more filling than crayfish—and much easier to catch.

"Two for me, none for you," Brennan joked.

"Not if I get there first," I shot back. Falling into comforting, well-worn banter, we headed up the dark path to the truck.

We never did see the camcorder propped in the trees, watching us go.

Chapter 2

By noon on Sunday, I would have cut off my ears for another swim. The Golden Fish was pretty much the only classy place to brunch in Granite Harbor, so a hungry, impatient crush of tourists and regulars milled around the fish statue in the restaurant's dark-paneled lobby. Crowds made me twitchy.

So did entitled divas.

"Ma'am, I'm sorry, but it'll be about forty minutes," I said, dropping my apologetic smile for a steelier expression. There was always someone who hadn't bothered with a reservation but nevertheless thought they were too good to wait. Like this woman. I'd had to repeat myself twice already.

Too Good To Wait narrowed her gaze.

"Look, we're on a schedule. Can't you squeeze us in?"

As if the people who'd been waiting half an hour were less important than her plans? Biting back an unprofessional sigh, I was about to ask pointedly if she wanted to be put on the wait list when the restaurant's heavy outer doors opened and my skin erupted in a sudden, familiar burn, the strength of which could only mean one thing: Douglas Murphy had arrived.

I gritted my teeth. Other than goose bumps, my flesh looked no different than usual, but to me Mr. Murphy's presence stung like a rash, as if I'd dropped into a bathtub of jellyfish. It strengthened as he approached, and I willed myself not to flinch. To the world, Douglas Murphy was a lot of things: respected businessman, doting father, mayor of Granite Harbor.

To me, he was a monster.

He didn't look like one: six feet of hearty Maine outdoorsman, our mayor was known for plain talk and a strong handshake. His detractors called him controlling and stubborn, but in this town, he was king. Though sighed over by Granite Harbor's middle-aged ladies for his rugged blond looks, as far as I knew he'd never cheated on his wife.

And I would know; I'd been stalking him for the past two years.

I doubted that as a high schooler Mr. Murphy had been voted Most Likely To Enslave A Whole Family, but twenty-two years ago that's exactly what he did. Stole my parents' sealskins, then Declan's when he was born, then Brennan's and mine a few years later. All our sealskins, locked away somewhere in his house.

For fifteen years, this man had owned me. He'd eventually been persuaded to set Brennan and me free, but refused to give up the rest of my family. I had to make him. Somehow. In the meantime, I had to play nice.

But not too nice.

Faking a smile was impossible in any case—it was all I

could do to hold my ground and pretend Mr. Murphy didn't scare me. I didn't greet him; he didn't expect me to. "Four," he barked, and I noticed the three be-suited men trailing in his wake. My skin burned, and the urge to spit on Mr. Murphy's expensive blue tie battled with the instinct to scram, but I'd handled this situation a hundred times before. Mr. Murphy often took his business or political associates here—The Golden Fish was, after all, his restaurant.

Yes, he owned that too. Sometimes it felt like he owned everything.

Smiling politely through my clenched jaw, I picked up four leather-bound menus; we always kept a table open for him. Mr. Murphy walked just behind me on the way through the dining room, and my heart pounded erratically—the pulse of prey. Holding tight to my facade of indifferent courtesy, I waited for the men to sit down, then handed out menus.

Mr. Murphy waited to take his until, stomach turning, I raised my chin and issued a crisp, "Here you go, sir," the way I was supposed to. It was by his permission that Brennan and I lived with my parents, and if I didn't play by his rules, he'd have them kick us out. Since he owned their sealskins, they had no choice but to do as they were told.

"Thank you, Cassandra. And send Declan out, please." Mr. Murphy gave his signature warm smile. Could no one else see the poison underneath?

"Sure thing. Enjoy your meal." My tone made it clear that what I really meant was *choke on it, please*. Mr. Murphy glanced at me sharply and I pivoted towards the kitchen before he could respond. My tiny spike of victory at having gotten under his skin cheered me, hollow though it was.

With every inch of space I put between us breathing got easier, but my skin still prickled painfully, reacting to his presence even across the restaurant. I made sure I was out of sight before I rubbed my arms, trying futilely to rid myself of the sensation.

Ducking into the kitchen, where Brennan glumly washed dishes, I approached our older brother Declan. Part chef, part manager, in the past few years Declan had turned this restaurant from a struggling diner to the type of place Boston food critics traveled up to visit. He'd been cooking the family meals ever since he was old enough to reach the stove, and as soon as he was allowed into the work-study program at school he'd spent the majority of each day in The Golden Fish's kitchens. People called him a culinary genius.

But I remembered one evening about three years ago, when I was a freshman and he a senior. The whole town knew that once he graduated he'd take over as head chef at The Golden Fish and, bewildered by career day at school, I'd told him he was lucky to have a job he loved waiting for him after graduation.

Declan's expression had curdled.

Don't you see anything, Sandy? he'd said. *I hate cooking.*

I'd asked him what he meant, but he wouldn't explain. It wasn't until later, when I knew the truth about our family and what we were, that I understood.

"Declan," I said now, and my older brother's back stiffened.

His hair was light brown like Brennan's, but wavy like mine, and the same freckles dusted his cheeks. It made him look young. I supposed he *was* still young, only twenty-one; he just seemed old because of the weight that seemed slung around his shoulders. People thought it was responsibility, or a young father's maturity. I knew better.

"I'm busy, Cassandra." He didn't look at me as he garnished a plate of sugar-dusted French toast. "What do you want?"

My lips tightened. *I want you to stop telling me to abandon you. I want Mr. Murphy to drop dead. I want you to call me Sandy again.*

"Mr. Murphy asked for you," was all I said.

The change was instantaneous. I hated this part, hated seeing my brother's face grow animated at the summons. He didn't even respond before handing his plate off to another chef and striding from the kitchen. I used to be like that too, even saw Mr. Murphy as a second father. It was part of what happened to selkies when a human owned their sealskin; they became devoted to their captor. Stockholm Syndrome, sort of, but stronger. Before I knew what we were, I hadn't even thought it odd how we all jumped to obey the whims of Mr. Murphy and his family. Watching it now sickened me.

Declan had been the one to set Brennan and me free from that prison. He wanted us to go live our lives, the lives he'd won for us, at sea. We had, for a few months: the summer between freshman and sophomore year. Then we'd returned, pretending to Mr. Murphy and our parents that all we wanted was to finish high school before leaving for good. The truth, of course, was that we'd never be happy knowing Declan and our parents were stuck on land, eternal slaves.

Everything we'd tried in the last two years to free them had failed, but I'd get them out of here. I'd get us all out of here. Somehow.

Back in the lobby, Too Good To Wait greeted me with a smile.

"Wait list?" I asked pointedly, but she slipped her palm onto my podium.

"Can you see if you haven't overlooked a table for me?" She withdrew her hand, leaving behind a fifty-dollar bill.

Ugh. I stared at the money, wishing I could be one of those principled people who'd shove her bribe back in her face and tell her to wait her turn like the rest of the world. Unfortunately, integrity wasn't something I could afford. Brennan and I had to buy our own groceries, plus our clothes and sundries like shampoo and toothpaste and school supplies. It was one of Mr. Murphy's more annoying rules we had to follow to be permitted to live with our parents. Working for our keep, he claimed, would help us be more independent. In reality, he wanted to cut down on the amount of time and money we could spend trying to free our family.

Mr. Murphy was no fool.

So odious as this woman's bribe was, and odious as I'd be for taking it, we needed the cash. At her smug expression I almost refused it anyway, but then I caught sight of my brother at Mr. Murphy's table. Declan was beginning to be known as far away as New York for his culinary skills, and Mr. Murphy liked to trot him out to impress people.

I watched them for a moment, the king and his jester, and nausea cut holes in my stomach. I had only until the end of the school year to free Declan and my parents, or I'd have to leave them to their prison forever. The deadline was still over a school term away, but behind me trailed two-years-plus of failure. Even the simplest of my so-far unsuccessful plans had taken weeks to put together, and I could practically feel the months ahead slipping away like water through my fingers. My throat constricted, panic tickling my gut.

I steadied myself with a mental image: Declan, Brennan, me and our parents out at sea, together. Happy. Free. I had to make that happen. Whatever it took, I vowed, and integrity be damned.

Palming the money, I forced a smile.

"It seems something's just opened up."

Chapter 3

Threading absently through the halls Monday morning, I inspected my just-returned math test. Apparently I had some work to do on no-limit equations, but other than that—

The shoulder hit me hard and sharp, just as my skin began to sting. I fell against a locker, barely keeping my grasp on my paper.

"Watch it," I snarled.

"We're supposed to keep trash out of the hallways," said a voice I knew too well. Ashlyn, red-haired tyrant of Granite Harbor High, smiled. "I'm just doing my part." Behind her, a trio of her cronies tittered.

Straightening, I raised a brow. "So how'd *you* do on the Calc test?" That was what this was about; Ashlyn couldn't stand when I ruined the curve, and I'd just done it again. I knew I'd struck home when Ashlyn's green eyes narrowed.

"Why don't you go f— "

"Hey, ladies," my brother interrupted, coming down the hallway. He stepped up beside me, shoulder to shoulder, and grinned lazily at Ashlyn and her friends. Ashlyn stilled, swapping her sneer for a cold stare. Three years ago, she and my brother had been the golden couple of Granite Harbor High, but *bitter exes* didn't begin to describe them now.

Behind Ashlyn, one of her friends flushed a bit. Brennan winked at the girl.

"Looking good, Katie."

"She's not going to Homecoming with you," Ashlyn snapped. "So don't even try." Brennan had a habit of asking out Ashlyn's friends, because it made Ashlyn furious when they said yes.

"Actually, I was thinking *we* could go." Brennan cocked his head rakishly at Ashlyn, his smile holding all the warmth of an ice pick. "For old time's sake. What do you say?"

Her cheeks bloomed with anger, and a smile ghosted across my lips. Ashlyn was a nasty piece of work, and everyone at school toed the line unless they wanted their reputation shot to pieces. Everyone, that is, except Brennan and me.

Why? Her last name was Murphy.

Yes, *that* Murphy. She was his daughter.

For a moment I thought she'd whirl and flounce off, but instead she stepped deliberately forward. The invisible jellyfish swarming my skin turned to piranhas, and it took all I had not to flinch. Beside me, Brennan tensed. Ashlyn's sharp gaze caught our reactions, and the corners of her mouth twitched up in satisfaction.

"That would be great, Brennan," she purred, and stretched out a hand towards his chest. "Pick me up at eight?"

The one thing that hurt worse than proximity to Ashlyn

was her touch, and Brennan jerked backwards before her fingers reached his shirt.

"Wait, I can't—I just remembered." He snapped his fingers with mock regret. "I have standards." He sauntered off, leaving me to witness the outraged gasps of Ashlyn's friends. Ashlyn, for her part, only rolled her eyes. Brennan's flight crowned her the victor of this micro-showdown.

I raised my chin, not backing down even though now she was closer than ever. Pain rippled over my skin, waves of barbed wire. It hadn't always been this way—growing up, I'd seen Ashlyn as a sister. We'd been inseparable. Now, it took effort not to cringe in her presence. Meeting her gaze, I let her read the hatred in mine.

Ashlyn tossed her hair, then led her friends down the thinning hallway. It wasn't retreat, though—the bell was about to ring. We both had American History next, so as much as it irked me, I was forced to follow her like a lost puppy.

I slid into my seat just as the bell sounded, and glanced over to where Ashlyn held court on the other side of the classroom. It was automatic, the instinct to keep her in my sights. Before we'd been freed, being near her and her family hadn't hurt; Brennan and I figured our allergic reaction came from the fact that she used to own us. At this distance, at least, she only made my skin itch a bit. Trying to dispel the sensation, I rubbed my arms.

"Hey, Cassandra," Mindy Stevens said from the seat next to me. We weren't friends—I didn't have those—but we weren't not-friends either, so I nodded in greeting. "You have a date to Homecoming yet?"

"Why, are you going to ask me?" I joked. The dance, next week, was all anyone seemed able to talk about.

"Ha, no. My friend wanted me to see if you might go with him if he asked." Her mouth tilted wryly—she knew I'd say no.

I sighed. This happened every once in a while, despite the very cold shoulder I turned towards any guy who took an interest.

"I'm not going."

"I know you don't, usually, but …" She handed me a folded bit of paper. "He wrote you a note."

The scrawled missive, from a guy I knew by name but not personally, compared my brown hair to tumbling silk, my blue eyes to lapis lazuli, and the freckles on my cheeks to dust from heaven. Holy crab shells. Maybe to another girl it would sound romantic, but to me … I shuddered. Mythology swarmed with human men, driven mad by desire, stealing selkie wives. Beauty wasn't a compliment to me—it was dangerous.

"Could you turn him down?" I crumpled the note. "Firmly."

Mindy made a face. "Sure. You finish last night's homework?"

We chatted and worked on the class warm-up questions until the teacher, Mr. Hayward, dropped a slip on my desk. "Seems you're wanted for a yearbook interview." He smiled at me. I was one of his favorite students, mostly because I at least pretended to care about our nation's history.

Although I actually did care. "But what about class?"

"You can get my notes," Mindy offered, so although I had no idea why yearbook would want to interview me—I avoided extracurricular and school activities like the proverbial plague—I grabbed my bag and headed back into the halls.

The slip told me to report to classroom 39B, in the English wing. I found it and went inside. Shakespeare quotes plastered the walls, and a girl with frizzy black hair and eyebrows that could use a tweeze or seven perched on the teacher's desk. She stared owlishly at me. Her messenger bag, covered with buttons, slouched on the floor, and she cradled a cell phone in her hands. I spared a moment for envy—everyone had smartphones now except for unfortunates like me who couldn't afford them.

"I'm Cassandra Kelleher." I held up the slip. "I got this note?"

"Hi," the girl said, then fell silent. Her dark eyes widened as she looked at me, like I was a priceless painting, or a mutant spider. Maybe both. Thinking of a painted mutant spider, I smiled.

"What's your name?" I prodded. "Are you with yearbook?"

"Leisel." The girl nodded. She wore a baggy aqua t-shirt with a sea turtle on the front. "Yes."

I waited, but the staring continued. It started to creep me out.

"Why does yearbook want to interview me? I'm not in any

clubs or anything." Except the club of Save the Selkies, with a roster of two, but we weren't exactly official.

"Um, have a seat?"

I shrugged and claimed a desk. Maybe she was waiting for other people, and would conduct a poll or something. Possibly about student jobs—it was common knowledge that I hostessed at The Golden Fish.

Then the other member of Save the Selkies walked in, and suddenly I knew this had nothing to do with part-time jobs.

"Hey, Cass." Spotting Leisel, Brennan raised a brow. "Who are you?"

I leapt to my feet. "What the hell is going on?" Why would this girl want to interview us, unless she somehow knew our secret? Instinctively I grabbed for the sharpened metal sticks in my hair, but paused when Brennan gave me his patented *chill already* look.

"Is this for a spread on siblings or something?" he asked.

Leisel had frozen at my outburst, but she managed to nod.

Oh. That made sense. I dropped my hands, feeling like an idiot. This was why Brennan called me paranoid. Besides, it wasn't like I could stab a classmate anyway. Attempting a smile, I reclaimed my seat.

"There's only a few questions." Leisel's voice shook; she probably wished she'd skipped this set of siblings. Brennan sat down next to me, and we answered her extremely mundane questions.

After ten minutes, she hesitated.

"We're done, but . . ." Leisel glanced at Brennan, her cheeks turning a little red, and I rolled my eyes. Despite playing no school sports, Brennan managed to have most of the female contingent of the school swooning over him. But Leisel, with her frizzy hair and baggy t-shirt, wasn't really his type.

He didn't really have a type these days, other than Ashlyn's friends. She'd forbidden them from accepting invitations or kisses from Brennan, and convincing her shallow hangers-on to betray her was a measure of revenge for what her father had done to our family. Futile, but Brennan said it made him feel better. For a little while, anyway.

"So we can go?" I said.

Leisel tapped at her phone.

"Actually, I wanted to show you something." She passed the phone gingerly to me. The screen showed a patch of nighttime forest, opening onto a riverbank. "I was recording this for a science project."

"About what?" And why was she showing us? I handed the phone to Brennan.

"I'm measuring the ambient light against noise throughout the month. It could help determine whether darkness is beneficial for recovering waterfront habitats, and—"

"Cass." My brother's voice held a jolt of alarm. He'd paused the video, and onscreen was …

Me. Standing on the silvery river bank. Wrapped in something that wasn't a towel. My brain tumbled to a halt.

"When did you take this?" Brennan asked.

Leisel nodded solemnly, as if answering his real question. "Saturday night."

Oh. Oh, no. No, no, no. Blood rushed from my head. This wasn't happening. This odd frizzy-haired yearbook girl with the crazy eyebrows was *not* holding video proof of Brennan and me *changing*. I was too shocked to even reach for my hair sticks, not that they'd do any good.

We sat there in silence, the wall clock ticking audibly, the air so thick I couldn't breathe. I stared at the screen. At that angle, it caught a wide expanse of river and bank. I was off to the left but clearly visible. It would have captured everything.

Finally Brennan rubbed his face. "Damn."

"That's helpful," I snapped.

Brennan raised his hands palms-up.

"And you want me to do what, exactly?"

In response, I grabbed the cell phone and threw it to the linoleum. Leaping up, I slammed my boot down on the screen. It cracked, and Leisel shrieked. I stepped on the phone again, with a satisfying crunch.

"*Wait*," Brennan said. Leisel had both her hands over her mouth, silent with horror. Somewhere beneath my panic I felt bad—that phone had to be expensive—but not that bad. If the sum of Leisel's problems totaled a broken phone, she was lucky.

Brennan held up two fingers. "First, you'd have to destroy the SIM card, not the phone. Wait," he said, because I'd snatched up the phone to dismantle it and do just that. "Secondly, she wouldn't have left her phone out in the woods all night, so the original recording is on a different device. She's probably uploaded the file to a computer already."

Leisel nodded, and my hands tightened around the broken phone. What was I supposed to do now?

"Third," Brennan continued inexorably, saying what I knew but didn't want to accept, "she already watched the video, so even if you destroy it, she still knows."

She knows about us. Leisel's furry black eyebrows suddenly seemed full of menace, despite the wideness of her eyes.

"I won't tell anyone," she whispered. "I swear."

Something not quite a laugh spilled from my throat. "And we're supposed to what, trust your word on that?" Then it hit me that she wasn't being nice—she was blackmailing us. "How much?" I snarled.

"What?"

"How much do you want?"

Leisel lowered her hands.

"I don't want anything."

Brennan raked his hair back from his forehead and stood. "Then why would you arrange this little viewing? Just for kicks?"

"What do you mean? You're— " Glancing at the closed door, Leisel lowered her voice. "You're *selkies!* I mean, that is just … so cool!"

My brain finally caught up with the situation, cobbling together a plan on the fly. I forced a laugh, which only sounded a smidge hysterical. "We are no such thing," I declared. "But you totally fell for it."

"Fell for what?"

"Our prank. Congrats—you're a moron."

Leisel flinched, then shook her head.

"You didn't even know my name when you walked in here. How would you even know about my project?"

I shrugged. "It's a hobby." That made no sense. Why wasn't Brennan backing me up? I cut him an entreating glare.

"I don't think she's buying it," he said.

For a second I was confused. "What are you doing?"

Brennan rubbed his face; when he looked at me again, his jaw had set.

"We're found out. We always knew what that meant, Cass."

I stared at the crystal-blue eyes, so like my own, and went still. *Oh.*

"You want us to leave."

"We have to." Brennan cocked his head at Leisel. "Before Miss Science Project makes us into an exposé."

"Wait—I'm not going to tell anyone." Leisel clutched her hands together. "I promise."

Brennan shook his head. "Maybe she means it, maybe she doesn't, but the fact is that neither of us will breathe easy again, knowing our secret is one girly gabfest away from being all over the school."

My breath caught painfully in my chest. He thought this would finally scare me into leaving before we had to. He wasn't even trying to control the situation; he just wanted to flee. My pulse beat faster, hot and angry.

Leisel said something, but I wasn't listening.

"You coward," I said to Brennan.

My brother's head snapped around. "Excuse me?"

I raised my chin, terrified that this was a moment we could never take back, but too furious to stop.

"You gave up months ago. You don't even care anymore, do you?" Not waiting for his answer, I turned to our videographer. "But you know what? This is simple." I took two steps forward, and Leisel shrank back against the teacher's desk. Slamming the busted phone down next to a mug of pens, I leaned over her. God, she looked so scared, and I felt like such a bully, but overriding any nicer instincts was my fear that she *could* force me to leave land, abandon my family to rot. I couldn't let that happen.

I stared into Leisel's wide dark eyes.

"If you so much as breathe a word to anyone, I will crush you like a bug. Got it?"

Leisel's mouth opened, but only a squeak emerged. I glared, and she managed to nod. Stepping back, I rounded on Brennan. Fear and fury made me shake.

"And you. Leave if you want. But I am not a coward, and I am not going anywhere."

Grabbing my bag, I stalked from the room before I could break down entirely.

Chapter 4

The rest of the morning was a blur. Leisel Somebody-or-other knew what I was. This couldn't be happening.

Would she stay quiet? What could I do if she didn't? I entertained visions of breaking into her house and destroying her computer, but what if she'd put the video on a flash drive, or uploaded it to a file-storing site online? Brennan was right—the damage was done.

Needing to know what kind of girl held my secrets, I took my lunch to the library and tracked down yearbooks from the last three years. It didn't take long to find her, situated at the beginning of the alphabet: Leisel Benton. A senior, like me. I should probably recognize her, but I hadn't paid much attention to my classmates in the last couple years.

With the help of the index, I looked up every picture or column Leisel appeared in. She'd authored a bunch of spreads from last year, mostly about groups like marching band and Mathletes. She herself had placed in every science fair, and participated in a coastal cleanup volunteer group.

A do-gooder. That was something. I looked her up in the

school newspaper, in the "Senior Special" issue where they'd listed student responses to questions like "Where do you see yourself in ten years?" and "What's your personal motto?"

Oddly, Leisel's answer to both questions was the same:

Saving the world, one starfish at a time.

Starfish. Huh. I traced the words with my index finger, and the pressure in my chest eased. Maybe Leisel hadn't been attempting blackmail. Maybe she wouldn't expose us. Plus, who would believe her? No one would accept that the video wasn't doctored. After a week of wild gossip, everyone would write Leisel off as a science dork who got duped. The end.

Okay. I paged through the yearbooks and newspapers for the rest of lunch, making a face every time Ashlyn Murphy's byline appeared. She'd been an editor of the yearbook and the weekly school newspaper for the last two years, as well as a producer of the student-run morning news and announcements program.

She'd finagled the positions not because of excellence or diligence, but because of her dad's clout. The media teachers were invited to the mayor's ball each winter, and Ashlyn approved or vetoed every story, spread, and news segment that the student body saw. It gave her a lot of power, without requiring a lot of work. The Murphy way.

Wondering what Ashlyn would say if she saw Leisel's video, a chill went down my neck.

After school, I headed straight for the truck and got in the long line to escape the parking lot bottleneck. Just as I rolled up to the stop sign, the passenger door opened.

Brennan swung in. "You weren't planning to wait for me?"

"I figured you were already halfway to Greenland." My voice was low and tight. I hadn't really thought he'd leave directly from school, but I didn't want to have this argument again, especially not if it ended with him telling me to take him to the coast so he could dive into the sea, never to return.

"We'll talk after work, okay?"

Did he hope to convince me then? "I'm not leaving."

"I know, alright? Neither am I."

"You're not?"

"We'll talk after work," Brennan repeated. I wanted to ask him what changed his mind, tell him what I'd found out about Leisel, but didn't dare chance it in the truck. We'd spent a significant chunk of our pooled money fund on a spy-tech gadget that supposedly would tell us whether our truck was bugged, but we still saved any sensitive discussions for places we knew were safe. In the past, even I had wondered whether I'd crossed the line into *too* paranoid, but not after today.

Declan always assigned us the afternoon shift at The Golden Fish, at Mr. Murphy's "suggestion," so we had to trade our daylight hours for minimum wage and a share of the tips. When we finally escaped, dark had stolen any remaining warmth from the sky. Brennan drove us home, parking in front of a tiny Cape Cod house on a quiet cul-de-sac. Inside the lit kitchen, my parents were preparing dinner—which they couldn't share with us, per Mr. Murphy's orders.

"Let's stow our stuff and make sandwiches," I said once out of the truck. "We can take them down the street and talk."

My brother made a face.

"What's the menu, peanut butter again?"

"Actually, I found cans of tuna half off yesterday, so I got a bunch."

Brennan gave me his fist to bump. "Score."

He acted like our earlier fight never happened. Maybe in his head it was resolved. Boys. Smiling a little, I followed him inside and tossed my bag by my desk. We each had one of the small first-floor bedrooms, while our parents slept upstairs. My room, like Brennan's, boasted only a bed, a bookshelf, a desk and a trash can. No knickknacks beyond school supplies, for three reasons: first, our parents had chucked all our belongings when we left after freshman year, so the normal accumulation of childhood had been purged. Second, we hadn't planned to be here for long, and third: we didn't want anything in our rooms that might hide a listening device.

In the kitchen, my dad spooned lentil stew over two bowls of rice while my mom poured iced tea. The table was only set for two, even though my brother and I usually made a point of eating with them.

"That smells great," I said.

My father, five-ten with dark hair that belied his age, covered the pot of stew with a pointed clink. My mother carried two glasses to the table without responding.

The silent treatment. Brennan and I got it most days—our parents wanted us at sea, not here. They thought it unnatural, and dangerous, for us to live on land when we had our sealskins, and begged us to go find their old selkie clan. They allowed us to stay here, but made no pretense about wanting us to leave.

Brennan and I made tuna sandwiches with cheap store-brand mayo and rolls I'd snagged from the discount bin. This week we'd been lucky; it was potato bread, soft and sweet.

Our parents hesitated between bites as we made for the front door instead of sitting down with them as usual, but said nothing. I followed Brennan outside. A block away, a little park containing swings and a slide and a flat metal merry-go-round huddled under the trees.

"So." I plunked myself down on one of the swings and bit into my sandwich so I wouldn't have to continue.

"Leisel says she wants to help us," Brennan said. I almost spit out my tuna.

"What?" I tried to say, then swallowed. "When did she say that?"

"After you left."

"You talked to her?" I gripped the cold metal swing chain. "What exactly did she say?"

"Well, she asked who Nicky was, for one."

"What did you tell her?"

Brennan scratched his ear. "I said he was my turtle, and— "

"I meant about *us!* Brennan, you— "

"Calm down. She just said she wanted to help us if she could."

"What did she mean? What did we say on that video?"

Brennan shrugged. "She caught the part where you said

have her hide her fear (emotion!)

our parents would die if we didn't free them. She figured out that meant their sealskins had been stolen."

"She did?"

"Well, she said if we were selkies, it stood to reason that at least one of our parents was too, and that if we wanted to free them, logically that meant they were captive. And she read a bunch of selkie myths, so ..." Brennan pushed himself backwards on the swing. "Leisel's a smart cookie."

I kicked the frost-bitten mulch beneath my feet.

"If she's smart, she'll keep her mouth shut and leave us alone."

"I think we should let her help."

Was he crazy? "She's a stranger."

"As is everyone, until you get to know them," Brennan pointed out dryly.

"But we can't trust her. We can't trust anyone." That was rule number one. Not to mention rules number two through infinity.

"She already knows about us. We don't really have a choice about that. And if she wants to help, why the hell not?"

"No. Just ... no." Did he really not see that letting Leisel into our world, even to "help," meant giving her more information? Meant letting her know our habits, letting her close enough to hurt us? What if she followed us when we went swimming? I shook my head. "We can't chance it."

Brennan opened his mouth as if to argue, then bit into his sandwich instead. We ate in silence. Darkness shrouded the playground, but street lamps lit the road to our house; the lanterns' soft halos cast us in even deeper shadow. Despite the icy temperature, we wore no coats—even in human form cold barely touched us.

My brother swallowed the last of his meal, brushed crumbs off his shirt, and stood.

"You're right, you know."

About Leisel? "Yeah." But my brother shot me a look.

"About me giving up. I had, pretty much. I mean, we're getting nowhere." Brennan paced across the mulch. "We're dead in the water, especially after the plumber scheme went belly-up."

I'd spent months offering bribes to any handyman who worked at the mayor's house. A plumber with a sick daughter was the only one who'd taken my money, in exchange for a promise to look for hidden rooms, passages, or safes. I'd told him it was for research on old houses. I doubted he'd believed me, but in any case, the plumber's only report was that Mrs. Murphy had watched him like a hawk, so he couldn't look anywhere but the work area. Shockingly, no hidden safes nestled under the bathroom sink. I'd offered him more money to try again next time, but last week he'd gotten cold feet and told me the next time I contacted him he'd tell the mayor. I doubted he would, or he'd have to confess to taking the first bribe, but that plan was definitively a bust.

Which sucked, because it had been my best idea in ages.

"We still have Plan A," I reminded Brennan. Plan A was stalk the Murphys until we discovered something to use as leverage to force them into returning the sealskins.

"If they haven't done anything blackmail-worthy in two years, I doubt they'll start now."

He was right, but … "We have to keep trying."

"The closest we came was getting their house key last year, but that didn't work either."

After stealing Ashlyn's key ring during a school assembly we'd thought ourselves close to victory, but Mr. Murphy changed all the locks before we could break in.

I pressed my forehead to the icy chain of the swing.

"They'll slip up. They have to."

"Dream on, Cass. It's never going to happen." He hurled chunk of mulch at the slide. "So yeah, I was just waiting for you to admit that we're beaten. Sue me."

I swallowed hard, afraid he'd talked himself into leaving. Afraid he'd talk me into going with him. "We knew this wouldn't be easy. We have to be strong."

Brennan laughed unhappily.

"You don't have Declan yelling at you every day."

"I thought he ignored you." Like he ignored me.

"Well, he doesn't. Whenever we're out of earshot of the rest of the kitchen staff he lectures me about how he sacrificed his own freedom for ours, and he doesn't want to see us squander it. He asks me how I think he feels, married into the Murphy viper nest."

That was the other complicated part about our family's relationship with the Murphys: Declan was married to Emily, Ashlyn's sweet but clueless older sister. It had been part of Declan's deal with Mr. Murphy, the one that set us free.

Brennan and I had been gone only a couple months, but when we returned, determined to free our family, we found Declan and Emily already married. They had a daughter now.

"How does he feel?"

"Like a traitor." Brennan chucked another bit of mulch at the slide. "But he did it for us. He got Emily wrapped around his little finger, then used her affections as leverage against her dad, for us. And now we're risking captivity again, for a 'fool's errand,' he says, when he quite likes it here, thank you very much."

At first, Brennan and I hadn't understood how Douglas Murphy could let his daughter marry a selkie when he seemed to think them fit only for servitude. But when we read up on the myths, we found they invariably claimed that selkies made great spouses. Forced to be loyal and attentive, how could they not?

Queasiness could not begin to describe my perspective on Declan's marriage.

"If he likes it here so much," I said, "why did he work so hard to keep you from winding up just like him?"

"I know." Brennan blew out his breath, a ghost in the shadows. "But they want us *gone*, Cass. They want us out there, living our little selkie lives at sea. They know we have less chance of saving them than we do the lobsters in The Golden Fish's tank, and they want to imagine us free and happy."

He was right, I knew he was right. But …

"I can't leave them," I said miserably.

Brennan settled into the neighboring swing.

"I know. So if Leisel can help, why not let her?"

I raised my head. "Why are you so eager to trust her?"

"I'm not. But face it, Cass—Leisel already knows about us. It's not like we're going to murder her to keep our secret." When I said nothing, he nudged my foot. "Right?"

My lips twisted.

"If we had it in us to kill, Mr. Murphy would be dead by now."

Brennan looked away. "I know." He took a breath. "Look, this could be our big chance. Our best chance." *Our last chance* hung unsaid in the cold night air.

"But what could she possibly do?"

"The Murphys don't know her, or know that she knows us. It could be useful."

He had a point. But if we let Leisel into our confidence, she'd have power over us. And I wasn't about to give anyone power over me ever again.

"I don't trust her," I said, and Brennan sighed.

"Just think about it, okay?"

I nodded, and we walked back to the house. My parents were watching the news on our old TV, like they always did; they'd go to bed at nine sharp. Their gazes followed us as we retreated to our respective rooms.

Ignoring Brennan's entreaty to think about Leisel, I tackled homework. After a bit I heard the TV click off and steps pad upstairs, but then a knock sounded at my door. "Come in," I called, and sat up in surprise when my mom entered. Over the last two years she'd been distant, as if motherly affection might make me hang on longer. Wearing a faded but clean sweater and dark slacks, she was beautiful in a quiet way. Her eyes were gray like the ocean, and as far off as the horizon.

"Everything okay?" I asked.

My mother walked over to my bed and sat down.

"You know, your father and I have a home, and each other. We're much better off than some in this country." She glanced out at the TV set in the living room. "Why, we were just watching about a family who lost everything in a tornado this summer. So sad."

I knew what she was getting at. "But you're trapped here. You'll never get to swim—"

"If you spend your days worrying about what you can't have, you'll drive yourself mad. We're fine. Go, Cassandra—before it's too late."

My throat tightened. "It's my life."

My mother's mouth flattened, fine lines spreading over her skin.

"You owe it to us to leave."

"We'll go as soon as we graduate, remember?"

For a moment anger flickered in the depths of my mother's ocean eyes. She knew as well as I did that my brother and I hadn't returned for our diplomas. But then the anger faded, her expression retreating to its usual passivity.

"You'd better." She went upstairs.

She and my father would rise at 5am to start their work day. On weekends they babysat for Declan's daughter Norah, and my mom knitted baby clothes and blankets while my dad ran errands. They were happy enough, as long as they kept busy. But when she thought no one was around, my mother would sing quietly to herself, mournful yearning songs of the sea. I'd thought it funny when I was growing up—silly mom, crying and crooning to her dishes again—but every time I heard her singing now it broke my heart.

Yes, they had it okay compared to some people, but it wasn't enough. This country was built on the concept of freedom as an inalienable right, and I wouldn't let my family be the exception.

My hands curled into fists. I owed it to them to leave? Bullshit.

But panic tugged at my scalp. Brennan was right that we were no closer to freeing our family than a year ago, two years ago. If we hadn't freed them by graduation …

Unable to focus on homework anymore, I turned out the lights. The slats of my blinds threw lines of moonlight across the opposite wall. They looked, unsubtly, like the bars of a cell.

In the morning, I caught Brennan's arm as we walked to our truck.

"Okay," I said. "Leisel's in."

Chapter 5

"There." Brennan pointed as I parked in the school lot.

A dozen or so cars over, Leisel Benton emerged from a blue minivan. "I see." We didn't speak again until we'd left the truck.

"You sure you don't want me to handle this?" Brennan murmured as we passed the school's sign, proclaiming this the proud home of the Granite Harbor Harpoons. No, a harpoon was not a proper mascot, and yes, there was a lobbyist group trying to get it changed to something less violent. So far no one could agree on anything.

"I got it," I said. "Just meet me here after school."

Brennan sauntered off, leaving me to meander after Leisel. She went straight to her locker, and I ducked into an alcove until she headed off to homeroom. When the coast was clear I sidled through the thinning crowd and surreptitiously slipped a note through the vents in Leisel's locker. My spy skills had been weak when I'd first attempted to deploy them two years ago, but now I could channel James Bond like a pro.

Yesterday, Brennan had noticed he and Leisel shared a

lunch period. I had English Lit, but ten minutes in I asked for a bathroom pass.

The bathroom I'd told Leisel to meet me in lay across the school from the cafeteria, lowering the chances anyone from lunch would stop by—an important consideration, because Ashlyn ate this period too.

I checked the hallway, then pushed open the bathroom door. Leisel waited by the sinks. She stood up straighter when she saw me.

"I got your note," she said unnecessarily.

I used my foot to wedge a rubber doorstop into place. Doubts clawed at me, but I owed it to my family to see if she could help. Besides, with her do-gooder background, who knew what Leisel might screw up if she tried to "help" without me directing her? This ship was already at sea, and if I wanted to control where it went I needed to be the one at the helm.

"Brennan said you want to help us." I leaned against the tile wall. "Why?"

"Because ..." Leisel's dark eyes lit with excitement. "Because you're selkies!" I winced, and she bit her lip. "I just ... I'll do whatever you want."

We fascinated her because of what we were. Would a science geek really be able to stay quiet about a previously unrecognized-by-science being for long? I pushed my queasiness aside.

"We do need help," I admitted, then held up a hand. "But that doesn't mean you get to know everything. I'm not going to lay out all of my family's secrets. You do what I say, when I say, and you don't ask questions." I sounded über-controlling, but couldn't help it. The only way I could even think of trusting this girl was if I stayed in control.

Leisel hesitated.

"But— "

"That's the deal. Are you in or out?"

Before Leisel could answer, someone tried to come in. The rubber wedge slipped, and I shoved my back against the door. "Find another bathroom," I called.

"Cass, open the door."

What was Brennan doing here? Annoyed, I let him in.

"You can't be here."

Brennan's lip twitched.

"And yet, somehow I still exist in the girls bathroom."

I elbowed him. "What are you doing?"

Brennan moved out of elbow range.

"I wanted to make sure you weren't murdering her."

Leisel's eyes widened owlishly.

"Did anyone see you leave the cafeteria?" I asked.

"No." Brennan dropped his backpack on the floor. "And Ashlyn's still there, so chill."

"Ashlyn?" Leisel asked.

"Ashlyn Murphy," Brennan told her.

"Like, the *mayor's* daughter Ashlyn Murphy? What does she have to do with this?"

That was exactly the kind of information I wanted to ration carefully, not lay out like a sardine smorgasbord. "*I* will explain after school." Glaring at Brennan, I hoped he'd caught the emphasis. "The Golden Fish is closed Tuesdays, so we don't have to work. Tell me where you live, and we'll pick you up."

Leisel frowned. "And go where?"

"The woods somewhere. Where no one can see us."

Leisel stared at me. A drop from the faucet plinked in the silence. Brennan grimaced and caught Leisel's eye.

"My sister has the inspired ability to make it sound like we plan to leave your body in the woods for wolves to devour. Sorry."

Leisel's lip quirked, but when she glanced at me her smile faded.

"No offense," she said, "but can we go somewhere more … public?"

"Thus defeating the point of a secret meeting?" Alright, considering my mildly deranged recent behavior I couldn't exactly blame Leisel for not wanting to go anywhere alone with me. But if she wouldn't … The impossibility of the situation made my stomach drop. "Look, this isn't going to work. Never mind. It's not your fight anyway."

Brennan's brows rose. "Now who's giving up?"

"Do you have a suggestion?" I shot back.

"I do," Leisel said. "What if *I* picked *you* up, and we went somewhere in my car?"

I shook my head. "I'm not going anywhere with— "

"This was what I was afraid of," Brennan said. "Go back to class. Leisel and I will work out the details for this afternoon."

"But I— "

He pulled me over to the door. "If you want this to work, you're going to have to let go a little."

I scowled. "The last time we *let go*, we wound up on video, remember?"

My brother exhaled slowly, as if mentally counting to ten. "Cass, you want her to just follow orders, no questions asked."

"And?"

"And nothing. She's going to want answers."

"She doesn't *get* answers. That's not part of the deal." And why was Brennan making us have this argument in front of the avidly-listening Leisel? "Can we talk about this later?"

Brennan waited a beat.

"Do you trust me?" he asked.

With my life, sure. Not to mess things up? Less sure.

"Yes," I said, "but— "

"Then let me handle this." Brennan chivvied me out into the hallway before I could mount an argument. I stared at the "Women" sign as the door swung shut. How had that just happened?

Torn between annoyance and worry, I trudged back to class.

When school ended I retrieved some books from my locker, then headed to the pick-up. After a couple minutes Brennan appeared at the window. When I lowered it, Brennan handed me a folded note. He winked, then headed towards the woods across the street.

I unfolded the paper. *Drop the car and meet us at the triple maple*, it said. *Don't worry—L will pick me up where no one can see.*

And he'd lead Leisel to the triple maple. She'd be outnumbered, but have the only car. The landmark he'd mentioned, where three big maples had fallen some years ago in a rough triangle, was a ten minute walk from our house, in a wildlife preservation area—secluded, but close enough to the neighborhood that you could hear people yell. Okay. That might work.

I followed directions and drove home, left the truck in the driveway, and hiked through the woods. When I neared the triple maple, I spotted Leisel and Brennan talking on one of the logs. My eyes narrowed. How could he just sit there with her, knowing she knew what we were? Sure, Leisel looked harmless, but so did sea anemones … until they stung you.

When I reached them, Brennan gestured at the quiet patch of woods.

"Great meeting place, right?"

Thirty feet away, Leisel's minivan waited at the end of the gravel trail. If anyone showed up, there were plenty of places Brennan and I could hide so no one would see us with Leisel. It *was* a good spot, but just being here with her made me uneasy, so I only shrugged.

"I've explained things to Leisel," Brennan said, "and we came up with a plan."

I blinked. "Already?"

"It's simple: Leisel will make friends with Ashlyn."

I laughed, then realized he wasn't joking. "What?"

"Then she can search the house for the sealskins during a sleepover. Or find out the front door code, or crack a window for us or something." Brennan grinned up at me, eyes alight. "Simple but brilliant, right?"

Thankfully, Leisel seemed more alive to the possibility that Princess Ashlyn might not jump at the opportunity to befriend a science nerd.

"Or I could work on a school project with Ashlyn?" she ventured. "For yearbook or something. To get me into the house."

Brennan shook his head. "Ashlyn's not allowed to have people over unless they're good friends."

"But she has parties, right?"

I snorted in disbelief.

"When have you ever heard of a party at Ashlyn's?"

"I don't really pay attention to that kind of stuff," she mumbled. "Is she not allowed to throw parties?"

"She's allowed," Brennan said, "but they're all carefully chaperoned. Her dad makes sure of that. It was fine when we were kids, but not so fun after middle school. Nowadays Ashlyn sponsors parties elsewhere."

"Sponsors?"

"She gets her older sister to buy her liquor, and stocks a party hosted by someone with fewer supervisional problems."

"Oh." Leisel stared at the leaf-strewn ground. "Then how am I supposed to get into her house?"

Brennan shrugged.

"Just make friends with her, and eventually she'll invite you over."

Leisel opened her mouth, then shut it. She'd gone a little pale. A girl like her would rather die than risk ridicule by so much as speaking to Ashlyn Murphy uninvited, but making her admit it in front of my brother would be cruel. I grabbed Brennan's arm.

"Can I talk to you for a second?"

"Sure."

I hauled him over to the parking lot. "What is your problem?"

"What? How is this a bad plan?"

"Does Leisel Benton really seem like she belongs in Ashlyn Murphy's inner circle?"

"Well, no. She's way too nice. But she's pretty, and— "

"Pretty?" Leisel wasn't a troll, but was he blind?

"And I bet if she just compliments Ashlyn enough she'll be fine. Ashlyn rotates friends every month."

"Because of you." Brennan's systematic sabotage of Ashlyn's friendships did mean she kept a lookout for new blood. Not that she shunned everyone who fell prey to Brennan's wiles; most of her current crowd had been lucky enough to be forgiven for their lapses. "But she can't just walk up and be Ashlyn's bestie out of the blue."

"Look, the surest way to get Leisel into that house is through Ashlyn. So let's make it happen." Brennan headed back to Leisel. I leaned against the minivan, watching him go. Annoyance at my brother warred with the knowledge that he was right. How else did I expect Leisel to get into the mayor's house—base a yearbook spread on him? She'd be watched closely, just like the plumber.

No, Ashlyn was the weak link. As far-fetched as it might seem, we had to finagle Leisel a spot in Ashlyn's inner circle.

Through the trees, I studied Leisel, and an idea unfurled. Back when I painted, my art teacher told me one of my strengths was seeing beauty in tangled landscapes. That hair could be fixed, same with those clothes. And, I realized, Brennan *was* right about Leisel being sort of pretty—she had good bones. Maybe I could do something about those eyebrows ...

It was worth a shot, anyway. I walked back over.

"Alright," I said. "Brennan, you're walking home. Leisel, come with me."

Brennan frowned. "I am *not* leaving you alone with her."

"Relax," I told him. "We're going shopping."

"Right now? Why?"

How could I put this delicately? "If we're going to try this, Leisel needs ... a new look."

"Oh, please." Brennan rolled his eyes.

"I'm serious," I said, and Leisel winced.

"What kind of new look?" Brennan asked.

"You want a list?" This would be like kicking a kitten, but I made myself harden. If Leisel couldn't handle me, she sure as hell couldn't handle Ashlyn Murphy. "Jeans she didn't borrow from her mom. Shoes not intended for the Appalachian Trail. A shirt without an animal on it." Today's baggy tee showcased a pair of swans.

"Cass." Brennan's eyes narrowed. "Stop it."

"A coat not made for senior citizens. Hair that wouldn't look at home on an electrified groundhog." I crossed my arms. "And trust me, I'm just getting started."

"What you're doing is being a bitch," Brennan shot back.

I looked at Leisel. "What do *you* think?" Brennan was a guy, and might not get it. But if Leisel was just as delusional, we might as well quit now. I didn't care how Leisel looked—and her nature-riffic hiker gear suited her in an odd way—but unless she could fit into the popular crowd, Ashlyn would never allow Leisel within ten yards of her lunch table, let alone her house.

Leisel did look like a kicked kitten, hunched on her log. She stared at her shoes a while before mumbling, "I think you're right." Then she raised her chin. "*And* I think you're being a bitch."

Brennan let out a choked laugh, smothered quickly as if he thought I might stalk off in a huff. Leisel's dark eyes were anxious but defiant, and I cocked my head, considering her. Seconds ticked by, but Leisel's gaze didn't waver.

Holy crab shells—maybe she had the attitude to pull this off after all.

"Alright," I said at last. A shred of real hope twisted painfully in my stomach. "Let's get this makeover montage on the road."

Chapter 6

Leisel and I wove through the racks of clothes like sharks circling each other.

I'd taken us to one of the discount department stores I'd used to replace my own wardrobe two years ago. Leisel picked half-heartedly through the shirts, but mostly darted glances at me. Except for the slight stalker-ish vibe, I didn't mind that she wasn't helping; I doubted she knew what to look for anyway.

I, thankfully, did. Though popularity was a phase of the past, I knew what was in style. My own personal clothing ran to clean lines and basic staples I wouldn't have to replace every season, but for Leisel I kept an eye out for trendier stuff.

As I picked through the racks, Leisel's gaze started to chafe.

"Stop staring," I finally said. "I'm not going to *change* right here in the store."

Leisel abandoned her pretense at shopping. "I just have a million questions. Like is your brother swimming right this second?"

"No. Why?" Did she think we spent every waking moment not at school as seals or something?

"When we left the meeting spot, he said he was going fishing."

"He is. To catch us dinner."

"But doesn't that mean— "

I raised a brow. "He's using a fishing rod."

"Oh." Leisel's enthusiasm was only momentarily stalled. "Do you always eat fish?"

"No." I pulled a cute pink top with a beaded design from the rack and pushed it at Leisel. "Here. Take this."

"How often do you go swimming? And— "

"Stop." My hands clenched on the hanger. "Stop asking questions."

"But ..."

"That was the deal. I let you help, you keep your mouth shut."

The silence lasted all of three seconds. "But you can't expect me not to be curious, right? I mean, you're a— " I shot her a glare, and she skipped over the word *selkie*. "—and it's almost unbelievable, but here you are, and I can't believe we've been going to school together for years and I never knew!"

"No one knows. That's kind of the point."

"Right. But I won't tell, I swear."

Gritting my teeth, I spotted an aqua sweater that would complement Leisel's dark hair. I passed it and the pink top to Leisel, added a couple more shirts, then moved on to the next rack.

"So why did the Murphys give you back your sealskin two years ago?" Leisel asked. "Brennan didn't explain that."

Declan's deal with the devil. "It's complicated."

"I mean, why you but not your parents? Because logically it would make more sense to keep all the sealskins, or none of them. I mean, it seems weird that he's okay with you hanging around while your parents are still — "

I whirled, tumbling Leisel into a pile of scarves.

"What is this to you, a *game?* Do you even hear what you're saying? This isn't some science project to figure out. This is my *family*."

Leisel clutched the shirts. "Sorry, I just— "

"Do you get what my life is like? I'm constantly worried someone will find out about us." I jabbed a finger at her. "And then yesterday my nightmare came true. *You* found out. And— " I cut myself off as Leisel's gaze dropped to my hand, which shook. Damn. Turning, I fled towards the pants section.

After a minute, Leisel appeared at my elbow. I shoved hangers one by one down the rack, ignoring their metallic skritches and trying to focus.

"Yeah. I get it," she said softly.

"Do you?" I pushed a pair of jeans at her. "Because I fail to see how you possibly could."

"Well, how can I when you won't tell me anything?" Her voice rose, but when I glared at her she lowered it. "You want me to befriend Ashlyn Don't-Cross-Me Murphy and infiltrate the freaking mayor's house, but you won't explain any of the details."

"Because they're none of your business."

Leisel rocked back onto her heels.

"If you don't trust me, why are you letting me help at all?"

"Because you have that video."

"Which you could have just ignored. Believe me, after you told me you'd squish me like a bug yesterday, I have no plans to share it. You could have just ignored me like everyone else."

Like everyone else? I frowned. The truth, of course, was that Brennan and I were desperate, but I didn't want to say that. Besides, Leisel was right that if I really thought she was dangerous I wouldn't be here right now, evaluating a rack of size-6 pants. What had inflicted my tiny fleck of trust in this girl?

"One starfish at a time," I finally said.

"What?"

"Your motto, in the newspaper." I handed her another two pairs of jeans. "What's that about, anyway?" We had enough clothes for a try-on session, so I headed for the dressing rooms. Leisel trailed behind.

"What do you mean?" she asked.

"Why starfish?" They had a deeper meaning for me, but Leisel couldn't know about that.

"It's from a parable." She fell silent as the dressing room monitor counted her items and gave her a number. We headed down the hall. "There's this beach after a storm, full of starfish that got stranded. They're all dehydrating in the sun. They're dying. And this guy is on the beach, picking up starfish one by one and throwing them back into the ocean. This other guy comes along and sees the first guy, and after a while he asks the first guy why he's wasting his time doing something so pointless. After all, he says, he can't possibly save all the starfish. There are thousands. Saving a few makes no difference."

I stopped in front of the dressing room at the end. "And?"

"And the first guy picks up a starfish, throws it in the ocean, and says, 'It made a difference to that one.'" Leisel flushed, then busied herself with hanging up all the clothes. "I know it's cheesy, but my mom's a biologist. She's sort of obsessed with saving the rainforest. That's where she is."

"The rainforest?"

Leisel shut the door, and I sat down in the fitting room opposite.

"Researching." Her voice was muffled as she changed. "In Brazil. They're looking into the population of poison frogs. Some of them are really endangered. We're worried they'll be extinct soon."

Leisel actually sounded distraught at the idea. It had never occurred to me to care about the possible extinction of far-off species, not with my family in more immediate danger.

"So she's saving the world one poison frog at a time?" Imagining Leisel's mom flinging poison frogs into a thick green jungle, I laughed.

There was a moment of quiet inside the dressing room, and then Leisel flung open her door. "My mother's work is not a joke." Her voice was low but angry. "You know what? I'm used to people at school being jerks, but I'm trying to help you. You can give me a makeover and boss me around, but you don't get to make fun of me."

"I wasn't making fun." How had I never heard of Leisel

Benton, crusader for starfish, before? "Are you like this at school?"

"Like what?"

"Feisty."

Leisel grimaced. "I wish."

"What do you mean?"

She turned to the mirror. "Outside of school, if I make someone mad I can just walk away. But at school … if I piss someone off there, I'm trapped. So mostly I just keep my head down. I'm good at playing Invisible Girl."

I didn't know what to say to that.

"Turn around," I directed, and she rotated so I could see her shirt better. Pink, with short fluttery sleeves, it was a vast improvement over her baggy t-shirts. "Looks great. Try on the next."

Leisel ducked back into her dressing room. If she crashed and burned trying to befriend Ashlyn, I reflected, Ashlyn could make her last few months of school hell. I frowned, wondering about Leisel's life. Her yearbook spreads told me about her extra-curriculars, but how did she spend the rest of her time? And with whom?

"You haven't told any of your friends about us, have you?"

"No." Leisel's voice was muffled again. "We don't really hang out except in school anyway." She opened the door; she now wore one of the new pairs of jeans, and the blue sweater. Turning to the mirror, she smoothed down the front of the sweater. Her unruly hair clashed with the shirt's sleek lines, but I tried to evaluate it independently.

"Do you really think there's any way I'm going to convince Ashlyn Murphy to be my friend?" Leisel asked. I hesitated too long, and Leisel seemed to shrink as her gaze found mine in the mirror. "I mean, your brother seemed sure, but …"

"But he's a boy, and has no idea what girls can be like with each other."

"Exactly." Leisel pushed a bushy lock of hair behind her ear. "I mean, her friends are all …"

"Horrid? Shallow? Ear-rendingly shrill?"

Leisel gazed at her reflection. "Pretty."

For a moment I forgot to see her as one more threat, or someone I might be able to use to free my family. Instead Leisel was just a girl who by her own admission didn't have close friends, whose mother was across the world, and who didn't think herself worthy of Ashlyn Murphy's time.

"You know what? You're pretty too." Doubt drenched Leisel's expression. "Don't worry—you'll see." I inspected her outfit. "The shirt is good, the jeans aren't. Try the next pair."

An hour or two flew by, and when we emerged Leisel had two pairs of jeans, black flats to replace her muddy sneakers, plus six shirts she wasn't quite sure she liked.

"I can't believe you made me buy the red one with the buttons," she muttered as we walked back to the minivan.

"What's wrong with that one?" It was crimson, fitted, and altogether something I wished I could buy for myself.

"The buttons don't even work! They're just for show."

I smiled. "Welcome to fashion." Somewhere over the course of the afternoon, my hackles had gone down. Leisel was sort of fun, and I hadn't been shopping for anything besides basics in forever. It was nice getting to choose trendier styles—and even nicer shopping with someone else's money.

And I'd realized that while I might not trust Leisel to guard my sealskin, she did seem genuine in her desire to fight against the evil Murphy empire.

"Now what?" Leisel asked when we'd stowed the bags.

"Time for a haircut." I led her back into the mall. Thankfully this place was a solid hour's drive from Granite Harbor, and in a run-down area, so there was nearly zero chance of anyone we knew seeing us together. I kept a sharp lookout anyway.

We found a salon, and I directed the hairstylist to trim Leisel's hair—as I'd suspected, her last haircut had been almost a year ago, and the split-ends were epic—and give her some face-framing angles. He blow-dried and straightened the result, and when we swung Leisel around to see her reflection, she stared in shock.

"Wow," she breathed, and the hairdresser beamed. "Wow." She touched her black hair, now stick straight to just below shoulder level. It made her look like a whole different person, and I smiled in satisfaction. Leisel was going to look awesome when I was done.

Lastly, we went to a pharmacy, where I had her pick up a straightening iron, some hair products, and makeup. "Nothing complicated," I promised, handing Leisel two packs of application sponges. She took them dubiously. "Just foundation and eye-liner. I'll show you how to apply it. Oh, and one more thing." I dropped the item into the basket Leisel carried.

"But I have tweezers."

I stopped her from returning them to the shelf.

"Not good ones, clearly."

Panic stole across Leisel's face.

"I am *not* plucking my eyebrows."

I raised mine. "Because you what, need them for warmth?"

"It hurts!"

"Ashlyn Murphy plucks her eyebrows." Well, that wasn't true. With Ashlyn's red hair, her eyebrows were naturally thin and tidy. But Leisel didn't know that.

Or maybe she did. She was shaking her head.

"No she doesn't. I overheard her in yearbook."

"But her friends do, don't they?" Was this really Leisel's sticking point? Even I plucked my brows, and I claimed not to care about my looks anymore. "Just buy the tweezers, okay?"

Leisel cocked her head. "If I pluck my eyebrows, will you answer my questions?"

We were back to that? Paranoia caught at me, but Leisel had been a really good sport about everything I'd put her through this afternoon. And with eyebrows like hers, plucking them was going to be hell.

"How many?" I asked, and Leisel's face lit up.

"Three."

"One," I countered, hiding my smile.

"Two."

I hesitated. "Fine, but I reserve the right to veto a question."

"Deal." Leisel dropped the tweezers in her basket and held out her free hand. Freezing, I only stared at it, and Leisel's face went red. "Sorry," she mumbled, and took off for the cash register.

I sighed. She probably thought she'd stepped on some big selkie taboo, that selkies didn't shake hands or something. Maybe they didn't—I had no idea. I went outside to wait, and when Leisel emerged, I nodded towards her minivan. She fell into step beside me.

"Sorry about the handshake," I said. "I know it's super paranoid, but I don't let anyone touch me unless I have to."

Leisel paused, and I swung around to meet her dark curious gaze.

"Do you think they might somehow *know* just by touching you?"

I shoved my hands into my jeans pockets. "I don't know. Maybe." It was more that while growing up I'd been ordered to shake hands and give hugs and even, when Ashlyn and I went on double dates, kiss guys regardless of whether I was into them. "Be nice to him for Chrissakes," she'd whispered more than once. My virginity was still intact, but I held no illusions: I'd have lost that too if I hadn't gotten my sealskin back when I did.

So now I touched no one if I could help it.

"Anyway." I smiled weakly. "Let's go attack your eyebrows, and then you get your questions. Okay?"

Leisel winced. "Did you have to use the word *attack?*" she muttered, and despite myself I laughed.

Chapter 7

The eyebrow plucking lesson, conducted by the lights of the fold-down visor mirrors in Leisel's minivan, didn't go too badly, and we returned to Granite Harbor as darkness fell.

"Let's stop by the Murphy house," I said, and gave her directions. When Leisel turned down the street, I pointed at a grand brick two-story. The columns flanking the double doors gleamed white, like huge fangs.

"There it is." My stomach twisted. Somewhere inside, my family's freedom was locked away. "The belly of the beast."

"Uh oh." Leisel cruised along the wrought-iron fence. "That's a big house."

"Yep. The fence goes all the way around the property, and is monitored by camera. The driveway gate can only be opened from inside the house unless you have the access code, and the front door has an alarm code you have to punch in. Different codes, by the way—we have the gate one but not the front door one."

"How did you get the gate code?"

"Digital camera with a telescoping lens." Which I'd had to

rent, costing two months of savings. "I took pictures of Ashlyn punching in the code. Her parents are too careful to let anyone see them do it."

"Ashlyn's not careful?"

"No. She doesn't know what we're trying to do. Or that we're selkies."

"Wait, what?"

"Ashlyn doesn't know about selkies." It was Ashlyn Murphy's one saving grace—she was spoiled and controlling but, unlike her father, she didn't understand the extent of her family's vileness. All she knew was that Brennan and I used to follow her every order, but now we wouldn't. And she hated us for that. "It was part of Mr. Murphy's deal."

"What deal?" When I didn't answer right away, Leisel raised a newly-elegant eyebrow. "That can be one of my two questions."

I hesitated. "There are really two deals."

"Oh, fine." She flashed an exasperated smile. "I'll spend both questions now."

I told Leisel to head back to the triple maple to drop me off, then explained about Declan's deal two years ago.

"So let me see if I've got this straight," Leisel said when I finished. "Your older brother, when he was your age, began to rebel against Mr. Murphy. He was dating Ashlyn's older sister Emily, who also doesn't know you're selkies, and who was in love with him."

"Still is, as far as I know." Sweet, clueless Emily, the only Murphy who still smiled at Brennan and me.

"But how did Declan find out he was a selkie? You said your parents weren't allowed to talk about it."

"I ... don't actually know," I said, surprised. "I never thought about it."

"And how did he rebel? Why could Declan rebel but not your parents?"

I didn't know that either. I frowned.

"Anyway, he did."

Leisel took the hint and moved on. "It was an election year, and the mayor couldn't afford any scandals, so when Declan offered to fall back into line, forever, in return for Mr. Murphy setting you and Brennan free, Mr. Murphy accepted."

I nodded. Leisel's expression told me she knew it wasn't that simple, but she didn't push for details. I could leave it at that, keep Leisel in the dark, but the afternoon had given me time to contemplate the difficulty of Leisel's mission. That the more I told her, the less chance she'd screw things up accidentally.

Besides, after hanging out with her all afternoon I was starting to think that Brennan was right, and that maybe, just maybe, Leisel could be trusted.

"At the time, the restaurant wasn't doing all that well," I said as Leisel turned off the road. "It was more of a dive then. And Emily almost got arrested for doing pot, because of Declan, and was telling her parents she and Declan would elope if they didn't give their blessing. So Declan promised to marry Emily and get her back on the straight and narrow, spend the rest of his life making her happy, and expand the business."

Leisel rolled to a stop at the end of the path and cut the

lights so we wouldn't be noticeable in the woods. "He had ideas for how to make The Golden Fish more profitable," I continued, "and how to launch a frozen seafood line for upscale grocery stores. Mr. Murphy knew it was way outside of my parents' capabilities. They might've been on land for twenty-some years, but though they can follow orders, they're not exactly business-savvy."

"I remember when the shrimp poppers came out last year," Leisel said contemplatively. "They're my mom's favorite. Sustainably sourced and everything."

"I've never had them. Not out of protest, just because we can't afford them." I explained how Brennan and I had to pay for our own food out of pocket. "Are they good?"

"Yeah." Leisel's brow scrunched "So I get that Declan was rebelling, but you said it was hard for him? Because of the … you called it the Haze?"

"That's what Brennan and I call it. When we got our sealskins back, it was like emerging from a suffocating mist." The Murphys' physical possession of our sealskins had, we'd realized, affected us mentally and emotionally. I remembered craving their approval—and when they'd been displeased, like when Ashlyn and I were caught sneaking wine freshman year, I hadn't slept until her parents forgave us.

Rebelling would have taken a lot of effort from Declan, and been exhausting. Painful, too. I'd rarely rebelled, but I remembered splitting headaches when I refused to do something Ashlyn wanted but which her father had expressly forbidden. The contradicting orders hurt.

"Then what was stopping the Murphys from just waiting Declan out?"

"His daughter's turning two next month. Do the math."

Leisel's face cleared. "Emily was pregnant."

"And her parents realized that if they didn't give in to Declan's deal, he could ruin Emily's life before they got him under control. They threatened to destroy his sealskin, but he said if they did, their hold on him would be over and he'd run off with Emily for good. They caved."

"And you and Brennan went free."

"Yep." And Declan married Emily, their daughter Norah becoming one more shackle. A cute one, but on the rare occasions I saw my niece, even though I knew she was innocent I couldn't help but view her as a chain throttling Declan's life. "That was just after freshman year ended. We spent the summer at sea."

"And then you came back."

"Which takes us to the second deal." Pushing the seat lever to recline, I propped my feet on the van's dash. "When Brennan and I showed up again, Douglas Murphy was concerned it was only to free the rest of our family. He's right, obviously, but we swore up and down that we just wanted to get our diplomas, and that since we weren't even eighteen yet we weren't prepared to be on our own in the world."

"And he agreed to let you stay?"

"We got lucky with the timing. At that point, the election was only a couple months off, and Declan and Emily were married. We pointed out that evicting his son-in-law's underage siblings from their home for no apparent reason wouldn't look good to voters. So he agreed to let us stay with our parents, and that we'd be safe from him trying to reclaim our sealskins, until graduation. With a few conditions—one of which is that we couldn't reveal our true selves to Ashlyn."

"Why?"

"I think he didn't want us trying to get Ashlyn on our side. Not that we even thought to try—at that point, we hated her."

"Even though she didn't know the truth?"

"Yeah." I wondered how things might have gone if we'd reacted differently, confided in Ashlyn instead of stonewalling her. But … "She'd owned us. Just being near her made us physically ill." I explained about my Murphy allergies.

"So you know whenever she's around?" Leisel looked fascinated again. "Wow. She literally makes you sick. No wonder you can't stand her."

"That and her personality," I said dryly. Even without the pain of being around her, Ashlyn was still Ashlyn. Self-centered and shallow, she'd always been her daddy's little princess. If we *had* told her the truth two years ago, there was a good chance she'd have sided with her father.

And now? Forget it.

"So Mr. Murphy hasn't tried to steal your sealskins again?" Leisel asked.

"So far." Not that we didn't take precautions, but for all his faults, Douglas Murphy had always been a man of his word. I didn't understand how someone who claimed to be principled could justify slavery, but somehow he managed.

For a while the minivan was silent.

"What's it like?" Leisel said finally. "Being a seal, I mean."

I turned my head to find her studying me avidly, like I was that painted mutant spider. My hackles went up.

"Natural," I said shortly. Leisel dropped her gaze.

"Sorry. I didn't mean to pry."

Yes she had, but I had to admit that if I were her, I'd be curious too.

"It took some getting used to," I said after a moment. "I can't count the number of times I've tried to scratch my face with hands I don't have." That made Leisel smile. "The first time I *changed*, it scared me silly—and it hurt." Though I didn't remember the physical pain of that day as much as I remembered Declan's face as he explained what we really were.

It was a warm June morning just after the close of freshman year. Declan had driven Brennan and me to the Lost Lighthouse, where we often fished in the shade of a curved, crumbling wall.

"You're selkies. We're all selkies," Declan had said, and the only reason I'd known what my older brother was talking about was because he'd made me and Brennan read a mythology book that morning before we piled into his van.

"Can't I be a harpy?" Brennan had asked, not taking Declan any more seriously than I had. "They sounded cooler."

"Don't be a moron," I'd said, laughing. "Harpies are girls."

God, I remembered that moment, that blissful second just before Declan tore our lives apart with the truth. I'd been happy, popular, my biggest worry what I would wear the next day to the movies—Ashlyn had finagled me a date with one of the hottest guys in school. Life had felt perfect.

Then Declan pulled a sack from the cargo hold of his van, and just like that, in the shadow of a half-destroyed lighthouse, my bliss dissolved forever.

Not that I wanted to go back. My former happiness had been numb, hollow. I might be miserable ninety percent of the time now, but at least I was *free* to be so. Free to be pissed off and scared, free to face the truth. I wouldn't trade it for a second.

Outside, the moonlit trees were pale slashes in the forest. I should head home, but it was warm in the van, and I felt oddly ... safe. Which was weird, since just this morning I'd been frightened of telling Leisel anything, but the fact that I'd opened up to someone and they hadn't turned out to be a threat made me almost giddy.

Plus, I hadn't had anyone to talk to besides my brother in two and a half years. I wanted to confess how powerless I felt all the time, complain about how expensive milk had gotten, and how it sucked not owning even a computer in the age of smart phones and tablets. But I curbed my impulse to share. Leisel was still largely an unknown quantity, and if she did by some miracle help us get out of here, I'd never see her again. It wasn't like we could be friends.

"I have a question of my own," I said, wanting to stall just a tiny bit longer. "You accepted what we are overnight. How?"

Leisel smiled faintly. "Well, I watched that video a lot."

"And what, you believe everything on YouTube?"

"No, obviously, but I took the video myself. And it's not as crazy as you might think. The ocean is full of unbelievable things. Have you ever seen a picture of a vampire squid?"

I shook my head.

"It looks like a Photoshop joke. But it's real. And pretending you're not what you are is silly. The proof is on the video." She sat up straighter. "Which I'm going to delete tonight when I get home. I swear."

"Thanks." But a tendril of suspicion marred my gratitude. How was I supposed to know for sure whether all copies were erased? There was no way to prove it, so was this just a ploy to gain my trust?

Suddenly I felt on edge again. Who was this girl, really? But Leisel's smile glimmered, earnest in the dark, and I tried not to let my knee-jerk paranoia ruin what we'd accomplished today. We'd bonded, sort of. That was good—Leisel was less likely to betray me if she thought we were friends.

I just had to remember that people like me couldn't afford friends.

"It's late." I lowered my feet from the dash and opened the door. "I still have Spanish homework to finish." Grabbing my bag, I hopped out.

"I'll see you and Brennan tomorrow?" Leisel asked.

"As soon as we get off shift." Leisel wasn't allowed out past 9pm on school nights, but on the drive back she'd come up with an alternate meeting place: her bedroom. Her house was a Cape Cod style like ours, but hers had a finished walk-out basement she'd claimed when she was ten. She said her dad, a veterinarian, went to bed as soon as they finished watching *Wild & Wonderful*, some nature show. "I've got the address."

"Great." But Leisel looked worried.

"You'll be fine tomorrow. Wear the aqua sweater. You'll look amazing, trust me." Her uncertain nod lacked the fire she'd shown earlier, so I rapped my knuckles on the door to catch her attention. "Remember, if you screw up, I'll chop you into fish sticks." I grimaced exaggeratedly to let her know I was kidding, and thankfully Leisel laughed.

"No pressure," she said, but she was smiling now.

I shut the door and trudged off into the dark.

Chapter 8

Wednesday night, Brennan and I snuck across the trimmed lawn of a house nestled in a secluded glen. We ducked around back and found the walk-out basement door.

"This had better be the right place," I muttered.

"You're the one who wrote down the address," Brennan said. "It's on you if we're greeted by an old guy and a baseball bat."

I shot him a look, then knocked. We both exhaled audibly when Leisel opened the door. Brennan flashed our co-conspirator a smile as we trooped inside. Her cheeks went a little red. Rolling my eyes at Brennan's effect on girls, I glanced around the room.

Animals were everywhere, from posters to calendars to books. Jungle leaves pattered Leisel's bedspread, little red and blue frogs peeking out here and there. A gift from her mom? A small desk held a lamp and a laptop, and I eyed the latter enviously for a moment.

Cozy and softly lit, the room boasted a full-size pair of windows on the walk-out side that made me feel like I wasn't in a basement at all. It was way better than my room, bare as a jail cell. Taking off my jacket, I sat down on the futon.

Brennan wandered around looking at stuff, bending to check out the books on her shelves.

"Where'd you park?" Leisel asked me.

"Around the bend, then cut across the woods to get here. Actually, we could have walked—it's only like two miles as the crow flies." Though that would add an hour of round-trip travel to this meeting, and I was already tired. "Is your dad asleep?"

"Yeah." She glanced at Brennan, her expression nervous. Hiding my smile, I wondered if she'd ever had a boy in her room before.

"You look awesome," I told her, because she did. In her sea-colored sweater, dark jeans and black flats, hair pin-straight and eyebrows tamed, Leisel would fit into any group she wanted. Sort of sad, really; now that I'd made her over, I doubted anyone could pick her out of a crowd.

But for our mission, that was perfect.

"You really like sea turtles, don't you?" Brennan asked, still perusing her shelves. "There are like twelve books here on them."

Leisel reddened. "Um. Yeah, I guess." She picked up a cell phone from her bedside table. "So I got my new phone today—should we exchange numbers?"

Brennan finally abandoned the bookcase. "We're getting new numbers in November, but sure." He flopped down on Leisel's bed.

Leisel pulled her desk chair over and sat down.

"New numbers?"

"We have to pay for our own cell phones," I said. "We're worried Mr. Murphy might try to track us with them, so we get pay-as-you-go burner phones and replace them every two months."

Or if we had a scare, like that time Brennan left his phone in The Golden Fish. It was gone when we doubled back, but magically reappeared in the lost-and-found the next day. Figuring Mr. Murphy had bugged it, we'd ditched that set pronto.

Remembering my vandalism of Leisel's old phone, I asked her how much I owed her.

"You don't have to pay me back," she said. "My dad got me a new one. Didn't even take it out of my allowance; I told him it got trampled in the hallway."

I opened my mouth to insist—it would be painfully expensive, but we weren't total charity cases, and if they gave out bitch awards I'd surely won a few by stomping on her phone—but before I could, Brennan asked Leisel her number. She recited it, and he punched it into his phone.

"I'm calling you Lady Turtle," he told her.

"No, you're not," I said. "That's obviously a fake name."

"So? I have everyone under false names." Brennan showed Leisel his screen. "See, Jeffrey Adams is House McLouse, because his house is literally the best I've ever seen for parties—they have a second-story balcony with a hot tub—but he cheats on his girlfriend all the time."

"He cheats on Stacey?" Leisel's eyes widened. "Everyone says they're the perfect couple!"

Brennan shrugged. "And Cass is here as Bossy van Grump."

Leisel laughed, and I swiped his phone.

"I am not!" But there was my current burner number. "Brennan!"

They were both laughing now, but Leisel at least attempted to stop when she saw my glare. "I'll put you in as my cousins Anna and Nate." She tapped at her phone. "They live in Tucson and I never actually call them, but no one else has to know that." She glanced over at me; I hadn't even gotten out my phone. "Did you already get my number?"

"Cass doesn't put in contacts," Brennan said before I could explain. "She punches the call in each time."

"Really?"

"I only ever call Brennan anyways," I said. "I memorize the number, and wipe the SIM card every day."

"Oh. Well, here." Leisel scrawled something on a post-it. "You can burn it after memorizing," she said with a grin. Brennan gave her his number, then got up to wander around again as I recited mine.

"Wow." Across the room, Brennan had opened the closet door and was staring inside. "Holy stuffed animal alert. You've got a whole zoo in here!"

Leisel's face flared crimson.

"Brennan, sit down," I said. "Stop going through her stuff." She'd obviously hidden the plush animals before we came. Noticing a lot of bare surfaces in her room, I wondered what else she'd thought too nerdy to show us.

"What?" Brennan grinned, then caught sight of Leisel's face. "Don't be embarrassed; I think it's cute you still have your stuffed animals." Reaching inside, he came out with a gray hippo the size of a cat. At my glare, he ambled over and settled on the bed again, nestling the hippo beside him. "Our parents trashed all of ours while we were gone." He looked at me. "Remember the twin pandas we used to have? You superglued a bow onto yours so we'd know it was a girl."

"You remember that?" I said, surprised.

"Of course. And then I glued an identical bow onto mine, and you got really mad. So then you added a necklace ..." He kept going with the story, our war of the pandas, and even though Brennan was getting us way off topic—we had plans to make, and couldn't stay here all night—I let him talk, because I'd forgotten most of the panda war and couldn't believe he recalled it in such detail. Plus, it was making Leisel relax again. By the time Brennan was done, we were all laughing.

"Anyway." Still smiling, I looked at Leisel. "How did lunch go today?"

She glanced at Brennan. "Good, I think. Ashlyn asked me to sit with her for the rest of the week, actually."

Brennan punched the air with the stuffed hippo. "Score!"

"She what?" That was way more progress than I'd expected on the first day. Had Leisel's makeover really done the trick—or was this suspiciously easy? "Why?"

"I think it was because of what Brennan did," Leisel said.

"What do you mean?" Brennan wasn't even supposed to be in the picture; at school Leisel couldn't know us, and vice versa.

"I went over to Ashlyn's table to talk about yearbook stuff, like we planned." Leisel grimaced. "At first she didn't even know who I was, which was embarrassing, but there was an empty seat so I just sat down and asked her about the accent colors for the junior photo sections. She seemed annoyed … until Brennan walked over."

I sucked in a breath. "He what?"

Brennan held up a placating hand. "I had an idea in homeroom this morning. Leisel worming her way into Ashlyn's good graces could take weeks, if not months, right? Except what if we could speed up the process?"

"How?"

"The Date and Ditch." Brennan spread his arms out wide, as if this explained everything, but I didn't get it.

Leisel looked confused too. "You mean where you ask Ashlyn's friends to dances and then leave them there after like half an hour?"

He lowered his arms. "So you've heard of it."

"It's almost a rite of passage. People take bets on who among Ashlyn's friends you'll ask out, and whether she'll say yes." Leisel paused. "Though I don't think anyone bets on her saying no anymore."

"Exactly. And I was thinking: Homecoming is next week, and what if— "

"Whoa," I broke in, finally understanding. "That's brilliant!"

My brother grinned. "Isn't it?"

"Isn't what?" Leisel asked.

Excitement made me jittery. "Brennan asks you to the Homecoming dance, and you say no." Leisel still looked confused. "See? You'd be the first of Ashlyn's friends to do that!"

"Thus proving yourself a better friend than any Ashlyn already has," Brennan finished. "She can't help but be impressed."

"Oh." Leisel's expression cleared. "That could work."

"Provided you are at least nominally Ashlyn's friend to start with." I glanced at Brennan. "What did you say to Ashlyn to make her invite Leisel to sit with her?"

"I just mentioned that I couldn't wait to see which lovely lady would accompany me to our final Homecoming dance."

"I bet she liked that." Imagining Ashlyn's irritation, I smiled.

"And I told Leisel I'd never seen her around before." Brennan grinned. "Then I left."

"I wasn't sure what to do, so I went back to talking about yearbook stuff," Leisel said. "Then Ashlyn told me she couldn't deal with it now, but I should come sit with them for the rest of the week." She leaned her elbows on her knees and propped her chin in her hands. "She wants to use me as a decoy friend, doesn't she?"

"Yep." Brennan absently patted the stuffed hippo. "She

tried the same trick last year with that foreign exchange student."

"And you totally fell for it," I said. Brennan shrugged.

"Marietta was hot." He turned back to Leisel. "Anyway, Ashlyn will adopt you until Homecoming, hoping it will keep me from asking out her real friends." He threw the hippo into the air, then caught him. "But you will prove to be the one person in Ashlyn's circle who refuses to put a hot date—" he pointed to himself, "—over friendship."

"Theoretically turning Leisel from a decoy friend into a real one," I concluded. If it worked, it would cut weeks, even months off our plan. "It's worth a shot."

"What if it doesn't work?" Leisel said. "What if she drops me after Homecoming anyway?"

"Why would she?" Brennan said, but Leisel and I exchanged glances.

"If she dumps you, we'll come up with another plan," I told her.

Leisel frowned, then swiped her laptop from her desk. "Actually, I think I have an idea for that. I found something the other day." Moving over to sit beside me on the futon, she pulled up a website with a simple landing page. "I was searching the web for anything on selkies, and this site came up."

Brennan hadn't moved from the bed. "Want to tell me and hippo what it says?"

"Silver Rescue League," I read. "So?"

Leisel moved the cursor over the word *Silver.* Now it read …

"Selkie Rescue League," I said softly.

Brennan sat up straighter. "What does that mean?"

"All it says on the site is 'Please contact us if you or someone you know needs help.'" Leisel looked up. "Don't you see? They're an organization that helps selkies! I thought maybe we could email them, and see if— "

"NO," Brennan and I said in unison. Leisel stopped short.

"Even if it's not a joke or something," I said, "there's no way we're telling some strangers about our family."

"But what if they could help?" Leisel asked. "I mean, what's the harm?"

"What if they're just pretending to be selkie-rescuers? What if they're really a group hunting for selkies to enslave, or a media group fishing for someone to make a story out of, or a government group looking for freaks to experiment on? That's just off the top of my head." I shook my head. "And even if I'm just paranoid and they do somehow happen to be genuine, how do we know they won't screw things up?"

Leisel hesitated. "We could be careful and just email them to ask— "

"Thus giving them information about us? No way." I shut the laptop for emphasis.

"But we don't have to mention your family by name, and I could send the email, so they'd never know anything unless we decide to."

I crossed my arms stubbornly, so Leisel looked at Brennan.

"No," he said. "I'm with Cass on this one. No contacting strangers unless we have to. Right now, we have a plan, and it's a really good one. Maybe if we get desperate later we'll come back to this."

"Okay." Leisel put the laptop back on her desk. "What now?"

"We'd better get some sleep," I said. After peeking out the door to make sure no one was watching, I went outside. As cozy as Leisel's room had been, I welcomed the crisp, cold air filling my lungs.

Brennan paused at the threshold to hand Leisel her stuffed animal.

"Sorry," he said. "I almost tried to steal your hippo."

"You could keep him if you want." Flushing, Leisel ducked her head.

Brennan smiled. "Goodnight, Lady Turtle." He walked around the corner of the house. I smiled goodbye to Leisel too, and followed.

"She's totally in love with you," I warned him. My brother shrugged his shoulders under his long-sleeve shirt.

"Chill, Cass. She's harmless. And cute."

"Don't toy with her, Brennan."

"I won't." He walked faster, getting ahead of me.

"I'm serious."

He raked his hand through his sandy brown hair.

"Will you chill?"

"I'm just saying," I muttered, walking in Brennan's footsteps on the cold leafy ground. I ran into him when he whirled, glaring.

"*I'm* just saying, stop trying to control me."

My mouth dropped open. "What?" But Brennan turned around again.

"Can we just go home? I'm tired." He walked into the dark.

I stared after him, not sure what had just happened. Was Brennan pissed at me? I knew I was bossy, but that was because he usually waited for me to tell him what to do. Frowning, I followed him to the truck in silence.

At home, I was getting ready for bed when my cell phone buzzed. I checked the screen—Leisel's number. Not wanting to talk in my house, I threw a blanket around my shoulders and went out into the backyard.

"What's wrong?" I asked.

"Nothing," Leisel said. "I just had a question."

"We're not supposed to call unless it's important."

"That's why I wanted to know … do you have another email address besides the ones through the school? So I can just email anything I find out?"

"We do, but we can't check it every day." I explained our computerless existence.

"Seriously?" Leisel sounded incredulous. "How do you survive without a computer?"

"Somehow we manage." Brennan and I used the school's library desktops to send email and type up papers. "Let's stick to texts. And don't forget to delete them."

"Okay." But Leisel didn't hang up. I gazed up at the stars, bright and far away, and waited. Finally she said, "I didn't want to ask in front of Brennan, but … why does he do it? The Date and Ditch, I mean."

I pulled the blanket tighter around my shoulders, though I wasn't cold.

"To get back at Ashlyn."

"But you said she doesn't know, right? About selkies, and what her dad is doing?"

"It's complicated. Brennan has his reasons." And they were none of Leisel's business.

"Yeah, but isn't it a little …"

"Douchey?" I supplied wryly.

Leisel laughed. "Yeah."

I shrugged, though she couldn't see me.

"Considering what her family has done to mine, I don't lose sleep over it."

"I just wondered if you'd ever thought of asking Ashlyn for help."

That startled a bark of laughter from me. "If you were lost in the woods, would you ask a bear for directions?"

Leisel was quiet. "I looked at our freshman yearbook," she finally said. "Ashlyn and Brennan were voted class couple, and you're beside Ashlyn in every picture she's in."

It was true. When we returned at the start of sophomore year, Brennan had rocked the school by dumping Ashlyn without ceremony or explanation. My own abandonment of Granite Harbor High's darling had proven less gossip-worthy, and by now most people had forgotten we'd ever been anything but enemies.

"We were best friends," I admitted. Back when I was a different person. My stomach turned. "I didn't have much of a choice, remember?"

"It just seemed like you three were close once."

Once upon a nightmare. But I understood what Leisel was saying.

"Trust me—she'd never help us. That bridge is long since burned." Even the ashes were cold. And with Ashlyn's father in her ear for the last two and a half years, telling her God-knew-what about us, I knew it could never be rebuilt. "Look, I have to get some sleep."

"Okay. Goodnight, *Anna*."

That made me smile. "Goodnight." I almost wished I'd done the fake-name thing with her and Brennan. But my phone had zero contacts, so even a false name would stand out.

That struck me, suddenly, as sad. *Safe*, I told myself. It was safer this way.

I stared up at the stars, letting the cold steady me, then went to bed.

Chapter 9

Brennan's plan went off without a hitch, and by the end of school on Friday, every hallway buzzed with the story.

Leisel said no to Brennan.

Leisel who?

Ashlyn's new friend. Brennan asked her to Homecoming at lunch.

And she said no? Sometimes it takes a few times, right?

But they talked for like ten minutes in the lunch line and afterwards.

And she still said no?

She told him she'd never date someone who was an asshole to her friend!

And Brennan had stormed off. Five people had asked me if it was true. I pretended not to know or care, but grinned inwardly all afternoon.

My brother and Leisel had practiced their charade yesterday—Brennan blew off his shift at The Golden Fish to meet with her. I'd worried his absence might make Mr. Murphy suspicious, but Brennan pointed out that he skipped work at least twice a month, so *not* skipping once in a while would look suspicious. Annoyingly, he had a point. I wished I had a history of absences too.

After school, Brennan and I met Leisel at the triple maple—we didn't have to be on shift at The Golden Fish until seven on Friday nights.

"It worked!" Leisel tumbled out of her minivan. "It totally worked! Ashlyn invited me to go to the dance with her friends in their limo!"

The tight anticipation in my chest gave way, and for a second I thought I might cry. Leisel was in. This might actually work. Sitting on the fence around the gravel lot, I put my hands over my face and took deep breaths.

"You should have gotten an Oscar," Brennan was saying when I wrenched myself under control. He high-fived Leisel. "Wait, what smells so amazing?"

Leisel dove back into her car, coming out with a box that smelled like cheese and pepperoni and oniony goodness. My mouth watered.

"I didn't actually get any lunch today, because of all the excitement, so I picked up a pizza on the way." Leisel brought it over. "Want some?"

"Oh my God, you are the best." Brennan snagged a slice as Leisel blushed and handed the box to me. I hesitated, remembering how I'd told her we had to buy our own food. Was this her idea of charity? But that hot, oozing cheese smelled so much better than cold pride, so after a moment I dug in too.

We celebrated and talked over plans for an hour or so, until Leisel had to meet her dad to go birdwatching.

"You're going to be there, right? At Homecoming?" Leisel asked me before getting into her minivan. "Just in case I need you?"

I didn't go to dances, so I shook my head.

"Why would you need me? You're doing great."

"Ashlyn's terrifying." Leisel's dark eyes pleaded with me. "All her friends are. I don't know what I'm doing. Please?"

I really didn't want to go. It wasn't like we'd be able to talk anyway, and I hated crowds. Back when I'd been under the Haze at Ashlyn's side, I'd been popular, the center of attention—or next to it, anyway—but now I preferred to be unseen.

But the taste of pepperoni lingered in my mouth, and if Leisel could actually get herself into Ashlyn's house and find our parents' sealskins, I'd owe her a lot more than moral support.

"Okay," I promised. "I'll be there."

That night during a break in my shift, I ducked into the kitchen to find Declan. Billy, the sous chef, pointed towards the hallway leading to Declan's office.

I hesitated—Mr. Murphy sometimes met with Declan in the evenings, and I'd rather avoid running into him. But it was way earlier than he usually visited, and Brennan whistled unconcernedly as he wiped counters, so the coast must be clear.

I approached Declan's open door quietly. The jellyfish-stung nausea that plagued me with Mr. Murphy's presence didn't strike, so I breathed a sigh of relief and walked in.

Declan, wearing a white chef's uniform, was studying a report or something on his computer. If he noticed my entrance, he didn't show it.

"Declan," I said. My brother's gaze, hazel like our dad's, flicked up.

"What do you want, Cassandra?"

"I need next Saturday night off of work."

He leaned back in his chair. "Why?"

"For Homecoming."

A long pause.

"I'll think about it." Declan returned his attention to his computer. "Go back to work."

I stared at my older brother, wishing … I don't know. That he'd yell at me like he yelled at Brennan, instead of treating me like an employee he barely knew. That I could free him, and repay his sacrifice, show him we weren't wasting it after all. But Declan ignored me, and finally I returned to the front of the restaurant.

At the end of my shift, Declan waved me down the hall and into his office. "So can I get next Saturday off already?" I asked, irked that he'd made me wait all night. "Because it's not that much to ask, and—"

As I crossed the room's threshold, itchy pain broke out over my skin. My stomach twisted up like eels, and I spun to find Mr. Murphy lounging in a leather chair at the far side of the office.

"What are you doing here?" Then I bit my tongue. "Sir."

"I own the place," Mr. Murphy reminded me mildly. Sipping from a lowball glass filled with amber liquid from the stash of expensive whiskey Declan kept on hand just for his visits, he wore his usual impeccable suit, accented with gleaming cufflinks. "Declan mentioned your request during the course of our meeting."

"I'm allowed a day off once in a while." I struggled for my usual show of defiant calm. "Aren't I?"

Mr. Murphy's glass clinked as he set it on the table.

"I think it's interesting that the night you want off just so happens to be the night I'll be out of town attending a fundraiser." He glanced at my brother. "Don't you think that's interesting?"

"Yes." Declan's eyes were slits. If he thought, as Mr. Murphy obviously did, that I was thinking of trying to break into the house—a clear violation of the Deal—why was he angry? Didn't he *want* me to free him?

Wrenching my features into an expressionless mask, I crossed my arms.

"It has nothing to do with you. It's the Homecoming dance."

"You haven't gone to the last couple," Mr. Murphy pointed out. "You can't expect me to believe you actually intend to spend the evening dancing with your classmates and drinking stale lemonade."

"This is the last Homecoming of high school. I want to go."

Mr. Murphy stood and walked deliberately closer. His shiny black shoes creaked; his blond hair gleamed in the lamplight. Pausing a step away, he studied me with a narrowed gaze. My skin stung so badly it was hard to stay still, but I stood my ground.

Finally Mr. Murphy raised a brow. "Very well."

"I can go?" I backed up, ready to be gone before he could change his mind. "Thank you, sir."

"Wait." Mr. Murphy held up a hand. "I want proof that you and your brother bought tickets."

"I don't have mine yet. And I don't know if Brennan's going." More importantly, I hadn't planned on actually buying a ticket—they were fifty dollars each, and I wasn't worried about sneaking in. Security was not exactly tight at Granite Harbor High.

"Of course he's going." Mr. Murphy scowled. "He always shows up, doesn't he? Skips work without notice to escort some idiot girl in an effort to make my daughter cry."

Ashlyn obviously kept her father well-informed.

"I don't think Brennan's doing that this year."

Mr. Murphy waved that off.

"One girl said no. I'm sure another will be happy to take her place. This is the deal—you show me the receipts for both tickets, and I'll give you the day off work."

I hesitated. "Or I could just skip too."

Mr. Murphy's mouth twisted in what passed for amusement.

"Brennan's dishwashing skills are hardly missed. But if you

skip, we'll have no choice but to hire another hostess, and I'm afraid there wouldn't be room for you anymore."

And as he'd made clear two years ago, when I'd tried — under a false name — to join the maid crew that cleaned his house, no other business in town would hire me. Damn. My pathetic dress budget had just been slashed even further.

"Fine," I ground out. "I'll show you the receipt Monday."

"See that you do." He gestured for me to go, but just as my hand grasped the knob, he cleared his throat. "Cassandra."

Forced to pause, I reluctantly met his gaze. Invisible knives cut at my skin, but I set my jaw. "Yes?"

"If I catch you or your brother anywhere near my house that night, you'll regret it. Do you understand?"

A chill chased down my spine. Mr. Murphy always kept his word.

"Yes, sir," I said, and fled.

Chapter 10

The day of the dance, Leisel was still nervous, so I snuck over that afternoon to help her get ready. At seven she was due at Ashlyn's friend Liz's house, where the parents would take pictures before the group went out to a pre-dance dinner.

"You excited?" I brushed sparkling shadow the color of stardust onto Leisel's eyelids. She wore a lacy blue sheath she'd found while shopping with Ashlyn on Tuesday. Her silver wristlet matched her heels. I'd smoothed her black hair into loose curls, now pinned up artistically.

"Are you kidding?" Leisel muttered, eyes closed. "This last week has been a minefield."

"You're doing great." Since she'd "proven" herself a true friend by turning Brennan down, Leisel was Ashlyn's new favorite pet. At the football game yesterday she'd been right next to Ashlyn on the bleachers, even after Ashlyn was crowned Homecoming Queen at halftime.

"Popularity is terrifying," Leisel said fervently.

Lips twitching, I put away the eye shadow.

"There you go." We stood up, and Leisel went to her full-length mirror. Her eyes, enlarged by black liner and highlighted by the silver shadow, went wide with wonder.

"Wow. I look so hot!" She laughed. "This is crazy. Thank you."

"The least I could do." I grinned.

Leisel shook her head, suddenly earnest.

"Seriously, thank you. I spent the last three years thinking it was my lot in life to be a frizzy-haired dork. I *never* thought I could look like this."

I smiled, touched but a little uncomfortable. "It's just clothes and hairspray." Looks were a mask; you couldn't trust them. They never showed the person underneath. I knew that better than most. But if it made Leisel happy, I was happy to be able to repay her a little for all she was doing.

"It's magic." Leisel went to one of her bookcases. "I have something for you, by the way." From a shelf holding cords and other gadgetry, she picked up a laptop twice the size of the sleek one on her desk. "My mom got me a new computer over the summer. I thought you and Brennan might want the old one."

Whoa. She wanted to give me a computer? It took me a stunned moment to shake my head.

"That's really nice, but no thanks."

"You don't want it?"

I craved that computer almost as much as the ocean, but … "I'm not a charity case," I said quietly. "Thanks, Leisel, but you're already helping us enough."

She pursed her lips, shiny with the berry gloss I'd taught her to apply.

"But you need this. It's ridiculous that I have no way to get in touch with you except through your phone. Besides, Brennan says the school computers are really slow; it probably takes you twice as long as it should to get research or homework done."

"We manage." And I didn't care that I hadn't seen the latest viral videos everyone giggled over. Though having a computer would let me track Ashlyn's movements more easily; she was always posting about what she was doing, and with whom. But I couldn't accept such an expensive present.

"I'm really not using it anymore." Leisel held the laptop out. "Take it."

"No thanks." But Leisel kept badgering me and finally, remembering Declan and my parents, I weakened. Why did I deserve pride when they had none? If the computer could help in even a small way, I'd be an idiot to turn it down.

"Could anyone trace it back to you?" I asked. That was possible, right? Not getting to surf the Internet all day like my peers meant I was sadly lacking in tech wizardry and know-how.

"Doubtful. I cleaned off all my animal stickers, wiped the drive and took off the registration label. No one should be able to tell you got it from me."

I hesitated one more time, then nodded.

"Thank you." My throat grew thick. The only gifts I got these days were when Brennan snagged me snacks from The Golden Fish's kitchen. I coughed to cover the hitch in my voice. "That's really nice of you."

Leisel put the computer in a plastic shopping bag, along with its power cord and a couple other attachments.

"One more thing." She glanced at me sideways. "Don't be mad, but I found a couple people on social networks who I think are in the Selkie Rescue League."

My warm fuzzies evaporated in a spike of panic.

"Leisel, if you emailed them I will never— "

"I didn't, I swear." Leisel went to her desk. "I just searched the site for people who mention the Silver Rescue League in their list of hobbies."

"Oh." That was smart. I peered over her shoulder at the page she'd pulled up on her laptop. A list of profiles. She pointed at each one—a woman in San Francisco, two people in Hawaii … Leisel tapped the second-to-last photo.

"Then there's this guy. He's in Boston."

Paul Alderson had dark auburn hair and cheekbones that could cut glass. Serious gray eyes. He was a freshman at Boston University, majoring in economics. His hobbies included reading, surfing, "anything outdoors," and, of course, the Silver Rescue League.

"Superhot, right?" Leisel giggled a little giddily and clicked through more pictures. "See this one where he's surfing?"

In the photo Paul stood shirtless on a sand dune next to his upright surfboard as he stared into the sun. Alright, he was hot.

"So you want to what, ask him out?" I teased, and Leisel flushed.

"No, but maybe we could set up an anonymous account and message him."

My brief moment of humor fled. "No offense, but we went over this. No."

"Right now we have all our eggs in one basket," Leisel argued. "Me. And to be honest, I don't know whether I can do this."

"You're doing amazing so far."

"But what if I *do* get into Ashlyn's house, but still can't find the sealskins? It might be good to have more than one plan in motion, you know? Not that we have to give them information about your family, but what if we anonymously asked this Paul guy about the SRL?" I didn't respond, and Leisel sighed. "Look, I know you and Brennan are paranoid about people finding out about you, and you have reason to be. But if there are people out here who could help, who might know what they're doing … Just think about it, okay?"

A voice called Leisel's name upstairs, and she grabbed her silver purse from the bed. "That's my dad. He's going to drive me over." Then she froze. "Wait, that's not nerdy, is it?"

My discomfort over Leisel's pushing ebbed, and I laughed. "Don't worry, you'll be fine."

Leisel gave me an anxious smile. "See you at the dance?"

"See you there."

Two hours later, I parked the pick-up in the school lot and stared through my windshield at the brightly-lit gym. Great.

I did *not* feel like going inside and pretending I belonged. Especially in my current crappy mood.

When I'd gotten home, I'd found an oak leaf on my desk—Brennan's sign that he'd gone out swimming. It made me furious. I desperately wanted to be out swimming with him—I hadn't been in the water in two weeks, which made me jumpy and anxious—but he knew I had to be here for Leisel. And swimming alone was dangerous. Even swimming together wasn't totally secure, as we'd found out, but using the buddy system at least made it a little safer. I didn't want Brennan out there risking discovery by himself. He knew that.

And he'd gone anyway. I was so mad I could spit.

I'd rather wrangle a walrus than attend my first dance since I'd been freed, but Leisel needed my moral support. With a sigh, I emerged from the safety of my truck.

The night was freezing—below, actually, the radio claimed—but I left my coat in the car. One time in middle school when Ashlyn and I played truth or dare, she'd dared me to run through a drift of snow wearing only my underwear. When I got back inside I hadn't even shivered. She'd laughed and called me a freak. I'd given her the same dare, and Ashlyn nearly turned blue. She'd called me a freak again, not laughing anymore. It was one of the first inklings I'd had that my life wasn't normal, but the Haze had blotted out any curiosity.

Squaring my shoulders, I walked to the gym entrance, handed my ticket over, and went inside. Ugh, it was crowded. The hallway by the lockers swarmed with people, everyone shouting over the music spilling from the open doors of the basketball court. A headache started immediately.

I wove my way through the crowd, trying not to touch anyone. It was a losing battle, but I finally shoved through to the basketball court. That room, cavernous with the overhead lights off and the bleachers pushed back, was thankfully less panic-inducing. A large crowd danced in the middle, and colored club lights swirled dizzyingly in the darkness, but plenty of space breathed at the edges of the room. I found a bare patch of wall and let my eyes adjust.

My classmates looked … happy. If I were normal, I could be one of them, rocking out to songs without a care in the world besides whether my date was going to kiss me tonight.

I remembered a middle-school dance I'd spent on the arm of Dave, a guy who was friends with Ashlyn's then-boyfriend—that was before she and Brennan got together. Dave and I had kissed, that night and afterwards. He'd been nice enough, but when Ashlyn broke up with her boyfriend, I'd dutifully broken up with Dave too, out of solidarity.

None of it had been my choice.

"Hey, Cassandra," called Mindy from History. I waved, and she walked over with her boyfriend Jaron. "I thought I saw you over here. I thought you weren't coming."

Right, I'd turned down her friend. "I heard there were free chips," I joked. Mindy's mouth tightened.

"Well, have fun." She hauled Jaron off.

Wow. My social skills had clearly atrophied during the last

two years. And Leisel looked up to me? Sighing, I went to find some punch.

Or not—Ashlyn and her friends crowded around the snacks table. *Found you.* Aborting my punch mission, I pretended to drink from the water fountain. Leisel looked a tiny bit gawky, but when Ashlyn whispered something in her ear, she laughed. I loitered until Leisel noticed me. She smiled a little bigger, then looked away. Moral support achieved.

Wandering back to the dance floor, I stood around feeling awkward. A guy I knew from Calculus class asked me to dance, but I told him no thanks. I used to love dancing almost as much as painting, but that was before. Under the Haze.

I refused to be anything like that girl anymore.

People were glancing at me, as if surprised to see the self-appointed outcast at a school event. It started to freak me out, and I pushed my way into the crowded hall. There had to be a lonely bathroom where I could hide out for a while.

Unfortunately, in the mess of people I managed to stumble into Ashlyn's friend Liz.

"Watch it," she snapped, then did a double take. She nudged the girl next to her, and I realized my skin felt jellyfish-stung—I hadn't noticed in the crush. My stomach sank even before Ashlyn turned around.

"Cassandra?" She looked genuinely puzzled. "What are *you* doing here?"

I shrugged. "I heard a monkey got voted Homecoming Queen, and wanted to see who it was. Any idea?"

Liz's mouth dropped open. Ashlyn's green eyes blazed.

"Nice dress," she said loudly. "Where'd you get it, the bargain bin?"

Not the cleverest of insults, but it hit home anyway because she was right. A couple girls to my left tittered, but I told myself that my dress, deep violet with thin straps that crisscrossed in the back, was fine. Sure, the fabric was cheap, but it was soft and clung. With my small cache of makeup employed, I looked good.

At least I'd thought I did.

The dance had put me sufficiently on edge that my well of retorts had run dry, but before I could flee James Owen, the Homecoming King, appeared between me and Ashlyn.

"Looking good, Cassandra." He smiled. "Want to dance?"

Ashlyn's eyes narrowed.

"Unbelievable." She glared at me. "You're here three seconds and you're already trying to steal my date."

"Whoa." Grinning, James put an arm around Ashlyn, then reached for me. "There's enough of this king to go around."

"Bite me," I snapped, slipping out of reach.

"Come back and I will," he teased. I knew he was just having fun—he wasn't a bad guy; even his ex-girlfriends stayed friends with him—but having anyone touch me without my permission made my skin crawl. I walked quickly down the hall. Turning the corner, I ducked the chaperon and made for the bathroom near the English wing.

The music behind me faded, and my clicking heels grew loud in the quiet. Slipping inside the blue bathroom door, I sighed in relief.

My phone buzzed in my purse.

Where are you? From Leisel, of course.

Girl's room, English, I texted back, then erased the message chain. Hopefully Leisel would remember to do the same.

A minute later, Leisel ducked into the bathroom.

"There you are. Don't worry, Ashlyn's dancing; she won't miss me for a few minutes." Her eyes widened. "Wow, you look awesome; no wonder James Owen was hitting on you."

"Thanks," I said wryly.

"No, really. You're gorgeous. I mean, you're always beautiful in that *I don't even care* kind of way, but— "

"And here I thought you were crushing on my brother," I joked. Still, the compliment made me feel better after Ashlyn's sneering. Then I realized Leisel looked stricken. "What?"

"Why would you say that?"

I raised a brow.

"You told him he could keep your hippo."

She winced. "God, I'm such a dork." Then she went pale. "You didn't tell him, did you? Please don't tell him."

"I won't." It was kinder not to mention that Brennan already knew. "But you realize he's … off limits, right? Because of … everything."

"Of course. I know it's pointless. Obviously." Avoiding my gaze, Leisel turned to the sink.

"Why'd you track me down?"

"Oh. Um, Ashlyn's actually sort of upset that you came."

"Yeah, I noticed."

Leisel turned on the faucet and washed her hands. "Well,

I think I'm doing okay, so ..." She trailed off, sudsing and rinsing industriously.

I blinked as I realized what she was saying. "You want me to leave?" After I'd spent a hundred dollars on tickets, plus sixty more on the dress and shoes, *and* been forced to beg Mr. Murphy for the night off? Anger heated my stomach. "I'm only here in the first place because *you* asked me to be."

Leisel turned off the faucet.

"I know, but Ashlyn's actually being really nice. And Valentino Remez asked me for the next slow dance! So I'm totally fine, you don't have to hang around." She dried her hands, then tossed the paper towel in the trash and made for the door as if she couldn't wait to get back.

What happened to *popularity is terrifying?* Just this afternoon Leisel had been practically throwing-up nervous. Now she looked like she was having the time of her life. She was the center of attention—or at least next to it. I frowned.

"Ashlyn is not your friend."

Leisel peeked into the hallway, towards the light and music and crowds.

"She is tonight." With a shrug, she slipped away.

My hand fisted at my side. Not that I even wanted to be here, but ... I exhaled in frustration, aware of a rising worry. What if Leisel succumbed to the lure of popularity, the fun of the spotlight? I'd shunned it for two years, but remembered how it felt. I'd made Leisel into someone Ashlyn wanted by her side ... maybe Leisel wanted to stay there.

But Ashlyn didn't really care about Leisel—she just liked

having a lackey who hadn't fallen for Brennan's smile. Couldn't Leisel see how Ashlyn was using her?

Like I was.

Oh, no. What if Leisel decided she cared more about Ashlyn than helping Brennan and me? What if she decided not to risk that friendship by searching Ashlyn's house—worse, what if she told Ashlyn what we were up to? I paced the length of the bathroom, then leaned against the far wall. The tiles were cold and hard against my bare shoulders.

What was I going to do if Leisel flaked?

I remembered the Silver Rescue League website, our backup plan. Leisel had shown me the profile of that guy, Paul something, who lived in Boston. Maybe I should email him after all.

The idea made me nearly break out in hives. I wasn't that tech-savvy, but what about IP-tracking? The SRL might find me even if I tried contacting them anonymously.

Then I had another idea. Boston was only like two hours away—what if I drove down and found Paul in person? I could ask him about the SRL without giving away any information about myself. No tech trail. Seeking out a stranger alone wasn't my favorite plan, but with my only other one dancing her butt off with Ashlyn Murphy and friends …

Brennan would be angry if I went by myself, but since he was off swimming, he'd lost his vote. Besides, I was tired of waiting. Waiting for Mr. Murphy to make a mistake, waiting for Leisel to help us. I wanted to *do* something.

A tiny thrill shot through me. It was Saturday night, and

I was all dressed up and ready to go. If I couldn't find Paul, all I'd waste was a tank of gas.

I stalked outside into the cold, cobbling together a plan. How could I prevent Paul from following me after I met him? How would I figure out whether to trust him? How could I keep myself safe while I decided?

Surmountable problems, I told myself. Jumping into my pick-up, I drove off to find some solutions.

Chapter 11

Holy crab shells, I loved the Internet.

It took me and my new laptop only twenty minutes on a coffee shop's wi-fi to track down Paul. People really did put everything online these days. Not that Paul himself posted his location to the minute, but his friends did, and one of them mentioned in a status update that Paul was, "with the group tonight, for once."

They were supposedly at a party in a townhouse near Boston University; I parked the pick-up a few blocks away. I'd exchanged the tiny dollar-bin Homecoming clutch for my normal black purse; though a tad shabby for my dress, it tucked up nicely under my arm and could hold the couple of items I'd grabbed from my bedroom before starting the two-hour drive.

I turned the corner onto the street the house was on—I didn't have the exact address, but I figured I'd know it as the one with the party.

Unfortunately there were two of those, right next to each other. Girls in tight shirts and guys in jeans flitted from one house to the other. Most held plastic cups as they party-hopped. I stared, feeling very much the high-schooler from a quiet Maine town. There had to be hundreds of people at this double-house party. My plan had seemed simple on the ride down: approach Paul obliquely—maybe "accidentally" spill my drink on him—then flirt outrageously until he suggested we find a room. Once I got him alone, I could interrogate him about the SRL.

But how the hell was I going to find Paul in a party this size?

A small park, little more than a square of grass with a few benches, nestled between two banks of townhouses across the street; I paused there to revise my plan. Actually, there wasn't much to revise, I realized. I'd just have to ask around for Paul. Someone had to point him out eventually. Then I'd channel James Bond and flirt him into submission.

Theoretically. I hadn't flirted in over two years, and suddenly I wondered if I could handle it. I'd have to touch him—a hand on his arm, more if we danced. Was I ready for this? Paul might get me a step closer to saving my family … or he might be useless.

Worse, he might be dangerous.

Wanting a moment to think, I searched the tiny park for an open bench. Two held couples making out, and on the third sat a guy reading on his phone. The bench beside his was empty. My heels clicked on the concrete—I'd thought my Homecoming finery would blend in, but now I realized the uniform seemed to be painted-on jeans and skin-flaunting tops. Maybe I should postpone my fact-finding mission until I'd planned more thoroughly.

As I passed the reading guy, the sound of my steps made him glance up, and I saw his face.

"Oh," I said, startled. "There you are."

Paul Alderson, recognizable even though his auburn hair was longer than in his profile photo, frowned. "Excuse me?"

Crap — my accidental-meeting scheme was toast now. Revise, revise, revise! "Um …" Glancing wildly back at the party, I blurted, "Your friends asked me to come out here and make you stop being lame." Yes. That was halfway plausible.

Paul held up his phone. "I'm reading."

"No joke." Could I talk him up out here? No — my interrogation plan required an absence of spectators. I pointed to the melee across the street. "But see, you're at a party. You've waived the right to do anything but dance and hit on drunk girls."

He raised one dark eyebrow.

"Drunk girls aren't really my type."

"Well, I don't get my twenty bucks from your friends unless you come back to the party and dance with me." Oh no, did I sound like a hooker? Too late now. I tossed my hair and smiled. "Help a girl out."

Paul's gaze slid down over my sparkly dress, then back up. I hadn't let anyone look at me like that in a long time, and heat flushed my limbs. Not sure whether to be flattered or offended, when Paul leaned forward I decided to just be grateful that he'd taken the bait. I stepped to the side to let him stand.

Instead, Paul withdrew his wallet from his pants pocket, pulled out a bill and handed it over. Andrew Jackson's green-ink face mocked me in the lamplight.

"There you go." Paul went back to reading.

Wow. Ashlyn's snotty comments aside, I knew I was hot. Most of the time I didn't put effort into looking good, but with this dress and my hair all dark, loose waves to the small of my back, convincing a guy to dance shouldn't be a problem.

Paul of the Silver Rescue League was starting to annoy me.

Narrowing my gaze, I studied him. Wearing a scuffed leather jacket over a dark shirt, Paul slouched casually on the bench as if oblivious to the cold. His phone, propped on one knee, threw faint light and shadow over the strong, sculpted planes of his face. Remembering the washboard abs from his surfing photo, I realized Paul must get hit on a lot. This was going to take more effort, and I wondered again whether I was up to the challenge.

More importantly, would whatever information I'd get be worth it?

I had no idea. Paul and the SRL were unidentified quantities. But I'd driven two hours to be here, the night was icy and invigorating, and Mr. I'd Rather Read didn't know who—or, more importantly, what—I was. Plus, my brother and Leisel weren't present to watch or interfere; I could handle this however I wanted.

I felt free, somehow. Determined. Dangerous.

Paul hadn't flicked to a new page yet despite his apparent focus on his phone, and my lips twitched. *Challenge accepted.*

Sitting down next to him, I crossed one long, mostly-bare leg over the other. Paul's head didn't move, but his gaze slid sideways. Now that I had his attention, I folded the twenty into thirds, then tucked the bill into the pocket of his leather coat.

Paul sat up straight at my touch. In the lamplight, his eyes flashed silver.

"I know *Zen and the Art of Surfing* or whatever isn't going to read itself," I said, "but how about we go back inside and you can *tell* me about gnarly waves instead of reading about them." Did surfers say gnarly anymore?

Paul's gaze sparked with wary interest.

"How'd you know I surf?"

I Internet-stalked you didn't strike the right chord. "Your friend told me, obviously." I gestured to the party-houses. "You're not really going to make me go back in there alone, are you?"

Paul gave me a dry look. "Would your ego survive?"

"Maybe, but—" *Think, Cassandra*. Why was he out here reading in the cold? "Everyone else is drunk and boring," I guessed. "But I promised my friends I'd stay to drag their smashed asses home at the end of the night."

For the first time, Paul's arms-length expression cracked.

"Me too, actually."

Score. "I'd suggest we stay out here, but frankly I'm freezing." I made myself shiver as if that were true.

Paul shifted, slipping his arm out of his sleeve. Realizing he was trying to lend me his coat, I held up a hand. "Unless you have a pair of pants for me too, that's not going to help. Besides, then *you'd* be cold." I smiled. "But points for offering."

Paul's lips quirked. He put his coat back on, but didn't move to get up.

"What's your name?" he asked.

I shook my head.

"I don't introduce myself outdoors." Another theatrical shiver.

Paul's grin transformed his serious features, and my pulse leapt. Maybe it was just that I'd been studying Paul closely for signs of danger or trustworthiness, focusing on him the way I didn't with any of the guys at school, but it struck me that if I were a normal girl instead of on a mission, I'd be all over that smile.

"Alright, you win." Standing, Paul slipped his phone into a pocket, then held out a hand.

I hesitated. Maneuvering Paul into an isolated room was clearly going to involve a certain amount of physical contact. Contact I remembered from freshman dates I hadn't really wanted to go on; contact on a level I hadn't suffered since getting my sealskin back.

The difference was, I reminded myself, that this time I was in control.

"Thanks." I slipped my palm into his.

Paul's hand was warm and made my skin tingle. He hauled me up beside him—even with my three-inch heels, he had a good two inches on me. That put him just over six feet tall. And judging from that surfing photo, it was all muscle. His long, lean frame set off alarm bells, but was that my intuition telling me not to trust him, or paranoia caused by two weeks without a swim? I reassured myself by surreptitiously patting my purse. Even Paul wouldn't be a match for its contents.

Paul led me across the street to the party house on the left. He kept my hand as we walked in—which was good, because the front room was crushed with people, flirting and spilling drinks and making out and yelling into each others' ears. My hackles went up immediately. Music pounded, and as we wove through the room I instinctively cringed away from anyone who brushed near.

Uh oh. I'd thought it would be easy to keep my distance, but this was worse than the Homecoming dance.

We went through the kitchen into the living room, which seemed to be the main dance floor. Paul shrugged his coat off, tossed it onto a pile, and pulled me with a grin into the crowd. I froze a smile on my face, trying not to betray how freaked I was by the sea of flailing strangers.

After a minute Paul bent his head to my ear.

"You okay? You look a little stressed out."

James Bond I clearly wasn't.

"There's just a lot of people," I muttered. "I have ... personal space issues."

"Oh." Paul moved an inch or two away. That wasn't the right message to send, so I grabbed his shirt on either side of his torso and pulled him closer.

"You're okay. It's everyone else." Under the dark blue fabric, his skin felt warm. Paul hesitated, then raised his head as if looking for something. He pushed us through the grinding dancers until we reached a pocket of space between two bookcases against the wall, and maneuvered me into it.

"Is this better?" he asked.

My breath came easier already. I nodded gratefully.

We danced. My nook protected me from people coming up behind, but movement from the middle of the room kept pressing Paul into me. Finally I gave up and looped my arm around his neck—after all, I needed him to want to get a room with me. My limbs were stiff at first, but our bodies touched practically from neck to knee, and as we moved together I loosened up. After a few minutes, I realized I was enjoying the feel of Paul's broad shoulders under my hands. For a moment, I could pretend to be a normal girl, dancing at a normal party with a normal guy who smelled of soap and salt and wind.

Paul lowered his head, his cheek brushing mine.

"By the way …" His breath, warm on my ear, stirred something way down in my stomach. "Where's your corsage?"

It took me a moment to realize my confusion had nothing to do with the way Paul's hands heated the soft fabric at my waist. I pulled back to meet his gray eyes.

"What do you mean?"

He eyed my shimmery dress. "You look like you got lost on your way to a high school dance," he teased, and I fought down a spike of alarm. Time to remember my casual flirting skills.

"The limo never showed," I joked.

The skin around Paul's eyes crinkled. "Pity."

"Yeah, I guess I'm stuck here." I trailed my hand down around his side until I could curl my fingers across the small of his back. Paul's breath hitched, and I felt a moment of giddy, unexpected power.

"Which of my friends asked you to put my book away?" Paul murmured. "Because I really need to thank them." He slid his hand up my back to my bare shoulder, and this time it was *my* breath that caught. I couldn't remember anymore which twitter handle had mentioned the party, so I gave a cheeky shrug.

"None of them. I just thought you needed to dance. With me." Though we weren't dancing much anymore, just swaying in our near-embrace.

Paul's eyes narrowed fractionally, but then his mouth quirked. "Sneaky. I like it." He brushed a lock of hair from my face. "You know, you never told me your name."

I hesitated. "Anna."

Paul cocked his head. "Is that really your name?"

"Um." Caught off guard, I knew by Paul's frown that my expression had given me away. I needed to get my head back to my real mission; Paul was way too sharp. "No," I admitted.

On my back, his hands tensed.

"Tell me your real name."

Thinking fast, I tossed my hair flirtatiously.

"I'll tell you later. If you impress me."

"I have to earn your name?" Paul raised a brow, but thankfully seemed to relax. "What do I have to do?"

"You'll think of something." I was about to suggest finding

a room to ourselves when Paul tilted his head down with a sudden quick grin.

"What about this?" He pressed his mouth to mine.

Surprise and heat flushed from my lips to my toes, but almost before I could register the sensation, I shoved him away.

Paul fell back a step, stunned. Damn my reflexes—I'd just undone twenty minutes of flirting. Besides ... wait, did I *want* him to kiss me again? I'd avoided touch for so long, but dancing with him ... Yes, I realized. I wanted that. My way, my choice.

"Sorry," Paul said over the music. "I just thought—"

Stepping forward, I grabbed him by the shirt, leaned up, and kissed him.

Paul responded instantly, threading the fingers of one hand through my hair and settling his other arm around my waist. He backed us up until my shoulders bumped solidly against the wall. His kiss burned, confident and intoxicating.

Suddenly Paul raised his head.

"Wait. If my friends didn't send you out to get me, how did you know I surf?"

For a moment I had no idea what he was talking about, but some part of my brain must still have been working, because only a second passed before a response slipped from my lips.

"Everyone knows you surf." I kissed him again, hard, so he'd stop thinking about the holes in my story. Paul hesitated, then seemed to give in, and we melted into each other against the wall.

It wasn't long before I forgot who was distracting whom.

His hands roamed my sides, my shoulders, my face. Everywhere he touched me burned. His lips trailed fire down my neck and across my collarbone. Somewhere in the back of my mind I knew I should stop this, but for a few minutes nothing existed beyond the music thrumming through my veins and his long, lean body pressed against mine. I'd never felt like this in my life, under the Haze or otherwise.

When we paused, gasping for air, Paul's eyes were half-lidded. He bent to kiss my neck just under my ear, and I swallowed, trying desperately to clear my head. I wasn't here to make out and feel normal for a night; I was here to grill Paul about the SRL. For my family.

Doused by the cold wave of reality, I wrenched myself from Paul's embrace. He looked surprised, so I made myself smile. My heart pounded—it was time. I pulled him towards the stairs.

The second floor held several rooms but too many people, so we went up to the third story. Fewer people here, and five closed doors. Heart racing, I led Paul to the farthest one. What was I going to do if the door was locked?

Abort and flee home. Flustered from the dance floor, I almost hoped …

But the door opened easily. The room was empty. In a party this crowded, that was a stroke of luck, but my stomach flip-flopped. Not that I didn't want answers, but my plan to coolly manipulate Paul into position now felt ludicrous. For all of the spy skills I'd acquired over the past two years, I wasn't sure I could do this.

But I was in too far to stop now. I straightened my spine, wiped my suddenly sweating brow, and pulled Paul into the room. Grabbing a sock from the floor — this looked like a guy's room, messy and … yes, those were boxers in a pile of clothes beside the desk — I hung it on the bedroom's outer doorknob. After closing the door, I flicked the flimsy handle-lock. There.

Turning to Paul, I paused at his expression. He had crossed his arms, and the heavy-lidded look was … gone.

"You've gone to a lot of trouble to get me alone, girl with no name," he observed quietly. "What is it that you want?"

"Uh …" I floundered. "Isn't it obvious what I want?" Despite my lack of exposure to the Internet, I wasn't totally ignorant of memes; I felt like someone had stamped me with a *Seduction: you're doing it wrong* stamp.

Time to abort? But I'd gotten him all the way up here, and the bed behind him had a wooden frame, made of spaced-apart slats with solid posts at each corner. It would be perfect … if only I could get Paul where I wanted him.

I took a deep breath and uttered the cheesiest line I could think of.

"I just want you."

Paul stilled, heat flaring to life in his eyes. Then we were kissing again and thank goodness I hadn't ruined the plan with my inept flirting but *oh God his hands were on my breasts now.* A surprised gasp emerged from my throat, and Paul's gray eyes gleamed.

Hastily I pulled him down, not to the bed but onto the floor beside the footboard. It was a clumsy maneuver, but Paul sat with a thump, leaning against the corner post. I fell more or less into his lap. Paul claimed my lips again, and his hands roamed distractingly, but I made myself focus. My purse, on the floor beside us, held the key to my plan.

Handcuffs, and not the toy kind.

I fumbled blindly in my purse with one hand until I found them. This was the point of no return: I'd have to be fast. Clutching the chain tight in my sweaty palm so it wouldn't clink, I slipped the cuffs around the bedpost and between two footboard slats.

Paul's hands dropped from the small of my back to the curve below. Breaking the kiss, I grabbed his wrists and pushed them behind him, into the open metal cuffs.

"Hey. What are you doing?" Paul tried to jerk his hands away.

Before he could, I snapped the cuffs closed.

Chapter 12

I scrambled off of Paul, hauling my purse—and me—out of kicking range. Paul tried to jerk his arms up, then twisted to look at his bound wrists.

"God*damn*it. Handcuffs?" He shoved at the bed, but the handcuff chain around the post was bracketed above and below by wooden slats, so he couldn't just lift the bed frame to free himself.

Giddy with adrenaline, I exhaled in relief. For a while there I'd worried he wouldn't fall for my faux-seduction wiles. "Serves you right for trying to sleep with some random girl you just met." Realizing my dress was skewed, riding way up on my thighs, I hastily straightened it.

Paul flushed. "I was *not* going to sleep with you. I knew you were up to something; I just wanted to see what your game was."

My victorious rush drained. He'd been suspicious all along? Even through all the kissing … and the freely roaming hands …

My eyes narrowed.

"Exactly how far were you willing to go with that?"

Paul scowled. "Care to explain what the hell is going on?"

"I just want to ask you a few questions." Maybe I should have felt bad for tying him up, but in my world, safety trumped manners. Besides, anyone in an organization that helped selkies would surely understand. If Paul proved trustworthy, I'd release him — no harm, no foul.

And if not, I could escape unhindered.

Paul jerked at his cuffs. "Untie me."

"Later."

"*Now.*"

"Relax, will you?" But Paul wrenched at the handcuffs, shoving at the bed with his back. "Stop that." He didn't, of course, but with the cuffs bounded on all sides by solid wood, there was no way for him to escape.

Paul knocked the bed against the wall. "Someone will hear this."

I shrugged. With the sock on the door, no one would investigate.

"Look, I just want to talk."

Paul kept struggling. Not sure what else to do, I waited for him to calm down. And for my pulse to slow. I could feel the echo of Paul's lips on my mouth, and his hands … a lot more places.

Finally Paul gave up his assault on the cuffs and glared at me. Dark auburn hair fell over his forehead, and his shoulders tensed, taut under his shirt.

"Alright, you've got my attention. What's this about?"

I leaned against the edge of the desk.

"Tell me about the Silver Rescue League."

Paul frowned. "What about it?"

I took a deep breath.

"Tell me what it has to do with selkies." There. The word was said. I searched Paul's face for a spark of recognition, but all I could tell for certain was that he was pissed.

"Selkies are mythological creatures," Paul said. "They're not real."

"The Silver Rescue League website is real," I countered. "Why does *Silver* turn into *Selkie* when you mouse over it?"

Paul's laugh sounded more annoyed than amused.

"Our web admin has a sense of humor and too much time on his hands."

My eyes narrowed. "Then what does the Silver *Rescue* League rescue?"

"The homeless."

That gave me pause. I wasn't sure I believed him … but nothing in Paul's angry posture indicated he was lying. And he stared at me like I might be an escaped mental patient. If the SRL did help selkies, wouldn't he be more … helpful?

With dismay, I realized Paul's explanation for the website thing was much more likely than an organization of people dedicated to aiding selkies out of the goodness of their hearts. In fact, as Paul looked at me with the carefully blank expression you gave the crazed or potentially dangerous, it felt downright ludicrous. Damn.

I'd let my hope take me for a ride, but this was a dead end.

"Well, then." I picked up my purse, squelching any drop of disappointment. It had been a long shot to begin with. "Thanks for the dance, and have a nice life." I headed for the door.

"If selkies *did* exist, we'd help them too," Paul said as my hand touched the handle. My chest seized.

Slowly, I turned around.

"What do you mean?"

Paul leaned back against the bedpost. "Why don't you undo these handcuffs, and I'll answer your questions." His voice was smooth now, suspiciously amiable. Was he screwing with me? Just trying to win his release?

"Answer my questions, and maybe I'll uncuff you."

Paul's mouth tightened.

"What's to stop me from yelling for help?"

Right. If he needed extra incentive to behave, it just so happened I'd brought some. Reaching into my purse, I pulled out a contact stun gun. Sleek, black and tipped with two silver metal prongs, it was twenty bucks of protection.

And, for the first time, intimidation.

"How about this?" I put my finger to the trigger.

Paul's eyes widened. "Those are illegal."

"No, they're not." I'd researched the laws.

"They are in Massachusetts," Paul said, and I froze. I'd only checked Maine's laws, where stun guns were allowed. Crap, could he be right?

Too late now. "Look— "

"Then you're not from around here."

Alarm snaked down my spine. Stepping closer, I brandished the stun gun.

"Tell me everything there is to know about the SRL."

Paul rattled his chained hands.

"Uncuff me, now."

I held up the stun gun pointedly, but he sucked in a huge breath, as if to bellow for help. Panicked, I leapt over and crouched beside him, thrusting the stun gun into his side.

"Don't," I said. "All I want are answers."

Paul searched my gaze, two inches from his. "Who *are* you?"

"You're not asking the questions here. Tell me about the Silver Rescue League."

"What is your name?"

Rattled, I snapped, "Answer me, or I'll tase you."

Paul's eyes flashed, and I knew I shouldn't have given him an ultimatum. He leaned over until his nose was half an inch from mine.

"You're bluffing."

I hesitated, but he was right—I wasn't about to torture him. My plan was a bust—I couldn't even be sure Paul *knew* about selkies, much less whether he and the SRL could be trusted. Disappointment churned in my stomach, but I'd suffered too much of that emotion over the past two years to crumble.

He wouldn't talk? So be it. Time to scram.

Before I could get up, something glass shattered in the hallway outside our room. The crash startled me, and my trigger finger tightened. The stun gun jerked to life, electricity shooting into Paul for a split second before I yanked the gun away. Too late; he yelped in pain.

Cursing, I scrambled backwards. "Sorry! I didn't— "

"I don't know who you think you are," Paul ground out, breathing hard, "but you are *so* going to jail for assault, not to mention carrying an illegal weapon."

"It was an accident!" I touched his side. "Are you okay?"

Paul jerked away, his eyes ablaze.

"Uncuff me, now, or I swear to God I will press charges."

Dead end was starting to look like an understatement for this night.

"Look, I didn't mean to— "

My phone rang, startling me again, but thankfully this time when my finger spasmed, electricity sparked harmlessly into the air. Cursing, I stood and threw the stun gun on the desk, sucked in a breath, and tried to get a hold of myself.

The phone rang again, and I snatched it from my purse. Leisel's number. Alarm shot through me, and I scrambled to answer.

"Are you okay? What's wrong?" Maybe I shouldn't have left her alone with Ashlyn & Co. after all. What if—

"I'm fine. I just got home. It all went great."

"Then why are you calling me?" My voice came out sharp; my nerves were beyond shot. I shoved hair out of my face and pressed my hand to my forehead. "What is it?" I said more calmly.

After a pause, Leisel said, "Ashlyn and Brennan had sex,

back when … you know. Ashlyn told me, on the ride home." I was silent, still panicked from Paul and not sure how to respond. "Did you know?"

"Yeah." Not from my brother; Brennan didn't talk about that part of his and Ashlyn's relationship, not even now. It was Ashlyn, back in freshman year, who had told me about her first time, *their* first time, even though I'd pointed out how much I didn't want to hear about my brother's sex life, thank you very much. I glanced over at Paul. "Look, I can't really talk right now."

"I just … hadn't realized. It's awful."

"I know." That was why I overlooked Brennan's Date & Ditch taunting of Ashlyn. I'd been close to her too, but I couldn't imagine how much worse he must feel. At the time, he'd thought he loved her. But to find out afterwards you didn't have a choice? I shuddered.

"I also wanted to say I'm sorry about earlier. I realized I sort of ditched you for Ashlyn."

"It sounds like you two bonded." Quite a bit, if Ashlyn was confiding her history with Brennan.

"Don't worry. I know who my real friends are. And thanks for showing up at the dance tonight. It meant a lot."

"No problem." Relief twitched through me—Leisel was back on board. Maybe she'd never wavered to begin with. I promised myself a swim soon, to manage my paranoia. On the floor Paul shifted, the chain between his cuffs rattling, and I told Leisel I had to go. We hung up, and I turned back to Paul. His mouth was set, his eyes hard like beachside granite. Crazy, to think that just twenty minutes ago we'd been all over each other.

But I really had just tased him. He wasn't hurt—a half-second burst was more shocking than painful—but no way would he help me now, if he even could. Tonight was an unqualified disaster, and it was time to get the hell out. Thanks to my precautions, Paul had no idea who I was, and no way to find me.

I smiled brightly.

"You know what? We're just going to pretend this never happened." Tossing my phone and my stun gun into my purse, I tucked it under my shoulder. "I was never here."

Paul gave a startled laugh. "You mean I tied *myself* to this bed?"

"You can keep the cuffs." I headed for the door.

"Wait! You can't just leave me here like this."

Oh, right. Pausing, I fished in my purse.

"Here's the key." I set it on the desk, out of reach of Paul. "Someone will come along eventually and let you out."

"Great." Paul stretched his legs out. "See you soon."

My brows shot up. "Um, no. You will *never* see me again."

"Want to bet? Because it's my new mission in life to track you down."

A chill went down my spine. Paul looked … determined.

"Please. You don't even know my name."

"I know you don't live in Massachusetts, and you have the accent of a Mainer. And I know your boyfriend Brennan cheated on you with some tramp named Ashlyn."

I stiffened—he'd overheard my conversation with Leisel? How? At least he'd misinterpreted what we'd said. "So?"

"So those aren't very common names. How many Ashlyns and Brennans do you think exist in the same network?"

Thank goodness Brennan wasn't in any social media stuff online. And Maine was a big state. "That's pretty weak."

"It's a start." Paul smiled grimly. "I'll find you. That's a promise."

I took a step back, thoroughly spooked now. But I couldn't leave without making sure he was afraid of me too. Swallowing hard, I pulled the stun gun out of my purse, walked over to kneel beside the bed, and jabbed him in the stomach. Paul inhaled, alarm flashing silver in his eyes, but I didn't push the button.

"Don't find me." Holding his gaze, I pressed the prongs against his abs. "Because if you do, I will tase you again. And *that's* a promise."

Paul's smugness evaporated; I could tell he knew I wasn't bluffing this time. Standing, I put the stun gun away and left.

"Hey," Paul yelled as I shut the door, but I could barely hear him over the music. No one in the hallway even looked up.

Leaving the sock on the handle, I slipped downstairs.

Chapter 13

I walked into American History on Tuesday to find a list of dire-sounding projects chalked in Mr. Hayward's blocky handwriting on the blackboard. I read the first few.

10-minute presentation on Lincoln's assassination.

Create a Union and Confederate soldier's uniform and kit, and contrast the differences.

Live debate the South's vs. the North's perspective on slavery in 1860.

Write a 20-page paper about Harriet Tubman.

They went on like that—we were covering the Civil War—and numbered about fifteen in all. This didn't look good. I exchanged dismayed glances with my classmates as we sat down.

When the bell rang, Mr. Hayward got up from his desk.

"New project, due the week before winter break," he said, surprising no one. We groaned anyway, and he waved it off good-naturedly. "I've assigned you a partner based on grades—specifically, your last test grade. You're paired with the person who got either the next higher or lower point score. That way no one person carries his or her team."

Well, that was a relief. Hopefully Mindy would be next to me, grade-wise—she was smart and easy to work with, and we'd gotten past the awkwardness from the Homecoming dance, mostly by pretending it never happened.

"You'll choose your assignment from the list on the board." Mr. Hayward checked his paper. "First up we have Cassandra Kelleher," he said, again to nobody's surprise. I crossed my fingers for Mindy. "With her partner, Ashlyn Murphy."

Ashlyn? This wasn't happening.

"What?" It took a moment, and a few swiveling heads, to realize I'd spoken aloud. "No way," I said before I could think better of it. A couple kids snickered. On the other side of the room, Ashlyn raised her hand.

"Mr. Hayward," she said. "Can you assign us different partners, please?"

"Is there a problem?" Mr. Hayward looked from me to Ashlyn.

"Yes," she said. "Cassandra's a bitch."

The room erupted in laughter, from choked giggles to outright guffaws. Mr. Hayward gave Ashlyn a severe look.

"Language, Miss Murphy. And for that, Cassandra will be the one to choose your assignment."

"But—"

"Your request for another partner is denied." He looked at me. "Cassandra? To the board, please."

"Actually, I second the change of partner suggestion. In fact—"

"Girls, it's just a class project. In your lives you'll be forced to work on many assignments with people you might not enjoy. Get used to it." Mr. Hayward tapped his watch. "Cassandra, we're waiting."

Reluctantly, I went to the board and scanned the list of projects. Which one would be the quickest? I hesitated at the 20-page paper. Ashlyn and I could do our parts individually and minimize our togetherness time.

"Choose the paper on Harriet Tubman," Ashlyn called. She'd probably come to the same conclusion, but my hand tightened on the chalk. I hadn't followed an order from Ashlyn Murphy in two and a half years, and I wasn't about to start now.

Casting a glance over the list again, my gaze stopped on one that hit close to home. Maybe too close, considering Ashlyn's and my history. Not that it mattered—I was the only one who would get the symbolism.

I drew a line through *Live debate the South's vs. the North's perspective on slavery in 1860.*

"Come *on*." Ashlyn groaned theatrically. "A debate? Seriously?" She put her head in her hands. "This is what I get for studying."

Half the class cracked up again, and Mr. Hayward sighed. "Because of your attitude, Ashlyn, Cassandra also gets to choose the side she's arguing."

I looked over at Ashlyn and raised my chin.

"The North."

"Surprise, she gave me the hard side," Ashlyn muttered.

"For you it should be easy." I reclaimed my seat as the class tittered. Across the room, Ashlyn lifted her head and frowned at me.

"Alright, girls, that's enough." Mr. Hayward marked his list. "On to the next lucky pair ... "

"Guess what?" Leisel said when Brennan and I showed up at her basement bedroom door that afternoon.

"You have blackmail material on Mr. Hayward so I can force him to change my partner?" I slouched inside.

"Cass got paired with Ashlyn for a History project," Brennan explained. Leisel winced.

"That sucks."

"Massively." I threw myself face-down on Leisel's frog-spattered bed. "So please tell me your *guess what* is good news."

"It is!" Leisel grinned when I rolled over to look at her. "Ashlyn's having a sleepover at her house this weekend. And I'm invited!"

"What?" I scrambled up off the bed, crummy History project forgotten. "You're kidding!"

"I'm not!" Leisel bounced on her toes in glee. Whooping, I joined in, and for a minute we jumped around like idiots.

"I have so many questions," she said when we calmed down. Her eyes got big. "Most importantly, what am I supposed to wear?"

"Wow." Smiling, Brennan shook his head. "If Leisel weren't going to help me cram for geometry, I'd flee from the imminent girl talk explosion."

"You're studying this afternoon?" I frowned. "I thought we were going swimming." Tuesday was our one afternoon a week off from the Golden Fish, and I wanted to spend it at sea. My paranoia last weekend proved that I desperately needed cold currents and my real form to center me. The kissing-and-tasing debacle would not have happened if I'd been more levelheaded.

"I swam on Saturday, remember? And I've got a test tomorrow."

"Since when do you care about tests?" Specifically, since when did schoolwork matter more than swimming to my slacker brother?

"I don't, but if I fail out Mr. Murphy will make our parents evict me, remember? And my grades are low enough in geometry that if I bomb this test …" Brennan crossed his eyes and pretended to shoot himself in the head.

"I can't go alone," I reminded him.

"Why not? I do. It's fun, trust me."

"And dangerous." Even without evil-minded humans prowling the shore, the ocean could be a rough place. Sharks and orcas and speedboats, oh my. Wasn't he the least bit worried for me?

"Stick to a lake," Brennan advised. "Or the rivers. They're safer."

I sighed. Rivers and lakes were great, but they sometimes

felt claustrophobic. I wanted to be free and unbounded for a few hours. Without a buddy, though, I was stuck in freshwater.

"Why do you get such good grades?" Leisel asked me. "Brennan said you're only pretending to care about your diplomas, so why waste all that time studying for straight A's?"

I made a face. "Because of Ashlyn."

"Somehow it always comes back to her," Brennan muttered. He scanned Leisel's pile of stuffed animals, now in what was probably their usual spot on her futon. "Hey, where's Hippo?"

"I hid him," Leisel said. "He was scared you might attack him again."

Brennan laughed.

"Aw, we fixed his ear. And he had fun being a football."

"Until you stepped on him." Leisel grinned, and I wondered when they'd had time to throw around a stuffed hippo. She turned back to me. "What do you mean, because of Ashlyn?"

"When we were in sixth grade, I got an A on a social studies test. Ashlyn got a C. She told me that no real friend of hers would get a better grade." It was stupid, a half-joking throwaway remark, but under the Haze … "I failed my next quiz, and kept my grades at or below hers from then on. I didn't even know why; I just thought I was being a good friend." Sometimes when I'd accidentally earned a better grade, my head would ache for hours.

"So when you returned, you started getting straight A's to spite her. I get it."

"It's not spite, exactly. It's just that now she can't tell me not to. No one can." Seeing as I'd never use my diploma, investing the significant time needed to ace my classes might be a futile protest, but it made me feel better. "Besides, it's not like I have any hobbies." Other than brainstorming sealskin-rescuing schemes, that is.

"Why don't you paint anymore? Brennan mentioned you used to."

I shot an annoyed glance at my brother, who was building a pyramid of stuffed animals on the futon. I hadn't shared his secrets; why was he sharing mine?

"Paint is expensive," I said shortly.

"Yeah, but why don't you take art at school?"

"Because I don't want to. The end," I added, in case she didn't get it. Painting was something I'd loved when under the Haze—and something Mrs. Murphy had praised me for. Remembering my joy at her approval disgusted me.

Leisel stuffed her hands awkwardly into her pockets and changed the subject. "You would not believe what hoops I have to jump through to go to this sleepover. Did you know Mr. Murphy is doing a background investigation on my family? Ashlyn's making me ask my parents for their social security numbers and everything so he can check us all out."

"Really?" Brennan said from the futon. "You mean Douglas Murphy is psycho?" He sounded so faux-bewildered that we all laughed.

"Ashlyn says he does that to everyone she asks over, which is why she doesn't hold that many sleepovers." Leisel glanced at

Brennan, then back at me. "You know, she says she feels like a prisoner sometimes."

After a pause, Brennan placed a small sea turtle on the top of his plush pyramid.

"Sympathy for Ashlyn?" He grimaced. "No offense, but vomit."

"Seconded." I grabbed my bag. "Brennan, when should I pick you up?"

"I'll walk home. Take the truck and go somewhere fun. Be careful."

"I will." Going outside into the cool autumn sun, I glanced reflexively around. Ever since my encounter with Paul, I couldn't help worrying that he would somehow make good on his threat to track me down. But he couldn't, I told myself.

Wondering which river to pick for the afternoon's swim, I headed for the truck.

"So what about Paul?" Leisel asked, and I whirled in alarm. She'd followed me outside.

"What about him?" Crap, how had she found out about last weekend? My hand went to my throat, where a hickey lurked under my turtleneck.

"Before the dance you said you'd think about whether we could contact him anonymously? To see if—"

"Oh." This is why I needed to go swimming, so I could think clearly again. I took a steadying breath. "Right. We're not contacting him. No way."

"But—"

"Look, I thought it over. My decision is that we can't

chance it." Leisel's brow scrunched, and I put a hand on her arm so she'd know how serious I was. "It's *my* family on the line, remember? It's my decision. Okay?"

Leisel nodded reluctantly.

"Okay."

"Because the last thing I need is you going behind my back— "

"No, I won't. I wouldn't. I promise."

I studied her carefully, but she seemed earnest.

"Good. Thanks." I wished I'd phrased everything a little nicer. I was just so tense. "If our plan with the sleepover works…" We'd be free. All of us. It was hard to imagine. "I don't know how we'd ever repay you."

"You don't have to." Leisel's dark gaze was shy. "That's what friends are for, right?"

An unexpected wistfulness wound through me. Would I ever lose my paranoia enough to have friends? Maybe after my family was free. Until then … On impulse, I hugged Leisel anyway. She deserved friends. "I'll come by later this week and draw the layout of Ashlyn's house for you, and we can talk pajamas and search strategy."

Looking a little surprised at my hug, Leisel headed back inside. I watched her go, then walked through the woods to the pick-up. Time, finally, for a swim.

First, though, I hit the pay phone by the library and called city hall.

"Mayor Murphy's office, how may I help you?" said his secretary.

"Is the mayor in?" I pitched my voice low and rough to disguise it. "I had a follow-up question about a meeting we had the other day."

"I'll put you through."

"Actually, I just got another call," I said quickly. "I'll call back later." Satisfied Mr. Murphy was too busy to follow me—not that he ever did, as far as I could tell—I hopped back into the truck.

Hiding a sealskin to be both secure and accessible wasn't the easiest thing in the world, but Brennan and I had half a dozen spots we trusted. Twenty minutes of driving and hiking found me at the current one, a hollowed-out, upright broken trunk of a fallen oak in the middle of nowhere. Inside lay two all-weather backpacks, tethered by carabiners to metal eye rings we'd sunk into the wood to keep even a nor'easter from lifting them out.

The backpacks looked identical, but I knew without opening them which one held my sealskin. I unhooked mine and left Brennan's alone. I hiked back to the truck, then drove an hour upstate along the coastal road. I should head inland; there were rivers and lakes all over the place. But I kept looking east. The ocean pulled at me—I wanted to taste salt and feel the tide and swim so far that dirt was just a memory.

I couldn't make myself turn away from the shore, so finally I pulled the truck over to the shoulder of the road. My hands shook, I wanted to be in the ocean so bad. Damn Brennan for not coming with me today.

As I sat there, though, something in me shifted. I belonged

to the sea. Brennan wasn't here, but so what? Screw Brennan, and screw the rivers. In the end, all you had was yourself. I was fast, and wary. I could do this. Alone.

Ocean it was.

I turned east with a grin. Quiet coves abounded up here, and it didn't take long to find an isolated shore. Ditching the truck in a copse of trees, I padded through the woods to the waterline, where rocks plunged down into calm, sparkling sea. I turned in a circle, searching for any sign of onlookers, but saw nothing beyond a squirrel rustling in the leaves. It eyed me curiously.

"Don't watch," I told him, but the squirrel only cocked his head. "Pervert." Shucking my clothes, I wrapped my sealskin around me, hid the backpack in a holly shrub, and waded into the water. It lapped at my calves, breathtakingly icy, full of brine and wind and freedom.

When fully submerged, I *changed*. Agony blinded me as my limbs reshaped and my sealskin sank into my flesh, covering and melding to my form as I became my other self. My true self. When the pain passed I stretched, my aches from the *change* fading quickly, and opened my eyes to sunlit blues and grays. Finally. The stress of the last couple weeks began to wash away; I felt lighter already, and not just from being more buoyant in water.

After making sure I knew how to find my haul-out spot again, I swam straight out to sea. Sailboats littered the surface, easy enough to avoid. Encountering a school of small shiny fish, I caught and ate one whole, savoring the firm flesh and crunch of bone. Then I dove deep, into the depths where light didn't penetrate, and listened to the ocean, felt it pressing on my fur, my skull.

If my family were here, if Leisel found the sealskins at the sleepover, this would be my life. I'd never have to see Mr. Murphy again, wouldn't even have to face Ashlyn on Monday to work on our History project. *Don't get too excited*, I warned myself, but it was hard not to think about the possibilities. My father could teach me how to open clams—try as we might, Brennan and I couldn't quite manage it—and my mom could sing unhindered under the light of the moon. We could all live the lives we were meant to. At sea.

Everything would be better then.

Vibrations picked up by my whiskers warned of something bigger than a fish approaching, and I went on high alert. Thankfully, the visitor turned out to be a seal, with two more behind. I relaxed, alarm turning to anticipation. Brennan and I came across seals occasionally, but maybe these would be selkies. So far we hadn't met any, but a girl could dream.

When the seals got within ten feet, they swam around me, grunting playfully. Catching the eye of one of the seals, I sent out a clear and distinct thought: *Be well of sea and sky.* My parents didn't speak of their selkie lives much—Mr. Murphy didn't allow them to—but one tidbit they'd shared were the proper greetings.

The seal stared back with big black eyes, devoid of comprehension. Wondering if I was bungling the mind-speech, I tried again.

No dice—after a minute or so, the trio left, swimming idly eastward.

Not selkies. Disappointed, I surfaced for a breath.

To the west, the sun was setting behind the land's ridged silhouette, and red-gold light melted the open water into flickering fire. I watched the sun disappear, then turned in a circle. The western clouds, still blazing pink and orange, faded in the giant sky to a rushing dark in the east, and suddenly I felt very alone.

The sea was too big for one person, no matter what form she took.

Seized by the hope that by the end of the weekend I'd be able to share it with the rest of my family, I headed back to shore.

Chapter 14

On Saturday afternoon, Brennan and I drove to The Golden Fish for our shift. Ashlyn's sleepover had already begun, and my insides twisted in knots.

"You think you'll miss anything?" Brennan asked as we walked towards the staff door by the kitchen. I slowed down; we wouldn't be able to talk freely once inside.

"What's to miss?"

Brennan half-smiled. "Pizza, for one."

I laughed.

"Okay, I'd miss pizza." I stopped, gazing at the whitewashed wooden paneling of the restaurant. "Do you really think …?" That after tonight we might not see this godforsaken place again? I couldn't even say it, but Brennan knew what I meant.

"I don't know. But it's a shot." We watched one of the kitchen workers take out a bag of trash. He waved at us, then went back inside.

"She'll text you when she finds something," Brennan said.

"If."

"Try not to freak out, okay?" Brennan tugged at a lock of my hair.

I nodded. Deep breaths, I told myself. Leisel wouldn't be able to search until everyone went to bed, so chances were slim she'd find the sealskins while we were on shift.

The evening was agony. Time crawled as I smiled fakely at customers, checked my phone, and stared at the fish statue in the entrance vestibule. The restaurant's namesake looked like solid gold, but if you rapped on it the jig was up—the trout was hollow plaster. My knuckles itched to smash the damn thing.

Leisel never texted.

Our shift ended at eleven, and I made myself walk calmly out to the truck, even though I was going crazy. What was happening at Ashlyn's house? Was Leisel searching? Had Mr. Murphy discovered her poking around and thrown her out?

Was she having too much fun at Ashlyn's side to try?

The scenarios careened from hopeful to disastrous, and when Brennan parked outside our parents' house I shot out of the truck and ran down the street to the playground. I couldn't be inside right now.

My brother followed more slowly. I threw myself on the flat metal merry-go-round, grabbed a handle, and kicked the mulch to start it rotating.

"I can't stand not knowing," I said when Brennan walked over.

"Should we text her?" Then Brennan shook his head. "No, of course not." He started to pace. "What do you think is—"

"I don't know." We waited, Brennan pacing around the jungle gym and me spinning slowly on the merry-go-round. I counted fifty rotations, then a hundred.

"What time is it?" Brennan asked, though he had his own phone.

I checked, then sighed. "Only midnight."

"They're probably not even asleep yet." Brennan collapsed on a swing. "They might not be for hours."

The seconds passed, sluggish in the dark. I let the merry-go-round ease to a stop. "Maybe we should go over there. Wait down the street in case she needs us."

Brennan leapt up. "Let's."

We tore back to the truck, then drove over. Brennan parked us around the corner, and we waited.

And waited.

I nibbled Fritos from a half-empty bag stashed in the console. Brennan drummed his fingers incessantly on the dash. The bug-detector device's power light glowed steadily, but we still didn't dare talk aloud, so I turned the radio on and we listened to a Saturday-night club mix of pop songs and commercials. Finally, as our pointless adrenaline turned into bleary yawns, Brennan switched off the music and leaned back in his seat.

"Wake me up," he muttered.

I leaned my forehead against the cold window, trying to stay awake.

Sometime later, I started upright when my phone bleeped and fell off the dash, vibrating with an incoming text. I snatched it from the floor mat and checked the screen. Leisel's number. I jabbed the button to read the text.

Nothing. Have to go to bed; her parents get up early.

I stared at the message, my brain too fuzzy or unwilling to comprehend it. But the words were there, and Brennan, who'd snapped awake too, read them over my shoulder. He cursed.

Tears filled my eyes, and I pressed the back of my hand across the bridge of my nose to keep them in. She'd failed. We'd failed.

My phone buzzed again in my hands.

BTW the alarm code for the doors is 73945.

A couple seconds later she texted a third time.

You okay? I'm sorry.

I stirred myself to type a response.

We're fine. Good try. See you later.

K, she texted back.

Beside me, Brennan punched the steering wheel. Thankfully our horn didn't work, so we didn't risk waking anyone. The time on my phone read 4:53AM. I put it in my pocket, then gestured for Brennan to follow me out of the truck. He slammed the door shut behind him, and I shot him a look.

We walked about twenty paces away.

"What now?" Brennan's question misted white in the icy morning air.

"She got the front door's alarm code. That's something."

"Not without the physical key. They changed the locks again over the summer, remember?"

"Yeah." Inhaling deeply, I blew out my breath and tried to regroup. We weren't beaten yet. There were still moves we could make. "I'm working with Ashlyn on that project; maybe I can get the key from her somehow."

Brennan stared down the dark street. "We're never getting out of here, are we?"

"We will; I promise. One day this will all just be a bad memory." He didn't look reassured. "She got inside. That's further than we've ever gotten before. She can try again later."

We stood there together for a minute. Birds sang in the pre-dawn darkness, and cold morning fog sank into my bones. Soon the sun would rise on another day of enslavement for my family. It tasted like stale Fritos and smelled of wood smoke from a nearby chimney.

Finally Brennan rubbed a hand over his face. "I'm exhausted." He trudged back to the truck. "Let's go."

Chapter 15

"You're late," I told Ashlyn on Monday as she sauntered through the door of the Big Buzz coffee shop for our History meeting. I'd rather have gone somewhere quieter, like the library, but on a federal holiday choices were limited.

"You're lucky I'm here at all." She tossed her hair. "Who gets up before noon when we're off school?"

"People who have to work the afternoon shift." My voice was sharp; my skin had begun to sting as soon as she walked in. "Pampered princesses like you might not understand."

Ashlyn rolled her eyes and went to order. I'd already bought the cheapest coffee on the menu, but had only drunk half of it. The other half would help me get Ashlyn's keys. Even across the coffee shop, her presence made my skin prickle, and I rubbed my arms under my thrift-store coat. Hopefully she wouldn't set me so far on edge that I wouldn't be able to concentrate.

Brennan and I had met up with Leisel for a blow-by-blow of her search yesterday after our brunch shift at The Golden Fish. God, that shift had blown chunks. Extra-slimy ones. Not that it was different than usual—it was hard because it was exactly the same.

But at least the night showed that we *could* get into the Murphy house. Or Leisel could. If she'd been invited over once, she would be again. She'd also discovered information about the rest of the security at the house. Ashlyn had apparently complained at length about her dad's police-state habits.

"Her mom won't allow cameras inside," Leisel had told us. "But there are cameras all around the exterior. Ashlyn said her dad doesn't mind her sneaking out as long as she locks up behind her, but the one time she left a window open for herself she was grounded for a week."

So far, the best plan was still for Leisel to get invited over again—she'd only been able to search the main floor and the basement, apparently—but in case we needed to launch a more daring assault, getting that front door key was, well, key.

Ashlyn returned with a drink in one hand and her phone in the other. I'd chosen a table beside the wall, with three chairs. The middle chair, its back to the room, was open; Ashlyn set her messenger bag on it and slumped into the seat opposite me. My skin burned. I swallowed hard and told myself to keep it together; I didn't want Ashlyn to know how much proximity to her hurt.

Ignoring me, Ashlyn slurped at her drink—a frappucino, despite the frozen temperatures outside—and tapped at her phone. I frowned.

"What are you doing?"

"Updating my status. Unlike some people I could mention,

I have friends." She glanced over, then helpfully read aloud as she typed. "*Big Buzz coffee with Cassandra 'Bite Me' Kelleher. Someone tell me this is just a bad dream.*" She set her phone on the table.

I snorted. "By *friends*, do you mean the same girls who make out with my brother behind your back?"

Ashlyn raised a slim red-blond brow.

"Haven't you heard? I've found a real friend. Someone immune to Brennan's dubious charms."

If I weren't suppressing the urge to cringe, I'd almost pity Ashlyn for calling Leisel her "real" friend. "Aw, you have a new lapdog? How cute. Do you let her carry your bags for you?"

Eyes narrowing, Ashlyn woke her phone back up.

"Cassandra … smells," she said as she typed, presumably adding it to her status. She turned the phone off with a smirk, and I rolled my eyes.

"That's why I miss you, Ashlyn. Your brilliant wit."

Something flashed in her green gaze, but Ashlyn shook her head.

"You know what? I am not letting you and whatever your damage is bother me today. Let's just get this over with."

"Fine."

Ashlyn pulled a binder from her messenger bag and opened it on the table.

"I talked to Mr. Hayward," she said. "He's going to moderate the debate. Basically, he'll ask questions, and we each answer them with our side's reasoning."

"Questions like what?"

"The example he gave me was: Why should or shouldn't slavery be abolished?"

I leaned back in my chair.

"Because it's morally abhorrent. I win."

"Well, obviously you're going to win the debate. The point is to talk about all aspects of the situation, to show we understand the South's predicament. I started a list of things to bring up."

"Their *predicament*? They wanted slaves to do all their work for them so they wouldn't have to. How is that a predicament?"

"Their economy depended on unpaid labor to harvest, among other things, cotton. If they had to start paying for it, they'd all go bankrupt."

Just like Mr. Murphy. Did Ashlyn know my parents still made minimum wage? And that if her dad lost control of Declan, he'd lose his business?

"What a tragedy that would be," I said bitterly.

Ashlyn put her hands on the table and spoke slowly, as if I might be insane.

"Look, we're not *actually* debating slavery, remember? No one thinks it's a good idea. But in 1860, people believed in it enough to die for the cause. So let's make a list of points to bring up in the debate so we both get an A. Can we do that without killing each other?"

"Fine." Actually, I had more important things to do. "Let me see your list." I reached across the table, making sure to bump my coffee cup. It toppled, spilling across Ashlyn's lap.

She cursed and leapt up, but the damage was done.

"What is your *problem?*" she screeched. Everyone in the shop turned to stare, and the barista hurried over with some napkins.

"Sorry." I hid my smile.

"This skirt cost ninety dollars!"

"You have way too much disposable income," I said sincerely.

"Come on, honey, it was an accident," the barista soothed before Ashlyn could go apoplectic. "I bet it'll come right out—I have Shout wipes behind the counter." She gave Ashlyn some, and Ashlyn stalked off towards the bathroom.

"Don't worry, I'll clean it up," I told the barista. With a sympathetic glance, she returned to the counter.

As soon as Ashlyn flounced around the corner, I grabbed a stack of napkins and wiped up the table. Standing, I made a show of patting down Ashlyn's bag and the chair it sat on, though they weren't wet.

Angling my body so the other coffee shop patrons couldn't see, I fished out Ashlyn's keychain, which held three keys and a car fob. One key was the type used at school, probably for the media room; one looked too small to be a house key. The third was the one I wanted.

Surreptitiously, I slipped a little metal mint box filled with modeling clay from my coat pocket. The two halves were separated by wax paper, and the surface of each side of clay was brushed with graphite powder. I loved the Internet—it could tell you how to do anything. I pulled off the wax paper, then carefully pressed Ashlyn's key into the clay. One side, then the other. Done. I brushed the excess graphite powder off the key, then tossed the bundle back into Ashlyn's purse.

When Ashlyn returned, I slouched innocently in my chair.

"Sorry about that." My skin stung with her approach. Knowing it would look apologetic, I allowed myself a wince. "It really was an accident."

Ashlyn shot me a glare as she reclaimed her seat.

"Can we just get back to work?"

"Whatever you want." Though with the key imprint burning a hole in my pocket, I really didn't care about the History project right now.

Ashlyn slapped her binder open again. Pulling her messenger bag onto her lap, she rummaged around and came up with a pen, then dropped the bag on the floor.

"Anyway, before the Civil War, the North was industrialized and could get along without slaves, but the South's economy depended on it. Landowners' livelihoods would collapse without slaves."

"You mean they were rich and entitled, and thought everyone should jump to obey them." I gave Ashlyn a razor smile. "Like you."

She tapped her pen on her notebook. "Even many whites who didn't own slaves supported slavery, you know. It meant that no matter how broke they were, they weren't the lowest rung of the social ladder."

"They saw slaves as sub-human."

"Like you," Ashlyn sniped. I bristled, but she was already looking at the next item on her list. "The tack I'll have to take is that the question of owning slaves comes down to a battle between states' rights and federal authority. The South believed that the federal government had no authority to interfere with their own personal rights."

"No one has the right to own another person."

"Sure, but that's a completely modern viewpoint. The South wasn't doing anything the Romans, Greeks and just about every other culture hadn't done before." She shrugged at my expression. "I'm just saying, slavery was common throughout history."

"So was dying of the plague." Damn, it hurt to sit here with her. I set my teeth against the pain itching across my skin. Even my face hurt.

Oblivious, Ashlyn slurped her frappucino. "Anyway, to the South it was unfair of the North to impose abolitionist laws that would decimate the South's economy."

"Please." I crossed my arms, feeling the tin in my coat pocket, and leaned as far back in my chair as I could. It didn't help much. "Is there a single reason for slavery that's not completely self-serving?"

"Well, some people thought non-whites weren't capable of caring for themselves, that they were safer and happier when they were owned by a good master."

"That's bullshit."

"Not completely." Ashlyn tapped her notebook thoughtfully. "Some people really aren't able to care for themselves. At the homeless shelter there's a dozen or so who I bet would be grateful if someone gave them a home and steady meals in exchange for their service." Ashlyn volunteered twice a month—not because she cared about the homeless, just to look good for college applications. "In fact, it might be the best thing that ever happened to them."

My eyes narrowed. I shouldn't make this personal, but she wasn't playing devil's advocate anymore—it sounded like Ashlyn believed what she was saying. Anger spun my pulse up to a hot beat.

"So you agree with your father?"

"What?" Ashlyn glanced up from her notebook. Pain danced across my skin, and my lip curled.

"You think some people were born to rule, while others were born to serve."

Ashlyn frowned. "I believe some people are natural leaders, while some are natural followers, if that's what you mean."

Behind me, the cafe door opened with a soft jingle. The barista at her counter cheerfully quipped with a regular. Newspapers rustled and conversations murmured, but suddenly all my attention fixed on my ex-best friend.

"And what about us?" Accusation darkened my voice. What about all the times she'd ordered me around throughout our childhood, and I'd obeyed without question? Did she really think that was *normal,* that I should be *grateful* for it?

Ashlyn sat up primly.

"I've always been a born leader."

I leaned forward with a flash of fury. "And you were happy to have me as your sl— "

"*You* were happy to follow me. Until you left. Is that what it was? You and Brennan left because I was too *bossy?*" Ashlyn's green eyes sparked with incredulous anger. She stared at me, but saw nothing.

"How are you so *blind?*" I ground out.

"How could you throw our entire friendship away over *nothing?*"

Nothing? My hands fisted. She was so clueless, so—

"Is this seat taken?" said a masculine voice upwards of my elbow.

"Yes," Ashlyn and I both snapped. Then I realized the voice sounded familiar.

No. It couldn't be. But when I glanced up, it definitely, horrifyingly was.

Paul Alderson sat down in the empty seat and smiled at me.

"Found you," he said.

Chapter 16

"Who the hell are you?" Ashlyn said. "Also, go away."

I just sat there, too shocked to respond. Paul's gray eyes gleamed with triumph. He leaned over and caught my left hand; before I knew what he was doing he'd snapped something cold and hard around my wrist.

I glanced down. *My handcuffs?*

Curses sprang to my lips. I tried to jerk my hand away, but the other cuff already circled Paul's right wrist. He'd chained us together.

"What the *hell*?" Ashlyn said.

Paul smiled at me.

"I wanted to return these. You left them in the bedroom."

Across the table, Ashlyn's jaw dropped open.

"Do you *know* him?" she asked me.

"I told you I'd find you," Paul said, clearly enjoying himself.

"Why?" My voice was faint, my brain stalled.

Paul raised a dark brow.

"What do you mean, why? You tracked me down out of the blue and asked me about—"

Moving instinctively, I lurched forward and clapped my free hand over his mouth. If he uttered the word *selkies* in front of Ashlyn …

"Don't," I said desperately. "Please."

Paul stilled at my touch. His lips were slightly parted under my hand, and his gray eyes, flecked with brown and green in the daylight, caught me like a net. Not because he'd startled me, though he had, but because as we stared at each other I read something in his gaze, a recognition he hadn't let show last weekend.

He knew selkies were real.

Paul pulled my palm away from his lips. "Can we go somewhere and talk?"

Conscious of Ashlyn watching in rapt confusion, I nodded.

"I have to go," I told her. "We'll finish this some other time." With my free hand I scooped my bag from the floor.

Ashlyn frowned at me in disbelief.

"Are you okay? I mean, is this guy a friend or—"

"Since when is it any of your business?" Harsh, but it had the intended effect—Ashlyn's expression hardened.

"Never mind."

My brain kicked back into gear as I dragged Paul out into the parking lot. My skin shuddered in relief as the pain from Ashlyn's proximity faded, but I barely noticed. Paul knew selkies were real, he'd known all along. That changed everything. Pissed that I'd read him wrong last weekend, and that he'd caused a scene in front of Ashlyn freaking Murphy of all people, I yanked on our handcuffed wrists.

"Where's the damn key?"

"There's my car." Paul headed for a sporty blue Audi across the lot. Tied to him, I was forced to follow.

"What the hell are you doing here? How did you find me?"

Paul tossed back a cool glance and hauled me forward.

"I think this time I'll be the one asking questions, Cassandra."

He knew my name. He knew my name and he'd tracked me down when he shouldn't have been able to and he knew selkies weren't a myth. Oh God, did Paul know *I* was a selkie? What if he planned to take my sealskin by force?

Panicked, I dug in my bag for my stun gun. As we reached his car, I yanked on the handcuffs, forcing Paul to swing around and face me. With my free hand, I jabbed the stun gun into his stomach.

Paul swore under his breath.

"You carry that with you in public?"

"That's sort of the point." I always had it, except at school. Right now I was blindingly grateful for my paranoia. "Hands up."

Paul half-raised his arms, pulling my cuffed left wrist into the air too.

"Put that away," he growled.

"Like hell. A guy dragging a girl to his car in handcuffs? I know how that story ends, and it's not pretty."

"I just want to talk." Paul's steely eyes narrowed. "And according to a certain person I could mention, handcuffing someone is a perfectly legitimate method of forcing a conversation."

"I told you what would happen if you came after me." I pressed the metal prongs harder into Paul's midsection. Under his gray long-sleeved shirt his abs tensed, but he didn't try to back away. His voice softened just a shade.

"I'm not going to hurt you, Cassandra."

"Then let me go."

Paul set his jaw stubbornly, so we stood together, too close for comfort, glaring at each other. The metal cuff bit into my wrist. What must we look like to spectators? At least with my back to the coffee shop, the stun gun was hidden from view.

"Why did you ask me about selkies?" Paul said.

"Why did you pretend not to know what I was talking about?"

He laughed without amusement. "You handcuffed me to a bed and threatened me with a taser. I wasn't really in the mood to share secrets."

"Then why are you here?"

Paul's gaze locked with mine.

"Because our web admin doesn't have a single speck of humor, and the Silver Rescue League doesn't rescue the homeless."

My breath lodged in my throat.

"Then what does it do?"

"Can we go somewhere private to talk?" Paul jerked his chin at the coffee shop, and I glanced over my shoulder. Ashlyn, sipping her frappucino, watched us from the window. Damn. I checked the sun's height, guessing at the time.

"I have to be at work in an hour."

"How about I drive us wherever you want to go, we'll talk, and afterward I can drop you at The Golden Fish?"

I stiffened. "How do you know where I work?"

"That's where people said I was most likely to find you. I was going to wait for you there until I saw Ashlyn's update online."

"How did you even find me? And her?"

In response, Paul glanced pointedly at his car. I wasn't getting more answers until we shed our audience. I hesitated, but if Paul was ready to tell me the truth, I wanted to hear it.

"I'm keeping the taser." Though I lowered it from his stomach.

"Fine." Paul fiddled with his keys. The Audi was a convertible, and the roof folded itself sleekly back into a compartment. "Hop on in."

I tugged on our joined wrists. "Don't you need to uncuff us?"

"Nope." His lips twitched in a smirk, and I realized that since his right hand was chained to my left, the cuffs didn't hinder his driving capabilities. Muttering a curse, I clambered into the passenger's seat. Paul followed, and I directed him to a state park by the shore. On the way, I texted Brennan so he'd know he didn't need to pick me up from the coffee shop.

"How did you find me?" I asked again, half from curiosity and half to stall for time to get my story together. No way was

I going to tell him about my family, at least not yet. Not until I knew what Paul and the SRL were about, and whether they could help us. I had Leisel and the house key—I didn't want some strangers mucking up my plan.

"Your friend on the phone mentioned a dance, so I checked out which high schools outside of Massachusetts but within a few hours' drive from Boston had Homecoming dances that night. I tracked down their yearbooks, and only one of them had an Ashlyn and a Brennan in the same grade. And next to Brennan Kelleher was you." Paul's smile was smug. "Cassandra Kelleher."

"What are you, a detective?" I sounded sour, but privately I couldn't help being impressed.

"Just determined. So why did you want to know about the SRL?"

Half a mile of winding road slid by before I answered.

"I have a friend," I said. "She sort of needs help."

Turning into the state park, Paul drove to the end of the lot, where we could just see the ocean over the grass and granite. He cut the engine.

"She's a selkie?"

"Yes. But I'm not telling you anything else about her, and nothing you threaten me with can change that. She'd kill me if she knew I was even talking to you." Ahead of us, boulders gave way to white-capped sea. Our hands lay chained together across the center console. "Now will you please uncuff me?"

"If I do, are you going to tase me?"

"Maybe I'll tase you if you don't." I waggled the stun gun in my free hand.

Paul's gray eyes were serious, but his lips twitched.

"Alright." Slipping a small silver key out of his pants pocket, he pulled my bound wrist to him. His touch made my skin tingle as he unlocked the cuff.

As soon as my hand was freed, I scrambled out of the convertible.

"Hey!" Paul threw open his door and jumped out too, muscles bunched as if he might tackle me. "Where are you going?"

"Nowhere. I just feel better with the car between us." And if I needed to, I could run for the woods. Paul might have longer legs, but he didn't know the area. I could lose him, if I had to. I raised my chin. "You wanted to talk. So talk."

Paul eyed me, then nodded.

"Alright," he said. "The Silver Rescue League's mission is to help selkies, both those at sea and trapped on land."

So there *were* organizations that helped people like me. Or so Paul said. But, my paranoia whispered, I couldn't trust some stranger's word. Even if Paul *was* telling the truth, what exactly did their grand mission entail?

"How many people are in it?"

"A couple dozen, all told."

I frowned. "Student council has more members than that."

Paul's mouth tightened. "We're small, but effective."

"Effective at doing what?"

"Helping selkies who are injured, and freeing them when

their sealskins have been stolen. Some other things, but those are the main efforts."

As he spoke, I studied him for signs of deception, but Paul met my gaze squarely. His limbs were relaxed, meaning he wasn't preparing to dash around the car and grab me, and my shoulders eased a bit.

"How did you get involved?"

Paul hesitated. "My father."

"He works for the SRL too?" Paul paused again, and my eyes narrowed. "Lie to me, and I'm out of here."

His jaw set, and for a moment I thought our talk was over. His gaze swept me like a stiff brush; my muscles grew tense, ready for flight.

Finally Paul let out a long breath.

"My father is a selkie," he said quietly.

Whoa. My jaw fell open—I don't know what I'd expected, but not *that*. Suddenly I noticed that despite the cold sea wind Paul wore no coat, just the gray long-sleeved shirt. Excitement leaped in my throat.

"Oh my God, are *you* a selkie?"

Paul shook his head.

"My mom is human. So am I."

Disappointment flickered only for a moment; Paul was still half-selkie, which was more selkie than I'd ever met before, beyond my family. He'd obviously inherited a resistance to cold from his dad. Plus heightened senses—that must have been how he'd overheard Leisel on the phone.

Kinship bubbled, fierce and sudden, in my breast. What would Paul say if *I* told him I was a selkie?

"Stop staring at me." Paul crossed his arms. "My point was that if you're helping a selkie, then I'm on your side. Now tell me about your friend."

His pushiness gave me pause; so did the realization that Paul's selkie dad could be just as fictional as my "friend." I really wanted to believe him, because if he was smart enough to find me, he might be smart enough to help free my family. But I'd read Paul wrong last weekend—what if I was reading him wrong now too?

If he *was* being honest, then sharing that fact about his dad had been a big step for him, but I didn't want to make a decision like this on impulse. Any of my own confessions could wait unless I was certain of Paul's motives.

The wind whipped my hair about, so I pulled it into a ponytail.

"Let's go down to the water." As I led the way down the rocky path, I wove my tale about my imaginary friend. I'd met her along the beach, I claimed, and we hunted shells and hung out a couple times a week. "She said some weird things about how she used to live at sea. I was curious and kept asking questions, so finally she told me how her husband had actually stolen her sealskin. I didn't know what she meant at first, but finally I figured it out. Once I got over how crazy it all was, I decided I had to free her."

We settled on a wide flat boulder, the sea frothing two feet below. Paul studied me quietly. Was he buying it? I tossed a pebble at the water. "I mean, she's not in any danger or anything, but I can tell she's miserable. And her being trapped as his wife … it's all sorts of screwed up." I caught myself—I could rant about this all day, but I didn't want to accidentally tip Paul off to the fact that it was really my older brother trapped in wedlock.

"Let me help." Paul's voice was deep and quiet.

I shook my head. "She made me promise not to tell anyone about her. She said if her master found out, he'd burn her sealskin." Even the idea made me shudder.

Paul put his hand on mine. "Let me help," he said again. "That's why you came down to Boston, right?"

"It's not your problem." My skin where we touched tingled. "You don't even know her. Trust me, I'm handling it."

Paul gave me a penetrating glance.

"Cassandra, I know you're not telling me everything." Alarmed, I pulled my hand away, but Paul made no any sudden moves. "You don't trust me, and that's fine. But know that I will do everything in my power to free a Bound selkie, may the ocean fill my lungs if I lie."

Was that last part some sort of selkie vow? The intensity with which Paul spoke it sent a shiver down my spine.

"Why is this so important to you?" Something in Paul's eyes told me it was more than simple right versus wrong. But he only shrugged.

"It just is. Look, I've helped free selkies before, and it can be dangerous. I don't want you or your friend to get hurt." The same intent emotion in his eyes vibrated in his voice, and something small but vital shifted inside of me. Maybe I could trust him after all.

Then I looked away. Yes, Paul seemed sincere … but I'd make him prove it before I put my family in his hands.

We'd start small. Extracting the mint tin from my coat pocket, I handed it over.

"I need a key made from that."

Paul peeked inside.

"Is this an imprint of the key to the Binder's house?"

"Binder?"

"That's what we call people who enslave selkies. They Bind them to their will by stealing their sealskins."

"Oh. Yeah, that's to his place. Can you get a key made?"

"I might know a guy." Paul slipped the tin into his jacket pocket. Anxiety washed over me, and I looked out at the horizon to hide it. If Paul didn't come through, I'd just given away the key to the Murphy's house.

"Cassandra." My name sounded warm on Paul's lips. I glanced over. The wind played with his dark auburn hair, and his eyes held a hint of amusement. "Can I get your number for when I have the key, or are you going to tase me again just for asking?"

Reminded of my attack, suspicion pricked at my nape.

"You seem to have forgiven me awfully quickly for that." I watched Paul's gaze for any indication of residual anger, but he only shrugged.

"To save a selkie, I'd endure that whole night again."

His voice was reassuringly serious. Then he smiled wickedly. "Especially the earlier bits."

That startled an embarrassed laugh from my throat. I looked away, knowing my cheeks were red. Thank goodness my hickey had disappeared after my swim last week. I gave Paul my number, which he punched into his phone. He told me his number; I said I'd remember it. A little silence fell, until Paul nodded contemplatively at the ocean.

"Makes you wonder, doesn't it? How many more of them are out there."

"Doesn't the SRL know?" But Paul shook his head.

"Not really. Selkies don't exactly fill out a census."

I shot him a glance. I was starting to believe him, and I wondered if, being half-selkie himself, he could tell I was one. Maybe not—I'd had no inkling about him. And because my key plan had required a pocket for the mint tin, I wore a coat today, so he wouldn't even know I didn't need it for warmth.

I cocked my head. "So your dad really is a selkie?" Paul nodded. "Have you met a lot of them?"

"A dozen or so, mostly members of my dad's pod. That's what you call a group of seals at sea, a pod."

"Oh," I said, as if I didn't know. I wondered if west-coast selkies called their pods *clans*, the way they did in the Atlantic, but the question didn't fit my role, so I had to let it go. It occurred to me that if Paul were all he claimed, he might know more about selkies than I did.

Paul told me he'd grown up in California, and his mom still lived there. I wondered why he'd chosen a college on the opposite coast, but before I could ask my phone chimed in my coat pocket.

I pulled it out. A text from Brennan read *you okay?* I glanced at Paul, who raised a brow but didn't try to see the screen. *I'm fine*, I texted back, then asked Paul to drive me to work. We returned to the car, and I had him drop me off a couple blocks away from The Golden Fish.

Paul pulled onto the shoulder of the road.

"It's admirable, you know." He touched the back of my hand. "What you're doing, helping her. Not everyone would. The Silver Rescue League could use more people like you."

Whoa. Paul had started off the day handcuffing me, and now he wanted me to join the SRL? For a moment I could picture myself, helping selkies and going to college. Maybe even hanging out with Paul. Remembering the feel of his body on mine as we'd danced, my cheeks warmed.

Then I dropped my gaze. Nice as the idea was, I wasn't that girl. Next year, if all went well, I'd be at sea with my family, and I'd never see Paul again.

"When do you think you'll have that key ready?"

"A few days. I'll bring it up." His jaw set stubbornly. "But I want to come with you when you rescue her. People who Bind selkies can be dangerous."

Didn't I know it. "We'll see." I got out of the car.

"By the way …" Paul's lips quirked. "I had a good time last weekend. All things considered." His eyes gleamed, as if recalling how I'd plastered myself against him. Heat pooled unbidden in my stomach, but I raised a cool brow.

“Fan of handcuffs, are you?”

Paul laughed. “See you soon, Cassandra.”

The wind tousled his hair as he drove away, the top of his Audi still down despite the chill. Feeling flushed, I waited until he disappeared from sight, then headed toward The Golden Fish. As I walked I thought over the last hour, replaying everything Paul had said. There was a chance his dad was as fake as my selkie friend, but the look in Paul’s eyes when he’d vowed to save her rang true.

Alright, I decided: when he brought me the key, I’d tell him it was my family I was trying to rescue. It wouldn’t hurt to have another person on Team Selkie, and maybe Paul’s Silver Rescue League knew helpful things like where Binders hid sealskins or how to get past alarm systems.

For once, I walked into The Golden Fish wearing a smile.

Brennan skipped work, so I had a coworker drop me off at home after my shift. Dusk was just easing into night, and between the hours on my feet, the meeting with Ashlyn, and the adrenaline roller coaster from Paul’s surprise visit, I was exhausted. And hungry—I’d forgotten to grab dinner at work.

Sandwich first, I promised myself, then bed.

Yawning, I walked up the front steps and opened the door. Hopefully Brennan hadn’t eaten all of the tuna yet. And I made a mental note to pick up more bread, because mold had started—

My skin prickled painfully, and I drew up short.

Douglas Murphy sat at my kitchen table.

Chapter 17

"What are *you* doing here?" The question shot out of my mouth before I could think better of it.

"Cassandra," my mom warned. "Be polite."

She and my father sat at the table with Mr. Murphy. My father scrawled on a pad of paper with the heading of Norah's Birthday Party—Declan's daughter turned two this Saturday. My parents' expressions were eager, their eyes bright; around the man who possessed their sealskins they came alive. I hated seeing my parents like this. Brennan and I avoided all family get-togethers so we wouldn't have to witness my mom and dad leaping to cater to the whims of the Murphy clan.

"Can I get you more tea?" my mom asked Mr. Murphy. My hands fisted at my sides.

"No thank you, Mara." Mr. Murphy stood. "Actually, Cassandra and I have something to discuss."

Alarm dug claws into my throat. Had Ashlyn told her father about Paul's visit? Could he somehow have figured out who Paul was and found the Silver Rescue League website? Or—my blood chilled. Brennan hadn't come in to work.

I'd figured he'd gone swimming, but what if something more sinister was going on?

"What's this about?"

"We'll talk in your room." Mr. Murphy's voice brooked no debate, and I stiffened. We could talk outside, or in the living room, but he'd chosen my bedroom as a power play to prove that nowhere was safe, not even where I slept, unless he allowed it to be.

Subtlety was not Mr. Murphy's forte.

"Of course." I tried to pretend it didn't bother me. My parents nodded placidly, and irritation surged. "Why shouldn't a grown man hang out with a teenage girl in her bedroom?" I muttered rhetorically. "That's not creepy." I went down the hallway before my parents could chastise me.

Mr. Murphy followed me into my room and sat on the twin bed with a faint smile. I hated that he found me more amusing than threatening. Leaving the door open, I leaned against my wall by the closet, as far away as I could get. For the second time today I had to grit my teeth against the pain scalding my skin.

Mr. Murphy gazed around the room as if cataloging my pitiful belongings, then focused on me.

"Ashlyn mentioned the project you two are working on for class."

That was why he was here, invading my space, making my stomach churn and my skin peel? At least it meant Brennan was okay. Hiding my relief, I crossed my arms.

"And you what, want to offer a first-person source on how beneficial it is to one's economy to own slaves?"

"Watch your tone, Cassandra." The sharp note in his voice warned me I'd crossed a line.

"Yes, sir," I muttered, hating myself as I looked away.

"I wanted to remind you of the deal." Mr. Murphy tapped his fingers on my desk. "My daughter is not to know what you and your family really are."

I blinked, confused about why he believed I needed reminding.

"You think I'd tell her?"

Mr. Murphy stood, and I instinctively flinched. "I think you're getting desperate. You know that after graduation, you and your brother will have to give up."

Alarmed, I shook my head.

"I don't know what you're talking about."

"Let's not play games, Cassandra. There was a brief time when you conned me into thinking you sincere about your diploma, and in a moment of weakness I agreed to our deal." He stepped forward, and the air in the room seemed to thicken and burn. "But let's be clear: I know what you're up to."

He didn't, not specifically. He couldn't. It was so hard to breathe.

"I'm not up to anything," I managed to say.

Mr. Murphy narrowed his cold blue eyes.

"If you attempt to get into my house, the deal is off. If you so much as mention the word *selkie* to Ashlyn, the deal is off. Do you understand?"

I hated him. I hated my fear. Mr. Murphy loomed, making me conscious of how much bigger he was. I hugged myself tighter as if that could stop my trembles, to no avail.

Trying to wrench myself under control, I nodded.

"I understand." He didn't move, and I choked out, "Sir."

Mr. Murphy stepped back with a satisfied smile.

"Good. I'll have your teacher assign you each a new partner, so that your word isn't threatened by … spirited debates." He turned towards the door.

I shuddered, wanting to do something, anything, to show him I wasn't afraid.

"Are you going to keep Ashlyn in the dark forever?"

At the threshold, Mr. Murphy paused.

"Of course not."

"Then what are you waiting for?"

"For you and your brother to leave, of course."

"Why?"

I kicked myself for prolonging the conversation when Mr. Murphy came back inside my room. His expression held a trace of annoyance. "Has it ever occurred to you that I am delaying telling my daughter the truth about what you are to protect you?" At my incredulous expression, his lips twisted. "You two were Ashlyn's prized possessions. Then you left, and she was inconsolable. I planned to tell her once the hubbub surrounding the wedding and Emily's baby died down, but then you two returned. You demanded to stay."

I couldn't believe what I was hearing. Did he really expect me to buy this load of crap?

"How is not telling Ashlyn protecting us?"

"I gave my word that your sealskins would be safe from my family until after graduation. Do you really think that if I told Ashlyn the truth, she'd wait very long before going after them on her own?"

The thought had occurred to me. It was the main reason I was afraid of Ashlyn discovering what we were. But the idea that Mr. Murphy thought he was protecting Brennan and me left me speechless. Did he expect me to be grateful?

The silence stretched, until finally Mr. Murphy cleared his throat.

"Of course, Cassandra, if you wish to rejoin your family, you have only to say so, or break the deal."

For a moment I couldn't believe he was actually suggesting what I thought he was suggesting. "You think I want to . . ." Be his slave again? I was so furious I could spit. "*Never.*"

"It was easy then, wasn't it? You were happy." Mr. Murphy raised his hands beseechingly. "You and your brother are so *angry* now, so troubled. You want to stay with your family more than anything. But they're not going anywhere. And why should they? Your parents are happy here."

I pressed back against my closet door. "You're insane."

"It's dangerous in the ocean. Here, I look out for them. I could do the same for you and your brother."

It was just what Ashlyn had mentioned earlier, the patronizing view that we couldn't take care of ourselves. We poor, dumb brutes.

Horrifyingly, Mr. Murphy appeared to believe it.

"Please leave," I whispered.

Mr. Murphy shrugged, then turned to go.

"Think about it, Cassandra. You miss them, don't you? You miss being a family. Say the word, and you could be at peace again."

I shook my head mutely, and finally he left.

Sinking to the carpet, I shook until I thought I'd break apart.

The next couple days were quiet. On Thursday I passed Declan in the kitchen of The Golden Fish at the start of my shift.

"Happy Halloween," I said.

My older brother just gave me a tight smile.

"Where's Brennan?"

"Um." I shrugged. He'd left an oak leaf on the driver's seat of the truck after school. He was probably in the water by now. He ditched more shifts than he showed up for these days. Declan scowled.

"If Brennan skips again this week he's fired. And don't forget that you're both working the party tomorrow night."

I made a face. "I haven't forgotten." Today was the actual date of Halloween, but Friday night was when the kids would make their rounds. The Golden Fish hosted an annual party, and anyone who showed up in costume got ten dollars off the cover charge. Kids and teens in costume got free soda.

My phone chimed an hour later. I finished seating a party

of four, then checked my message on the way back to the hostess podium.

Your present is ready. Where are you going to be tomorrow night?

From Paul's number. A grin stole over my face. Paul had gotten that done way faster than I could have; my plan had been to ship the wax imprints to a business I'd found online, with a minimum two-week turnaround.

Working, I texted. *Come in costume. Something that covers your face.* That way even if Mr. Murphy showed, Paul wouldn't draw his eye. Paul could give me the key and meet Brennan at the same time. I realized I was looking forward to seeing him.

You don't like my face? Paul texted, and I bit back a smile. Unable to think of anything clever before I had to seat the next group, I settled for a winking smiley face. Were we text-flirting? Faintly flushed, I dove back into work.

The rest of my shift passed quickly, and as I drove home I wasn't even annoyed at Brennan for ditching me again. At home my parents nodded to me stonily, back to their usual habit of ignoring me in the hopes that I would see reason and leave land. Brennan and I were out of bread and milk, so I ate a few scoops of cereal dry. Except for the TV the house was quiet. I was caught up on homework, and had at least two hours until bed.

Needing to see a friendly face, I decided to walk over to Leisel's. She'd told me to stop by anytime, and she was always at home after dark on a school night. Plus, I hadn't had a chance to tell her about Paul's visit. I hadn't even told Brennan yet.

Part of it was that I didn't want to get anyone's hopes up until I had the key, and part of it was figuring out how to explain about meeting Paul in Boston without mentioning the making out and handcuffs part.

Besides, Brennan had been pretty scarce this week, even after I told him about Mr. Murphy's drop-in. I could have used his support in case Mr. Murphy came by again to press his point, but … oh well. At least now I had Leisel for support, and it was about time I brought her up to speed on Paul. Between Brennan, Leisel, Paul and me, we could figure out a plan to kick Mr. Murphy's ass.

The fab four, I thought, and grinned.

The dark woods were friendlier than my house, and I inhaled deeply as I traipsed through the forest. I jumped over a little stream, then picked through a thicket of brambles—in a month or so, everything would be covered in snow. I loved the winter, when the ice and wind kept most people inside.

Skirting the few houses near Leisel's, I approached from the back. At the edge of her yard, I paused to wave up at the stars. Maybe sometime soon I'd see them from far out to sea.

Stealing silently across the lawn, I jogged over to Leisel's basement door.

"Trick or treat," I said as I went in. "You will not believe what—"

My voice died, and I drew up short at the scene in front of me. No. Please, no. I wanted to be seeing anything else: an F on a test, a shark, even Mr. Murphy.

Anything besides Brennan and Leisel making out on her futon.

Chapter 18

Leisel scrambled up, her face reddening instantly.

"Cassandra, hi, I didn't know—"

"What are you *doing*?"

"Calm down, Cass," my brother said, but I didn't look at him.

"You … *bitch*."

"Whoa." Brennan leapt up. "That's enough."

Leisel raked a frantic hand through her mussed hair. "We were just …"

"Just what?" A thought occurred to me: Brennan had been skipping work a lot lately. What if he hadn't been swimming like I'd thought? "How long has this been going on?"

"That's none of your business," Brennan said. I stared at him in disbelief.

"What are you, crazy?"

"How exactly is who I make out with your business?"

"Usually it's not, but I'm talking about *her*. How could you do this?" Leisel was key to our escape plan—the one which ended with her never seeing us again. Was Brennan *trying* to give her a reason not to see that plan to fruition?

"Broken record alert: it's none of your business." Brennan's raised voice made Leisel wince.

"Please be quiet," she said. "If my dad hears you …"

Fury consumed me. I couldn't believe I'd let this happen right under my nose. Or, more accurately, behind my back. So much for Leisel's innocent do-goodery, her *that's what friends are for* smiles.

"I'll catch up with you later," Brennan told Leisel. He squeezed her hand, then headed for the door. "Come on, Cass. Let's go." Leisel bit her lip, looking agonized. I stared at her for a long, icy moment, then went after my brother.

I caught up to him in the woods, before the first bramble thicket.

"What the hell were you thinking?" My breath puffed white in the spidery moonlight. Brennan didn't stop walking.

"What? She likes me, I like her. What is the big deal?"

"The big deal is that we don't belong here, Brennan! We're going to leave, forever, as soon as we get the rest of our family's sealskins."

"If." Brennan ducked under a branch. "Look, I'm the one who kept saying we should leave. So why are you—"

"How do you think Leisel will feel when you suddenly ditch her?"

"We're not getting married, Cass. We're having a little fun."

"You can't get attached."

"I'm not attached," Brennan muttered, but I grabbed his arm. His face had guilt written on it as if with a Sharpie.

"You are! There are plenty of girls to make out with if all you wanted was some fun, but you choose the *one* girl who knows our secret. The one girl who is *supposed* to be helping us leave."

"What is your point?"

"Do you really think she's motivated to help us when that means she'd never see you again?"

Brennan rolled his eyes.

"We haven't made any promises to each other. Leisel knows this is casual."

"She's never had a boyfriend before, and it's been obvious from the start that she likes you. No matter what she says, this isn't casual for her."

Unfortunately, that seemed to make my brother more happy than concerned. "Well, I like her too," he said, and my anger welled over.

"Do you really think she'll let you leave, Brennan?"

"It's not up to her."

"It is if she steals your sealskin."

"She wouldn't."

"If the guy she's fallen for with threatens to leave … God, Brennan, how can you be this naïve?"

My brother yanked his arm away.

"You know what? This isn't about Leisel. This is about you."

"What?"

"You're not afraid Leisel will steal my sealskin. You're terrified that *I'll* fall for *her*, and decide to stay on land when the rest of you leave."

"That's crazy. You wouldn't." My brother didn't respond, and my spine went cold. "Brennan?"

His blue eyes pierced the gloom.

"It's my choice whether I go or stay, Cassandra."

I shook my head in disbelief. "We've worked for two years to free our family. To be at sea with them. That's where we belong, not here trapped in these fake lives and— "

"You don't *get* it." Brennan took a step backward. "You always have to control everything, Cass, and I'm tired of being bossed around."

"You can't stay here. Please. Brennan, you— "

"I'm not planning on it. Alright? So calm down. But stop acting like you have the right to control what I do. You're as bad as Mr. Murphy." Brennan stalked off, leaving me feeling sucker-punched.

Fear and anger swamped me in waves. Brennan staying behind was something I'd never even considered. He'd said he didn't plan to, but … Ice snaked through my body. What if, by the time we found our family's sealskins, Brennan had fallen so hard for Leisel that he'd changed his mind?

I'd hoped Leisel would help put my family back together. Instead, she might tear us apart.

I had to act quickly. Thank goodness Paul had the key—with that and the access codes, there was nothing stopping Brennan, Paul and me from searching the Murphy

✓ * shouldn't she be hurt? more emotion would help w/ likeability

house as soon as possible. In fact, my niece's birthday party this Saturday would be the perfect opportunity. The Murphys would be out all day—we'd have hours to take the house apart. Without Leisel.

The fab four was down to three.

No loss there, I told myself as I stalked after Brennan. Leisel had already searched the Murphy house, with no luck. Though … oh, no. I stumbled to a halt, barely seeing the pine-scented woods. If Leisel had fallen for Brennan, had she even searched the house during that sleepover like she'd claimed? After all, there was no way to tell. Maybe she'd simply lain in her sleeping bag next to Ashlyn's all night and texted me before dawn, pretending to have tried and failed.

My phone rang, and I jumped, hitting a branch.

Leisel's number. Narrowing my eyes, I picked up.

"You have a lot of nerve." I skirted a bramble thicket, wishing I could toss Leisel right in the middle of it.

"Look, I'm not going to apologize. It wasn't a secret." She sounded matter-of-fact, but her voice trembled.

"If you and my brother hooking up wasn't a secret, why didn't you tell me?"

"You never told me about Paul."

Thrown, I stopped with a crunch of leaves underfoot. "What?"

"Ashlyn told me about Monday. When Paul came up to you at the coffee shop. She didn't know who he was, but I recognized his description."

Alarm flared. "You didn't tell her about him, did you?"

"Of course not. And I didn't tell Brennan either. But why'd you lie about contacting Paul? You said we couldn't."

I'd been going to tell her all about Paul and the key tonight, but I didn't trust her anymore. I concocted a cover story off the cuff.

"Alright, I contacted him, and he tracked me up here. But it's a dead end; they can't help us. After we left the coffee shop, I told Paul I'd been playing a practical joke on him, pretending to know a selkie. It took a while to convince him, but he finally bought it and went home."

Leisel hesitated, as if unconvinced.

"Are you sure he won't come back?"

"Positive."

"If he does, tell me. I can be there next time. So you don't have to face him alone."

Leisel still thought she was on the team. "Right."

"Ashlyn was worried about you, you know."

Rage built in me. First Leisel thought she could take my brother from us, and now she thought she knew who was on our side and who wasn't. She'd sympathized with Ashlyn from the beginning, wanted to tell her the truth, even though she knew of the deal. Didn't she understand how dangerous, in so many ways, it would be to trust Ashlyn with anything?

"If you tell her one goddamn thing about us—" I cut myself off. I couldn't go ballistic, couldn't alienate Leisel or she might stop listening to me altogether. I made my tone a shade lighter. "I will personally feed you to an alligator."

"We don't have alligators in Maine." There was a smile in Leisel's voice. "But she really seemed like— "

"Leisel!"

"Fine." Leisel sighed. "Look, I'm sorry I didn't mention … what's going on with Brennan."

"It's over now. You know that, right?" Silence on the line made my fingernails dig into my palm. "He's leaving, Leisel. You're supposed to be helping with that, remember?"

"I know. And I am."

"You and Brennan are over now," I repeated, but Leisel didn't rush to agree.

"This is why Brennan said not to tell you," she muttered.

"I thought it wasn't a secret."

"It just sort of happened, Cassandra. We didn't plan it or anything."

"But it's over now." If she swore that, pledged on her life that she'd stop entangling Brennan in anything that might tear him from his family, I'd think about trusting her again. She wasn't a bad person—she was probably the best person I knew. But … "I need you to promise."

To my left, an owl hooted in the shadows. Moonlight pooled in a clearing just in front of me, but I closed my eyes, willing Leisel to do the right thing.

"I can't," Leisel said.

My heart went cold.

"Whatever's between Brennan and me is between us," she continued. "I know it— "

"Exactly how hard did you look for those sealskins during the sleepover?"

Leisel inhaled sharply. I could picture her shocked face, as if I'd slapped her.

"If you knew me at all, you would never ask that."

After what I just witnessed … "I'm asking."

A long silence.

"Sometimes you really are a bitch, you know that?" Leisel said.

I hung up. Fury washed through me. How dare she pretend to my face to be selfless, to be on our side? All along, she'd been building her own dream. Now she had Brennan at her beck and call, and popularity through Ashlyn. Freeing my family would leave her with nothing, and a different anger surged—this time at myself for being so monumentally stupid.

Then the wave of emotion drained, leaving with only terror. Leisel could ruin everything, in more ways than one. If I let her.

But I wouldn't.

Stalking through the moonlit clearing, I plunged into darkness.

Chapter 19

"You are wearing a beard," a familiar voice said.

I glanced up from The Golden Fish's coat check station, a deep closet off one side of the entry vestibule with its gilded statue. It was Friday, the night after Halloween, and Paul smiled from behind a white mask that covered half his face. I raised a brow.

"And what exactly are you supposed to be?"

He rotated to show off his long black cape.

"The Phantom from *Phantom of the Opera*, obviously. Have you ever seen it?"

I shook my head. "I don't go to a lot of movies."

Paul winced.

"Not the movie; that was lame. The play. It's amazing."

"Our high school did *Bye Bye Birdie* freshman year. I think that's the only play I've ever seen."

"Really?" Paul shook his head. "We'll have to fix that sometime."

He said it easily, a casual flirtation, but I stiffened. Last night's blow-up showed the danger of letting people get too close. Maybe Brennan wasn't in love with Leisel yet, but he wasn't being careful. It made me question my own feelings for Paul. Not that I'd even admitted any feelings, but my pulse quickened when he spoke, and even in a half-mask and cape, Paul looked too good for my own comfort.

But I wasn't the girl he thought I was, who could go to plays and make plans for the future. My plan, my future, was the ocean.

Paul rapped his knuckles on the golden fish statue. It echoed hollowly.

"I'm guessing this is the restaurant's mascot."

"My brother and I call him Clamchops." Brennan had named him when we were seven. We'd loved the fish then; now I hated it.

Paul laughed, then eyed me again.

"So you are … Moses?"

"Yep." I wore a long striped tunic, tied with a rope around my waist. My feet sported flip-flops, and from the table I picked up my two "stone" tablets cut from gray Styrofoam.

"Complete with wig and beard." Paul looked simultaneously impressed and amused. From behind tufts of fluffy white cotton, I winked at him.

"Sexy, right?" I'd put together the costume two years ago, when Mr. Murphy made Declan assign me to work this party. The shapeless robe, plus the beard and wig combo, kept the male partiers from hitting on me no matter how drunk they got.

Plus, I hoped the subtext irritated Mr. Murphy. *Set my people free, dammit.*

Speaking of which … I lowered my voice.

"Did you bring the key?"

Paul glanced into the restaurant, where the Halloween party was in full swing. "Is there somewhere we can talk?"

Just then a couple came through the outer door, along with a blast of icy air. They gaily handed over their coats in exchange for a numbered slip. They joined the party and, tucking my foam tablets under my shoulder and draping the coats over my arm, I gestured for Paul to follow me around the counter.

I hung up the coats, then led Paul deeper into the closet. Outerwear packed the walls, creating a cozy cavern of wool and synthetics and what I fervently hoped was faux-fur. The closet right-angled about ten feet in, creating an L, and at the end, where no one could see us from the coat-check counter, I turned to face Paul.

"So," I said. "Key?"

Paul cocked his head, studying my costume.

"Do you have a pocket under that robe? Not that I'm picturing what's under your robe," he added, though the playful heat in his gaze suggested otherwise. My breath caught, but I carefully exhaled to steady myself. Tonight wasn't like the one in Boston; I didn't get a reprieve from my normal life. I had to keep my distance from Paul—no matter how hot he looked tonight.

I hugged the foam tablets to me like a shield.

"I'm wearing jeans and a t-shirt." The robe was really just

a blanket with a hole cut out for my head. Belted at my waist with the rope, it was nearly as good as a costume at the party store, and about a quarter of the price.

"Oh. In that case, let me help, since your hands are full with those tablets." He stepped forward, the two-inch-thick foam pinned between our bodies, and slipped his hand through the lengths of fabric. I froze as his fingers found the back pocket of my jeans and tucked what I guessed was the new key inside.

Before I could register more than the heat of his touch, he stepped back. I found myself slightly disappointed. Get a grip, I told myself.

"Thanks." My voice was a little thick, and Paul's eyes gleamed, as if he could hear my racing heartbeat.

But all he said was, "When are you planning to use it?"

"Tomorrow."

"I'm coming with you." The side of Paul's face not covered by his mask turned serious, and my head tilted in bemusement. Even Brennan didn't seem to care much these days about watching my back, but Paul wanted to be there for me. Forget keeping my distance; I suddenly wanted to kiss him senseless. But once I told Paul about being a selkie … would he still look at me like this? I hugged my foam tablets tighter and ducked my head.

"Okay."

"I'll get a hotel room for tonight, then."

When had it gotten so hot in here? "There's a motel on the—"

The bell chimed at the coat-check counter. Swearing under

my breath, I muttered for Paul to stay put, then sidled past him. There wasn't enough room, and I had to grab Paul's arm for balance or fall into the rack of coats. Where we touched tingled as if with static electricity.

As I rounded the corner, the feeling intensified abruptly, pain jerking my thoughts away from Paul.

A Murphy was here.

Douglas and Shannon, to be specific. The mayor wore the get-up of a king; his wife wore a ball gown and powdered wig, complete with crown. They always went as some royal couple; I didn't bother to guess which one they were this year. Instead, I braced myself against the wave of itchy pain and approached the counter.

"Cassandra." Mr. Murphy frowned, ever suspicious. "What were you doing back there?"

"Some coats fell down." I forced myself to breathe evenly as I set my foam tablets on the table. "Did you want me to take yours?" I asked, though they never left their belongings where I could access them. Their coats and Mrs. Murphy's designer purse would be hung by Declan himself in his locked office.

The royal couple turned without answering and walked grandly into the mass of townspeople. It would be a night of glad-handing, I could see. The jellyfish-pain faded a bit, but even after the crowd swallowed the Murphys I could feel them nearby. I slipped back into the comforting dark of the closet. As I rounded the bend I rubbed my bare arms and wished for a dip in the ocean. After a run-in with the Murphys, water was the only thing that really washed them from my skin.

“Sorry about that, I—” I broke off; a foot away, Paul grinned at me. “What?”

“I don’t know how you pull off looking hot in a beard, but you do.”

My jittery unease turned at once to heat, and before I could even think twice, I stepped forward and kissed him.

Of course, I’d forgotten I was wearing the beard and wig, so Paul got a mouthful of fluffy white cotton. Laughing, he pulled the headpiece from my face and shed his own mask too. Then his arms were around me. Our lips met, and I pushed him back against the cushion of coats. His hands found their way under my robe, his electric touch washing off the latest Murphy run-in. Who needed water when Paul was here?

But as my unease faded, my head cleared. What was I doing? I couldn’t get close to Paul when I’d yelled at Brennan for doing the same with Leisel. Paul, at least, was trustworthy—I hoped—but if we succeeded in freeing my family tomorrow, he’d never see me again. I needed to tell him the truth about that, about me, but not in a closet when anyone could ring that stupid bell.

I tore my lips free.

“Wow,” Paul said, breathing hard.

“What?” I was a bit breathless too.

“I’m just surprised not to be handcuffed to anything.”

I laughed. “I have to get back to work, but can you meet me outside around back in forty-five minutes? I get a break then.” Swiping our costume pieces from the floor, I handed Paul his mask and settled my wig on my head.

Paul reached up to adjust my beard.

"See you then."

I kept watch as Paul slipped out of the closet, and when my break came, I headed for the kitchen. Brennan was washing pots and pans in his normal t-shirt and apron—the kitchen staff didn't have to wear costumes.

"You got a minute?" I stopped beside him. "I need to talk to you outside."

"Sort of busy, Moses." Brennan grabbed a dirty saucepot and plunged it into soapy water.

"It's important." From his sidelong glance, I could tell he thought I just wanted to yell at him about Leisel. "It's not what you think."

Brennan shrugged.

"Give me a few minutes."

"Okay." I ducked outside and looked for Paul. Spotting him by the far corner of the building, I waved and headed over. My stomach fluttered.

I was going to tell him about my family. About me. Nervous energy shot across my skin—what would Paul think when he found out I was a selkie? So far the only person in the world besides Douglas and Shannon Murphy who knew about us was Leisel.

And look how that turned out, whispered my paranoid side. Now I had to worry that Leisel might try to keep my brother on land. What would Paul do? He clearly liked me—a lot, if even tasing him hadn't put him off—and those myths I'd read, of selkie girls being enslaved by men in search of a wife, shivered through my head. But Paul worked to save selkies. He'd never Bind one himself. And despite the coat closet, we had no future anyway. It was almost like I was breaking up with him.

I steeled myself—best to rip the band-aid off now.

Paul smiled when I reached him, but before he could speak I took off my cotton beard and stepped into the shadow of the building.

"I have to tell you something."

Paul grimaced. "I have to confess something too, and I should do it before we free your friend."

I hesitated, then shrugged. "Confess away." Anything to delay my own confession; I was more nervous than I'd anticipated.

Paul grimaced, looking towards the starlit ocean beyond the pier beside the restaurant.

"She might react a little weirdly to me."

"Why?"

"Ex-masters cause a physical reaction in free selkies—they can't stand to be around someone who has Bound one of their own. So she might run as soon as she gets her sealskin back. Of course, they do that anyway, because—"

"Wait. What are you saying?"

"I Bound a selkie once." Paul winced. "Don't look at me like that. It was only—"

I stared at his moving lips, but wasn't listening anymore. My blood went cold.

"Cassandra?" Paul said, and I snapped my attention back

to him. His eyes, shadowed in the dark, studied me. "Say something."

I was saved by Brennan coming out the kitchen door. Acting on instinct, and the split-second realization that if Paul had Bound a selkie I didn't want him anywhere near my own family's sealskins, I grabbed his sleeve and pulled us out of sight. Knowing we were still within earshot of my brother's keen hearing, I didn't stop tugging until we'd crossed the parking lot and ducked behind a van.

"Sorry, I didn't want him to see us," I muttered, then stepped away. Paul had Bound a selkie. It kept flashing through my head. I'd made out with him. I'd been about to trust him with my secret, my family.

Not anymore.

"Anyway, I just wanted to let you know," Paul said. "In case your selkie friend runs from me once she's freed."

"Right." I felt like running too. How had I not known? Why hadn't I reacted physically to Paul the way I did to Ashlyn and Mr. Murphy?

Except, I realized, I had. The way my skin tingled when Paul touched me—what if it was more than attraction? What if it was a remnant of what he'd done?

"In fact, she probably won't wait to say goodbye to you either," Paul was saying. "Selkies who are Bound act differently when they're free. Their personality changes. She might not even consider you her friend anymore."

"Oh." I barely heard him.

"I just want you to be prepared. There's a good chance that after we free her, you'll never see her again."

"Okay." I wanted to throw up.

Paul glanced in the direction of the restaurant.

"That was your brother back there, right?" I stiffened in alarm until I remembered Paul had found me via our yearbook pictures. I nodded. "He doesn't know about your friend, does he?" I shook my head, and the skin around Paul's eyes creased in sympathy. "It's hard, keeping their secret. But we have to, for now at least."

"For now?" I had to keep him talking while I figured out what to do. I didn't trust Paul anymore—or at least, I didn't trust myself to judge him. My attraction seemed to be overwhelming my better judgment. He'd enslaved another person, however briefly. Maybe he was sincere, maybe he really did want to help, but I knew if Paul came along tomorrow I'd only worry about his intentions towards my family's sealskins.

But, I realized, Brennan and I could search by ourselves. We had the key—we didn't need Paul. I'd let him on Team Selkie because I'd liked him, because I'd been impressed by his smarts and persistence, because I'd started to trust him. But now all that was toast.

Brennan and I were in this alone again.

Paul was still talking; I listened with half an ear.

"My mom and I and the rest of the SRL have been debating how, or whether, to introduce selkies to the modern world. They can't hide in the ocean forever undetected; there's already a video online from Australia of a selkie merging."

That caught my attention. “A video?” Then I frowned. “Merging?”

“When they merge with their sealskin to take aquatic form.”

That sounded so very textbook. Dry.

“When they become who they really are.” I glanced at the sea beyond the pier. “There’s a video?”

“No one thinks it’s real, but eventually more videos will surface. The world is becoming a smaller place, oceans included. At some point within the next few decades, the world is going to realize that selkies are not myths.”

“What then?” If Leisel had put her video online, I realized, Paul would already know about me.

“Depends on how it’s handled, I guess. But for now, we keep their secrets.”

“Right.”

Paul studied me. “So we’re still on for this weekend?”

“Actually, that was what I had to tell you,” I improvised. “My work schedule for the weekend changed. Now I’m on shift tomorrow and off Sunday. Can you come up then instead?”

“Sure.”

I backed toward the restaurant. “You should go. I don’t want my brothers seeing you, or they’ll ask who you are.”

“Are they always nosy when you have a boyfriend?”

My heart jumped. Boyfriend. Paul’s smile told me he knew he was being just a little presumptuous, but considering our kiss … I supposed if I were a normal girl, after we freed my fake selkie friend Paul would ask me out. He'd take me to prom. I'd visit him in Boston.

"Goodbye, Paul."

Slapping a false smile on my lips, I walked away.

"Hey," Brennan said when I stopped by. "Where were you? I— "

"Ditch your burner." Paul had my number, and I didn't want him to have a link to us anymore. It would only be for one day, but with the recent revelations about Paul and Leisel, I was going to let paranoia reign. I'd stomped on my SIM card and thrown my phone into the dumpster on my way inside the restaurant.

"Why? We still have another week before— "

"Something spooked me." Brennan rolled his eyes. "Look, I don't want to order you around like I'm *Mr. Murphy* or anything— "

"Cass, I didn't mean that— "

"—but will you please just trust me?"

Brennan set a clean martini glass on the counter next to an army of cutlery.

"We don't have enough money for new phones." His tone was carefully light. "Someone spent too much on her Homecoming dress."

"Someone *else* has been skipping work, so we didn't get paid as much last week. We'll just have to do without until we earn enough for new phones." Worried he might insist on bringing Leisel along, I didn't tell him about my plan for tomorrow, not yet. "Please?"

"Okay," Brennan said. "Why are you—"

"Gotta get back to work." I left him to his dishes. In the morning, I'd catch Brennan before breakfast and tell him that we were going to finish this war the way we'd started it: together.

Team Selkie was down to two.

Chapter 20

I woke on Saturday full of terrified determination. Despite the shocks of the past couple days, I'd slept deeply, and was ready to launch a full-on assault of the Murphy stronghold with Brennan. I went to wake him up.

My brother's room was empty.

An oak leaf lay on his neatly made bed—he'd gone out. *Oh, no.* Panic started a low thrum in my throat. I had to find him. But was Brennan swimming or with Leisel?

Either way, since I'd insisted we ditch our phones last night I didn't even have a way to call him. I never used the house phone, worried Mr. Murphy might have bugged it. I could head to the pay phone by the library and call Leisel to see if my brother was with her, but time was slipping by—Norah's birthday party was scheduled to start soon. From my parents' schedule I knew there would be story-time, cake, and arts-and-crafts sessions. The party would last until noon, and once the kids went home my parents would look after Norah while the Murphys, including Ashlyn, took Emily and Declan out for a late lunch.

I didn't have time to track my brother down, not if I was going to take advantage of the empty house. It likely wouldn't be empty again until … cold sweat broke out on my brow. I didn't know the next time the Murphy house was guaranteed to be undefended.

It had to be today.

The mansion was a lot to search all by myself, and for a moment I considered asking Leisel for help. But although I'd had a couple days to calm down about her sneaking around with Brennan behind my back, I couldn't shrug off my unease at the thought of her getting her hands on my family's sealskins.

Not that it mattered if I couldn't find them.

I'd find them, I told myself. And I'd do it without Leisel, without Paul—even if I trusted him, which I wasn't sure I did, he was hours away in Boston—and without my flaky brother.

I'd do it on my own.

Pocketing the key Paul had given me and grabbing the supplies hidden under my bed, I dashed outside, worried Brennan might have taken the truck. But it was there. That meant Brennan might have walked over to Leisel's, and I thought again about calling her.

No. Brennan had abandoned me again, and I was fed up with his lack of dependability. Besides, if Leisel came I'd worry whether she was sabotaging us, and Brennan would be angry with me for questioning her motives. He thought I was just paranoid, and hadn't really believed I could pull off this rescue for a long time.

But I could do it. I had the key, I had my plan, I had the time.

And I had no one to slow me down.

I drove to Emily and Declan's house, which was twice the size of my parents', and watched from half a block away as people arrived. Ashlyn was always required to at least show up at family parties, but I knew she'd split after twenty minutes and go shopping with her friends until lunch. When she parked her car and walked inside, I drove to the Murphy's street.

From Leisel's information, I knew a camera watched the gate across the driveway, so I parked a block away. I checked for any neighbors, then adjusted my disguise. I wore a sweater-dress similar to one Ashlyn owned, and I'd picked up a coppery wig with the last of Brennan's and my money. Big sunglasses and gloves from The Golden Fish's lost-and-found, along with dollar-store leggings and ankle boots Emily had given my mother last winter, completed the look.

As far as the cameras were concerned, I'd just be Ashlyn dropping in. My stash also contained a hat and preppy button-down for Brennan's disguise, but they were useless now. I waited another ten minutes, using my laptop and a neighbor's unprotected wi-fi signal to watch Ashlyn's online profile until she updated it from *Happy Birthday to my cute niece Norah* to *Shoppingsville, here I come*, and then I stowed the laptop in the truck's center console.

Here we go.

I walked up to the pedestrian gate beside the driveway and

punched in the code for entry. The wrought iron slid smoothly open, and I hurried through.

If Leisel's information could be trusted, Mr. Murphy could access the live feed from his phone, but I was betting he'd be too distracted by Norah's party to wonder why "Ashlyn" was walking up the drive instead of coming in with her car, if he even noticed at all. He'd see the back-up recording on his computer later, but by then it would be too late. And once I was inside the house he shouldn't be able to see me.

I hoped.

This all depended on whether Ashlyn had told Leisel the truth about her house's security, and whether she even knew about all of it. If Mr. Murphy had a camera inside his daughter wasn't aware of, I was swimming into a shark's maw.

But this was my one chance, and I had to take it.

Adrenaline scorched my veins, but I coached myself to walk calmly instead of breaking into a run. It seemed to take forever to round the dolphin fountain in the middle of the driveway loop. Finally I approached the door, making sure to angle my head so the camera would catch only my wig. Slipping Paul's key from my purse, I said a silent prayer that it would work.

It did, thank God. My limbs felt like jelly as I turned the knob. Inside, I punched the alarm code Leisel had given me into the access box by the coat closet. The status indicator flashed to green. I nudged the front door closed with an audible click, then leaned against the dark carved wood.

I was in.

The Murphy house lay before me, big and empty and

silent but for the hum of electronics most people wouldn't be able to hear. I hadn't been inside this building since discovering the truth. For two years I'd tried and failed to breach these walls. Now the rooms were defenseless.

My family's sealskins were here somewhere; all I had to do was find them. And I'd better, because just by being here I'd broken the agreement. When Mr. Murphy found out …

I shoved the fear aside. By the time Mr. Murphy realized what I'd done, my family and I would be long gone.

Since Leisel claimed she'd already searched the main floor and the basement, I ran upstairs. Some of the selkie myths I'd read mentioned sealskins hidden in the eaves or roof timbers, so I yanked open the pull-down staircase in the guest bedroom and started with the attic. Unfortunately, the unfinished space beneath the roof proved to hold only spiders, bundles of extra insulation—I unrolled them, but found nothing inside—and spare flooring planks.

I moved on to my next best guess, the master bedroom suite. *Where evil slept.* The room was painted green, the four-poster bed done up in shades of gold and cream. On the wall a picture of the Murphy family crest, all apple trees and gilded lions, shone regally. With plush carpet and dark wood furniture, the whole room felt elegant and serene.

My parents' room, by contrast, was dingy white, with mismatched cast-off furniture and a threadbare rug older than I was. As I stared at the Murphys' chic, expensive bedroom, a familiar rage bubbled in my throat. I'd had to swallow it for two years, but I was finally here, in the house that pretended innocence but guarded my parents' enslavement.

With a growl, I dashed downstairs to the garage and seized a sledgehammer. This house deserved to fall, and if that's what it took to free my parents, I was more than happy to oblige.

The first crash of the sledgehammer into the wall of the master bedroom made my heart sing, so I did it again, and again. I tried not to smash any load-bearing beams—yet—but when I stopped to catch my breath the walls were a mess of drywall and insulation, and the framed crest lay on the floor in a pile of shattered glass. A couple dresser drawers were locked, but instead of taking the time to pick them—a skill Brennan and I had practiced for months—I just smashed them open instead. Though my attack ultimately yielded no hidden safes, a rush of satisfaction buoyed my spirits as I turned to the bed.

Hoping the sealskins would be tucked inside, I cut open the mattress and box springs with my switchblade. Nothing. I tore open the pillows and comforter, but as creepy as it would be to picture the Murphys sleeping under my parents' sealskins, they weren't there either. I ransacked the closet and dresser drawers, then checked under and behind all the furniture. Still nothing.

Finally I wiped my brow and surveyed the pockmarked, broken—and maddeningly empty—room. Damn. I'd really hoped the sealskins would be here. Fear shot down my spine, but I ignored it. There were still plenty of places to search.

I highly doubted the sealskins would be bundled next to the spare towels and toothbrushes, but I tore apart the guest room and hall bathroom anyway. After slamming the sledgehammer through any open space in the hallway, paying particular attention to the linen closet, I went into Ashlyn's room.

At the end of freshman year the walls had been sky blue, except for the long side, on which I'd painted a giant mural of the beach. Not one of our rocky, cold Maine beaches, but a Florida beach, with a bright sun and golden sand and a sign saying Key West. We'd talked all the time about road-tripping to the Keys as soon as our parents would let us, and one day as a surprise I'd painted the mural for Ashlyn. It was the kind of thing I did back then, to make my best friend happy.

In any case, the beach was gone. Now the dark purple walls held bookcases and a giant flat-screen TV. One of the bookcases was crammed with DVDs—most I'd never seen, not having had time for TV or access to streaming video in the last couple years, but I recognized a couple shows Ashlyn and I had watched together. I paused at the DVDs of *Gilmore Girls*, remembering our TV marathons. They'd been good times—but when there was popcorn to fetch, guess who'd leapt up to fetch it?

I couldn't believe Ashlyn still had no idea what was going on right under her nose, and a spike of fury gave me the strength to topple the shelves, sending books and DVDs crashing to the carpet. I only wished I could crush Mr. Murphy under their weight. I bashed in the now-bare walls, there and behind Ashlyn's dressers, which were full of clothes upon clothes I'd never be able to afford. No secret safes.

In the back of her closet, however, I came across a surprise.

Not sealskins, unfortunately. Paintings.

My paintings. I'd thought they were all destroyed after Brennan and I left, but Ashlyn had saved nearly twenty of them, ranging from a three-inch-square watercolor of a butterfly to a huge canvas depicting the Golden Fish restaurant on its pier.

I flipped through them, unexpectedly transported again to that time a few years ago when I loved to paint and adored my best friend and didn't worry about anything. One painting showed two dolphins leaping above the white-frothed waves, and I remembered the day I'd given it to Ashlyn. Emotion tightened my throat.

I flipped to the next painting—a stylized self-portrait of myself—and my breath stopped. Over my face one word had been scrawled dozens of times in what looked like permanent marker: *bitch*.

Rosy-colored memories fading, I recalled Ashlyn's anger at the coffee shop last Monday. *How could you throw our friendship away over nothing?* To her I was the girl who callously cut her out of my life for no reason. My stomach twisted as I thought of all the ways Brennan and I had hurt her over the years, but what was done was done. Ashlyn had every right to hate me, and I had no doubt she did.

It didn't matter: I had to free my family. Now. I couldn't afford to get sidetracked by memories. I surged to my feet and headed for Ashlyn's door, but found myself pausing by her dresser.

I wonder . . .

I'd already checked the drawers, but on impulse I opened the top one again. This was where Ashlyn kept her jewelry. I searched quickly through the compartmentalized organizers.

After I'd painted Ashlyn her beach mural, she'd surprised me with a gift too: matching necklaces. We'd just spent a weekend down on Cape Cod, and Ashlyn had been obsessed with starfish. We'd found dozens that weekend, including one that had been cut in half, probably by a boat propeller. Distraught, Ashlyn had flagged down a passing lifeguard to see if there was anything we could do to help the poor creature. He'd told her that in fact, starfish could regenerate limbs that were torn off. So long as part of the center was still alive, it could regrow itself entirely. Ashlyn had been fascinated.

In the back of Ashlyn's drawer, stuffed under a mess of tarnished bracelets, I found what I was looking for: a starfish pendant on a slim chain. I dangled the shiny starfish in the air. When she'd given me its match, she'd told me it represented our friendship. No matter what happened, Ashlyn promised, our friendship would regrow itself. Best friends forever.

For the last two years, thinking of this necklace was like eating bad clams. Our starfish friendship was hacked apart, ruined by the truth: I'd been her slave, not her friend, and she'd been too oblivious to notice.

It burned, still, that she couldn't see what was in front of her, that she'd bought her father's explanation that Brennan and I had gotten into drugs and spent our missing summer in rehab or something; rumors had mangled the story so that I hardly remembered which was the "official" version.

Fetching a notepad from Ashlyn's desk, I scrawled a note:

We're selkies, you idiot.

I hesitated, nearly throwing the note away, but why shouldn't Ashlyn know the truth now? I'd already broken her father's deal. In for a droplet, in for the ocean. I left the note and necklace on Ashlyn's dresser.

Padding downstairs, I took a deep breath. A glance at the clock made my heart seize—time was slipping by way too fast, and the house had given up no secrets yet. The professionally decorated downstairs loomed, pristine and mocking.

Fury and desperation caught me like a riptide, turning me into a vengeful wave of destruction. I tore recklessly through the couches in the den, upended bookcases in the library, and scattered dishware in the kitchen to access the cabinets. I smashed the walls, pulled down paintings, and even rolled up rugs in case a safe might be hidden in the hardwood floors.

Finding a hidden nook behind a false panel in the dining room's china cabinet, I nearly had a joyous heart attack, but it wound up holding only a bundle of government bonds and a handgun. The handgun was heavy and made of cold black metal. Not new, or at least it didn't look like the shiny pistols you saw in movies, it still emanated threat. I almost left it untouched, but it occurred to me to remove the bullets in case Mr. Murphy ever wound up pointing the gun in my direction.

Gingerly, I picked it up. It took me a while to figure out how to release, empty, and re-seat the clip, and by the time I set the gun back in its nook I was shaking.

I took a deep breath, replaced the false panel, and stood.

Onward.

I searched the closets, the game room, the pantry, the three-car garage.

Nothing, nothing, *nothing*.

I checked my watch—after one now—and tried to choke down a tidal wave of panic. Today was my only chance. There was no way to pretend I'd never been here; Mr. Murphy would know I broke my end of the agreement, and the deal would be off. Brennan and I would have to leave, so we wouldn't be—

Oh God. Even the idea of being captured again made me reach for an ornamental trash can. I retched, then wiped my mouth on a tablecloth and fought back despair.

Wait—I hadn't searched the basement yet! I scrambled up and dashed downstairs. The basement ran the whole footprint of the house; on one side was a utility sink and two small windows. I flipped the overheads on, and by the light of four bare bulbs I peered around at the stacks of furniture, boxes and toys.

The sealskins had to be here; there was nowhere else left.

Leisel claimed she'd searched the basement during that sleepover, but maybe I'd been right—maybe she'd just said that to keep Brennan from suspecting how much she *didn't* want him gone.

I was tearing through crates of Christmas decorations when the bellowing started upstairs.

"Cassandra! Brennan!" Then a string of curses.

Mr. Murphy. I clutched a box of glass ornaments. *Oh, no.*

It dawned on me, suddenly and sickeningly, that I'd failed.

My grand plan had yielded nothing; my family was not free, would never be free.

I had to get out of here.

The thought of what Mr. Murphy would do if he found me broke my paralysis: shoving a crate under one of the tiny windows, I smashed a ceramic Santa statue against the glass. The statue broke, but so did the window. I bashed the pane open. Chucking the ruined Santa aside, I tossed a yellow baby blanket over the sill, then clambered onto the crate and pulled myself through the opening. Glass cut into me, slicing my arms and back, but I ignored the pain. If Mr. Murphy caught me …

Outside the day was sunny, impossibly so. My breath came in rasps, desperation and fear and failure all clawing at my throat. I blinked to clear my eyes. The basement window looked out the back of the house, so I took off running towards the front.

Rounding the corner, I slammed into someone. Ashlyn. We fell to the ground, but I shoved her away and scrambled up before she could do more than shriek.

"Cassandra!" she called, but the wrought-iron gate across the driveway gaped wide, and I pelted through it without a backwards glance for the drops of blood in my wake.

Chapter 21

Nine minutes later I charged into my parents' house, screaming my head off for Brennan. If he wasn't here, I didn't know what I'd—

"Cass." Brennan jumped up from the living room couch, where he'd been watching TV. His eyes widened at the blood on my sweater-dress. "What happened?"

"We have to go." Tears streamed down my cheeks. I'd held them back in the truck, but now that I had to tell Brennan what had happened …

Before I could, someone charged through the door. I shrieked, sure it was Mr. Murphy, but it was only Declan.

"You." My older brother's gaze snagged on my bloody arms, but then he pointed at Brennan. "And you. Let's go. Now."

"What? Where?" Brennan was already shoving his feet into his sneakers.

"You two are getting your sealskins and leaving."

"What happened?" Brennan asked again. Declan turned to me.

"Keys," he barked. I held out the pick-up's key, which he tossed to Brennan. "Cassandra is coming with me so I can keep an eye on her. You take the truck and get your sealskins. Meet us at Shiny Hollow." It was a fishing spot that wasn't popular in the winter. "Then I'll drive you both to the ocean."

I swallowed hard. "Declan, I— "

"Now!"

Brennan shot me a bewildered look, then took off running out the door. Declan grabbed my arm and towed me outside. His minivan waited on the street, still idling. I felt numb, and though my arms throbbed, I barely felt the wounds.

Declan put me in the front seat of his van, slammed the door, and jogged around to the driver's side. My niece's teething ring lay in a plastic bag on the floor. I stared at it, feeling dull and beaten. I'd failed.

"How could you do this?" Declan threw the van into gear. "What the hell were you thinking?"

That broke me out of my stupor.

"You know what I was trying to do."

"You broke the deal, Cassandra. You and Brennan can never come back." My older brother's jaw set.

"How can we leave you here?"

"I'm fine. I have Norah. And Emily."

My gaze dropped to the teething ring. He did seem content when around Norah, but otherwise … "You can't honestly tell me you're happy."

"Happy enough."

"Like mom and dad are happy?" I said, knowing he'd

proved my point. They were only "happy" because of the Haze, and because they were making the best of an awful situation. "She still cries at night, Declan. I hear her."

"We're fine. You two should be gone." Declan punched the rim of the steering wheel, making me jump. "Do you have any idea how much I sacrificed to give you this chance?"

"If you're *happy*, it's not a sacrifice, is it?"

As we entered the patch of grass that passed for a parking lot at Shiny Hollow, Declan stomped on the brakes. The minivan lurched to a halt.

"You spoiled little brat. Grow up, Cassandra. This isn't a fairy tale, where we all swim off into the sunset together. This is real life, and sometimes the good guys get screwed. All you can do is win what battles you can. I fought that battle for you and Brennan, and you are damn well not going to waste it."

"But—"

"I don't want to hear it." Declan held up a hand. "I love you, Cassandra, but I never want to see you again. I let you hang around as long as I thought you were safe, but not anymore. You're gone. Today."

Blinking back tears, I crossed my arms over my chest. We waited for Brennan in awful silence, Declan staring at the dashboard clock.

Finally our silver pick-up pulled into the grassy area. Brennan hopped out with our two backpacks in his arms. He motioned for Declan to roll down his window. Declan cracked it impatiently.

"We're not coming back here, are we?" Brennan asked.

Declan shook his head. Brennan hurled the truck's keys as far as he could into the woods, then clambered into the minivan's backseat. He handed my backpack to me; I clutched it, my heart swelling as always when reunited with the piece that made me whole.

Declan got back on the road, heading north.

"Where are we going?" Brennan asked.

"The Lost Lighthouse," Declan said. That was where he'd sent us off to sea two and a half years ago. He'd been calm then, and patient. Now he was just angry.

"So it's time to go. For good." Brennan leaned forward in the back seat. "Don't I have any say in this?"

"No," Declan snapped. "Your sister saw to that."

"We need to make a stop so I can say goodbye to someone." Brennan's voice was serious, but Declan punched the steering wheel again.

"Goddamnit, Brennan, I'm in too much pain for your jokes right now." My older brother breathed shallowly as he drove. His forehead was slick with sweat, deep brackets etched around his mouth.

"You're not supposed to be taking us to the Lost Lighthouse, are you?" I asked, and Declan shook his head. "You're supposed to be taking us and our sealskins to Mr. Murphy." My brother probably had standing orders for this sort of situation. Declan nodded, and my arms clenched around my backpack. "He won't suspect that you're disobeying?"

"On the contrary. He's probably only two minutes behind us."

"*What?*" Brennan and I said in unison.

"He has GPS trackers on all our cars. Except for your truck."

"Why not our truck?" Brennan asked.

"Because Douglas doesn't make false promises, and he promised he would leave you two alone so long as you held up your end of the bargain."

I heard the castigation in Declan's voice. "Dec, I couldn't *not* try."

He sighed.

"I know." His voice gentled. "I'd have done the same, okay? But it's over. You gave it your best shot." He gave a bark of laughter. "Hell, I'm surprised that house is still standing, with all the holes you put in it."

Brennan leaned forward again. I could feel him looking at me.

"You were there?" I asked, surprised. Declan nodded.

"Douglas told me not to come—I guess he was afraid you'd actually succeeded—But Emily said we could go to the house. She didn't know what was going on, of course. Once I heard your truck start on the street, I realized before they did that you'd left, so I ran out to my car and followed without waiting for Em."

He pulled over to the side of the road, onto the wide gravel shoulder—we'd reached the Lost Lighthouse. It wasn't an official landmark or anything, and might not have even been a lighthouse to begin with. Nothing remained of the structure that had once stood by the sea except for a foundation set into the granite and one curved wall about four feet high. We'd often fished from the rock ledges here when we were growing up, and one day Brennan and I had made up the story that the rest of the lighthouse had gone for a swim and forgotten where it belonged. We'd pretended it was wandering at sea, and would someday come home.

Now it just looked like the broken wreck it was.

Declan cut the engine. "Come on," he told Brennan. "Cassandra can change in the van." Brennan squeezed my shoulder before getting out, and the boys walked towards the line where granite gave way to gray-blue sea.

I sat quietly for a minute, shaking, starting to feel the pain from the glass cuts. They were shallow, and would heal when I *changed*. What hurt more was the unavoidable knowledge that I'd failed. It was like a baseball bat against my ribcage, hitting anew with every breath.

Swallowing tears, I divested myself of my sweaterdress, leggings, underwear and boots, then pulled my sealskin from my backpack and wrapped it around me. I opened the car door; cold air shivered on my bare limbs. I felt numb, rattled. Blood trickled down my arms, but I didn't care.

I picked my way across the granite to my brothers. Declan wore a long-sleeve button-down and black slacks—his going-out clothes from lunch. His hair and Brennan's, the same driftwood brown, blew back and forth in the wind. Brennan was naked to the waist, his sealskin wrapped towel-like around his hips. His gaze went to my arms, and I realized I should have wiped off the blood to keep from worrying him.

Not that it mattered. We were going.

I stopped in the shadow of the broken wall and looked at Declan. My brave older brother, who'd given up so much for us, and was sacrificing more right now by not turning us in.

"What's he going to do to you for this?" I asked.

Declan shook his head.

"That's not your concern."

"Declan …" I didn't know what to say. Sorry, a million times over.

My older brother wrapped me in his arms. He hadn't spoken to me as anything but my boss in two years, but now he hugged me close. It punched a hole in my self-control.

"It's okay, Sandy," he murmured. Hearing my nickname from childhood, I choked back tears. "Douglas needs me—there's only so much he can do. Once you're gone, he'll calm down. Just … never come back. Please. Be happy, out at sea. Find our people."

I opened my mouth, but all that came out was a sob. I stifled it against Declan's shirt.

"Promise me, Sandy."

I couldn't speak, so I just clutched Declan tighter. This was all my fault. If I'd trusted Paul, or Leisel, or both of them, would this still be happening? The sealskins were somewhere in the Murphys' basement—they had to be. But I had been so determined to do everything myself, and I'd run out of time. I wondered what Paul would think when I didn't return his calls, when I didn't show up to meet him tomorrow. And Leisel. She'd have no way of knowing whether we were dead or just gone.

I wished ... but just then Declan stiffened, turning towards the road.

"He's here."

I raised my head; I could hear it now too, the rumble of an expensive sedan. Fear shot through me as Declan stepped away. My bare feet felt glued to the icy granite. All I had to do was leap into the ocean and *change*, and I'd be free.

But not Declan.

Mr. Murphy's car careened around the bend in the road, then screeched to a stop behind Declan's minivan. Mr. Murphy emerged, his motions taut with fury.

The wind picked up, tearing at my hair. Brennan pulled me to the edge of the sea. It splashed happily at our feet, welcoming. Oblivious. I cast one last glance back at my older brother. Declan jerked his head at the ocean.

"Go," he said. Fifty yards behind him, Mr. Murphy stalked over from the road.

Brennan tugged at my hand. "I'm not going until you do, Cass. Come on." His voice was rough, trying to disguise his fear. Mr. Murphy was our worst nightmare, but Brennan didn't budge from my side. I hated to leave Declan behind, but if I stayed any longer, Mr. Murphy would take us all.

I turned and dove.

Chapter 22

An hour up the coast, I tried to make Brennan stop so we could *change* to human form and regroup. I wanted to explain what I'd done. Apologize. But Brennan ignored any thoughts I sent his way. I tried swimming in front of him, but he ducked under me and kept heading north, leaving me no choice but to follow or get separated.

He didn't stop swimming for a day and a half.

When Brennan finally hauled out in a deserted rocky cove next to snow-covered woods, I was too exhausted to do anything besides sleep.

I woke to early morning light and Brennan nudging my side.

Come on, Cass. Let's keep moving.

Brennan, we have to talk, I thought, but he swam determinedly out of sight.

I hauled myself out of the water and *changed*. The air felt colder to my human skin, but I wrapped my sealskin around me, got to my feet, and picked my way across the gravel to a frost-coated boulder. I sat down to wait. My cuts from the broken window had healed.

After a couple minutes Brennan, still in seal form, surfaced a dozen yards out. He slapped the surface with a front flipper and grunted, his meaning clear even without mindspeech. I shook my head stubbornly.

"Get out here and talk to me," I called. Brennan slapped the water again and swam away at the surface so I could see him. I didn't budge. A handful of minutes later he returned and let out a wordless bellow of frustration.

"I'm not going anywhere until you talk to me," I said.

This went on for at least a half an hour, but eventually Brennan gave in and *changed* into human form. He wrapped his sealskin around his torso and stood, seawater surging gently around his knees.

"Come on, Cass. Let's *go*."

"Where are we?" Farther north than we'd been since that summer, for sure. Nothing looked familiar in winter. Snow edged the forest loam behind me, and a lone songbird chirped to the dawn breaking over the ocean's horizon. Brennan shrugged.

"Don't know. Canada by now, maybe."

"We have to talk."

"Later."

"What, did you promise Declan you wouldn't let me stop until we reached the North Pole?" I was half-joking, but Brennan's expression told me that this, or something like it, was precisely the promise he'd made. "No. We have to talk."

"We can't go back. Declan was clear about that. So don't try to convince me, Cass."

"You don't even know what happened."

"Dec gave me the highlights. You fucked up, Cass. You crossed the line with Mr. Murphy—and because of that, I didn't even get to say goodbye to Leisel before we left. Have you even thought about that once?"

"I'm sorry." Disaster didn't begin to cover how badly my big move turned out.

"Sorry doesn't help. She'll think …"

"We didn't get to say goodbye to our parents either." Though they'd be overjoyed to know we'd finally left. Brennan's grimace told me he knew that too.

"They said their goodbyes to us a long time ago. But Leisel …" He shook his head. "Whatever. It just sucks."

His focus on Leisel made my jaw set.

"What about abandoning our family? Doesn't that suck more?"

"Look, if you tore the house apart like Declan said but still couldn't find the sealskins, we'll never find them. It's over."

"That's not true. I barely got started searching the basement, so— "

"Stop!" Brennan shouted it into the cold landscape. "We lost, Cass. We have to stop now, while we at least have *our* freedom."

"But— "

"It's what our parents want. It's what Declan wants."

I searched his face. "Is it what you want?"

Brennan looked south along the coast, as if he could somehow see through the rocks and trees and distance. "What I want," he said bitterly, "is to never see a Murphy again."

"I'm not giving up." I had to fix this.

"There's nothing left to try, Cass."

"There might be. Like I said, I never searched the basement."

"So? If the sealskins were there, Mr. Murphy will have moved them by now."

I'd opened my mouth to continue my arguments, but that stopped me.

"Shit, you're right," I said after a moment.

"And besides, we're never getting near that house again." Brennan paced in the shallows, kicking up saltwater spray. "I doubt even Leisel would get in anytime soon—they wouldn't let Ashlyn have people over until the house was fixed up."

My determination had blazed bright like a candle when I'd marched up this beach, but now it wavered in the gale of Brennan's reasoning.

Then I realized something—Brennan wasn't saying no anymore. He was stating problems ... meaning he'd put at least some thought into how to overcome them. Which meant that despite his protests, he didn't want to give up yet either.

My flame of determination steadied.

"It's time to get some outside help," I said, and Brennan paused.

"What help?"

"Did Leisel tell you I went to see someone from the Silver Rescue League?"

"You what? When?"

"The weekend of Homecoming. I drove to Boston and tracked down a guy named Paul."

"Why didn't you tell me?"

"It, ah … it didn't go very well. I didn't think Paul could track me back to Granite Harbor, but he did." I told Brennan how I'd asked Paul to prove his good intentions by making a key out of the wax imprints I'd gotten from Ashlyn. I thought my brother might be impressed, but instead he looked … pissed.

"Are you kidding me, Cass? You flip out when I tell Leisel *anything*, but you blab to this stranger about our family without even running it by me?"

Put that way it sounded sort of bad, but I crossed my arms.

"One, I didn't tell him about our family, just asked him to get the key. And second, you've been AWOL for the last few weeks, so no, I didn't run it past you."

"I've been home every night!"

"When you're not making out with Leisel!" I rushed on before he could explode. "Look, we needed help, so yes, I asked Paul to get us the key."

"So why didn't you include *Paul* in your breaking-and-smashing plan?"

I bit my lip. With the clarity of our swim and my thoughts over the last day, shunning Paul's help felt like one of the dumber decisions I'd made.

"He told me that he'd stolen a selkie's sealskin once."

Brennan recoiled. "What?"

Okay, from the look on my brother's face, maybe my own knee-jerk reaction hadn't been totally off base. "I don't know the whole story, or how long it was for, or why. " I shook my head. "Thing is, I think he's sincere in wanting to help selkies."

"How do you know?"

"His dad is a selkie."

Brennan's brows shot up.

"His dad's a selkie, but he enslaved one?"

"Like I said, I don't know the whole story."

"He might've been lying about his dad."

"I know, but I don't think he was." I sighed. "I should have brought him along. Maybe with two of us, we'd have had time to find the sealskins."

Brennan frowned.

"Why didn't you bring *me*?"

"I was going to, but you went swimming that morning before I could find you."

"Why didn't you tell me beforehand? Leisel and I would have …" Brennan caught sight of my expression. Comprehension flickered across his face, followed swiftly by anger. "Are you telling me you cut me out because of your stupid paranoia about Leisel?"

My anger rose to meet his, pulling me to my feet. "You were talking about *staying*, Brennan. For her. I couldn't …" I broke off, emotion clogging my throat.

"Couldn't what?"

"Couldn't let that happen."

My brother's blue eyes narrowed.

"Where I go, and why, isn't your decision, Cass."

"I'm just trying to keep our family from tearing apart," I said. "Even more than it already has. Can't you see that?"

Brennan's hands clenched, but then he gave a little shake of his head. "Let's keep going. We have to find a selkie tribe to join up with."

We'd always said this was what we'd do if things got too dangerous, or we hadn't freed our family by graduation. We'd tried. Our parents and brother would spend the rest of their days in captivity, but hey, we'd given it a shot, right?

Like hell. Maybe Brennan could live with that, but I couldn't.

"I'm going back," I said quietly.

"No, you're not."

"Where I go, and why, isn't your decision." My brother scowled, not liking his own words thrown back at him, but I reclaimed my seat on my boulder. "Look, from what Paul told me, the Silver Rescue League has freed selkies before. I want to see if they can help."

Brennan raked a hand through his dripping hair, then turned toward the sun. Rising pink in the east, it cast dawn shadows over the beach. "I'm going north, Cass," he said without looking at me. His shoulders set; he'd made up his mind.

I swallowed hard, tears pricking my eyes. My twin had been by my side since the day we'd discovered our true natures. I wasn't sure I knew who I was without him. But if he swam away from our family … I wasn't going with him. Pressure built in my throat and my voice, when I spoke, was ragged.

"You're right, Brennan. I can't control where you go. So go. Find a tribe. I'll catch up with you when I've freed our family." Staring at my bare knees, I struggled to keep the tears at bay.

Our little cove was quiet but for the idle surge of waves on rocks, and birds rustling in the woods behind me. The sun edged higher, drying my skin, my hair. Finally I heard Brennan move. Anguished, I glanced up, not wanting to miss the last sight I might ever have of him.

But Brennan didn't dive into the water. Instead, he stalked over and dropped down beside me on my boulder.

"God, you're such a little snot, you know that?" He gave a frustrated growl. "All brave and shit. It's embarrassing. I can't have my little sister showing me up."

"I'm only eleven minutes younger," I said automatically, then paused, hardly daring to hope. "Does this mean…"

"Yeah, I'm coming with you." Brennan nudged my shoulder. "But we're bringing Leisel into the loop."

I hesitated. "Brennan …"

"Cass."

"I know you like her and everything, but …"

"I showed her my sealskin," Brennan said. I sucked in a horrified breath.

"Why would you do that?"

"Because I trust her, obviously. With my life."

"What about our family's lives?"

Brennan met my gaze steadily. "Those too."

I couldn't imagine even swimming around a human, let alone allowing anyone near my sealskin. My head spun.

"Wasn't it scary?"

"Yeah. But you have to trust someone." His mouth quirked. "And Leisel is proof that not everyone in the world is awful."

"Are you in love with her?"

Brennan's gaze darkened, but he answered calmly.

"When it came time to leave, did I hesitate?"

He had me there. Despite how close he obviously felt to Leisel, he *had* left when push came to shove, and I suddenly felt ashamed for not trusting him. Or her. Maybe Leisel *was* in love with my brother—but when I tried to picture sweet, conservation-crazy Leisel stealing his sealskin, I couldn't. Was it so bad, them enjoying each other's company for the time they had? If it made them happy, it was none of my business.

"I'm sorry I tried to interfere with you and her," I said finally.

"You were just trying to look out for me. I know that."

Did that mean he forgave me? I bumped his shoulder, and he laughed and bumped me back. I smiled, relieved.

Then a thought struck me.

"You didn't show her *my* sealskin, did you?"

Brennan tugged at a lock of my hair.

"Of course not. But do you really think she would have stolen it?"

The idea now seemed ludicrous in comparison to the very real danger of Mr. Murphy, and I ducked my head.

"No." I sighed. "I'm sorry. I just saw how much she liked you, and I got scared. I should have told you both about the plan earlier. Maybe then Declan would be here with us, instead of ..." Instead of suffering whatever punishment Mr. Murphy was meting out for his disobedience. I felt cold again.

Brennan set his shoulders.

"Let's go hunt; I'm starving. Then we can make a plan, get a good night's sleep, and head out tomorrow. This time, giving up isn't an option—but Cass, we have to be on the same page."

"Okay. I'll try not to be so paranoid."

Brennan shook his head.

"Don't stop being you. In our situation, a little paranoia is a good thing. But we have to work together. That means you stop keeping things from me, and I ..."

"Stop saying things like, 'We're never getting out of here'?" I gave a wry smile. "Because that was not so great for morale."

My brother looked away.

"I was going to say that I'll stop being a coward."

My smile faded. "You're not a coward."

Brennan grimaced. "If I'm not, it's because you won't let me be. In any case, I'll suppress the morale-killers. Deal?" He held out his hand.

I shouldn't feel this happy—tomorrow we'd swim back into Granite Harbor, now a much more dangerous place than when we'd left. Who knew how many weeks or months of struggle lay ahead of us: I'd declared a war with Mr. Murphy, and neither of us would stop until we won.

But Brennan and I were a team again; I wouldn't be going to war alone.

I shook my brother's hand.

"Deal."

Chapter 23

We reached Granite Harbor's coastline as dusk fell.

Brennan led us up a river to a bend I recognized—we'd left a cache here. It was something we'd put together when we'd first returned to land two-and-a-half years ago. We'd bought three batches of cheap clothing, Swiss army knives, and granola bars, and hid them at different places near water in case we were forced to abandon our belongings.

We'd never had to touch them before, and I hoped our caches were still intact. Brennan *changed*, then waded out of the river while I waited, all senses on high alert.

Finally I heard the rapping of stones through the water, the all-clear signal, and surfaced. Brennan, sealskin slung around his waist, held up the heavy-duty trash bag in which we'd stored our stuff. The sides looked like black Swiss cheese.

"The squirrels got into the granola bars, but our clothes are still fine." He dumped everything onto a bare patch of riverbank. "Mostly. Come on out." Leaving my bundle on a log, he disappeared into the woods to get dressed.

I swam into the shallows, *changed*, and once the agony

faded quickly threw on clothes. Black, thick sweatsuit material, the top and bottom weren't the height of fashion, but we'd scored them for a dollar each. No underwear, but Brennan should have found twenty dollars tied around the Swiss army knife. Maybe we could buy some.

My pants had a hole chewed through them, but luckily it was down by my shin. My shirt had a similar hole on my shoulder. Damn squirrels. Despite the gaps, the cold fabric warmed against my skin. I pulled on a pair of thick black socks, then bundled my sealskin into the chewed-up plastic bag. When Brennan reappeared, he stowed his sealskin with mine.

We got our bearings and started toward Leisel's. We were several miles away, so it took over an hour to pick our way through the deepening dark, giving any houses a wide berth. Even though Mr. Murphy couldn't know we'd returned, fear skated across my skin. If he caught us, there'd be no deals anymore.

When we neared Leisel's house, it was full dark. We stashed our sealskins in a hollow log, crept across the lawn, and knocked on the door of Leisel's bedroom. After a few moments, the curtains shifted, and Leisel's face appeared behind the glass. Her eyes bugged out when she saw us.

She threw open the door.

"Ohmigod!" And then she was hugging Brennan. "I was so worried." Releasing Brennan, she threw her arms around me. "But you're okay. You're okay."

I met Brennan's gaze as I hugged Leisel back. Fine, I'd been wrong about her. After days in the water, my head felt clear again; sometimes I forgot how twisty my brain got if I went too long between swims. I'd let my paranoia run wild.

I'd been wrong to cut Paul out of my plan too. He'd Bound a selkie—but, remembering his serious gray eyes, I knew there must have been a good reason. I'd been worried my own feelings about him had warped my judgment, but now I wished I'd told him the truth—and demanded the whole story—that night at The Golden Fish.

"We need your help," I said when Leisel let me go.

"Of course." Inside, Leisel gave me clean underwear and a sports bra, along with non-holey yoga pants and a T-shirt. The shirt, pink and splashed with parakeets, was part of Leisel's old nature-nerd wardrobe, but it made me smile. She gave me a dark blue hoodie to wear over it, and I changed in her closet.

I emerged to find Brennan and Leisel sitting together on her futon. Their faces pressed cheek to cheek, not kissing, just resting, and something stabbed at me. Worry, maybe—though Brennan hadn't hesitated on Saturday, what happened now that we would be depending on Leisel more than ever? What if he fell for her?

But it wasn't my business; I'd sworn not to interfere anymore. And part of what I felt, I realized, was jealousy. They looked so close. She'd seen him swim; they trusted each other. I'd never had that, and with my paranoid nature, I knew I never would.

I cleared my throat. Cheeks reddening, Leisel sat up out of Brennan's arms.

"So what happened to you guys?" she said.

"First things first." Brennan smiled at her. "You have any food?"

"Of course, you're hungry after *changing*. I'll get some sandwiches." Leisel dashed up her stairs and disappeared.

I worked a brush through my mess of tangled hair. Brennan tapped his fingers on his knee, lost in thought—and wearing one of his own sweaters. My eyes narrowed.

"At what point did you start leaving clothing here?"

Brennan glanced at me but didn't answer. Biting my tongue, I kept working on my hair, and by the time Leisel returned with a tray of food, I had it smoothed out and bound back in a ponytail.

Leisel set the tray on her bed. She'd brought deli ham, Swiss cheese, hamburger rolls and a suite of ketchup, mustard and mayo. Brennan made himself a sandwich, smothered it with way too much mustard, and settled back onto the futon. My stomach rumbled. Throwing together some layers of ham and Swiss, sans condiments, I bit into it with a groan.

"Thank you," I said as I chewed. Leisel waited until we'd each wolfed down a sandwich before asking Brennan what had happened.

"What do you know?" He made himself another sandwich, and Leisel helpfully drizzled the mustard for him.

"Well, you didn't show on Sunday, but I figured something came up. I didn't realize anything had happened until Monday when neither of you came to school." Leisel looked over at me. "Ashlyn told everyone that you've been abusing prescription drugs, and went ballistic and tore up her house when her dad had his doctor cut you off. She says you and Brennan were sent to rehab across the country."

"Ashlyn will believe anything her dad tells her." So much for my note.

"I don't know about that." Leisel frowned. "I kept bringing it up, and finally she told me we'd talk in a couple of days about what was really going on."

Brennan lowered his sandwich and met my gaze.

"Do you think she knows?" he said.

I considered. "Mr. Murphy told me he always planned to tell Ashlyn the truth once we were gone for good. Maybe he did."

"So what happened?" Leisel looked from Brennan to me. "Did you really break into Ashlyn's house?"

I told her how I'd asked Paul to make a copy of Ashlyn's key for me, how Paul confessed he'd Bound a selkie so I didn't trust him to come with me, and how Brennan had been gone that morning, so I'd broken in alone. I finished with Mr. Murphy showing up to chase me off. Brennan picked up the story, explaining how Declan forced us to leave.

"Why didn't you grab me?" Leisel asked when he finished. "To help you search. I wasn't doing anything on Saturday."

"We had to ditch our phones," I hedged. "There wasn't time."

"She didn't tell you because of me," Brennan said. "Us, I mean."

Leisel's brow wrinkled. I tensed—did Brennan have to

make this more awkward than necessary?—but couldn't think of anything to say as Leisel's expression cleared.

"Oh," she said.

The last bite of my sandwich stuck in my throat.

"I should have told you," I muttered.

"It's okay," Leisel said softly. She looked like I'd punched her.

"Sometimes I just get mega-paranoid," I tried to explain. "I—"

"What's done is done," Brennan interrupted. "Let's move on. Cassandra is going to call Paul and get the Silver Rescue League up here. If both of you searched the house and came up empty, we need all the help we can get." He took Leisel's hand. "We're going to stay in the water, but we were hoping you would be our on-land eyes and ears."

"Of course." Twining her fingers with Brennan's, Leisel glanced at the dark beyond her window. "You can stay here tonight, at least, can't you?"

Brennan looked at me. "It's up to you, Cass."

I hesitated. "What do you think?"

My brother met my gaze squarely.

"I think we're safe here."

After a moment, I nodded.

"Okay," I told Leisel. "If you think your dad won't find us …"

She shook her head. "He never comes in without knocking, and I'll lock the door just in case. There's room on the bed with me, and there's the futon—"

"Brennan gets the futon," I said quickly. I'd promised not to interfere, but no way were they sharing a bed with me sleeping two feet away.

The three of us hashed out a plan, and I borrowed Leisel's phone. She and Brennan held hands on the futon while I dialed Paul's number.

He picked up after two rings.

"Hello?"

"It's Cassandra."

"*Cassandra.*" His voice lowered urgently. "Where are you? Are you okay? You never answered your phone on Sunday, and I went by The Golden Fish, but they said you'd left town and weren't coming back. What the hell is going on?"

"I'm okay." Conscious of Brennan and Leisel listening, I walked across the room.

"Where are you? I'm getting in the car; I'll drive up now."

"No, wait. Hold on a sec." I bit my lip. "You know the selkie we were going to rescue together? She's not a friend. She's my parents."

A pause. "Which one?"

"Both. And my older brother, Declan. They're all Bound."

"Both? But that would mean …"

Seconds ticked by. "Go on."

"If both your parents are selkies, that would mean … you're a selkie."

I took a deep breath. "Yes."

A couple seconds passed. I wondered what Paul was thinking. I didn't look over at the futon, but I knew that while

Leisel could only follow my half of the conversation, Brennan's selkie senses meant he could hear the whole thing. I hoped Paul wouldn't say anything to tip Brennan off that our history included more than just talking. I just hadn't been able to bring myself to tell my brother about the kissing, or the tasing.

"What the hell are you trying to pull?" Paul finally said. I frowned.

"What do you mean?"

"You can't be a selkie."

"Well, I am."

"Impossible. You don't act anything like a selkie."

I could practically feel Brennan narrow his eyes at me. "Look, Paul, I need your help. I need the Silver Rescue League."

"Is this a joke? Because I don't think I'm getting it. Why— "

"It's not a joke!" Leisel winced at my shout and put a finger to her lips. "It's not a joke," I repeated more quietly. "And refusing to believe me is not helping."

Silence on the line, and then an exhalation of breath. "I'm listening." Paul's voice was dark, quiet. Angry, or just absorbing what I'd said?

"Can you meet us up here tomorrow morning to talk?"

"Who's us?"

"Me and my brother Brennan. And Leisel." She planned to claim illness—apparently her dad usually let her stay home from school by herself when she didn't feel well; he'd be just down the road at his vet practice.

"Your brother Brennan … who is also a selkie?"

"Yep."

"And who the hell is Leisel?"

"A classmate. A friend. She's the only one who knows about us. Besides you, now."

A long moment passed. "You really expect me to believe you're a selkie? That this isn't another one of your lies?"

I winced, but couldn't blame him for being suspicious. Then again, he'd Bound a selkie, so I wasn't the only one who had to explain past actions.

"It's the truth. Are you going to help us or not?"

Paul didn't answer for so long I thought he might have hung up, but when I pulled the phone from my ear, the call was still active.

"What time?" he said at last. Relief made me light-headed.

"Nine." I gave him Leisel's address, and told him to park around the corner.

"I'll see you there."

"Okay." I didn't mention that we were actually going to meet in the woods—Brennan had encouraged me to let my paranoia-flag fly, so I wasn't telling Paul the location where we'd meet in advance. Leisel would greet Paul at her house and fill him in about our family's situation. If he reacted badly, she'd tell him the meeting was off, and if he seemed trustworthy to her, she'd bring him to us.

"Cassandra, are you … serious about this?" Paul's voice held a note of bewilderment in its uneasy depths.

"I am." He didn't respond, so after a few seconds I said, "Goodnight, Paul."

"Goodnight, Cassandra." He hung up.

Turning to the futon, I pretended not to see the questions in Brennan's gaze.

"All set," I said. "He'll be here."

"What now?" Leisel asked.

I shrugged, and faked a smile. "I hope you don't kick in your sleep."

Chapter 24

The next day, Brennan and I trudged into the woods a half hour before Paul was scheduled to show up. We waited in a little clearing brushed with frost; I sat on a fallen log next to a holly tree. Among its deep green leaves nestled clusters of red berries, glistening like drops of oil paint. Brennan paced, while I wondered whether to mention how I'd noticed him and Leisel cuddling on the futon this morning.

Deciding to keep quiet—*not my business*, I told myself—I stared at the walkie-talkie Leisel had given me, part of a set she and her dad used when hiking or birdwatching.

Finally it came alive.

"He's here, over," Leisel's voice intoned. I pressed the *talk* button.

"Got it."

"You're supposed to say 'Roger that.'"

I smiled. "Roger that. Over."

Brennan had paused to watch me answer Leisel, but now he resumed his pacing. I waited nervously, wondering how

Paul was taking everything, and worrying that Brennan and Leisel were closer now than ever.

Finally I couldn't help myself.

"You guys were cuddling on the— "

"Don't start with me," Brennan snapped, not pausing in his march around the clearing. Wishing I'd kept my mouth shut, I fidgeted with my shoe laces—unfortunately, no adjustment was going to keep Leisel's old sneakers from pinching, as they were almost a full size too small—and plucked at the long-sleeve shirt she'd given me. It was an unflattering tan, with horses galloping across the front. I'd almost asked for that awesome red shirt we'd bought for her a few weeks ago, but I didn't want her or Brennan thinking I was dressing up for Paul.

After a while, the walkie-talkie emitted a burst of static.

"On our way," Leisel said. "Over."

So Paul had passed muster, at least in Leisel's judgment. I clutched the walkie-talkie.

"We're waiting. Over."

After a few minutes, figures appeared through the trees. Spotting them, Brennan walked over to me. I stood up and studied Paul as my brother must see him, as a stranger. Paul moved quietly through the frostbitten forest; his form was tall and lean, clad in jeans, a blue sweater and his leather jacket. The morning sun pulled red tones from his dark hair.

What did he think of me? Last week he'd kissed me, teased me, but then I'd been a normal girl, albeit one who wanted to save a selkie. Now he knew the truth, and didn't look happy about it. His gray gaze slid over me coolly.

I regretted not asking for the crimson shirt.

Leisel and Paul stepped into the clearing, and Paul nodded to me.

"Cassandra," he said. Not quite a greeting, I returned it with my own nod.

"Paul." Feeling awkward, I gestured to Brennan. "This is my brother."

Brennan stepped forward and held out his hand. Surprise flashed across Paul's face, but he clasped Brennan's palm.

"Cass says you belong to a group that helps selkies," Brennan said.

"The Silver Rescue League." Paul swept his gaze over Brennan as if searching for signs of selkie-ness. The silence stretched.

"Well, we could use your help," Brennan prodded.

Paul studied my brother for a moment more, then turned to me.

"Prove it," he said.

"Excuse me?"

"Prove you're a selkie, that you're not just trying to hoodwink me or something."

I frowned. "Why would I lie about this?"

"I don't know. I have a hard time figuring out why you do anything."

Alright, I deserved that. But I crossed my arms.

"If you think I'm showing you my sealskin, you're very sadly mistaken."

We stood there, at a standoff. I could feel Brennan and

Leisel casting glances between us, but kept my gaze on Paul's. Finally his expression altered subtly.

"You're not lying this time, are you?" he asked.

"Is that so hard to believe?"

He opened his mouth, then closed it. Opened it again.

"I just can't believe I didn't know." He looked down at his hand, flexing it. I remembered those hands all over me, and hoped I wasn't blushing.

"Leisel filled you in about my family, right?" I said, and Paul nodded. "My parents have been Bound for over two decades, and if we can't free them, they'll be slaves for the rest of their lives. Can you or can you not help us?"

"Yes, we can help. We *will* help." He hesitated. "But now isn't the best time."

Brennan frowned. "How is now not *exactly* the best time?"

"What I meant is that most of the group is in Hawaii right now. They have another case."

"The case of the tropical selkie?" Brennan sounded half-amused, half-angry. Mostly impatient. "When will they be done?"

"As you can imagine, freeing a Bound selkie isn't something you can set a clear schedule for. They're hoping two or three weeks will be all they need."

"But what about us?" I asked.

"From what Leisel told me, your family's situation is stable, right? No one's being abused physically?"

Brennan and I exchanged glances.

"You want us to wait," my brother said.

"I can call my mother tonight," Paul said, "but I know what she'll say. She'll tell me to offer you shelter at our house and wait for the team to arrive."

"Your house?" I asked.

"The SRL has a safe-house up the coast a bit. We want to make it a safe haul-out spot for selkies. Leisel said you can't go back to your parents' house, or this Mr. Murphy might attack you." He waited for my nod. "You should stay at the SRL house, with me."

"We'd planned to stay at sea," I told him.

"But— "

"This isn't a discussion," Brennan said. "No offense, but we're safer on our own."

"Look, you want our help. Our organization can protect you. If you're willing to trust us to help your family, why not stay with me?"

"Because you Bound a selkie," Brennan said. Paul shot me a glance, searching and edged with anger, but he couldn't be surprised that I'd told my brother his secret.

"Why did you?" I asked.

Paul shook his head. "It's complicated."

My brow rose. "I bet if you try *really* hard, you could uncomplicate it for us."

"It's also personal." Before we could respond, Paul put his hand to his chest. "Look, I'd never do it again. I swear it on the fiery trenches and the sea-swallowed moon, and all the whiskers of my ancestors."

We stared at him.

"Well, thank the seas," Brennan drawled. "He swore on his ancestor's whiskers."

Leisel smothered a giggle. Paul's eyes narrowed.

"It's a traditional selkie oath." He took in our expressions, and his cheekbones colored. "At least, it is on the west coast."

Brennan snorted. "What do you think?" he asked me, not bothering to lower his voice—I'd told him how Paul seemed to have our selkie hearing. "Do we call the whole thing off?"

Paul crossed his arms, still flushed but meeting my gaze squarely. I wanted to trust him. Without Paul, we had no plan. His refusal to tell us his "That time I Bound a selkie" story wasn't winning him any points, but the solemnity with which he'd spoken that vow … as silly as it sounded, Paul seemed to mean it.

Still. I took a deep breath.

"We'll let the SRL help. But we'll stay at sea while we wait."

"That might not be for weeks," Paul said. "Look, it's your call, but from what Leisel told me, there's an angry guy out there who wouldn't hesitate to hurt you. It's safer if— "

"Mr. Murphy doesn't know we're back," Brennan cut in. "And he won't know, unless someone tells him. I'm not about to put my sealskin and my sister's at the mercy of some guy who Bound a selkie, for whatever reason."

Jaw set, Paul turned to me.

"You know I wouldn't hurt you."

I hesitated. His eyes were dark with whatever memory our questions stirred up, and his quiet intensity reminded me of our talk by the sea. But Paul still seemed angry that I was a selkie, and with his refusal to explain his past … paranoia curled over my skin like a cold wind.

"Can you really say that either of us knows the other at all?" I said.

Paul's expression tightened. His voice turned crisp.

"I guess not." He slipped his phone out of his pocket, tapped, and handed it over. "Here are some pictures of the house taken from the water. I'll be here through the weekend if you change your minds." He was careful not to let his fingers brush mine. I flicked through the snapshots, mostly to avoid Paul's gaze. The house boasted a wrap-around deck, the railing painted an odd, bright blue.

Brennan barely glanced at the phone. "We won't change our minds."

"How should I contact you?"

"When your team gets here, talk to Leisel. We'll check in with her."

"How?"

"That's not really any of your business, is it?"

Paul held up his hands. "Your call."

A few paces away, Leisel checked her watch.

"Are we done here?" she asked. "My dad's going to call the house soon to check on me, and if I don't answer he might come home."

I met Paul's gaze. His was grim, and my stomach tightened. My splash of paranoia had faded; I might not know Paul very well, but I knew I'd hurt him.

But we'd never be anything to each other anyway. Maybe it was better like this.

"Yeah." I handed his phone back. "I guess we're done."

Paul slipped his phone into his pocket, then paused as if about to say something. *Be safe*, maybe, or *so all that time I was kissing a selkie?* Heat crept up my neck.

Without a word, Paul turned to go.

Chapter 25

After seeing Paul off and fielding a call from her dad, Leisel drove us to Shiny Hollow. Our truck was still there, dinged and dirty but quietly solid.

"Cass, why don't you go find the keys?" Brennan said, not moving from the front seat of Leisel's minivan.

"You're the one who threw them."

"I need to talk to Leisel. In private."

I opened my mouth to scoff—no way was I doing all the work while they made out or whatever—but at his set jaw I thought better of it. Getting out of the car, I struck out into the woods.

I searched around the trees where I thought I remembered Brennan throwing the keys, bending to scoop through the leaves with my hands. Was I even in the right spot? But when I looked back at Leisel's van, thinking I'd insist on some help, Brennan and Leisel weren't making out. Instead they were talking—or Brennan was. As I watched, Leisel's face grew pinched. She glanced out the windshield at me, and I hastily returned to searching.

Deciding to get organized—no telling when the others would come help, if ever—I started in one spot and shuffled in an expanding spiral, dodging trees and a log and peering into a holly bush's sphere of sharp leaves.

Wait. There.

Of course the keychain lay in the center of the holly bush. Right by the roots. I pulled the hood of Leisel's sweatshirt over my head and lifted a branch so I could crawl in.

Five minutes later, slightly punctured but victorious, I returned to the car with the pick-up's keys in hand. I jangled them at Brennan through the windshield. He said something to Leisel, who nodded. Were her eyes watery? Before I could get a better look, Brennan kissed her on the cheek and got out of the car.

"What happened?" I asked.

"We broke up." Ignoring my shocked expression, Brennan plucked the keys from my hands and headed to the truck. I stood there feeling pole-axed, though I wasn't sure why. Maybe because they'd both seemed so happy to be reunited last night. I'd been worried Brennan would fall for Leisel, but he'd broken things off early.

That was … good, right?

Leisel didn't look like she saw it that way. She was trying to keep her poker face, but her jaunty wave goodbye was spoiled by the tear she had to swipe off her cheek.

I jogged over, and she rolled down the window.

"Are you okay?" I asked.

"Like you care. This is what you wanted, right?" Then her eyes filled. "Never mind. It wouldn't have worked anyway."

My heart twisted for her. This was exactly why I'd thought they shouldn't get involved in the first place. I tried to think of something to make her feel better, but came up empty.

Leisel sniffled, then glanced up.

"Are we still friends, Cassandra? Because I honestly have no idea."

Sweet, earnest Leisel was much too nice for the likes of paranoid, stone-hearted me. How could she even *want* to be my friend?

"If you can forgive me for being sort of a bitch," I said.

That won me only half a smile.

"You haven't even apologized yet."

I winced. "I'm not sure it's a one-time thing. But I'm sorry I didn't ask you to search the house with me. I should have trusted you."

Leisel glanced at Brennan in the pick-up. Her eyes filled again. "Be safe out there, okay?" She rolled her window up, and I walked over to the truck. Brennan stared straight ahead, but as I got in I realized he was watching Leisel leave in the rear-view mirror.

I touched his shoulder. "You alright?"

"I'm fine." He executed a jolting three-point turn. "Where to? Straight to the water, or …"

"I was thinking maybe we could go see Declan."

Brennan flashed me a hint of a smile.

"Great minds think alike."

"I mean, I'm sure he's fine— "

"Yeah. But let's go check, just to be sure."

It was past tourist season, so The Golden Fish didn't open for lunch on weekdays. Brennan drove us to the fish market, where Declan often went to pick out supplies for the evening, but he wasn't there.

"Try his house," I suggested, then noticed that the light on our bug detector device, wedged on the dash, wasn't on. I fiddled with it, but … "Next time we're on land remind me to get new batteries for this thing," I said as we cruised down Declan's street.

Brennan parked two houses away.

"Watch the car." He jumped out, leaving the engine idling. I slid into the driver's seat in case we needed to make a run for it. Brennan snuck up to the bushes flanking the living room window and peeked in. After a moment, he dashed back to the truck.

"He's fine. Didn't see any bruises," he said, and I relaxed a little. I'd worried Mr. Murphy might have punished Declan for my stunt.

"Okay, let's go."

I drove us to the pay phone by the library, to call they mayor's office. Mr. Murphy's secretary said he was in a meeting. Satisfied that Mr. Murphy was busy and blissfully unaware of our return, I turned the truck north.

Ten minutes above Portland, I parked in a deserted stretch of forest that led to a river rolling sluggishly toward the sea.

Grabbing the tote bags Leisel had given us to hold our sealskins and clothing, we trudged through the woods.

When we reached the water's edge, I cleared my throat.

"So we head north, hug the coast, and come back in a week to check in?"

Brennan nodded and shouldered his bag. "See you in the water."

"Hey," I said. "Are you really okay? About Leisel?"

"Are you really asking, or do you just want me to say yes?"

I looked away. "It's for the best, right?" Brennan belonged at sea; Leisel belonged on land. It was simple and unavoidable.

My brother sighed. "I'll feel better once we get into the water." He headed downstream to find a place to swap his clothes for his sealskin. There was a useful shrub where I stood, so I waited until my brother was out of sight, then shucked my clothes. Swathed in my sealskin, I tucked my clothes into the bag and the bag into the shrub. Padding on bare feet over the cold hard bank, I waded into the river, ducked underneath the surface, and *changed.*

Relief hit as soon as the pain faded. I'd been so worried about coming back, depending on Leisel and Paul to help us, but everything was turning out alright so far. It would be a couple weeks until the SRL could come to Maine, but our family wasn't in any immediate danger, and a month or so more under Mr. Murphy's thumb wouldn't hurt them. Soon the SRL would save them.

All I had to do was wait.

It felt odd, and freeing—for the next week, Brennan and I

could just swim and relax and hang out. Have fun, even. Chase fish, roll in the waves.

And wonder about Paul.

He'd been so different at the meeting. I'd thrown him a shock, but … was he mad I'd lied to him, or that I was a selkie? Maybe both. But he had no leg to stand on, with his *It's complicated* line. How did he expect us to trust him without knowing what had happened?

It annoyed me that he'd looked hot as usual while I'd been stuck in old sneakers and a horse shirt.

"You there, Cass?" Brennan's voice was blurred a bit since I was underwater, but comprehensible. I surfaced and slapped a front flipper on the water to catch his attention. He waved, and stepped towards the bank.

Behind him, a shadow loomed.

I yelped a reflexive alarm. Brennan started to turn, but he was too slow.

Mr. Murphy knocked him to the dirt with a baseball bat.

I shot like a harpoon for the shore. *Changing* would take too long, but … as Mr. Murphy and Brennan wrestled on the frozen bank, I lumbered out of the water and launched myself at them. Mr. Murphy cursed; I angled my snout towards his voice, then bit down hard. Blood filled my mouth—I'd gotten his shoulder. He yelled, then rolled away, and I lost my purchase. Brennan cried out as Mr. Murphy's fist hit his jaw. I tried to crawl towards them, but seals aren't nimble on land and I was reduced to dragging myself with my front flippers.

Just as I reached him again, Mr. Murphy snatched his

baseball bat from where it had fallen in the underbrush. Before I could lurch away, he struck out. Pain blinded me, exploding in my side, then my head. I screamed, trying to roll towards the river, but Mr. Murphy hit me again.

Then Brennan was there. He shoved me into the water and launched himself at Mr. Murphy. They tumbled against a tree, fists flying.

"Go, Cass!" Brennan yelled. "Get out of here!"

Blackness ate at the edges of my vision. My head felt sawed in two, and my ribs stabbed at me as I wriggled into deeper water. I made my way across to the other bank, out of reach. Pain hit me in waves. I couldn't fight, not in this condition—not in this form.

But I couldn't leave Brennan. Maybe I could *change* … but a jolt of nausea hit me, and I floated at the surface of the river, breathing shallowly and trying to stay conscious.

When I could raise my head, barely, I saw the struggle was over.

Oh, no. Brennan lay against the trunk of a tree, his hair mussed, dirt on his skin. His nose was bloody, his eyes closed. My heart went into a panic, but then Brennan opened his eyes. He didn't move, and after a moment I saw why.

Two paces away, Mr. Murphy held up a length of fur. And a knife—he was threatening to shred Brennan's sealskin.

He had my brother.

Horror built in my throat, and between that and the pain I nearly blacked out right there. Mr. Murphy said something but, hurt and half-hidden in reeds, I couldn't hear him. After a moment Mr. Murphy turned toward the river and looked around.

For me, I realized, and ducked under the surface.

Blood seeped through the water, red tendrils in the gray. I could taste the blood, mine along with Mr. Murphy's. My vision faded in and out, and any thoughts of charging onto the bank and rescuing Brennan were rendered impossible by the stabbing in my torso.

I had to get to safety, or Mr. Murphy would have us both.

Hoping I could swim far enough away by the time I lost consciousness, I summoned the last of my strength and kicked my hind flippers to push me downstream.

Chapter 26

When I came to, the scent of water and frozen sedge flooded my nose. I lifted my head. My whiskers brushed the ground—I was in seal form. I lay heavily in cold mud, a few inches of water chilling my belly. Winter-bare skeletons of reeds and cattails struggled through the ice of the half-frozen shore.

Hunger tore at me. Something terrible had happened, I knew hazily. I needed food to heal, but could barely move. I wriggled backwards, pushing the mud with my front flippers until fully submerged. My body ached, the pain shooting through my limbs so intense I almost passed out again, but I poked my nose out of the water and breathed shallowly until the feeling ebbed.

I tasted the water—fresh. A current tugged at me, slight but discernible. A river. The sun glared high overhead. How long had I been out? The attack had been—

The attack. Mr. Murphy.

He had Brennan.

Oh, God.

Horror threatened to drown me, and if I were in human

form I'd have sobbed. As it was I let out a soft whine before I cut myself off. I couldn't risk alerting anyone nearby to my presence.

Changing from seal to human form and back again healed small injuries, but I was badly hurt, and too exhausted to make more than one *change*. It took energy, and I had none.

I needed help. But crawling to Leisel's wasn't an option—I was too weak.

Paul. I remembered the coastline and the house from his pictures, his safe harbor for selkies. Preoccupied with the meeting, I hadn't paid all that much attention, but I remembered the blue of the deck railing, which should be easy to spot from sea. In any case, finding that house was my only shot.

I made my way painfully downriver and out into the ocean, then turned north. Progress was slow: anything larger than a crab sent me into hiding, as I was in no condition to fight, or even flee. I hugged the coastline, poking my head out of the water every fifty feet or so, searching for the distinctive railing of Paul's SRL house.

It took what felt like hours. Several times I had to pull myself into a little nook of rocky shoreline and rest—I fell asleep twice. But I kept going, pushing past the pain in my head and shoulder and ribs. Finally, one time when I raised my head from the water, the house on the shore looked familiar.

Was it the right one? I squinted uncertainly.

The deck railing was blue. That was it. It had to be.

I tried to drag myself from the water, but nearly fainted when I put any weight on my left flipper. Still in the shallows,

I braced myself and *changed.* The pain from the transformation washed over me, merging with the pain from my injuries. Normally *changing* healed me at least a little, but this time I felt even worse when it was over. Wrapping my sealskin around me, I pushed myself to my feet.

The house before me was light gray and made of clapboard, with a black roof and a chimney on one side. To my right up the beach, a pier jutted into the water. The blue deck curled around the side and back of the house, where a figure sat reading on a lounge chair. Paul, or so I hoped. He hadn't noticed me yet.

A moment of panic hit me—what if this was the wrong house? What if I'd washed up on some stranger's property, and they were going to find me naked but for a sealskin on their beach?—but I choked it down. I was at the end of my strength, and not in any shape to run.

I'd have to trust whoever was on that deck to help me.

I staggered forward, but even that was too much. I swayed in the cold air.

"Paul," I croaked out. Too quietly—he'd never hear me. But on the deck, the figure looked up.

My strength gave out, and I fell to my knees. Granite and sand cut into my skin, barely registering in the struggle to keep from toppling over completely. "Paul," I said again. Dark spots swam in my vision, and I felt simultaneously burning up and cold as the bottom of the sea. My hair dripped bits of ice onto my skin.

The figure was close now, and ... yes, that was Paul's voice saying my name. Relief hit, and it was like I'd cut the only cord keeping me upright.

Clutching my sealskin, I blacked out.

Chapter 27

My eyes opened to a pale blue ceiling. At first I thought it was the sky, but then I noticed the cream-colored walls featuring framed seashells. I turned my head, which was a mistake—gasping in pain, I squeezed my eyes shut. My shoulder throbbed, along with most of my torso. I knew better than to move.

When my eyes opened again, Paul sat in the chair by the window. It was dark outside, the room lit softly by a table lamp. When Paul saw me awake, he put his book down.

"Cassandra?"

"Paul," I croaked. God, my throat hurt. My teeth hurt. Everything hurt.

"Are you alright?" Paul scooted his chair over to the bed.

My mouth opened to answer, but then it hit me. The attack. Swimming up the coast. Collapsing practically into Paul's arms. My eyes welled, and the room blurred.

"Don't try to move." Paul touched my arm, which like the rest of me was shaking. "You have a sprained shoulder, and I think a couple cracked ribs. I can't do an X-ray or anything, but I don't think they're broken. Your head has a nasty bump. Can you look at me?" He pointed a tiny flashlight at my left pupil, then my right. "You don't seem to have a concussion. I called my mom to talk me through first aid, and she says you should be okay if you rest and go through a couple of merge and separation cycles."

I barely heard him. "My brother," I managed to say through my shakes. "Brennan."

"He didn't come to the beach. I searched for him once I got you inside, but … What happened?"

"Mr. Murphy happened." I didn't have the energy to say more. Shifting, I realized that under the covers, I was wrapped in a light blue robe. And nothing else. I lurched upright. "Where's my sealskin?"

"Right next to you."

I turned, and there it was, folded neatly on the side table. I grabbed for it, bundling the comforting weight against my chest under the covers. *Home.* My head swam, pain stabbing at me like shark's teeth, and I fell back onto the bed. Paul reached out, then hesitated. He withdrew his hand.

"Do you want something for the pain?"

"God, yes." When he came back, he set the pills and a glass of water on my table. "I need help sitting up," I said weakly.

Paul's gaze drifted to my sealskin lump under the covers.

"What?" I asked.

"Selkies don't usually let anyone near their sealskins if they can help it."

He was right, but at this point I didn't have a choice.

Besides, if he'd wanted to steal my sealskin, he'd had plenty of opportunity. Too tired to point this out, I sighed.

"Please, Paul."

After a moment, he leaned over and slid his arms around me. I tried to hold onto him so he could pull me upright, but let out a cry as I strained my injured shoulder. Paul froze, his head next to mine, and I bit back tears. I let my hurt arm cradle my sealskin between us, and grabbed onto Paul with the other.

"Okay," I said in his ear. Paul gently eased me into a sitting position and rearranged the pillows behind me. I swallowed the pain pills and some water, and closed my eyes as I waited for them to take effect.

When my headache lessened to a level where I could think clearly, I opened my eyes to find Paul waiting patiently.

"Mr. Murphy followed us somehow." Haltingly, I told Paul about the attack.

"When did that happen, Friday afternoon?" Paul grimaced. "That was two days ago. You showed up this morning; it's Sunday evening now. I called your friend Leisel, but she hasn't heard from Brennan. She said she'd call if she found out anything."

My eyes squeezed shut. Behind the lids, every possible outcome of the attack enacted itself in lurid detail, and I opened my eyes to cast a desperate look at Paul.

"Can't you go and see if he's okay?"

"Leisel has a better chance of finding out than I do. And I need to stay with you; I'm worried about that bump on your head."

The injury throbbed despite the pills, but what hurt more was not knowing whether my brother was alright. My last sight of him, crushed against the foot of that tree, with Mr. Murphy hulking over him … Before I could stop myself I let out a moan. I bit my lip hard to keep from breaking down, but tear splashed onto the covers anyway.

Paul reached out, then withdrew his hand again. My stomach twisted.

"You don't want to touch me now that you know I'm a selkie?"

Paul dropped his gaze.

"It's sort of policy," he muttered. I looked away, shivering and clutching my sealskin. I hated being like this, weak and whimpering, but fear ripped through me. I couldn't stop shaking.

After a minute, Paul muttered a curse before shifting his hip from the chair to the bed. Facing me, he cautiously wrapped his arms around me and my sealskin.

"Is this okay?" he asked.

I leaned into him, grateful for his solid warmth.

"What about your policy?"

"Screw the policy."

That made me snort, which sent pain stabbing through my skull. I dropped my forehead to Paul's shoulder, pressing into his sweater as if that could erase the attack from existence.

"What if he's not okay?" My breath hiccupped. "What if Brennan's …"

Dead. I couldn't say it.

"You saw Mr. Murphy take his sealskin, right?" Paul rubbed my good arm. My skin tingled, reminding me that he'd Bound a selkie once, but I was too worried about my brother to care. "Brennan should be alright, if Mr. Murphy intends to keep him captive."

"What if he doesn't? What if he shredded Brennan's sealskin right there? Or what if he killed him, and I left Brennan there to die?"

"Shhh." Paul hugged me closer, and for a few minutes I cried silently into his shirt. He didn't try to tell me it would be okay, just stroked my back and pressed the uninjured side of my head to his rough cheek.

After a while his solid warmth steadied me, and my tears ebbed.

"The best thing you can do right now is eat, rest, and heal." Paul disentangled himself and eased off the bed. "I'll go get you something."

I spent the rest of the evening sleeping or choking down food. At first Paul brought me a plate of tuna, diced into bite-sized cubes but unavoidably raw.

"Are you trying to make me throw up?" I asked incredulously. My stomach turned just looking at the cold pile of fish. "I am so not in the mood for sushi."

"Most selkies only …" Flushing, Paul fetched me a bowl of tomato soup and a box of crackers.

I ate slowly, then napped, then devoured a plate of mac and cheese. Napped again. When I woke, Paul asked if I wanted to try a "merge and separation cycle." Feeling stronger now and knowing a *change* cycle would help heal me, I said yes.

"I'll help you down to the shore," Paul said.

"Or I could just do it here. Go wait in the hall."

Paul blinked, then went out and shut the door.

I usually *changed* in water, but that was for safety, not because it was necessary to spur the metamorphosis. Easing the covers down, I unbelted my robe and slipped it gingerly over my arms, then spread my sealskin over my bare skin.

The *change* was hard this time. I lay there panting in seal form for a few minutes, then *changed* back to my human self. Oof. Exhaustion swamped me, but my head felt a little better. I slipped my robe back on, dragged the covers up, and called out to Paul.

He opened the door.

"You okay?"

"Need sandwiches." I closed my eyes.

Sometime later, Paul woke me by gently shaking my good shoulder. I sat up, pausing to let a spate of dizziness fade. My head hurt less now, and my ribs barely creaked as I breathed. Early morning light shone through the bedroom's window, and on the side table, a plate of PB&J sandwiches tickled my nose. My stomach rumbled.

"What is it?" I asked Paul. He held up his phone.

"I thought you'd want to know. I heard from Leisel."

Panic hit me, and hope so sharp I gasped. "My brother — "

"He's okay." Paul squeezed my hand. "Brennan's alive."

Chapter 28

Alive but not free, it seemed.

"How is Bound defined as okay?" I asked Paul a few hours later. I could walk now, thanks to a second *change* cycle I'd managed after Leisel's phone call, but my hands still shook whenever I thought about the attack. And my brother's fate. Huddled at the kitchen table, I clutched a glass of orange juice. "He's trapped."

"But not dead or seriously injured." Paul spread cream cheese on the freshly toasted cinnamon-raisin bagels he'd picked up earlier. We'd already had breakfast, but we were having a second, Hobbit-style. "That's better than we'd hoped. And with Ashlyn watching out for him, you have to admit things are a lot less grim than they could be."

Ashlyn. My mind still reeled from that information. Leisel's phone call had been short, because it was Monday morning and she was at school—with Ashlyn and Brennan. I wasn't clear on the details, but the gist was that although Mr. Murphy had indeed Bound Brennan, Ashlyn wanted to help us. She, Leisel and Brennan were coming to see Paul and me as soon as school let out.

Ashlyn on our side was something I couldn't quite wrap my brain around.

"Do you think she's sincere, or playing us?" I asked. Paul shot me one of his glances, the kind he'd been giving me all morning. The kind that said *I don't know what to make of you anymore.* I didn't know what to make of him, either. I was in his house—my sealskin had been literally in his hands—and I was vulnerable, still healing. But I felt safer with Paul than I had in … well, years. Which was weird, since I knew he'd Bound a selkie. Then again, he'd had all night to make off with my sealskin if he'd wanted, and I found it difficult to work up even a smidge of my usual paranoia.

"You know Ashlyn better than I do," Paul pointed out.

"She claims she wants to help, but then why hasn't she given Brennan his sealskin back yet?"

Paul slid a bagel over to me.

"Maybe it would anger her father. Maybe he hasn't told her where the sealskins are. Maybe they're not kept all together, and she wouldn't be able to free the rest of your family if she tips her hand now."

"Alright, voice of reason," I said dryly. "I'm just worried."

"Do you have some reason to think she would fake trying to help you?"

"Brennan and I haven't been the nicest to her in the last couple of years." As Paul ate, I filled him in on how we'd cut her out of our lives, and Brennan's Date-and-Ditch assholery. "She hates us, and I don't blame her. I really don't see how she could just forgive us for all that."

"Maybe now that she has an explanation for why two people she loved turned on her, she understands." Paul nodded to my bagel. "Eat. I'll make coffee, and afterwards, I have more stuff for you to read." He'd been giving me various bits of Selkie Rescue League's collected research about the ocean, especially when he discovered a gap in my knowledge about, say, what fish species now contained unsafe levels of mercury in their flesh thanks to pollution.

"It better not be like your last pamphlet." I frowned at my bagel as Paul abandoned me for the counter. "*11 Ways To Die Horribly In The Ocean* is not my idea of breakfast reading. Or even Second Breakfast reading."

Paul shot me a glance while he filled the water reservoir.

"What kind of pamphlet do you want?"

"*How To Start a Fire Using Fishbones And A Chunk Of Ice* would be pretty useful."

I thought I saw Paul's mouth twitch, but he turned away before I could be sure.

"I'll see what I can find," he said, scooping coffee grounds. I never drank coffee, not being able to afford it, but he thought the caffeine might help with my recovery. He wore a heathered gray shirt, and hadn't bothered to throw on his coat when he went out earlier for supplies, though it had been close to freezing. A selkie's resistance to cold.

"What happened with the selkie you Bound?" I said it as casually as I could, but Paul's shoulders went still. After a moment, he pushed the start button on the coffeemaker. It started to gurgle.

"I wondered when you were going to bring that up again." He watched the brown liquid spit into the pot.

"You pretty much saved my life, Paul. You can't possibly be worried I'd judge anything you say right now."

Paul turned. Propping my chin on my hands, I put on my best non-judgy face, and finally he walked back over.

"It was my brother." He sat down heavily.

"Your brother?"

"Half-brother, anyway. My father has three children with a selkie woman, at least the last I knew of their pod. One was—is—around my age. Theo. The pod visited a few times a year, so we sort of grew up together."

He'd grown up with selkies. My lip quirked in bemusement.

"I forget that you know more selkies than I do."

"Theo and I were close. We explored together, raced each other, that kind of stuff. I snuck him chocolate chip cookies—he could eat a whole sleeve of Chips Ahoy in two minutes flat—and he taught me to catch fish with my bare hands." A smile ghosted across his lips, but didn't reach his eyes.

"What happened?"

The coffee had finished by now, and Paul grabbed two mugs from the cabinet. His voice was low but steady as he poured. "The last time they visited, we fought—we always squabbled and pushed, like brothers do. But that time, Theo was bigger; he'd had a growth spurt, and I hadn't, and … it didn't end well for me." He doctored the two mugs with milk from the fridge, then tore open a couple of sugar packets, the kind you get from restaurants.

"What were you fighting about?"

"No idea. I was twelve, so it was probably something stupid, like who got to be king of the rock pile." He brought the mugs over and set one in front of me. It was lopsided and glazed in a streaky lavender, obviously handmade. "Anyway, we got into a wrestling match, and worse than the bruises was how Theo kept making fun of how scrawny I was."

Uh oh. I sat up straight.

"Please tell me you didn't steal his sealskin just to get back at him."

Paul met my gaze grimly. "I stole his sealskin to get back at him."

Sweet, fragrant steam tickled my nose. I felt sick. "You stole his freedom just because he made fun of you? How immature can you—" I cut myself off: he'd been twelve. A twelve-year-old boy was pretty much the definition of immaturity. One time when Brennan and I were that age he'd put a bag of fish entrails in my pillow, and when I plopped my head down … Yes, twelve-year-old boys were idiots, but that was no excuse.

I opened my mouth to say that, then paused. Paul wore no expression, but I knew a thing or two about masks, and underneath his lay a deep well of pain that told me he expected and even agreed with my condemnation. But here I was, eating food he'd given me and wearing one of his sweaters, which was too big but warm and soft. Paul had been there for me when I was vulnerable, and I owed him more than knee-jerk judginess.

Curling my hands around the horrifying handmade mug, I took a steadying breath.

"Then what?"

Paul frowned, as if surprised I wasn't flying off the handle, then shrugged.

"I hid it under my bed, went back to the beach and spent an hour ordering Theo around. Generally being a brat about it. But after the thrill of winning the fight wore off, what I'd done scared me. Theo acted so different. Empty. It was like—"

"I know how it feels." I couldn't help a shudder. Paul's gaze flicked up to mine, then away.

"Right. I gave him his sealskin back, but it was too late; the damage was done." He picked up his mug, a chipped and perhaps even more lopsided version of mine. "The whole pod knew, and they left before I could apologize. I never saw Theo again, or any of them."

"Ever?"

"Can you blame them?" Paul sounded calm, but bitterness twisted his lips. In one fell swoop, an idiotic mistake had cost him his brother, his father, his whole ocean family. It was wrong to take the sealskin, obviously, but … if I'd had a way to get back at Brennan for his fish-guts pillow, would I have been able to resist? I knew from experience how vicious sibling squabbles could get, and how awful I'd always felt until Brennan and I made up.

But Paul hadn't been able to apologize.

He was a year ahead of me, so probably eighteen. That was six years of not being able to make things right. He could shout sorries until his throat gave out—and probably had—but the sea wouldn't hear them.

Paul's expression was still masked, but I knew without being told that on the quiet, cold nights when I brooded about my family, when everyone tortured themselves with their unhappiest memories, this was what Paul thought about.

On impulse I slid off my chair, ducked around the table, and kissed Paul on the cheek. He froze, surprise cracking his mask.

"What was that for?"

"You looked like you needed it."

Paul blinked, then said almost angrily, "How can you stand to be near me?" I cocked my head in question. "We—the SRL—thought that selkies had a physical reaction to people who've Bound selkies. They can always tell—it hurts them."

"Oh. Yeah, I know what you mean." I hesitated, a little embarrassed to admit that the effect his nearness had on me was decidedly not of the "ow" variety. With him staring at me I shifted, conscious that the bundle of clothing Paul had given me had not included a bra. The sweater was thick, but … I was about to cross my arms over my chest when Paul laced the fingers of his right hand with my left. He held up our hands pointedly.

"So how can you stand to touch me, let alone kiss me?"

My face felt hot. "It's tough," I deadpanned. "But somehow I manage." Paul's gray eyes sharpened, and I realized now was probably not the best time for jokes. "It sucks to be near one of the Murphys, but with you it's not so bad. Hardly noticeable, actually." My hand in his tingled, but not unpleasantly. "The thing with your brother happened years ago, right? Maybe it fades over time."

Paul hesitated. "Huh."

I squeezed his fingers.

"Thanks for telling me about your brother."

Paul's face went masklike again, but this time I couldn't read it. He let go of my hand. "You should rest," he muttered, and went to clean up the kitchen. After a moment I reclaimed my seat, confused and a little hurt but not sure why I should be.

"When are they coming?" I asked Paul a couple hours later. He was reading a textbook on one of the deck chairs—he'd told his professors he had mono and was taking the week off school, but still had to keep up with the material—while I paced circles around the house in fleece-lined slippers. My shoulder still hurt and my ribs twinged, but my headache was finally banished by ibuprofen.

"Still around three-thirty." Paul lifted his head. "Is the bump on your head interfering with your memory?"

"No, I know they have to wait until school's out. I'm just ..."

"Nervous."

I walked up the three steps from the rocky winter-brown

lawn to the deck. "I can't believe Brennan's really okay." Though it was sinking in. He would be here soon, whole and in front of me so I could see for myself. Weird, to think I might have Ashlyn of all people to thank for that.

Under the relief, unease twisted my gut. Would Brennan be different, now that he was Bound? I didn't like to remember how we used to be, and though I wanted to see Brennan, I wasn't sure I could handle it if he was … empty, like Paul had called his brother. Shuddering, I tried to think about anything else.

The pacing had tired me out, so I leaned against the wooden railing. The deck wrapped around one side of the house so you could see the driveway, empty but for Paul's car. I cast a glance at Paul from under my lashes, but he'd gone back to reading. Since our talk at Second Breakfast, he'd made sure not to touch me more than was strictly necessary, though I'd caught him looking my way more than once, gray eyes thoughtful but grim. Maybe he regretted telling me about his brother.

I wished he'd smile, but he didn't treat me as anything more than a selkie in need of help. Which, of course, I was. But although my thoughts kept wandering to the feel of his hand on mine earlier—not to mention those moments in The Golden Fish's coat closet—Paul seemed irritatingly indifferent to me now.

I cast about for a topic to distract myself.

"How many houses like this does the SRL have?"

Paul glanced up from his book. His dark hair shifted in the breeze coming in from the sea. "Half a dozen. Three on the west coast, two on the east, one in Hawaii. We're in negotiations to buy one in Ireland."

Ireland. Where selkie myths abounded. I wondered if I'd ever see it. The farthest Brennan and I had wandered during our summer at sea was, we thought, Greenland. With all the icy isles north of Maine, it was hard to tell when you left one country for another.

"Do they belong to the Silver Rescue League, or to the individual members? And how do you get the money for them? It's got to be hard to fund-raise for selkies."

"There's a trust. My mom and the two other founders put it together, and our CFO manages our investments."

I raised my brows. The cottage wasn't huge, but seaside property wasn't cheap. And the SRL had other properties too, scattered around the country. All of that was paid for by three people? "Hm."

"Hm?"

"I just realized something. Though I guess I should have known when I saw your car. Question: have you ever 'summered' in a foreign country?" Paul reddened—that was a yes. I grinned. "You are spoiled rich, aren't you?"

Paul hesitated, then closed his textbook and put it aside.

"My mom's first husband was wealthy. He divorced her when she got pregnant with me. The settlement was generous." His expression had gone carefully blank; the source of his money was clearly a touchy subject.

"How did your parents meet?"

"The same way people usually meet selkies." Paul stood

and went to the other side of the deck, facing away. He didn't look at me as he continued, though thanks to my selkie hearing his words were perfectly audible. "A deserted moonlit beach. She was going for a run. They hit it off."

Tension in his back belied his easy tone. "Sounds romantic," I said cautiously.

Paul turned to face me, leaning against the blue railing.

"You think so?"

His features were set in stone, as if I were to blame for … something.

"Are you mad at me?" I asked.

Paul looked away. "Why would I be mad at you?"

"For being what I am?"

A moment passed, of sunlight and cold silence. Then, "No."

"Well, *that* was convincing." A muscle jumped in Paul's jaw, and I crossed my arms. "Look, I'm sorry I lied to you. I—"

"I get why you lied to me. I do. I get why you did all of it. But will you *please* knock it off now?" The annoyed exasperation in his voice made me frown.

"Knock what off?"

Paul's gaze swept across the deck to lock with mine.

"Making me want to kiss you."

Confusion dissolved into heat; my heart beat out an increasing tempo.

"You want to kiss me?"

"You know I do."

Suddenly I felt buoyant as sea foam. I was alive, and Brennan was sort of okay and on his way to me, and somehow we'd survived and I was bursting with the need to kiss Paul like crazy. I couldn't stop the smile sneaking onto my lips.

"Then why are you all the way over there?"

Paul's gray eyes sparked with what almost seemed like anger, but his muscles tensed under his skin and I knew he would come over even before he stalked across the deck, grabbed the railing on either side of me, and covered my mouth with his.

The kiss was deep from the start, pushing me back against the rough pine. Grabbing the sides of Paul's shirt to pull him closer, I fit his torso to mine, kind of glad now for my lack of a bra. Paul made a sound deep in his throat that sent fire all the way to my toes. My hands slipped down and under his shirt. His skin was hot, his back taut muscle. I curled my fingertips over the hollow of his spine.

Paul broke his mouth away.

"What are you doing to me?" he said raggedly, raising his right hand from the wooden railing to cup my jaw.

"Same thing you're doing to me," I said, and kissed him again. His mouth opened, and my own lips parted. Paul kissed me hard, and though my ribs twinged, I only shifted a little to spare them. The world outside his arms disappeared. Closing my eyes, I heard nothing but our heartbeats, felt nothing but his touch.

This was just what I needed, and I didn't want to stop. I'd never wanted anyone this much, never allowed myself to get this far. Never trusted anyone enough. But I could trust Paul;

he'd proven that a million times over. I sank deeper into the kiss.

Suddenly Paul was yanked backwards.

By my very angry brother.

Chapter 29

"Get away from her!"

Brennan swung Paul around, then punched him in the jaw. Paul staggered backwards. Stunned, I pushed off from the railing.

"Stop! Brennan, wait." Dimly, I realized Leisel and Ashlyn stood on the deck in the shadow of the house; I hadn't even heard them arrive.

Brennan advanced on Paul, who threw up an arm to block the next punch. I rushed over and put myself between them, wincing as I wrenched my still-healing shoulder trying to pull Brennan away.

"Stop," I said, and this time my brother paused. His hands were fists, his eyes wild.

"He was attacking you," he growled.

"He wasn't." I towed him backwards, sparing a moment for blinding gratitude at this proof that my brother was alive and whole, if possessed of unfortunate timing. "We were just kissing."

That brought Brennan up short.

"Why would you be kissing him? Leisel said you were hurt."

My cheeks burned. "I was. I am—but I'm healing." Meanwhile Brennan sported a bruise on his cheek and a split lip, plus who knew what other injuries hidden by clothing. He hadn't had the benefit of a healing *change*.

Brennan jerked his chin at Paul, who eyed us warily. "He doesn't have your sealskin?" I shook my head, and Brennan seemed to deflate. His fists dropped. "Jesus, Cass, I just saw him on you and thought—"

"I'm fine, I swear."

Brennan sank down at the edge of the stairs and dropped his head in his hands. I flung myself next to him.

"Are you okay?"

He didn't answer, and I threw my arms around him. Of course he wasn't okay. My brother's worst nightmare was being Bound again, and because of my insistence on coming back, it had come true. Guilt twisted like an eel in my stomach.

"Brennan, I'm sorry. So, so sorry. This is all my fault." I babbled apologies until Brennan gripped my hand.

"It's not your fault, Cass."

"It is. If I hadn't—"

"You didn't do this. Mr. Murphy did." His back stiffened as if in pain. Then he shook it off. "If this had happened to you instead, would *you* blame *me*?"

"If it had happened to me, wouldn't you blame yourself?"

Brennan sighed, then tugged a lock of my hair.

"I'm fine." Getting to his feet, he added, "Thanks to Ashlyn."

Just the name made me realize my skin prickled with jellyfish stings. I turned to find her, Leisel, and Paul watching us. Ashlyn's eyes were narrowed, Leisel's wide and dark. Paul was rubbing his jaw.

After an awkward moment, Leisel made introductions between Paul and Ashlyn.

"You're Mr. Murphy's daughter," Paul said.

"The bitch who owns Brennan at the moment. Yep, that's me." She looked Paul up and down. "And you're Handcuff Guy."

"Wait, what?" Brennan said.

"I told you they sort of met," I muttered.

"You didn't tell me his nickname was *Handcuff Guy*."

Everyone looked at Paul, who held up his hands. "At least I'm not Taser Girl."

All eyes turned to me.

"You guys must have some wild times," Ashlyn drawled.

"I may have accidentally tased Paul the first time I met him," I said through gritted teeth. "Is it really important right now? I want to know what's been going on the past two days."

Brennan eyed Paul suspiciously, but dropped it. We gathered around the deck's table, a disk of weathered plastic. I sat next to Brennan, wanting to keep him close, and Ashlyn took the seat on his other side. I stiffened—she was close enough now that my skin sang with pain, as if she'd painted it with acid. Plus, I didn't like her peremptory attitude, like she belonged next to Brennan—or the other way around. Leisel bristled at Ashlyn's chair choice too, but Ashlyn ignored both of us and drummed her nails on the table. Paul took the seat next to me, and after a moment Leisel flopped into the remaining chair.

"So when Mr. Murphy—" Brennan broke off with a wince. "Damn. Ash, maybe you ...?"

"What's wrong?" I asked, alarmed.

"It hurts him to speak ill of my father," Ashlyn said. She clasped her hands together on the table. "My dad brought Brennan home Friday night. After you tore up my house and left town, he put a GPS tracker on your truck, in case you came back. He noticed on Friday when it started moving. He followed you, catching up when you headed into the woods, and ... well, you know that part better than I do."

Her recitation was matter-of-fact, as if the events of the past few days barely bothered her. It rankled.

"He attacked us with a baseball bat," I said. "Your dad attacked us with a baseball bat, beat me half to death, and took Brennan's sealskin from him."

Silence descended like flies on a corpse.

"You say that like it's my fault." Ashlyn's eyes were hard bits of emerald, but spots of red dusted her cheeks. "Well, I had nothing to do with it, and I'm helping you now. So back off, Cassandra."

Brennan's hand sought mine. "She's right," he muttered. Anger surged in my chest—not at him, but because even if he meant it, he sounded just like we used to, back when we agreed with anything Ashlyn said.

As nauseous as it made me to see him like this, though, it was true that Ashlyn wasn't to blame for her father's actions. My instinct to fight and snipe stemmed from old habits, plus the difficulty of being near her. Brennan must not feel it, being Bound, but my skin burned, and I dearly wanted to throw up. Or run away. Instead I bit my tongue, squeezed Brennan's hand, and nodded for Ashlyn to go on.

"Brennan wasn't cooperating, and my dad said he was going to burn Brennan's sealskin. So I said I wanted Brennan for my own again." I couldn't help but bristle at that, and Ashlyn snapped, "Cut out the glare of death, Cassandra. The only way to win my dad's game is to pretend I'm on his side."

"Win?" This wasn't a game.

"Free your family. My dad told me about you, about what you are, after you left. Emily bought his story that you were bipolar and abusing prescription drugs, but …" Her expression changed.

"But what?"

Ashlyn fumbled at her neck. From under her sweater, she pulled a pendant on a golden chain: a starfish.

"I got your note," she said simply.

The starfish, *our* starfish, gleamed in the afternoon light, symbolizing our hacked-up friendship long after it should have given up and died.

"When did you leave Ashlyn a note?" Leisel asked.

"In my disaster-area room," Ashlyn said, and tucked the necklace back under her sweater.

"What did it say?"

"None of your business," Ashlyn snapped. Leisel flinched back in her chair.

"Selkies," I said softly. "I told her we were selkies."

"I didn't quite believe it, but I knew something more was going on," Ashlyn said. "Something beyond my dad's normal crazy-uptightness. So I made him tell me the truth. Selkies, sealskins, stealing them. He says it's my *heritage*." She made a face.

"You're Irish, right?" Paul asked. Ashlyn nodded.

"My dad's family came over about a hundred years ago. Every election year, my dad goes on and on about the better life this country gave us. What he apparently fails to mention is that we come from a long line of slave-owners."

"Binding selkies was common in the Old Country," Paul said. "Still is, as far as we can tell, particularly on isolated islands where the modern world hasn't quite reached."

"Anyway, I didn't know what to do. Arguing with my dad only gets me grounded, so I told him I understood. That I thought he was right." Ashlyn looked at me. "I finally knew why you two acted the way you did, but you were gone, and if I wanted to finish the job myself, my dad had to believe I was on his side."

I sat up straighter. "Finish the job? You mean …"

"Free your parents."

"And Declan," Brennan added.

Ashlyn hesitated. "Declan might want to stay, you know. After all, he's got Emily and Norah."

"He only married Emily to fulfill his side of the deal and free us," I said.

"But he loves her."

I barely knew how to respond to that. Thankfully, Paul stepped in.

"If he does, it's a side effect of his stolen sealskin. It's in his best interest to love her, to please his master, so loving her makes him happy. But if he had his sealskin back, he'd leave without even saying goodbye."

Ashlyn shot him an annoyed glance.

"And you're, what, a selkie expert?"

"It's the truth. If you're serious about helping, you're going to have to accept it."

Ashlyn scowled, but after a few moments she looked away.

"There's really no chance he'd stay for her?"

Paul shook his head. "Afraid not."

Ashlyn shoved her chair back from the table and jumped up to pace.

"This *sucks*. My sister is the sweetest person in the world, but she's going to get her life ripped apart." Every time she moved towards the stairs, my stinging skin eased a bit.

"Her life is built on lies," I said, gritting my teeth as she stalked close again.

"And so is mine," Ashlyn snapped.

She didn't have to watch her parents suffocated under a Haze that left them bland shadows of the people I knew they must be. I let the pain on my skin stoke the fire in my belly. "Am I supposed to feel sorry for you?"

Ashlyn whirled and jabbed a finger in my direction.

"Do you think I wanted all of this dumped in my lap? When you two disappeared after freshman year, I thought I couldn't feel any worse. Then you came back and proved me wrong. It's been two years of Brennan asking all my friends out and you shooting me dirty looks, and I never knew *why*. I figured that was as low as it could get."

My stomach twisted. I wasn't proud of how we'd acted.

"Look—" I started, but Ashlyn ignored me.

"Now I know the truth, and I feel even worse. But no—I don't give a damn whether you feel sorry for me; I just want you out of my life. You and your whole goddamned family. The faster we can find those sealskins and send you all out to sea, the better."

She stalked towards the stairs again, but this time kept going, down and across the rocky shore. Seizing a stone, she hurled it at the ocean.

Leisel stood up.

"I'll go talk to her."

"Do you think she'll speak to you?" I asked. I hadn't missed the cold shoulder Ashlyn was giving Leisel. She must have been furious when she realized Leisel had only befriended her as a step in helping us. And lord knew how she felt about Brennan and Leisel's relationship, if they'd told her.

"I don't know. Does it mean I shouldn't try?" Leisel zipped up her coat against the wind—of the five of us, she and Ashlyn were the only ones wearing more than a sweater—and went down the stairs.

Beside me, Brennan closed his eyes and tilted his head back to catch the afternoon sun. He looked tired, tense lines bracketing his eyes and mouth. Worried, I scanned his bruised face. So far, he didn't seem much different than usual, except for not being able to speak against Mr. Murphy.

"How does it feel? Being Bound again?"

"Shitty," Brennan muttered. I bit my lip.

"Worse than before?"

"Yeah. I think because now I know what's going on. It's weird—I keep wanting to just obey and be happy, and it gives me a headache not to. It's hard to fight it. I think the only reason I'm able to is because Ashlyn told me I could."

Across the table, Paul studied my brother uncomfortably.

"Do you still feel like … yourself?" I asked, but before Brennan could do more than shrug, Ashlyn and Leisel clattered up the steps.

"Still want to help us?" I said, trying to ignore the fresh outbreak of pain stinging my skin.

Ashlyn shoved her hands in her coat pockets.

"Nah, I changed my mind. Brennan, let's go."

Without warning Brennan surged to his feet, shoving his chair loudly over the wood, and I bristled. Ashlyn sighed.

"Whoa. Sit down, Brennan. I was kidding."

Brennan reclaimed his seat. His jaw was set, but he didn't say anything.

"That's not funny," I snapped, shaken.

"None of this is funny." Ashlyn flopped down in her chair. Anger flickered in her eyes. "Did it ever occur to you to ask me for help?"

I looked away. Leisel had suggested it. Maybe we should have listened.

"They wouldn't be able to," Paul said. "Because of the after-effects of the Haze."

"Technical term, is that?" Ashlyn said tartly.

"It's what Brennan and I call it," I said. "Because when we were freed, it felt like coming out of a suffocating fog."

Ashlyn eyed Brennan, still staring resolutely at the table, and subsided.

Paul cleared his throat. "The SRL calls it the Bonding Effect. The Bond takes hold when the master, or Binder, possesses the sealskin in his or her hands and issues an order. Then, so long as the sealskin remains hidden in the Binder's home, the selkie remains under the Bond, which encourages them to obey. They essentially become different people: passive, willing."

Ashlyn had the grace to look uncomfortable.

"This all sounds like magic to me," she muttered. "It's ridiculous. Impossible."

Leisel rested her elbows on the table.

"My mom said that when she was in the Amazon, she saw native shamans bring a man back to life long after their own doctor said there was no hope."

"So?" Ashlyn said coldly. Whatever Leisel had said to make Ashlyn return to the table obviously hadn't thawed the freeze between them. Leisel flushed.

"So there are a lot of impossible things in the world. A bumblebee's flight, for instance."

"What do bumblebees have to do with selkies?" Ashlyn snapped, but Leisel didn't flinch this time.

"Their wings are mathematically incapable of supporting their bodies in flight. Yet they do. Isn't that a sort of magic?"

"Don't get her started on vampire squids," I joked. Leisel shot me a tiny smile.

"Okay, fine," Ashlyn said. "So selkies can be mind-controlled or whatever through their sealskins. But once you were free, you didn't even think of telling me? I mean, Brennan said my dad forbade it, but I don't understand why—"

"Being near you is like bathing in jellyfish," I said bluntly. Ashlyn narrowed her eyes.

"Gee, thanks."

"I'm not saying it to be mean."

"Could have fooled me."

"That would be the after-effect of the Bond that I was talking about," Paul said, stepping in. "Free selkies have a physical reaction to those who've Bound selkies." His gaze found mine briefly before returning to Ashlyn. "We think it fades over time, but any selkie would have a hard time being near you, let alone trusting you."

"But I never stole any sealskins," Ashlyn said. Paul shrugged.

"They're in your house. If you gave orders, over time the Bond would include you as a master."

"Great. I'm an accidental slaver." Ashlyn put her head in her hands. "Fucking great."

There was silence for a moment, and then Brennan turned to me.

"Question," he said. "Why exactly were you kissing Paul earlier?"

My cheeks went hot.

Ashlyn raised her head with a smirk. "I can think of a couple reasons."

"It just sort of happened." I straightened. "Let's talk about how we're going to find the—"

"Because what I saw was an ex-Binder taking advantage of a selkie." Brennan looked at Paul. "One who was injured and vulnerable."

The accusation lay in the air, its ugliness nearly visible.

"Wait a second—" I started, but Paul cut me off.

"*I* was taking advantage of *her*? Try the other way around."

I paused. "Wait, what?"

Paul's glare hit me like granite. "You Thralled me."

Silence fell. I shot a glance at the others, but they seemed just as confused as I was. "You say that like it means something."

His eyes narrowed. "Selkies who are in possession of their sealskins have a sort of power over humans. Kind of a reverse of the Bond, though weaker. They can make people do what they want, to an extent. Seals, too—selkies can Thrall seals into hunting for them."

"Really?" All those seals I'd met could have been fetching

me fish? "Huh." Then I realized what he was saying. "Wait a second. You think I *brainwashed* you into kissing me?"

"Why else would I be *taking advantage* of you?"

This was unbelievable. "Maybe because I'm hot?"

Ashlyn laughed, then sobered. "Hold on. Selkies can convince people to do things?" She looked at Brennan. "Things like … saying yes to a date they'd otherwise refuse?"

"Yes. Exactly like that." Paul leaned back in his chair. "In the myths, selkies would come ashore and Thrall land-folk into sleeping with them."

"Please," I scoffed. "Or they just showed up naked and the 'land-folk' fell into bed willingly."

"That happened a lot too," Paul allowed. "But so did Thrall-induced sex."

"In myths," I shot back, incensed. Was he really accusing me of forced kissing or something? "Name one person that's happened to in real life, ever."

"My mother," Paul said flatly.

Silence again, this time of the horrified variety. Paul didn't look like he was kidding, and dismay drowned my indignation. No wonder he'd been weird when I asked how his parents met. But did he really think … I swallowed hard.

"I wasn't Thralling you. I don't even know how to do that."

"Sounds like your brother does."

"I didn't realize that's what I was doing," Brennan said. He glanced at Ashlyn. "I just thought your friends were shallow."

"So did I." Ashlyn stared at the table. "Interesting."

"Hey, this Thrall thing wouldn't work on Mr. Murphy, would it?" Leisel asked hopefully, but Paul shook his head.

"It's not hard to overcome if you know about it and have a strong will. And— "

"*You* know about it," I interrupted, some of my outrage returning. "Are you saying you're weak-willed?"

"The strength of a selkie's ability to Thrall depends on a lot of things," Paul said through his teeth. "And— "

"This is fun and all, but it's getting late," Ashlyn broke in. "My dad thinks I'm at a yearbook meeting, but if Brennan and I don't show up at the house soon, he might get suspicious. Shouldn't we be working out a plan?"

"The plan hasn't changed," Paul said. "Except now Ashlyn looks out for Brennan as we wait for my mom and the others. She told me last night that it shouldn't be more than a couple weeks."

"Weeks?" My hands curled into fists. "You want my brother to be Bound for a couple *weeks*? That's— "

"I'd survive," Brennan said, exchanging a glance with Ashlyn, "except unfortunately, we can't wait that long. Mr. Murphy told me he's going to burn my sealskin on Friday."

I sucked in a horrified breath.

"Unless— " Ashlyn started to add.

"No 'unless,'" Brennan snapped. "That is not happening."

"Unless what?" I asked, but at Brennan's glare Ashlyn held up her hands and stayed silent. "*What?*"

It was Leisel who finally answered.

"Unless you turn yourself in."

Chapter 30

I fell back in my chair.

"Oh." When had it gotten so hard to breathe?

"How does your father even know Cassandra's alive?" Paul asked. He'd gone rigid in his seat. "She was in pretty poor shape when she got here."

"I don't think he thought he hurt her that badly," Ashlyn said.

"In any case, it's out of the question," Brennan said. "We'll just have to hope he's bluffing, or launch an attack ourselves before then." Paul shook his head, and Brennan's gaze narrowed. "What are we waiting for, anyway? What exactly can the rest of the SRL do that you can't?"

"Deactivate the security cameras, for one."

"Maybe Ashlyn could ask her dad how to do that," Leisel suggested.

Ashlyn grimaced. "No, my dad would get suspicious. He won't even tell my mom the password for the camera system, and he trusts her."

"Well, Cass is *not* handing over her sealskin," Brennan said.

Ashlyn tapped her polished nails thoughtfully on the table. "What if she did?"

Brennan's head whipped around towards her. "Ashlyn—"

"Be quiet," she ordered, and Brennan's mouth snapped shut. Leisel and I bristled, but she ignored us. "Think about it. If Cassandra gave me her sealskin and I took it to my dad, he'd finally be convinced that I'm on board the Slavery's Awesome boat."

She was crazy.

"He'd never believe that I'd just turn my freedom over to you," I said.

"Actually, he's convinced that you *want* to be owned. He thinks you're miserable without your family, and that it's just a matter of time before you come to your senses."

I'd opened my mouth to argue but, remembering the little chat I'd had with Mr. Murphy in my room, I paused. Ashlyn had a point.

"How could he attack them if he thinks that?" Leisel said.

Ashlyn frowned.

"I'm not saying he's not willing to help your realization along. But when he was trying to get Brennan to behave, he seemed surprised that Brennan wasn't thrilled to be back in the fold."

"I thought he was just messing with my head," Brennan muttered. "But yeah, he kept asking me *wasn't I happier now?*"

"The way he explained it to me, he thinks he's doing your

family a favor." Ashlyn wore a lemon-sucking expression. "He thinks he's saving them—against their will, but according to him selkies don't know what's best for them—from an early, brutal death at sea. Anyway, in order to add Cassandra's sealskin to the stash, he'll have to show me where they're all hidden. And then I can free everyone."

Horrible, how logical that sounded.

"Why would he show you now, if he didn't when he brought Brennan in?" Paul asked.

"He'd already hidden Brennan's sealskin by the time I saw him," Ashlyn said. "He said I didn't need to know anyway, not until I was ready to take over 'custodianship.' That's what he calls it. But I'll tell him that since I brought Cass in, I want to be an equal custodian."

"No," Brennan said. "We're not risking Cass's sealskin."

"Well, it's that or hope my dad's bluffing." Ashlyn looked around the table. "Which I guess we could do. The worst that happens is that he follows through and burns Brennan's sealskin. Which would suck, but Brennan wouldn't, like, die or anything. Right?"

Brennan and I exchanged glances, horrified but unsure. What *would* happen if our sealskins were destroyed?

Paul cleared his throat.

"There've been two cases of sealskin destruction that we know of. Plus half a dozen unconfirmed stories from the last couple decades. In one case, the selkie's sealskin was burned, and in the other it was shredded beyond repair."

Recalling Mr. Murphy holding a knife to Brennan's

sealskin, my stomach clenched. "What happened to the selkies?"

"One of them threw herself off a cliff. The other walked into the water and drowned himself."

Silence fell. Brennan had turned a little green.

"So we can't wait," I said, then had another thought. "What if we used a decoy sealskin?" That could work, right? Because there was no way I could hand my sealskin over to Ashlyn. Just no way.

Paul considered, then shook his head.

"If he knows you, knows how you act with and without possession of your sealskin … I doubt he'd buy it. Being Bound is more than just obeying. The Haze, as you call it, is hard to fake. Besides, there's the after-effect. Do you really think you'd be able to pretend not to be in pain?"

I'd forgotten about that, and I sank back against my chair. "Probably not." I could barely stand my ground with Mr. Murphy in the room, let alone fake an eagerness to obey. He'd know within seconds.

"So we use the real sealskin," Ashlyn concluded.

"No!" Brennan slammed his hand on the table, making everyone jump. "Didn't you hear me? We're not risking Cass!" Then he screwed his eyes shut and groaned. "I could seriously use some painkillers right now."

"Are you okay?" Leisel asked anxiously.

"Fighting the Bond causes physical pain," Paul explained, and headed inside for ibuprofen. Ashlyn's gaze rested briefly on Brennan, then swept to me.

"Cassandra, it's your decision."

I stared at her. No. God, no. Of course the answer was no.

Except . . .

Suddenly I couldn't be at the table even considering this. I scrambled up, and ran down the steps to the shore. I didn't stop until I was up to my knees in the surf. The ocean swirled around my calves, cold and heavy, comforting me.

I couldn't do it. I couldn't give up my sealskin, my freedom, my very *being*, to Ashlyn of all people. Not voluntarily. I didn't trust her, not that much. But I couldn't come up with another plan that had even a remote possibility of success, at least not before Mr. Murphy's deadline.

Could we try option two, and hope he was bluffing? Maybe Brennan could convince Mr. Murphy I was dead . . .

If that didn't work, though, Brennan would lose his sealskin. For good.

Forever.

The thought of chancing it turned my spine to ice. I stared to the east, but the horizon was empty, even of clouds. Certainly of answers.

I felt a frisson across my skin, and hoped it was Paul approaching. But the tingle turned into a full-blown jellyfish bath, and I braced myself. Ashlyn.

"I know you think my plan sucks," she said. "But it'll work."

I turned, hands fisting at my sides. Ashlyn wore a black wool coat that fell to her knees and boasted a line of teal piping, a trend for designer coats this winter I'd never even hoped to afford. She wore a matching knit hat that set off her coppery hair and its expert cut. Her make-up was as perfect as her manicure, and compared to her I felt every inch the bedraggled refugee I was.

"You'd just love it, wouldn't you? Ordering me around, having both of us under your thumb?"

Ashlyn sighed. "It's not like that."

"No? You aren't loving the fact that Brennan has to obey you now?"

Ashlyn swiped at the red hair blowing across her face.

"I'll admit, when my dad told me he'd captured Brennan again, that he was under our control, I thought about revenge. But that ended the moment I saw Brennan tied to a chair in the shed."

The image flashed before my eyes; she meant the utility shed in the backyard, filled with pool cleaner and gardening tools. I could picture my brother there, bound, *Bound*, and surrounded by sharp things meant for trimming plants but which could just as easily slice flesh.

Ashlyn stepped to the edge of the water, just beyond where the waves could mar her expensive leather boots.

"I'd never actually been afraid of my dad before that moment, you know. Sure, he's always been controlling. Possessive. Big Brother-y, with the cameras and the extra security. But he's never been … scary." She inhaled, then released her breath. It froze in the air, briefly visible before the breeze snatched it away. "He was scary that day."

The image of Mr. Murphy looming over Brennan with his baseball bat haunted me.

"I remember."

"He was trying to talk some 'sense' into Brennan, who was fighting the Bond. Not thrashing about or anything, just sitting there, refusing to obey. My dad told me that if Brennan was 'too far gone' to cooperate, he was going to burn Brennan's sealskin. So I said I wanted Brennan as my own, the way Emily had Declan. My dad didn't think I could get Brennan to obey, but I whispered in Brennan's ear for him to behave until I could get him out of there."

I waited, but Ashlyn seemed done with her story.

"And what?"

"And so my dad ordered Brennan around for the afternoon, then turned him over to me."

"But why would Brennan trust you like that?" It made no sense.

Ashlyn shrugged. "Look, we both want the same thing: you and your family out of my life. Let's make it happen."

My throat felt tight. She seemed sincere, and that scared me.

It meant I no longer had an easy reason to say no.

"What exactly is the plan, beyond me handing over my freedom to you?" I hedged. "Your dad shows you where the sealskins are hidden, we grab them and run?"

Ashlyn snorted.

"Take them while he's there? Yeah, that sounds safe."

I paused. "You think your dad would hurt you?"

"It's not me I'm thinking of." Ashlyn's face, framed by teal and copper, was inscrutable. "Anyway, Leisel had a good idea. Once I know where the sealskins are, I'll put sleeping pills in my parents' dinner. When they're asleep, we'll get the sealskins and free your family."

I turned the scenario over in my head.

"That sounds so simple." And easy. But just as easy for Ashlyn to screw us over, if she wanted to.

That was the crux, wasn't it? I'd have to trust her—but I wasn't good at figuring out who to trust.

Then again … I looked down at the water, at the sea ruining the slippers Paul had given me. He'd claimed they were old, dumped in a closet with the loose pants I wore, but I'd spotted the price tags in the kitchen trash can. He must have bought them while I was napping.

Paul was someone I'd trust with my sealskin. If I were honest, I'd known it in the woods last Friday. I hadn't spoken up, because Paul was being cagey about his past, but if I'd believed in that trust, Brennan might not have been captured. And if I'd trusted Leisel, she and Brennan might have been with me when I broke into the Murphy house, and my family might be free right now.

So it wasn't that I didn't know who to trust—it was just that I'd refused to. I'd lacked the courage.

Fine. I'd hand my sealskin over to Paul, or even Leisel, this second if it would help. It would scare me to death, but I'd do it. But Ashlyn? How could I trust the girl I'd spent two years hating, who'd spent two years hating me right back? She knew the truth now, but what did she really want out of this? If I gave her my sealskin, she could have everything the way it was: Brennan as her devoted boyfriend, and me as her slavish best friend. She'd be Ashlyn, master of selkies, on top of the world once more. She'd follow in her father's footsteps and win his approval the way she'd always wanted.

Except …

I studied Ashlyn out of the corner of my eye. She stood on a chunk of granite, just out of reach of the waves that eddied about my calves. The wind had tangled her copper hair around her shoulders. The tip of her nose looked nearly blue—she must be freezing. She brooded at the water without seeming to see it, and I felt an unwilling sympathy. I knew how it felt to have your whole life shredded by the truth.

And beneath her coat, beneath her sweater, she wore a golden starfish as if it still meant something to her.

"You kept my paintings," I said.

Ashlyn's head turned absently, like she'd forgotten I was there. Then her green eyes sharpened.

"Just waiting to cash them in."

I snorted. It was an old joke, that my amateurish middle-school art would one day be worth a fortune. Every time I'd finished a painting, Ashlyn would hold it above her head and crow, "Going once, going twice, going three times … *sold*, for three *million* dollars!" Or two million. Or eight-point-five.

"I think the self-portrait might not be worth much anymore," I said, remembering the word *bitch* scrawled over my face with black sharpie.

Ashlyn raised a brow.

"Really? I think it's improved."

Unwillingly, one side of my mouth quirked up; I turned back to the ocean to hide it. Damn Ashlyn for making me want to laugh when just standing near her hurt. Damn her for reminding me how fun our friendship had been, even though it had been founded on lies. For the last two years I'd only seen her, only *allowed* myself to see her, as dangerous. A copy of her father.

But was that really Ashlyn?

Sure, she'd been bossy, she'd been petulant, she'd thoroughly enjoyed being the Earth to my moon. She'd also been snarky and loyal and protective. She'd treated me like a sister, and she'd loved Brennan with all her heart. I remembered the way she'd talk about him, eyes shining. I remembered how bewildered and hurt she was when we cut her out of our lives. I remembered the day she came crying to our doorstep, begging to know what she'd done wrong, why we wouldn't speak to her anymore. My parents let her in, because they had to, but Brennan and I literally ran away, out of the house and down the street, from her painful presence.

Neither of us was the person we'd been back when we'd called each other *best friend*. But fundamentally, I knew Ashlyn was not the type to settle. Not for forced devotion, not for forced friendship. And as much as my paranoia painted Ashlyn as a clone of her father, deep down I knew it wasn't true.

"If we'd come to you two years ago, would you have helped us?" It wouldn't bring back the lost time, but I wanted to know.

Ashlyn's mouth went tight.

"Let's not do this—rehash the past. It is what it is. We're not friends, and we never were. I get that, finally. That's not why I'm helping you."

"Then why?"

Ashlyn shrugged.

"You called me blind, in the coffee shop. Now I see."

Was it really that simple? Not for everyone. But maybe for Ashlyn.

Swallowing hard, I turned to the horizon. I still wasn't sure I could bring myself to put my sealskin in her hands; my very being rebelled at the thought. It was unnatural. But what if her plan worked? Could I live with myself if I passed up the best chance we might ever get? My skin crawled painfully with Ashlyn so close, and all I wanted was to run away, jump into the ocean and never return.

Cowardice lay metallic on my tongue, but I took a deep breath. My entire family was on the line, and I couldn't fail them.

"I'll do it," I said.

Ashlyn let out a low whistle.

"Alright," she said, "but you're the one who has to tell Brennan."

Chapter 31

Plans were made despite Brennan's grumblings, and I walked him, Leisel, and Ashlyn around the side of the house to say goodbye. Paul waited on the deck.

Halfway to the minivan, Brennan caught my arm.

"I don't like the idea of leaving you here with him. Can't you stay with Leisel tonight?"

"I'll be fine." I had things to say to Paul—and only some of them were curse words. I needed to get to the bottom of this Thrall stuff. Did he really think ...

"He Bound a selkie," Brennan said. "Have you forgotten about that?"

On the deck, Paul poked at his phone and pretended we weren't within earshot. I met my brother's worried blue gaze.

"He told me what happened."

"Care to share?" Brennan asked, but Paul's past wasn't mine to tell.

"You told me we could trust Leisel, and you were right. Now I'm telling you that we can trust Paul."

Brennan's mouth tightened, but he didn't argue. "Did

you really tase him when you met him?" At my nod, Brennan looked towards the deck. "Hey Paul. Just want you to know that I have a taser too. You touch my sister again— "

"Actually," Ashlyn interrupted, "my dad confiscated all the weapons in your rooms."

"Whatever. I'll find another one."

"Cut it out." My cheeks felt sunburned. "I don't need you to defend my honor or whatever you think you're doing." But he ignored me.

"Hear me, Paul? If you so much as— " Brennan broke off as Ashlyn grabbed his hand.

"Alright, slugger, let's go."

He followed her to the minivan, suddenly meek. Leisel and I exchanged unhappy glances. I wondered how she was doing with all this. It had to be hard for her too—she and Brennan had only broken up a few days ago, after all, and with Ashlyn acting so possessive ... But there was nothing to say that would help.

"Hold on," she muttered, and trudged after them. Grabbing something from the trunk, she returned with a backpack. "I wasn't sure you'd have decent clothes here, so I brought you some of my stuff I thought might fit."

I dug into the bag. "You brought me a bra!"

"It might be a little small."

"It's fabulous, thank you." Spotting a flash of crimson fabric, I looked up in delight. "Is this the shirt we bought?"

Leisel smiled. "I think you like it better than I do."

I dropped the bag and drowned her in a fierce hug. The

minivan's horn beeped, startling us; behind the windshield, Ashlyn glared impatiently.

"Ashlyn's pretty pissed at you," I observed. Leisel shrugged, her shoulders taking on the bit of steel that always surprised me.

"I've done nothing I regret."

That struck me as a lovely thing to be able to say. I sighed. "Brennan seems to think I'll regret staying here tonight."

"He's just worried."

"He shouldn't be. If Paul wanted to steal my sealskin, he could have."

Leisel gave me a wry glance.

"I think Brennan's worried about more than your sealskin."

Heat crept up my neck.

"From how Paul tells it, *his* virtue is in more danger than mine."

Leisel cocked her head. "Is that even something you're thinking of? With Paul?"

"Of course not." But Leisel kept looking at me. Maybe it was just a secret-sharing kind of day, because I found myself murmuring, "I've never … you know. Before."

"Oh. Me neither." Awkwardness descended. Leisel glanced at the house. "I guess it might be nicer in a bed than …" She faltered. "What do selkies do?"

"Never really thought about it." Logically, I supposed, they kept to beaches. Hard, rocky beaches. I frowned.

"Hey!" Ashlyn waved from the minivan's passenger side. "Are you deaf? Let's go!"

Leisel made a face, then headed for the van. I watched them leave, feeling sick even after Ashlyn's stinging presence drove away. How could I yield my sealskin, my freedom, to her? Shoving my panic down, I went inside.

Paul wasn't in the living room, or his bedroom. I checked on my sealskin, tucked between my mattress and box springs, then changed into the bra and red shirt, along with black stretchy yoga pants that were way better than the shapeless slacks I'd been wearing. Leisel had even included a comb, so I ran it through my hair before throwing it up in a ponytail.

Back in the main rooms, I thought I'd find Paul reading somewhere, but he remained conspicuously absent. I fetched up next to the kitchen table in confused annoyance. Had he gone for a nighttime stroll?

Then I heard a sound, plastic and hollow, coming from behind a door I'd assumed was a pantry. Instead, opening it revealed stairs leading into a finished rec room. I padded silently down the steps. Paul, his back to me, stood at one end of a ping pong table that had been shoved against the far wall so he could hit the ball against the side of the room. The ping pong ball bounced over the net, and Paul swung hard, sending the ball off into the corner without hitting the table. He didn't go get it, instead grabbing another from a pile in a bowl.

"You are getting your ass kicked by a wall," I said. "That's embarrassing."

Paul turned. He scanned me from head to toe, and I thought he'd comment on my new outfit, but all he said was, "This wall competed in the Olympics."

My lip quirked.

"That's not so bad, then."

"Want to play?" He tossed the ball my way. I caught it, then walked to the other side of the table and helped Paul pull it a couple feet out. Another paddle lay on a bookshelf, and I picked it up. But when Paul served, I didn't move, and the ball sailed by me to join the dozen others on the floor.

"You do actually have to raise your arms, Cassandra."

I met Paul's amused gaze.

"Do you really think I Thralled you?" I asked, and his smile faded.

"You seriously had no idea what I was talking about?"

I shook my head. "Could I have done it accidentally? Like Brennan?" Was everything between us false? Was the only reason guys asked me out because I unknowingly sent out Selkie Thrall Spores or whatever? It was too embarrassing to even consider.

Paul grimaced doubtfully.

"My father said it took concentration. Like ping pong." He tapped his paddle pointedly on the table. I retrieved the ball from the corner of the room and served. We played for a while. Distracted by my musings, I focused more on keeping a volley going than on winning. I *had* really wanted Paul to come over and kiss me earlier, so maybe I'd concentrated on it enough to—

"No, I don't think you Thralled me," Paul said finally. "My dad had one of his friends Thrall me when I was younger, so I could learn to recognize and ignore it."

I caught the ball in mid-air, annoyed now.

"So why did you say all that? You acted like I was some kind of predator, hunting hot defenseless college guys."

"The last time I had any contact with selkies I was twelve. I thought at first that maybe I'd misremembered what a Thrall felt like." Paul waved his paddle around. "This whole thing has sort of thrown me for a loop. You're nothing like what I know selkies to be, Cassandra."

"What do you mean?"

"Most selkies would pick raw tuna over mac and cheese, for one. And no selkie I've ever heard of would let a human near their sealskin voluntarily."

I caught his eye. "I trust you."

"What about Ashlyn?"

Suddenly my throat closed, choking me.

"Oh, God. I can't believe I agreed to that." I covered my face with my hands. The paddle smelled like rubber and old wood, and served as a decent shield. I didn't want Paul to see me cry. Sucking in deep breaths, I tried to regain the determination I'd felt earlier when I'd made the decision, but it was a losing battle.

The first tear was about to fall when I felt Paul's arms encircle me. He pulled me close, and I stood there in his arms until my shudders subsided.

"I have to do it," I said at last, more to myself than Paul. "It's the only way."

Paul rested his chin against my temple.

"See? You're different from most selkies. None of them would make this kind of sacrifice."

Sacrifice. If my hands were empty I'd have clutched at his shirt, so maybe it was a good thing I still held the ping pong ball and paddle.

"You mean none of them are this stupid."

Paul pulled back, but only to take my face in his hands. His fingers threaded through the hair at my temples, and his thumbs brushed my cheeks. With anyone else I'd have pushed away, but I let his tingling touch steady me.

"Brave," he said. "Not stupid. Brave."

I felt not even a tiny bit brave, but before I could say that, Paul released me.

"What do you want for dinner?"

My mouth twisted. "My last meal?"

"I'll get anything you want. Well, anything you want that I can find around here. This place is not exactly a take-out mecca."

I considered. "Pizza. And the chocolatiest dessert you can find."

An hour later, we settled on the couch to dig in. Giving the pizza place our address probably wouldn't pose a threat, since there was virtually no chance of Mr. Murphy even knowing about this house, let alone finding me here, but Paul had taken the precaution of picking up our meal anyway. I approved.

The pizza place hadn't offered any chocolate to speak of, so he'd bought pre-made brownies at a grocery store. I approved of that too.

Halfway through my second slice of double-veggie with extra cheese—so nice, not to have to worry about the cost of toppings—I shot Paul a glance.

"I'm not really that different than other selkies, right?"

"You are." He piled stray cheese onto his crust. "You and your brother."

"Well, we grew up on land, so …"

"It's more than that." Paul waved his slice in the air for emphasis. "Freed selkies are … wild. Mysterious. They're the type of people you find dancing naked on the beach under the light of a full moon."

I raised my brows. "Like hippies?"

Paul laughed. "Yeah, I guess. But without drugs."

"So I'm not mysterious enough for you?" I said, hiding my smile.

"That's not what I meant. Selkie culture is the same, largely, as it's been for centuries. They don't understand phones, much less the Internet. I tried to show Theo a video game once, and he freaked out. They think it's black magic or something." Paul sobered. "Their justice code leaves something to be desired, too."

Figuring he was talking about his parents, I asked, "If your dad Thralled your mom, why is she so dedicated to helping selkies?"

Paul chewed slowly before answering.

"She doesn't blame them all for one selkie's actions."

"But she let your dad visit, even though ..."

"She says the line got very blurred." Paul grimaced at my expression. "I don't really get it either. In any case, she never went down to the beach by herself, or allowed herself to be alone with any of the selkies of the pod my dad belonged to. And she made them swear not to Thrall any humans, at least while they were staying on our beach. But she said that just because he'd done something wrong didn't make him a bad person, and she wanted me to know my father."

We ate in silence for a minute. I didn't know what to make of Paul's parents' relationship, especially considering how it seemed to have started, but I wondered what it would be like, to have parents who were free and not Bound to jump at the whims of their captors.

"What was he like?" I asked. Paul shrugged.

"He was a good dad, mostly—I only saw him every other month at best, but some of my friends had dads like that too, only theirs were high-powered businessmen who cared more about their companies than their kids. I always felt lucky that I had my secret family. My dad loved me. The whole pod loved me." Paul's mouth tightened. "Right up until they tried to kill me."

I choked on my pizza.

"Wait, what?"

"Selkies have one punishment for Binders: death. After I set Theo free, he dove into the sea before I could apologize. I tried to go after him, but as soon as the rest of the pod saw me they could tell. The after-effect. I can still see my dad recoil.

I tried to tell them what happened, but they wouldn't listen. They dragged me into the water and tried to drown me."

"Even your dad?"

"He didn't stop them. Thankfully, my mom saw me running with Theo's sealskin and knew enough to grab a tranquilizer gun. She and my stepdad scared them off and pulled me from the water. I was unconscious, but after some CPR I coughed up the water in my lungs and was okay."

Feeling sick, I put my plate of pizza down on the coffee table. Paul's mouth twisted.

"Didn't mean to ruin your appetite."

"I'm so sorry, Paul. That sucks." And then I felt dumb. "I know, that's the understatement of the year. I just …"

"It was a long time ago." Paul pushed off of the couch. "I'll get us some brownies."

We talked all through the evening, until finally I yawned.

"You should sleep," Paul said. "You need to be rested for tomorrow."

I drew my legs in and hugged them. "Ugh, I don't want to think about tomorrow." Fear curdled my stomach, disrupting the lovely warmth from moments before.

"You don't have to do this, you know," Paul said quietly.

"If it means freeing my parents, my brothers … then yeah, I do." But holy crab shells, I dreaded handing my sealskin over tomorrow.

Paul leaned over and brushed my cheekbone with his lips.

"What was that for?" I asked, startled.

He wore a slight smile. "You looked like you needed it."

Our gazes locked, faces inches away, and I was suddenly anything but tired. After hours of talk, I felt closer to him than I'd ever felt with anyone, and I wanted … something. Something more than goodnight.

Before I could close the space between us, Paul stood up from the couch.

"Get some rest," he said. "I'll clean up."

Rattled, I fled. In the bathroom I splashed icy water on my overheated skin, then brushed my teeth. After I spit, I paused to look at my toothbrush. There were no toothbrushes at sea, and my stomach knotted. For the first time, I wasn't sure I wanted to live without something so useful, and smart, and …

I shook my head to clear it. This wasn't about toothbrushes, but I had bigger things to worry about. Like tomorrow, and our terrifying plan. If it worked, it'd be worth it—but what if it didn't?

I flicked off the light in the hallway, then went into my room. Without turning on the overhead, I walked straight to the window to stare at the moonlit sea, trying to regain my calm. It didn't help, and finally I sighed and turned on the bedside lamp to find my robe. Light flooded the room, revealing a surprise on the bedspread.

Slippers. Fleece-lined slippers that looked just like the ones I'd ruined earlier today. Paul must have picked up a new pair when he went out for pizza.

My breath caught, and before I knew it I was running into the hall. The lights were off, but movement sounded from the direction of the kitchen. I dashed along the corridor.

Rounding the corner into the living room, I collided with a tall, solid form that made my skin hum with electricity. Paul. I'd almost knocked him over, and we held onto each other to stay upright.

"You alright?" he asked, laughing a little. "Where are you running to?"

You, I thought, but couldn't say it, because I was already on tiptoes, my lips already finding his. He hesitated only a moment before kissing me back, his hands sliding up my arms and around my shoulders to pull me against him. I pressed forward, and he walked back in the darkness until his legs bumped something—the couch, I realized, and then we were tumbling onto the soft cushions.

Wrapped in his strong arms, I kissed him with everything I had. His touch sent shivers of electricity through my waist and back and other places that made me quickly forget anything but him. He tasted like brownies and midnight, and smelled like the sea.

He felt like *home*, which startled me so much that I raised my head, breaking the kiss. Lying under me on the couch, Paul breathed as hard as I did; his heartbeat raced under my hand.

"Thank you for the slippers," I managed to say.

Paul kissed my collarbone, left bare by the low neckline of my shirt.

"I figured you'd like them more than flowers." A hint of a smile curved his lips, and my fingers rose to trace it. At my touch, his body tensed beneath mine.

"You were right," I said, and kissed him again.

Chapter 32

The next morning as we ate—leftover pizza and brownies—I tried to stop glancing at Paul, but it was impossible. My cheeks were tender from the stubble on his jaw, and echoes of his touch whispered across my skin. It was a welcome distraction from what would happen later today.

Paul caught my latest stare.

"What?" he asked.

"I wish I could paint you." Immediately, I wanted to unsay it; my face felt as red as my pizza sauce. But it was true, my fingers itched to paint Paul. I wanted to capture everything from last night.

A slight, bemused smile crossed his lips.

"You paint?"

"Not anymore. I used to. When I was Bound." I ducked my head. "When I got my sealskin back, I didn't want to be anything like my former self. I changed everything I could—I even dyed my hair black, but it went back to brown after a *change* cycle." I figured a tattoo would disappear too. I'd gotten my ears pierced with Ashlyn in sixth grade, but those holes were long gone. "Silly, I guess. I sort of wish I'd kept painting. I'm probably awful now." When had my explanation turned into babbling?

"Cassandra." Paul took my hand. "You won't turn into her again."

I felt like a clam was stuck in my throat. "Isn't that sort of the point? Once I give my sealskin to Ashlyn …"

"You'll still be you."

"Will I? What if I lose myself?" What if I wasn't as strong as Brennan? What if I couldn't do this?

"You need something to focus on. Isn't that what Brennan said he did?"

"Yeah." Yesterday, once Brennan had been forced to accept Ashlyn's plan and the overall strategy was set, we'd talked a different sort of strategy. He'd confided that whenever he felt his will slipping, he'd focus on the fact that he didn't know whether I'd survived Mr. Murphy's attack. "Brennan used a cut on his hand to remind him." Staring at it had, he said, given him the strength to resist Mr. Murphy's orders. I held out my hands. "I don't have so much as a bruise anymore. Maybe I could draw something in pen?" But even as I said it I shook my head. Part of the plan was the cover story that I'd spent the time since the attack in the woods and the water, alone, so pen marks wouldn't fit.

Paul slid a finger up my arm. Electric tingles riveted my attention; I had no idea what he was doing, but I wasn't about to ask him to stop. His thumb traced my skin, stopping at a pair of freckles set close together just to the left of the inside center of my wrist.

"These freckles," he said.

"What about them?"

"Use them as a focal point."

"That's ridiculous," I said, but Paul raised his brows.

"What are the two things you want most in the world?"

"Freedom. My family." I didn't even need to think.

"Then that's what we'll name them." Paul tapped the left-most freckle. "That one's Freedom, and the other is Family. When you need to, look at them and focus." He released my hand and picked up his half-eaten slice of pizza. "Think that'll work?"

I gazed at the twin freckles on my wrist. Freedom and Family. I set my jaw.

"I'll make it work."

"This is going to blow serious chunks," I told Leisel a few hours later as we waited in a cul-de-sac that accessed one of Granite Harbor High's cross-country trails. Brennan and Ashlyn were due to meet us here after school let out. I paced across the cul-de-sac. Despite a swim earlier, my nerves were strung tighter than a sail-line on a windy day. "What if Mr. Murphy doesn't buy it?"

"He will." Leisel had used a yearbook pass to get out of class early and wait with me after Paul dropped me off. Perched on the curb, she was trying hard to look reassuring, but worry peeked through her attempt at a smile. "You look the part, and Ashlyn will take care of the rest."

Paul and I had tracked down another of Brennan's and my clothing caches before he dropped me off, so I wore a cheap black sweatsuit. This one had fewer holes chewed through it, at least. Leisel had crumbled leaves over me, and we'd streaked my hands and face with dirt. My bare feet were scratched, my hair a mess. I felt like an urchin from a Dickens novel.

Was it enough? It had to be.

Pacing was making me more wound up, not less, and finally I threw myself onto the curb between Leisel and the black garbage bag that now contained my sealskin.

"So did anything happen with you and Paul last night?" she asked. I just shrugged. With Ashlyn's arrival imminent, I couldn't let thoughts of last night distract me anymore. *Focus.* I grabbed my left hand with my right and stared at the twin freckles. Next to me, Leisel sighed. "I thought he'd at least stay and wait with you."

I shook my head. "His car might attract attention." Picking up a pine twig from the ground, I stripped the needles off one by one. "How's Brennan today?"

Leisel was silent, and I glanced up to see her grimace.

"They were holding hands at lunch. I had to just sit there."

My stomach clenched.

"Did Ashlyn order him around?"

"She told him to throw her trash away for her. Then when he came back she kissed him on the cheek. I almost threw up." Leisel stared at her hands, pressed together in her lap. "Everyone acts like they're star-crossed lovers, like them fighting for two years was just proof that they were meant to be. Ashlyn's friend Liz says that if they'd stopped loving each other, they wouldn't have been so angry."

"That's bullshit."

"Is it?" Leisel's voice went very quiet. "He looks at her differently now."

"That's just the Bond. I promise. You're the one he cares about."

She bit her lip like she might cry.

"It doesn't matter anyways, I guess."

I wished there were some magical words to make it better. "I'm sorry I was such a jerk, before. About you guys. You made him happy. This farce with Ashlyn doesn't make him happy."

Leisel's gaze narrowed. "Could have fooled me."

I turned to find the silver pick-up pulling into the cul-de-sac. Ashlyn, smiling, sat next to my brother … who was laughing. I winced on Leisel's behalf, but then a cold numbness crawled through my bones, pushing out everything but dread. It was time. The truck rolled to a stop, and I picked up the squirrel-ravaged garbage bag containing my sealskin. It lay heavy and comforting in my arms.

"It would be a tragedy," Leisel muttered as we stood. I shot her a confused look.

"What?"

"I'm in charge of sending the pictures for the yearbook's Homecoming spread. I was just thinking how tragic it would be if, in the picture of Ashlyn accepting her crown, she somehow had ink across her teeth." Leisel grinned fiercely, and I gave a choked laugh just as Ashlyn swung down from the truck.

"What's so funny?" Ashlyn asked.

"Nothing," Leisel said, and the green gaze narrowed on me. My skin stung.

"Cassandra, you tell me." Her voice held the peremptory tone that always made my teeth ache.

"Don't hold your breath."

Ashlyn arched a brow.

"You might want to get used to me ordering you around," she said mildly, and my stomach knotted. "Come on, Brennan," she called behind her. My brother hopped obediently out of the pick-up. It was like a flashback to freshman year, and nausea hit me like a rogue wave.

Whirling, I made it onto the dirt before retching up the tuna sandwich I'd had before Paul dropped me off. I felt hands on my hair—Leisel, holding it back.

"You okay?" she murmured. I wiped my mouth on my sweatsuit sleeve, which was gross, then tried to scrape my sleeve on the ground. Some dirt and slime remained, smelling foul, but I decided it wouldn't hurt my cover story. In fact, it would likely help.

Ashlyn spared me a glance as I stood and picked my bag up again.

"Are you done proving how sick I make you, or should we come back later?"

Later. I wished I could put this off a day or two—Mr. Murphy's deadline wasn't until Friday, after all—but I shook my head. It had to be today, had to be now, or I'd lose my nerve.

"Let's do this," I said. Everyone waited, but I didn't relinquish my hold on my bag.

"Take your time," Ashlyn said. I couldn't tell whether she was being snarky or serious. My bones ached to flee, and for a moment I thought I would. But then I remembered Paul calling me brave, and Declan's face as he'd watched me leave without him. My gaze caught on the scabs marring Brennan's hands, and something inside me stilled. I could do this. I had to do this. For them.

Fighting every single one of my instincts, I reached out and placed the bag containing my sealskin into Ashlyn's hands. She took it doubtfully, nose wrinkling at all the dirt. My muscles screamed with the urge to snatch the bag back before she could …

"Sit down," Ashlyn ordered, and as Paul would say, the Bond took effect. In Brennan's words, the Haze descended.

I let out a cry of pain.

Disorientation hit, and with it an odd floating sensation. When my vision cleared, I was sitting on the pavement. I hardly felt my anger and fear anymore. It wasn't that the emotions were gone, but they were … blurred. I was still myself, but it was like part of me stood in a bare clearing surrounded by fog. The rest of me waited somewhere outside the clearing, unseen.

I remembered this.

Before it had felt normal, like life.

Now it felt *wrong*.

"Are you okay?" Leisel crouched next to me, but I couldn't answer. My gaze fixed like superglue on the girl who held my sealskin.

Ashlyn slung the bag over her shoulder. A pang of desolation hit, but it was dull and hard to hold onto. I lost it in the mist. Ashlyn's green eyes as she studied me were bright and sharp and ... beautiful. I wished I had eyes like that.

"You have pretty eyes," I said, looking up at her.

Ashlyn's brow pinched.

"I think that means it worked," she said.

"Cass, are you okay?" Brennan asked.

"Sure," I agreed automatically, looking to Ashlyn as if for confirmation. Somewhere outside my mental clearing, I was screaming. What had I done? I wanted to grab my sealskin back. But it was hers now, and I didn't want to make her angry.

No. *No!* I lurched to my knees, fists ready. Then I stopped, remembering that I wasn't supposed to punch my way to freedom. The plan. I sank back to the ground, barely aware of Leisel hovering next to me. The Haze battled with the urge to leap at Ashlyn, but finally numbness began to win. I could feel myself slipping away, and my inner panic scrabbled futilely, finding no purchase, until my gaze caught on my wrist. *Freedom. Family.* For a moment the Haze lessened. I stared at my wrist, letting the two freckles anchor me. Ridiculous as it was, it sort of worked; I felt like I could fight off the Haze, if I needed to.

But per the plan, I wasn't supposed to fight. My job was to convince Mr. Murphy that I'd given my sealskin to Ashlyn freely, without ulterior motives. So for the next ten minutes I patiently listened to everything Ashlyn said, how I was to behave and what I was to say when we reached her house, and then I bundled myself obediently between her and Brennan on the front bench of the pick-up.

"You okay?" Leisel asked through the window. "You seem a little …"

Blank. That's what I felt like, as if all my sharp edges had been erased.

"She's fine," Ashlyn said impatiently, and pushed the button to close the window. Leisel's expression pinched; she shoved her hands into her coat pocket as Brennan backed us up.

"Seriously, though, are you alright?" Ashlyn asked when we'd left Leisel behind.

I considered, then shrugged.

"It feels like old times. Except now that doesn't make me want to hurl." I smiled ruefully. "Too bad I don't have my starfish necklace."

Ashlyn frowned, as if hardly able to believe I'd said that without sarcasm. "What happened to it?"

"I was wearing it when Declan gave us our sealskins back. I guess it fell off when I *changed* that first time; I never saw it again." I glanced at the trash bag Ashlyn held in her lap. My head hurt to think about it, but I bet I could ignore the pain long enough to snatch my sealskin back. The plan, however, required me not to, so with difficulty I looked away.

"So did anything happen with Paul last night?" Ashlyn

asked, just as Leisel had. But unlike with Leisel, the answer popped out of my mouth before I could even think of whether to stop it.

"We hooked up."

The truck lurched as Brennan slammed on the brakes. "You *what*?" he yelped. Behind us, a car horn blared.

Ashlyn's green eyes were wide. "Like, all the way?"

I hesitated, but couldn't help answering.

"No. Pretty close, though."

"I am *so* going to tase that guy," Brennan said through gritted teeth. My cheeks felt on fire—this was not a conversation I wanted to have around anyone, let alone my brother. I should be angry at Ashlyn, but with the Haze, all I felt was embarrassed.

We were still stopped, and more car horns sounded behind us.

"Chill, Brennan," Ashlyn said. "And keep driving."

Brennan obeyed only the second part of her order.

"He took advantage of her!"

Ashlyn rolled her eyes. "Cass doesn't let anyone take advantage of her."

"*You're* taking advantage of her," Brennan shot back.

"What are you talking about?"

"You know she'd never have told you if you weren't holding her sealskin."

"Oh." The amusement drained from Ashlyn's expression. Part of me didn't want her to feel bad about it, and I cast about for something to derail the insane urge to apologize.

A horrible thought struck me, and I went rigid in my seat.

"Hey, the truck isn't bugged anymore, is it?"

"No. I made my dad promise. And Brennan says the bug-detector is working." Ashlyn still looked troubled, and I tried to think of something to say.

"Who's Liz dating these days?"

Ashlyn gave me an odd look. "Don't tell me you care."

"I don't?" If she didn't want me to care, then I didn't.

She muttered a curse. "You know, I always thought you were just scatterbrained, or joking, when you said shit like that before."

"Maybe I was," I said agreeably.

"Be quiet, Cassandra," Ashlyn said, and I fell silent. For a moment, I thought *This sucks.* I wanted to be at sea. Underneath the complacency from the Haze, humiliation crawled over my skin, and my hands itched to snatch the bag from Ashlyn's lap. Finally I twisted my fingers together to keep them still. I stared at my wrist and mentally chanted *Freedom, Family* over and over.

It helped, and by the time we reached the house I felt almost normal again. Brennan drove us through the gates and parked behind Ashlyn's car. We all piled out. The asphalt driveway chilled my bare feet.

"Here." Ashlyn held out her schoolbag. "Carry my stuff." She cradled my sealskin, still swathed in its dirty garbage bag. Taking her messenger bag, I looked up at the house. The fortress. It had beaten me last time, and a stab of dread made me balk.

"Come on," Ashlyn said from the doorway, and my feet started me forward in automatic obedience.

Mr. Murphy must have spent a fortune to get repairs handled so quickly, because the foyer bore no sign of my assault on the house, unless you knew that the paint was a shade creamier this time around. The dining room to our right was similarly recovered, the drywall repaired and wallpapered over. The pattern was different now, blue and gold stripes instead of the old garnet paisley. To the left, the front sitting room had new couches to replace the ones I'd slashed up.

"Dad, I've got a surprise for you," Ashlyn called. There was noise in the living room, and then Douglas Murphy appeared at the end of the hall.

When he saw me, he stopped dead. A bruise bloomed on his jaw, and his hand went as if in reflex to the shoulder I'd bitten.

"What is she doing here?" Then he noticed my scruffy appearance, and the garbage bag in Ashlyn's arms. He went still, like a hawk sighting a field mouse. "What's that?"

Ashlyn walked over and put my sealskin in her father's arms.

Chapter 33

Two hours later, I lifted my face to the shower spray. Water poured over my skin, comforting like the sea. When I was younger, I'd taken epically long showers. Now I knew why.

After a mind-numbing session of what Mr. Murphy called "obedience exercises"—*pick up the litter along the street, Cassandra. Fetch me a Coke, Cassandra. Put the Coke back, Cassandra*—Ashlyn had finally ordered me to go upstairs and clean the forest dirt off of myself. A respite, sorely needed. I felt tired. And underneath that, violated. Humiliated.

Bereft.

Throughout the afternoon, the loss of my sealskin squeezed me like a noose, split seconds when I couldn't breathe for the ache of loss. I hadn't forgotten anything. I hadn't wanted to apologize to Mr. Murphy for biting him, or for wrecking the house, or for all my transgressions, large or trivial, over the last two years.

But I had. The need to obey, to make nice and win his approval was so strong I wondered if I could even hope to fight it like Brennan had. But the plan required me not to fight, so

I didn't try. Instead I groveled, and when Mr. Murphy finally gave his grudging forgiveness, relief washed over me.

"Thank you for being so kind to me and my family," I'd said, wondering all the while how it was that I wasn't choking on the words. They flowed from my mouth smoothly, as if part of me even meant them. Whenever I thought of rebellion, my head would hurt, and with each order I obeyed it became more difficult to consider refusing. Pressing a thumb into the two freckles on my wrist helped keep my wits about me, but only to a point.

When I'd handed Mr. Murphy his Coke earlier he'd looked at me and asked, easily and calmly, "Tell me your secret plan, Cassandra."

I'd nearly spit it out right there.

The only reason I hadn't was because behind Mr. Murphy, Ashlyn shook her head, telling me with her wide eyes not to answer. That, and the coaching from earlier, let me frown in confusion—and pain; my head hurt from the conflicting orders—and say, "I don't have one. Not anymore."

My head still ached from the lie. I held my breath and let the water pound at my pores. It was almost good to have that rebellion to hold onto; painful as it was, it centered me. *Don't tell him. Don't tell him. Freedom. Family.* It kept me from losing any more of myself in the rush of orders stripping me away.

"Cassandra, come on," Ashlyn called through the bathroom door. I went on eager alert, like a bird dog waiting for instruction. "Get dressed ASAP and come downstairs; dinner's on its way."

"I'll be right out," I said, already turning the water off. I missed it immediately, but if Ashlyn wanted me downstairs, that's where I needed to be. Mr. Murphy was having shrimp linguine alfredo sent over from The Golden Fish.

I was toweling off before I realized I hadn't rinsed the conditioner from my hair. But Ashlyn wanted me downstairs, so …

I stopped, dripping, and pinched my freckled wrist as hard as I could. I let the pain focus me. *Don't lose yourself.*

Gritting my teeth, I turned on the water and got back in the shower.

When Mrs. Murphy arrived home, she greeted me like a long-lost daughter. Mr. Murphy had called her with the news, I gathered. She hugged me, and though part of me wanted to spit in her perfectly made up face, I only asked if I could hang up her coat.

One of The Golden Fish's waiters arrived with the shrimp linguine, waved at Brennan and me, and left. Ashlyn dished everything up, and I focused on looking as innocent as possible as I set the plates on the table in the order she instructed. I felt an odd swelling of affection for her. Ashlyn was my best friend. She'd take care of me.

We sat down to eat. Mr. Murphy claimed the head of the table, of course, with his wife at the other end. Brennan and Ashlyn sat across from me. We bowed our heads, and Mr. Murphy said grace.

"Well, this is nice," Mrs. Murphy said as we dug in. "Just like it used to be. How did it all happen?"

Mr. Murphy twirled sauce-coated linguine around his fork, then brought it to his mouth. I frowned. The Haze gave me a sort of knee-jerk loyalty to him, but I stuffed my mouth with pasta so I wouldn't feel the need to warn him about the sleeping pills.

As we ate, Ashlyn ran down the cover story, which she'd told her father earlier. She explained how I'd left a note on Brennan's car for him to meet me after school. Thinking I was plotting a rescue attempt, Ashlyn had gone with him. Instead, upon hearing about Mr. Murphy's ultimatum, I'd confessed how tired I was of running and hiding, and had decided to rejoin my family instead of live miserably alone.

"She gave me her sealskin, and I went back inside to get her a granola bar from the vending machine. She was starving—she can't fish that well by herself," Ashlyn said.

"Cass and I never really learned," Brennan said with a straight face. My brother, who could eat his weight in trout in less than an hour, managed to look embarrassed. "That summer we were gone, most of the time we wound up scavenging garbage."

Mrs. Murphy made a moue of sympathy at me. We'd concocted the lie to appeal to their twisted sensibilities, that we needed to be cared for.

"Have you told Declan yet?" Ashlyn asked her father. "How's he taking it?"

Mr. Murphy's face tightened. "He'll settle down soon. He

knew it was only a matter of time before these two got caught again."

Declan would think his sacrifice had been for nothing. Guilt should be gouging my insides, but I only felt vaguely sad. I shoveled more pasta into my mouth.

"So are you and Brennan officially 'dating' again?" Mrs. Murphy asked Ashlyn. "Or are you going to wait until Brennan's been back at school for a bit?"

"I thought we'd dive right in," Ashlyn said brightly, taking Brennan's hand. Her mother frowned.

"It might make people talk, being so sudden and all."

Ashlyn shrugged. "He and Cass disappeared for a week and you told people they went to rehab. The gossip is already flying. I'm telling everyone that Brennan's walking the straight and narrow for me, and we're both helping Cass through her struggle with prescription drugs."

Mr. Murphy looked at me.

"How do you feel about that, Cassandra?"

I met his sharp blue eyes and willed my mind to go blank.

"I just want things to go back to normal," I said, as Ashlyn had coached me to.

When we finished dinner, Mr. Murphy—was he looking tired?—told Ashlyn to send us home. In the foyer, Brennan grabbed his bookbag from the floor next to the stairs. Having no coat or purse, I just followed Ashlyn to the door.

She opened it, and cold air swirled around me.

"I'm so glad we're friends again, Cassandra," Ashlyn said

loudly. "Go home and get some sleep. Tomorrow morning, bring me a coffee before school."

"What kind?" I asked automatically.

"Skinny vanilla latte." She sounded so serious that worry spiked beneath the Haze, but Ashlyn was already turning to Brennan.

"Goodnight, hon," she said cheerfully, moving in for a hug.

Brennan kissed her instead, right on the lips, and for a second everyone froze.

Ashlyn jerked her head away.

"What are you doing?" she said.

"I— " Brennan looked as surprised as the rest of us. Ashlyn glanced at her parents, watching with raised brows, and flushed.

"That's moving a little fast. We only just got back together, remember?"

Brennan mumbled an apology, and Ashlyn pushed us outside. When she closed the door I felt … lost. My sealskin, my master, were inside that house, and I wanted to be there too. I'd felt the same, without understanding why, when I was younger, always preferring Ashlyn's house to mine.

Brennan's cheeks were red as we walked to the truck. I didn't comment. He drove us out to the street and down half a block, where Leisel and Paul waited. Wearing a hooded parka, Leisel waved as we came to a stop. I met Paul's gaze, which rested on me questioningly. He stepped up to the passenger's side window, and I rolled down the glass.

"Hi," he said. "Are you okay?"

I showed him my wrist, the two freckles, and shrugged.

Brennan got out of the truck. He and Paul would go with Ashlyn into the house and get the sealskins, while Leisel and I gathered my parents and Declan. We'd all meet at The Golden Fish.

Paul gave me a last searching look, then stepped away from my window. Pulling two stun guns from a pocket, he held one up.

"You should have this when we go in," he said to Brennan, "but if I give it to you are you going to use it on me?" After a hesitation, my brother shook his head. "Swear?" Paul said suspiciously.

"I swear I won't tase you," Brennan said, and punched him in the nose.

His fist didn't hit squarely, because Paul ducked at the last moment, but the blow was enough to send spots of blood flying in the glow of the streetlamp.

"*Brennan*." I scrambled from the car. "Stop it!"

Paul had dropped the stun guns and was holding his nose, cursing. Brennan picked one up; I rushed between them.

"Stop being an ass," I snapped at my brother.

"I warned him."

This was because of what I'd said in the truck earlier? "You are the *last* person who has any say in who I— "

"What the hell is going on out here?" Ashlyn came jogging up, her face a picture of exasperation. "You'll wake the neighborhood—or worse, my parents."

"Brennan punched Paul." Leisel's eyes were wide. "I'm not entirely sure why."

Ashlyn glanced at me and sighed. "Great. Brennan, give me that taser." He did, automatically. She handed it to me.

"I need that," Brennan said. "I'm going in with you, remember?"

"No, you're not, because Paul's going in too, and you apparently can't play nice with Paul. New plan: Cass comes with us, while you and Leisel go get your family." She cut off his protest. "We don't have time to argue, so just go."

Brennan went rigid, fighting the order. It hurt to watch, knowing he must be in pain. I put a hand on Ashlyn's arm.

"Maybe we could both— "

"Shut up, Cassandra." She shook off my hand.

"Hey," Paul said sharply. "Don't— "

"I am the only one here who knows where the sealskins are," Ashlyn said, not tearing her gaze from Brennan. "If you all don't shut up and listen to me, I'll call this whole plan off and the Kellehers can stay Bound forever."

My horrified intake of breath was matched by three others.

"You wouldn't," Brennan said, but Ashlyn stepped deliberately forward. Nose to nose, she stared my brother down.

"Get in your truck, Brennan. Drive to your parents' house and pick them up, then pick up Declan. Wait for us at The Golden Fish."

Brennan stared at her for a long, agonizing moment, then wheeled and stalked to the pick-up. Leisel cast a murderous glance at Ashlyn and went after him. The slamming doors were loud enough to make me wince.

When the truck disappeared around a corner, Ashlyn waved us after her. We headed back to the house.

"Sorry about that," I said to Paul.

"Tasers and fists," he muttered, but flashed me a smile. "Don't worry, you're worth it."

Warmth flooded me, even with the Haze, and I paused. Paul paused too, reaching for my hand.

"You two coming?" Ashlyn called back, and before I knew it, I'd trotted past Paul like he didn't exist. With an effort I stopped, pain digging into my skull, but Paul caught up to Ashlyn and put her between us. We walked up the steps.

"So where are the sealskins?" Paul asked Ashlyn. His expression held no reaction to my zombie-like obedience, but inwardly I cringed.

"The fireplace." Ashlyn led us inside and down the twisty hall to the den. "There's a safe built in the bricks."

At the entrance to the den, I looked around. I'd spent probably thousands of hours here when Ashlyn and I were younger, watching movies, doing homework. For a while I'd even had an easel set up in one of the corners. I'd torn up the walls and couch during my rampage, but had never thought to do more than check up the chimney to make sure it was empty.

Ashlyn walked over to the fireplace, which boasted one of those fake woodpiles with flames really fueled by gas. Raised to knee level by two feet of bricks, it had kept us warm on winter sleepovers all through my childhood.

"There's a safe in there?" The brick base looked pretty solid to me.

"Yup. You press three of the bricks in a certain order. He showed me." Ashlyn knelt next to the left side and put a finger on the bottom-most brick by the wall. She counted over one brick, then up two. "It starts with this one." She pressed. Nothing visible happened, but she counted over two bricks and pressed again. Then she pressed the one to the left.

An electronic beep sounded in the quiet, and we all waited anxiously.

And waited.

After fifteen seconds, Ashlyn frowned and tried again. Same result.

"What's supposed to happen?" Paul asked.

"The magnetic lock is supposed to disengage, and the door should swing open." She and Paul pried at the bricks, to no avail. I gripped my stun gun, uneasiness building in my throat. Ashlyn entered the code a third time, but the result was the same.

Muttering a curse, Ashlyn sat back on her heels.

"That paranoid bastard," she said, and I understood what had happened. *Oh, no.* Panic fluttered in my throat like a trapped seagull.

"What?" Paul said.

Ashlyn only slammed a fist onto the unhelpful brick, so I answered for her.

"Her dad changed the code."

Chapter 34

Paul jumped to his feet. "My car's a block away. I brought a sledgehammer."

"Wait." Ashlyn got up too. "There's one in the garage. Cass tore up half my house with it." She paused. "Though on second thought, my dad installed a lock on the tool cabinet."

Paul pulled a small bundle from his pocket. "I brought lock picks."

"Well aren't you handy." They set off in the direction of the garage.

Should I follow? I felt … frozen. Now that I knew where the sealskins were, I couldn't leave them. But maybe Ashlyn wanted me with her …

"What should I do?" I asked. Paul was in the hall already, but Ashlyn paused at the entrance of the den. She waved at the couch.

"Sit down and count to a hundred. We'll be back by then."

She left, and I sank down onto the leather couch. I wasn't going to count—such a dumb order—but it hurt not to. I fought the Haze for a couple seconds, then wondered why I was bothering.

"One," I said softly to no one.

Ashlyn and Paul returned at sixty-seven. Wearing safety glasses, Paul carried my friend the sledgehammer, Ashlyn a crowbar. Without fanfare, Paul raised the sledgehammer over his shoulder and brought it down with a mighty crash. I jumped at the noise.

So did Ashlyn. "Cass, go to the bottom of the stairs and keep a lookout. Shout if you hear anyone move upstairs."

I yearned with every inch of myself to stay and watch the brick shatter and crumble, but my feet took me out to the hallway, where I gazed obediently up the stairwell. Mr. Murphy's presence seemed to fill the darkness upstairs, as if he were a slumbering dragon.

Straining to hear movement, I flinched with every crash from the den. Where would we go, if the dragon woke? There'd be no escape this time.

After an agonized eternity, I finally heard Paul's voice.

"Got it!" Then a screech of tearing metal.

My heart pounded, but my feet wouldn't move.

"Ashlyn?" I said, my voice strangled.

"Oh. Come here, Cass."

I dashed down the hall. The fireplace was rubble, shards of brick and mortar, and in the middle a metal box yawned open. Holding her crowbar, Ashlyn wiped damp copper hair from her forehead while Paul knelt next to a large black duffel that he'd apparently just extracted from the chewed-up safe. He unzipped the top as I dove down next to him.

I plunged my hands into the bag. As soon as I touched fur, the fog of obedience lifted. I clutched my sealskin, all silver-gray and spotted with white, to my chest. *Mine.* The Haze tore apart, the cobwebs dissolving.

Water. I had to get to the water. I nearly tripped on the thick carpet in my haste to flee, but as I passed the couch a scrap of my brain remembered that I couldn't leave yet. Wrenching myself to the side, I hurled myself onto the cushions. Curled around my sealskin, I pressed my forehead into the cool leather and sucked in deep gasping breaths. *It's okay,* I told myself. *You're free. It's over. You're okay.* There was no need to run. I repeated that to myself and fought my instincts for control. I had to finish this.

Seconds or minutes or hours later, I raised my head. Passive, blank Cassandra was gone; the jagged edges of my fear and fury gouged deep. I welcomed them. Less welcome was Ashlyn's presence, which once more felt like an acid bath. Ow. She and Paul stood by the wrecked fireplace, watching me. The duffel bag sat at Ashlyn's feet.

She'd owned me. She still owned my family. I wanted to kill her. The urge knocked me breathless, and my hands clenched into claws. I wanted to tear out her eyes and fill her lungs with water for what she'd done. From my throat came a low growl.

Paul put himself between us.

"You're feeling the after-effect of the Bond," he said carefully. "Ashlyn's helping you, remember?" His expression was so odd, like he wasn't sure he knew me anymore. Like I might be dangerous. Suddenly I remembered that his selkie family *had* tried to kill him. I had to get a grip.

But it was hard to focus in the rush of rage, and the scrabbling animalistic fear screaming at me to flee. I wanted to do something to show Paul I was the same girl from yesterday, that today hadn't changed me, but the pain from Ashlyn's presence, noxious and jarring, made me cringe. Shame hit too, because of how I was acting, and because he'd seen me jump to answer Ashlyn's orders, seen me look to her for approval. I burned, hot tears pressing against my eyes, and shook with the effort it took not to give in to them.

"I'm okay," I said hoarsely, but didn't move. If I got up right now, I wasn't sure whether I'd run down the hallway to the glass doors leading to the deck—and from there, a half-mile sprint to the sea—or leap at Ashlyn like a wild animal.

"We need to get out of here," Ashlyn said, peeking around Paul. "Brennan texted; he's got your parents. They're on their way to pick up Declan." She slipped her phone back into her jeans pocket and held up her crowbar. "Am I going to need this to defend myself, Cass?"

Before I could help it, I growled again. Both of them tensed, staring at me.

"I just need a few minutes," I said.

"We can't stay here," Ashlyn insisted. "Get up, Cass."

"Don't tell me what to do," I muttered. I'd never follow an order of hers again.

Paul studied me inscrutably before whispering something in Ashlyn's ear. She raised a brow, then shrugged.

"Cass," she said. "I order you to stay on the couch."

Reflexive anger made me snarl. "I know you're reverse-psychologizing me," I said, but as dumb as it was, it worked: my arms and legs unlocked, and I stood. "Give me those sealskins."

Paul picked up the duffel bag and walked towards me, but halfway across the room he stopped, eyes widening at something over my shoulder. Ashlyn gasped, and I realized with horror that the sick pain I felt at her nearness came from behind as well. I turned.

Mr. Murphy loomed in the doorway, a gun in his hand.

"You betrayed me," he said, and for a crazy moment I thought he was talking to me—after all, that was where the gun was pointed. But when I tore my gaze from its deadly black menace, he was looking at Ashlyn.

"Put the gun down, Dad." Her voice quavered. "You don't want to do this."

He blinked, eyelids drooping, then fought the effect of the sleeping pills with a shudder. His gun hand didn't waver.

"You drugged me. To free them. Why, Ashlyn?"

"Why?" She stared at him incredulously. "Because you're psychotic, and I can't sit by while you hold people hostage! Do you get how messed up that is?"

His mouth dropped open in outrage.

"It's our *heritage*." He raised a hand, cutting off her protest, and pointed at Paul. "Whoever you are, give me those sealskins. Ashlyn, go upstairs to your room. I'll deal with you later."

"Go to my *room*?" Ashlyn screeched. "Do you even hear yourself? I'm in the middle of trying to stop a human rights violation, and you want me to toddle up to my *room*?"

As she ranted, I slipped my hand into my pocket underneath my sweater, where I'd shoved the stun gun earlier. But I didn't dare move to use it, not with the pistol's black eye pointed with deadly precision at the sealskin I clutched to my chest.

Then I realized something. The gun Mr. Murphy held was the same one from the secret nook in the china cabinet.

The one I'd emptied a week ago.

Moving on instinct, I dropped my sealskin and sprang forward, stun gun thrust out before me.

Light flashed before my face, and a shot cracked the night in two.

Chapter 35

Something hissed by my right ear, and I heard a crash. Colliding with Mr. Murphy, I pressed the stun gun's trigger, but even fighting sleeping pills he was too fast. He wrenched himself to the side, and the stun gun's energy crackled into empty air. Before I could try again his fist connected with my stomach. Pain exploded in my midsection, and I collapsed to the carpet.

"Cassandra!" Paul tossed the sealskins to Ashlyn and charged forward, but Mr. Murphy aimed the pistol at Paul, forcing him to freeze.

Gasping for breath, I scrabbled for my stun gun, but Mr. Murphy kicked it away. Seizing me by my hair, he dragged me up from the floor.

"Now," he snarled, "let's try this again." The cold metal of the gun bit hard into my temple, and my heart hammered. Belatedly, I realized that of course he would have checked and reloaded the hidden pistol sometime in the last week. "Ashlyn, bring those to me, or— "

The doorbell sounded, making everyone flinch. If Mr.

Murphy's trigger finger was as jumpy as mine had been I'd have died right there, but he only held my hair tighter.

"Douglas!" It was Declan's voice outside. He pounded on the door. "Wake up and get out here!"

Mr. Murphy cursed.

"Go home, Declan," he yelled. "That's an order."

"Screw your orders." Declan's roar was slurred, as if he were drunk. He continued to beat against the front door. "Keep your end of the bargain, or I'll— "

"I *did* keep my end of the bargain! It's your damned siblings who didn't keep theirs. Go home or I'll burn their sealskins."

The pounding stopped. Then, in the foyer, glass shattered. One of the tall decorative panels flanking the door, I guessed. An alarm began to sound.

Mr. Murphy cursed again, and the cold metal of the gun left my head. He still held my hair, but this distraction was the best chance I was going to get. Twisting in his grasp, I bit down as hard as I could on his wrist.

He yelled in pain and knocked me away from him. Everyone was shouting now; I scrambled up just in time for Paul and Ashlyn to shove me out of the room with them. We ran for the doors to the back deck.

When we reached them, though, the handle wouldn't turn.

"It's deadbolted," Ashlyn shrieked. "My keys are in my purse— "

A shot whistled by us, shattering a glass bowl on the counter. I whirled to see Mr. Murphy aim again, but then he was tackled by a tall blur. Declan.

Paul, who'd wound up carrying all the sealskins, pushed Ashlyn and me down the hallway. To one side was the door to the basement; recalling the windows I'd smashed though last time to escape, I grabbed for the knob. It opened, thank the holy high seas, and I shoved Paul through it.

"Wait," Ashlyn said, but another gunshot made her leap downstairs with us. I closed the door and flicked the lock, then ran down and across the box-strewn basement. Paul followed on my heels.

"Smash the windows with your crowbar," I shouted at Ashlyn, but she stopped halfway across the room. When I fetched up underneath the windows, I saw why.

Mr. Murphy had bolted a metal grate across each pane of glass.

Oh, no. Panic iced my spine. We were trapped.

Crashes and shouting from upstairs made us all jump. "Hide," Paul said, and pushed me behind a pile of boxes. Throwing the duffel bag down, he pulled his stun gun out. "Maybe we can find some tools."

A yelp of pain from above launched my heart into my throat. My brother was up there, and I had to help him. "Keep these safe," I told Paul. Leaving him to guard the sealskins, I grabbed the stun gun and ran for the bottom of the stairs. Just as I reached the bottom step, an anguished cry from somewhere in the house was cut off by another gunshot.

I froze. Above us, silence reigned. The fight seemed to be over … but who had won?

"Declan?" I called, ears straining for any sound.

Approaching footsteps made me start up the stairs, but when an itchy pain stole over my skin, horrified realization dawned: Mr. Murphy. Remembering the truncated cry, I couldn't stop a whimper. What had he done to my brother?

I backed away from the stairs as Mr. Murphy tried the door. It was locked, but I knew the flimsy handle wouldn't hold. My shoulders bumped into a refrigerator, the spare used for overflow drinks and frozen meals. I ducked behind it just as the basement door crashed open.

"Cassandra," Mr. Murphy growled. "I want those sealskins." He waited, then came slowly down the steps. It sounded like he was limping. "I know you're down here, you little bitch. You won't escape this time."

I crouched behind the fridge, wincing with every creak of the stairs and trying not to panic. What was I going to do, hope he'd walk past me so I could leap at him again? He was careful, and smart, and he'd check behind the refrigerator before going further into the basement. Taser versus gun was like paper against fire.

But I had no choice, and I gripped my stun gun, listening to Mr. Murphy's footsteps and waiting until the last possible moment. Just when I was about to run out of time, Paul stood up across the room.

"Hey," he shouted, waving his arms. I couldn't see Mr. Murphy, but I heard the scrape of his shoe as he pivoted away from my hiding spot. Paul caught my eye and nodded.

I leapt out from behind the fridge.

This time when I pulled the stun gun's trigger, it connected solidly with Mr. Murphy's torso. He let out a yell of pain, but I dodged his flailing arms and clung to him like a barnacle, shooting electricity into his side.

Finally he slumped unconscious to the ground, and I scrambled away.

Paul and Ashlyn raced over.

"Are you okay?" Paul said. I nodded, and he turned to Ashlyn. "We need rope, or zip ties or something."

Ashlyn, staring numbly at her father's crumpled form, didn't answer. My stalled brain stuttered to life, and I dashed for the stairs. *Declan*. My feet took the steps so fast I stumbled and barked my shin, but I kept going. The hallway was dark and filled with awful quiet.

"Declan!" I called, but there was no response.

The house looked like someone had gone on a smaller-scale version of my own rampage: chairs were toppled, one with its leg broken as it lay on its side in the dining room. A painting lay on the floor, its frame splintered. A tall decorative vase was smashed, shards leading into the main foyer.

I followed the carnage into the front sitting room, and a scream caught in my throat. My older brother lay on his back, in a pool of throw pillows and blood. His face was covered in red from a gash on his temple.

With a wordless cry, I threw myself down and grabbed his shoulder. "Wake up. Declan, please wake up. We beat him. It's over. Please, please wake up." But my brother lay still.

Tears filled my eyes, ruining my vision; I seized Declan's wrist and searched frantically for a pulse, but couldn't feel one. No. No, no, *no*. We'd finally won—my brother had his freedom at long last. He couldn't be ... Horror built in my throat, and I fell backwards with a sob.

"Cassandra?" I heard. Paul's voice, but I was crying too hard to answer. I felt Ashlyn's stinging presence approach, and raised my head as she appeared in the doorway with Paul.

"We've got my dad tied up downstairs," Ashlyn said. "Are you—" she stopped when she saw Declan's motionless form.

"He's ..." My voice broke. I couldn't say it.

Paul knelt by Declan's side and gripped his wrist. Miserably, I waited for him to tell me what I already knew.

"There's a pulse," Paul said, and met my startled gaze. "Very faint."

"He's alive?" Hope seized me like a vise as I grabbed my brother's other hand. I couldn't feel anything, but after I swiped the liquid from my eyes I could see Declan's chest rise fractionally. Joy stabbed at me, quickly eroded by fear: although Declan wasn't past death's door, he was clearly at the threshold.

Paul muttered about stopping the bleeding—there was a nasty shard of porcelain in Declan's side, among other injuries—but I turned to Ashlyn, still clutching the duffel bag in the doorway.

"Give me his sealskin," I told her.

Paul paused, then shook his head.

"Even if he weren't too injured to merge, he can't while he's unconscious."

"Give me his sealskin!"

Ashlyn stumbled over.

"I don't know which one it is." But she dropped to her knees next to me and opened the bag. "Here's yours, and—"

"It'll be the smallest one," I said, and she came up with a tiny, pale thing that would barely cover a raccoon. "That's it." Mine had been that size when I'd first gotten it back two-and-a-half years ago. It seemed so fragile.

"Cut his shirt off," I told Paul. I wasn't sure what I was doing, but I knew that if anything could help Declan, it would be his sealskin.

Paul didn't question me; he slipped a switchblade from a pocket and sawed the front of Declan's sweater open. Taking the small, pale bundle from Ashlyn, I placed the soft skin on Declan's bare chest and pressed it to him with both hands. We waited, the acrid scent of gunshot residue mixing nauseatingly with blood.

Declan's chest rose once under my palms, then shuddered down. I stared, willing it to rise again, but it didn't.

A choked cry clogged my throat. The sight of Declan standing between me and Mr. Murphy at the Lost Lighthouse rose up, along with every other memory I had of him: teaching me to make grilled cheese when I was twelve, taking Brennan and me fishing every weekend of freshman year, the look in his eyes when he'd told me what I really was. All those moments and a thousand more passed though me in half a heartbeat's span before, desperately trying to remember how CPR worked, I shoved sharply down on the sealskin covering Declan's chest.

With a violent shudder and a gasp of breath, my brother opened his eyes.

Chapter 36

An hour later, I stood in the shadow of The Golden Fish and watched Declan *change* for the first time. The water roiled, white in the darkness, and I lost sight of him. The harbor surface calmed.

"It's over." Knee-deep in water next to me, Brennan hugged his sealskin against his chest. The shorefront parking lot behind us was bathed in orange from the old-timey-looking but electric lanterns that decorated Granite Harbor's downtown. Fifty yards to the south, sailboats peeked over the marina's fence, and next to the restaurant a lone pier stretched over the water; diners could reserve a slip during dinner hours, so they barely had to disembark from their yachts to enjoy a five-star meal. The slips were empty now, of course.

Our parents had seized their sealskins and dived off the pier as soon as the duffel bag came out, but Brennan had been able to hold off long enough to help carry Declan, bleeding but insistent, into the water.

We hadn't been entirely sure he'd make the *change* successfully, but after a few moments, his head popped up a dozen yards out. In seal form Declan was painfully thin, but I remembered Brennan—and me too, probably—looking like that when we first got our sealskins back. He'd heal.

My heart too full for speech, I reached for Brennan's hand. My family was finally, unbelievably, free. The weeks and months and years of worry still clung to my shoulders, but the worst slid away like layers of mud.

Everything would be alright now.

Far out in the harbor beyond Declan, two domes broke the moonlit surface of the ocean. Our parents. I couldn't wait to get to know them as they really were. Couldn't wait to be a real family.

Brennan squeezed my fingers. "We'd better say our goodbyes." Turning, he walked over to Paul's car, where Ashlyn, Paul and Leisel stood. Leisel shivered in her hooded parka; Paul stared at the spot where Declan had disappeared with a satisfied expression, as if he'd scrubbed some of the black marks from his conscience today. Wrapped in her designer coat and teal gloves, Ashlyn wore the ice princess expression, remote and haughty, that she'd perfected over the last two years.

Brennan gave Ashlyn a wide berth, not even looking at her. When we'd filled him in on our close call he'd been guilt-stricken, saying he should have been at the house, not me. And he blamed Ashlyn for the last-minute switch. It wasn't fair, but newly freed, he wasn't thinking in terms of fair.

Brennan smiled at Leisel, then shook hands with Paul as I waded from the water. They joked about the punches, Brennan offering to let Paul get in a shot before we left. I listened with half an ear and watched Ashlyn.

Her ice princess mask didn't budge, but suddenly she wheeled and walked to her car, parked further up the lot. Declan had gone ballistic when she'd tried to help bandage his side, so she'd kept her distance afterward, even driving over separately.

I couldn't stand being near her either now, but it wasn't her fault, and I could tell my brothers' attitudes—and mine—hurt her. Gritting my teeth against the familiar jellyfish-bath sensation, I jogged over.

"Sorry," I said. "Brennan just—"

"Hates me." Ashlyn shrugged carelessly, but her voice was bitter. "You both hate me. I get it. You don't have to explain."

"I don't hate you."

"Yes, you do."

I did, sort of, but it was the instinctive, animalistic fight-or-flight reaction her ex-Binder presence spurred. Underneath, I knew she'd sacrificed a lot for us today. Right now all I felt was numb, but once it sank in that I'd finally regained my family, I knew I'd feel guilty that she'd lost hers.

"Not totally."

"Whatever." The momentary crack in her mask disappeared. But underneath, I knew she was still shattered.

"What are you going to do?" She couldn't go home.

Ashlyn wrinkled her nose. "Buy new flats, I guess. You've ruined those." She meant the waterlogged shoes I'd borrowed earlier; I'd forgotten to take them off before helping Declan into the shallows. "I don't suppose you intend to reimburse me for them."

"Ashlyn, be serious."

"I am serious. They were expensive."

"Will you stop it?" But Ashlyn only tossed her hair.

"Cass, you almost ready?" Brennan called. He stood at the end of the pier with Leisel. Paul waited by his car, but I couldn't let Ashlyn go without thanking her, no matter how hard she was making it to do so.

When I turned back to her, Ashlyn's expression hardened. "You want to know what I'm going to do? I'm going to try and figure out how to tell my sister that her husband abandoned her and their daughter without even a backwards glance." Her lip curled. "Who does that?"

My gratitude evaporated.

"Can you blame him? Your father nearly killed us all tonight."

She looked out to sea. "Thanks for reminding me. I'd nearly forgotten."

Why was she making this impossible? Our starfish friendship would never grow back its limbs, but when it counted, she'd been there for me. I tried one last time. "Ashlyn, I—"

"Go away, Cassandra." Turning, Ashlyn got into her car and shut the door. She took out her phone, then started tapping. I stared incredulously. What, was her status in dire need of updating?

A splash caught my attention—on the pier, Leisel stood

alone. Brennan must have jumped in. I needed to wrap this up, but Ashlyn was still pointedly ignoring me.

Fine.

I jogged back to Paul. Behind him, inside the restaurant's lobby, I could see that gaudy hollow trout shining in the glow of the emergency lights. For the last two years, the statue had seemed to mock me. Not tonight. Now, it was Clamchops once more, my friend from childhood.

"She's just processing," Paul said as I reached him. "Her father's actions are a lot to deal with."

"I know. But does she have to be such a …" I cut myself off, frustrated and worried. "You can give her a place to stay, right?"

"Yeah. She's almost eighteen. We'll figure out something."

And then it was time for goodbye. I tried to memorize Paul's face: the cut of his cheekbones, the set of his jaw, the somber look in his gray eyes. I wished again to paint him—but I couldn't take a painting with me, any more than I could take the real thing.

"Here." Paul passed me a slip of paper. "I set up an email account for us. I don't know if you'll ever get a chance to check it, but I'll email you the location of the house we're buying in Ireland, as soon as it's settled. If you and your family are ever in the area, it should be a safe haul-out spot. Like the one in Canada."

He'd shown me pictures of the Canadian shoreline this morning, and given me landmarks to navigate by. I didn't think I'd be able to find the SRL's house there any more than I would some house in Ireland, but I memorized the email address and password anyway.

Returning the paper, I kept Paul's hand and gathered my breath. I couldn't believe I'd never see him again. There was so much I needed to say, but Paul shook his head before I could get out a word.

"Don't."

"Don't what?"

"Don't waste another second not kissing me goodbye," he said, and pulled me into his arms.

It was a kiss made up of a thousand moments, from that first dance in Boston to The Golden Fish's coat closet to last night on the couch. A kiss built from suspicion and trust, worry and comfort, secrets kept and told. A kiss that made the stars sing and my heart blaze with light.

It was a kiss almost good enough to stay for.

Then Paul released me, and it was over. I tasted salt on my lips, and wiped my eyes before retrieving my sealskin from the car.

Before I turned to the pier I searched Paul's silver gaze, hoping he could read in mine all the things I couldn't say. His mouth curved, ever so slightly, so maybe he could.

Paul had braved tasers, fists and bullets for me, and it hurt to walk away. Somehow, I did.

At the end of the pier, legs dangling off the edge, Leisel stared at the water. I sat down next to her and slipped off Ashlyn's shoes.

"Remember when you threatened to crush me like a bug?" she asked, dark eyes shining with tears and laughter.

Throat tight, I looped my free arm in hers.

"Thank you," I managed to say.

Leisel gave me a lopsided smile.

"Be safe out there."

Nodding, I withdrew my arm and turned my attention to the water two feet beneath my toes.

It was time.

A dream, I thought. This felt like a dream, with the cool breeze and wide open night. Was my family really out there in the ocean, free after all these years?

Cradling my sealskin, I scooted forward and dropped into the water. The sea rushed up to claim me. Once submerged, I pulled off the rest of my clothes, wrapped my sealskin about me, and *changed.* Eleven seconds of agony hit, but I welcomed them.

The pain cleared. Now in seal form, I found Brennan waiting, and together we surfaced. Still perched on the pier's edge, Leisel waved. Ashlyn had come out to see us off after all, and she stared at us with a shell-shocked frown. By the corner post, Paul found my gaze.

Brennan ducked under the ocean's surface, diving deep, then coming back up. The water shifted, and … Oh no, he was going to—

Saltwater drenched everyone as he exploded into the air and splashed down. I rolled my eyes, and heard Leisel laugh.

Paul smiled as he wiped the spray from his face. Heart full and aching, I raised a flipper in farewell. He inclined his head.

I dove.

Meeting my brother in the depths, I cocked my head.

Ready?

Ready, Brennan replied.

We set out after our family, the moonlit horizon, and freedom.

Thanks for reading!

If you want more people to discover the awesomeness of *Wavecrossed*, review it online! It makes a huge difference to writers like me, and as a bonus, if you email me with a link to your review, I'll send you cute pictures of my kitten. See? Now you're interested :) My email's on my website: www.andreacolt.com. Trust me, he's worth it.

Another reason to review: it'll get me to write the sequel, *Seaswept*, faster!

In *Seaswept*, Cassandra and Brennan finally have what they always wanted: freedom, their family, and the ocean. Unfortunately, fitting into a selkie clan isn't as easy as they'd thought. Hello, culture shock. When a reunion with their landlocked friends coincides with a dangerous power struggle at sea, Cassandra is forced to decide where, and with whom, she really belongs.

Sign up at www.andreacolt.com to be emailed when *Seaswept* and other new books are released!

Acknowledgements

This book has been a part of my life for a long time, and a lot of people had a hand in shaping it. Or, as it were, a paw: I dedicated the book to my late feline friend Winston, a gorgeous, vocal black-and-white kitty with green eyes who loved to sit on the arm of my writing chair. He supervised this book through all its drafts, and meowed encouragement the whole way. It was tough finishing up without him. Love you, buddy!

Vicki Wenderlich, artist and editor extraordinaire, had better get used to being featured in my acknowledgments pages, because she's read and torn apart everything I've ever written, and I'm so grateful. She also created the cover, which I want to hang on my wall. For more on her, visit her website: www.vickiwenderlich.com

Thanks to Christine Wells, for declaring each of the three completely different versions of this book excellent. I swear I'll print out all three for you soon.

Thanks to Caroline Richmond, for speedily offering feedback whenever I begged, and Robin Talley, whose critique in part made me decide to rewrite the entire book from scratch (again). Thanks also to Ray Wenderlich and Lindsay Smith, whose comments and advice were invaluable in shaping Cassandra's story.

I'd never survive without my writer friends who've cheered me on and kept me sane, so thanks to the above ladies and also Jessica Spotswood and Miranda Kenneally, and all the DC MafYA members. Your encouragement means so much.

Thanks to Jessica Sperlongano for the copyediting help!

A cheesy thank you to my mother, for being my favorite mother.

And, finally, thank you to all my readers. I'm still shocked to realize I have fans, so an ocean-sized thank you to everyone who has reviewed, tweeted or otherwise talked up my book(s). Every time you do, I feel like I'm a selkie getting her sealskin back.

About the Author

Andrea Colt grew up reading fantasy novels, majored in mechanical engineering, then decided that words were way more fun to tinker with than gears. She lives in northern Virginia with her husband and feline muses. Don't invite her over, or she'll eat all your cheese :)

Visit www.andreacolt.com to get to know her better.

Excerpt:

Torched, by Andrea Colt

Cheerleader Rose Whitfield's senior year goes up in smoke when she's framed for arson. Believing the culprit to be her neighbor Paxton, with whom she's been feuding since middle school, she sets out to clear her name, get her life back and take Paxton down hard — not necessarily in that order.

Chapter 1

Usually you feel flames before they burn you. You smell them: the post-Homecoming bonfire in the woods, the love letters in a trash can, the cookies forgotten in the oven (which is also what grounded for two weeks smells like, by the way).

The only scents tickling my nose on Friday morning, however, were coffee and wind. I set my latte back into its cup-holder, then swerved into Alina's ludicrously expensive driveway. It wasn't literally paved with money, but considering the textured Italian marble under my tires, moolah-blocks might have been cheaper. I gunned the engine to get up the hill, then slammed on the brakes when I reached the stone lion snarling from the corner of the mansion. Almost before the wheels even stopped I was texting Alina.

Vroom vroom. I punched send, abandoned my phone to the center console, and ran through a cheer routine — well, as much as I could without actually getting out of my seat — while I waited. The Homecoming game was a scant week away, and as head cheerleader, it was on my bared shoulders if our new choreography fell flatter than a punctured football.

I punched the air, pretending it was the face of the drive-thru barista who'd given me the stink-eye along with my *grande* this morning. It was the cheerleading uniform, obviously, because usually she rewarded my smile with professional-grade apathy.

She must be one of *those* people. You know, the ones who buy into all the stereotypes about cheerleaders: we're mean, vapid bottle blondes who carve up the lower rungs of the high school social ladder with our stilettos to distract ourselves from our hollow centers. We care about the girl in the mirror first, money second, and our star-quarterback boyfriend third.

I've heard it all, and I'm sure there are cheerleaders who feed that image. I've tangled with a couple myself, at competitions. But you know what? I'm not that girl. First of all, no one wears stilettos at my school unless she wants to break her idiot neck on the cobblestone courtyard, and my strawberry-blonde hair is completely natural. Well, except for a tiny bit of highlighting, but in California that totally counts.

Second, if you check out the GPA rankings, the name at the top belongs to yours truly: Rose Whitfield. Yup, if all goes well, this May the Petalina Panthers will crown a cheerleader valedictorian. Stick *that* in your Never Thought I'd See The Day file.

And third, I wouldn't date the quarterback if you paid me.

No, my boyfriend co-captains the soccer team. And the debate team. Yeah, he's an overachiever, but so am I. We were made for each other.

I finished mouthing my cheer as Alina ran through the

mansion's massive double doors. She tossed her bag into the back of my convertible, then threw herself into the passenger seat.

"Thank the freaking pixies you're here, Rose," she said. "Seven A.M. and my parents are already fighting like caged monkeys." She slumped against the leather headrest.

"Orangutans or gorillas?" I studied what I could see of my best friend's face. Her designer sunglasses were hot enough to make all other shades melt from envy, but their oversized proportions weren't helping me figure out how upset Alina was.

"Whatever kind throw shit at each other." She sounded tired. Battered. I tensed.

"Like vases-and-dishes shit, or metaphorical?" I tried not to sound too worried, but Alina slid her sunglasses down to glare at me.

"Relax, social worker. Mom just thinks dad shagged his secretary." She reached for her coffee, wedged as always with two sugar packets in the cup-holder. The glimpse of her eyes told me today hadn't been a crying day, at least, and she sounded better already. Relieved, I grabbed my coffee again too.

"Ouch. Did he?"

"Hope not. So cliché, you know?" Alina tore the tops off her packets and dumped the sugar in her coffee. "He'll probably crash on the boat this weekend, give mom some space to cool down. Which means she's going to want me to hang out with her tonight." She groaned theatrically as I put the car in gear.

"You want me to launch Operation Moral Support?" Alina's mom usually didn't sob around company, so even my almost-family presence would help. Besides, her strawberry margaritas were beyond tasty, and she didn't bother pretending to care that we were only seventeen.

"Don't you and Ryan have a date?" Alina said.

"He'd understand." Coffee in one hand, I eased the car around the fountain in the driveway loop. Ryan Appleton, aforementioned boyfriend, was the other half of my soul. We'd met over the summer, at Alina's family's Fourth of July party, and it was swoon at first sight for me. Ryan is tall, lean and deliciously broody when he's not flashing his high-voltage smile. And when he noticed me … well, let's just say I clean up nice too: Ryan tripped over a chair and spilled Coke all over his twelve-year-old sister. I found towels, helped Ryan's sister raid Alina's closet for a clean skirt, and wound up kissing Ryan by the time the fireworks faded.

Like I said. Made for each other.

Alina grinned. "Because your love is like an oak tree, right?"

I sighed. "I never should have shown you that poem." But I couldn't hide my smile. Ryan had written the sonnet to celebrate our three-month anniversary.

"It grows in dirt!" Alina crowed.

"It has deep roots," I corrected, trying for a scowl and failing. The poem *was* kind of ridiculous, but totally sweet nonetheless. "You want me to come over or not? I can always walk over to see Ryan after your mom goes to bed." How fabulous was it that his family had moved next door to Alina? So convenient.

"Nah, go be all blissy-kissy," Alina said as I turned out of her driveway. "I'll make my mom take me shopping. Retail therapy always puts her in a forgiving mood. Plus, I need new slouchy boots.

My grey ones have a scratch." She shivered. "Little cold for top-down, isn't it?"

"No point in having a convertible if you're not going to flaunt it, right?" I grinned. The car was second-hand, but well-maintained and a powder blue that matched my eyes. I loved it more than Alina loved slouchy boots, and that was saying something. I'd even named it.

"That's my girl." Alina drummed her teal manicured nails on the armrest. "We're driving the Jag next week, though. Yearbook is going to go photo-crazy."

"My Cloudmonster isn't good enough for Spirit Week?" I pouted, but I wasn't really mad. Whenever delusions of grandeur swamped my head, Alina and her racks of designer clothes, her costs-more-than-some-houses car and her three-figure weekly allowance knocked me back to earth. I ought to be jealous, but Alina thought it was as ludicrous as I did when her parents took private jets to Maui for the weekend.

Alina shivered again. "Why is it so cold this morning?" She took off her sunglasses, and I saw she'd matched her eyeliner to her nail polish. No mascara, though—she didn't need it. She'd inherited her mom's long, thick lashes, along with Hispanic genes that gave Alina an effortless year-round tan I'd never match no matter how I tried.

"It'll heat up by noon," I said. "Besides, why are *you* complaining? I'm the one in a skirt."

"Yeah, about that." Alina eyed me askance. "You do remember Homecoming isn't until *next* Friday, right?"

"We're giving a demo for the middle school squad during lunch. No time to change."

Behind us, a car horn blared. I recognized the tone, and since we hadn't made the turn from Alina's street onto the main road yet, I slammed on the brakes. Alina yelled a curse as coffee slopped onto her jeans, but I was already twisting in my seat and grinning at the figure that hopped out of the SUV now idling behind us.

"Morning, ladies," Ryan called as he jogged over. He wore an olive long-sleeve tee and smelled like French toast as he leaned on the top of my door. He'd probably made his sister breakfast; how adorable was that? "I wanted to kiss you hello, since I won't be seeing you in the parking lot before school." Ryan arched a brow. "Seems someone siphoned the gas out of Paxton's car last night, so I have to go pick him up."

"Aw, do you have to?" Paxton Callaway was my neighbor, and Ryan's friend from summer camp a couple years ago. I was not pleased about either of these facts, and hadn't known about the latter when I met Ryan. Paxton and I had been enemies ever since he threw cranberry juice all over me in eighth grade. I'd responded to his senseless violence by planting gum on his bus seat. Relations had only grown chillier with time.

"I thought you guys promised to play nice." Ryan's mouth was smiley, but his voice held a serious note.

I widened my eyes.

"What makes you think *I* had anything to do with this ghastly crime?"

Okay, so Paxton and I had been forced to bury the hatchet when Ryan asked us to for his sake, but we hadn't shoveled too much dirt on top. I'd thought our unwritten agreement drew the line just after verbal insults thinly disguised as humor, but the rotting egg in my gym bag last week certainly hadn't put itself there.

Ryan was trying to keep his serious face, but finally he grinned and kissed me. "You are way too cute in that uniform for me to yell at you."

Oh, his voice got all rumbly when he said that. I sighed against his lips.

"Thanks a lot, Rose," Alina said next to me. "Look at my damn jeans." I could hear rustling, as though she were blotting Breakfast Blend with a napkin. I probably shouldn't have stomped on the brakes so hard.

"Sorry," I said, looking up into Ryan's green, green eyes. "Love made me do it."

"I'm going to chop down your freaking love-oak and mulch it," Alina muttered.

Ryan's gaze cut to Alina, then back to me. Oh, crap. He was mad now, and I knew why. The air felt stuck in my lungs. Ryan straightened up from the door.

"You showed her my letter?" It wasn't really a question. He started to say something more, then shut his mouth and walked away. I tore off my seat belt and scrambled from the car.

"Ryan, wait." Halfway back to his SUV, he turned as I caught up. "It was really sweet. I couldn't help but tell her." Ryan *hated* the whole girls-gab-about-everything concept the rest of the world took for granted. I wanted to shout how awesome he was from the roof of the school, but he liked to keep things private. Not that we didn't engage in our share of PDA, but showing his letter to Alina? Not on the Allowed list.

"I didn't write it for her. I wrote it for you." Ryan shoved his hands in his pockets. "We've talked about this, Rose."

We had, several times, though the verb I'd have used was "fought." I tended to be an open book to my friends, but Ryan had Boundaries. Learning them, and sticking to them, sometimes felt like walking around a maze of prickly-bush hedges. Blindfolded.

"She's my best friend," I said. And she'd promised on her beloved pug Piper's life never to let on that I'd shown her that damn poem. "I don't understand why the poem has to be a secret. You meant it, right?"

"That's not the point, Rose." Behind Ryan, his little sister rapped on the windshield. "I have to go. We're gonna be late already." He turned away without a goodbye kiss. I walked quickly back to Cloudmonster and hid my hurt as the SUV roared past.

"Is he mad?" Alina asked as I jerked my car into drive.

"No, he's buying me flowers," I snapped. "I think the note will read, 'Your friends suck, and so do you. Hate, Ryan.'"

"It slipped. I didn't mean to."

Too furious to respond, I drove in silence. I shouldn't have shown Alina the letter. Why couldn't I just savor Ryan's awesomeness on my own? Then again, even though I knew it was kind of typecast cheerleader-ish, I liked showing off, whether it was my stellar backflip, my curve-breaking test grades, or the fact that the hands-down most amazing guy in school loved me. Why should I have to keep quiet just because Ryan was afraid of the word "whipped"?

"Spaghetti," Alina said suddenly.

Was that supposed to make sense? Sometimes we had contests about who could name the most types of something—Alina was the reigning champion in the cheese category, but I'd smothered her in trees—but I was way too mad to play now.

Thirty seconds later, my willpower broke like an egg. "Manicotti," I said, loading my voice with acid to make it clear I was still upset. But Alina shook her head.

"My mom threw a Tupperware of spaghetti and sauce at my dad this morning," she said. "Nothing shattered, so at least they're learning, right? But my favorite jeans got splattered."

Oh. And then I'd stained her second favorite jeans. It wasn't really about the jeans, though. I got that. The coffee spill had just tipped her over the edge. I wanted to get Alina to talk about it—she tended to bottle things up if I let her—but just before school was not a good time for a crying jag.

"Rigatoni?" I offered, accepting her tacit apology. Alina smiled.

"Fusilli."

By the time we reached the parking lot of the Petalina Panthers, I'd stumped her with Rotelle. Alina practically tore her hair out trying to name another pasta in time, but then the clock ticked forward and she officially lost. I let out a whoop, startling some juniors, and pulled into our spot.

I cut the engine and hit the button to slide Cloudmonster's top into place.

"You think if I seduce Ryan after the Homecoming dance he'll forgive me?" I said as the machinery hummed. Alina twisted to retrieve our bags from the backseat.

"You were already planning to do that." She handed me my messenger bag. I hugged it.

"Not as far as he knows."

"Why you won't just wait until prom to lose your virginity like normal people, I don't know."

"Prom is passé. Besides, half our class has lost theirs already." I desperately wanted to be closer to Ryan, and we'd done almost everything anyway. His SUV had a very comfy backseat, but Homecoming weekend my parents were going out of town. They were away this weekend too, but empty house *plus* a dance? It was fate.

We got out of the car, and I patted Cloudmonster as I locked him. Just as the beep sounded, I noticed Mr. Haverton, my AP Psych teacher, walking towards us wearing his habitual frown. He pointed at the ground.

"Girls, chalking isn't permitted until Spirit Week," he said.

When I saw what he was talking about, I smiled. In front of Cloudmonster's bumper, the sidewalk was decorated with two red flowers, along with "The Roses" in elaborate script.

Did I mention that Alina's last name was Rose? Yeah, it led to punning by people who thought they were clever, but my first name being Alina's last was actually what brought us together in middle school. My mom had splurged on a designer bag for me, a black backpack emblazoned with *Rose* in pink.

Alina had stopped me at the entrance to the cafeteria. "Cool bag," she'd said, and asked where I got it. This was a Huge Deal, since Alina was as popular then as she was now, and since I was officially a dork for all of sixth and seventh grade. I'd stammered out the designer name, then added, "My name's Rose," as if Alina wouldn't know.

Maybe she didn't, because Alina had given me a once-over,

like she'd never seen me even though we'd had chorus together the year before. The summer before eighth grade, however, I'd done the caterpillar to butterfly thing—braces finally off, hair tamed by a flat iron, and new clothes that shouted style the way my ratty T-shirts decidedly hadn't. I think my mom finally took her gaze away from her reflection long enough to be horrified that her only child was unsightly. She hadn't wasted time fixing the problem, but until that day, when Alina asked if I wanted to sit with her, no one at school had bought my transformation.

I shrugged at Mr. Haverton. "We plead not guilty, officer."

"Then who's behind this?"

The only person I knew with enough artistic talent and suck-up-itude to do this was Lindsay Bonner, a junior cheerleader angling to be my sidekick in the run-up to nationals, which would put her in a prime spot to take over the squad captainship next year. I don't know if Alina came to the same conclusion, but she tossed her head.

"What can I say? We've got fans, Mr. H." Alina snapped her fingers and turned to me. "Linguini! Damn, how could I forget linguini?"

Mr. Haverton frowned at her in confusion, then sighed and walked away. I shouldered my bag and glanced around, but Ryan's SUV didn't show. It was getting close to bell-time. He *was* going to be late, and I felt bad. Ryan wasn't supposed to be a casualty in my latest skirmish with Paxton, and with the whole oak-poem debacle, I had a lot of apologizing to do.

"We'd better hustle," Alina said, then noticed my expression. "Don't worry, Rose. Ryan loves you. And with the Homecoming thing, you're golden."

I bit my lip, then pictured Ryan's green eyes and relaxed. Alina was right: I was worrying over nothing. Straightening, I gave her a cocky grin. "Gold? Try platinum."

Alina rolled her eyes, and we booked it to homeroom.

Twenty-four hours later, though, I wasn't platinum, or gold, or even silver.

And neither was my jail cell.

Find out more about *Torched* at www.andreacolt.com

Excerpt:

One by Leigh Ann Kopans

Young-adult science fiction novel about a girl with only half a superpower, and the boy who makes her fly.

Chapter 1

Most nights, and some mornings before sunrise, I sneak to the back of the shed, and I practice. I push myself off the ground, telling my body to go weightless, and hover. An inch, two, six, a foot. I stay there for seconds, then minutes.

I can't generate enough tension between my body and the air to take a step — can't even make myself drift. I'd give anything just to be able to float along like a freaking ghost.

I'm a One — a half-superpowered freak. It's the same sad story for all of us. Every superpower is made up of at least two distinct abilities. A kid can only fly if she can make her body light and then somehow propel herself forward.

Two powers. Not one.

Every One puts up with getting teased at Superior High, waiting for their second ability to show up. While they do, that One power starts to fade. There are still shimmers of it, but after a while, the kid quits trying and the One fizzles into nothingness. Then their disappointed Super parents ship them off to Nelson "Normal" High, like mine did.

Here's my secret – I never quit trying.

This morning, standing in our weedy backyard surrounded by a chorus of crickets, behind the ancient shed with chipping red paint, I go weightless. It happens so fast that I feel like I'm being pushed upward. My heart jumps.

Maybe…

I try to move, try to resist the air or push it away from me, and…nothing. I've been practicing so much that I've gotten fast at going light. So I'm a speedy floater. Great.

I could hover here forever, until my muscles strain, then burn, then ache, then tremble, weeping and getting eaten alive by mosquitoes. I'd just end up collapsing on the grass.

Nevertheless, I smile when I have to will some weight into my body to keep from floating above the shed. I definitely cleared three feet this time. Four years of hard work, and I can float an extra two feet.

Maybe by the time I'm eighty, I can say "hi" to the folks taking hot air balloon rides at the Nebraska State Fair.

I've watched all the old-school cartoons about misfit superhero kids that just need to work on developing their powers in order to totally rule. But I'm not a freaking X-Man. I know I can't work on my One power hard enough for it to become something better, something more. And it's not like I can magically give myself a Second.

I know. I know.

But my body whispers to me. It tells me I can fly, if only I'm brave enough, strong enough, determined enough.

I sigh and trudge back to the house, being careful to dry the dew from my shoes before heading in to get ready for my first day at Normal.

Dad slows the car as Nelson High comes into view. It's about a third of the size of Superior High, and the building's face is shot through with mossy cracks, dull with years of dirt the groundskeepers didn't bother to power wash before the first day. It's a strange contrast to the slick solar panels that blanket the roof, glinting silver-blue and reflecting the sky full of white, fluffy clouds. Most people think these older-model panels are hideous, but I always love it when a building's roof looks like an extension of the sky.

I can't take my eyes off the school, but I can feel Dad looking at me from the driver's seat.

"Dad." I pat his knee, a little awkwardly. "I'm just going to school. A different one, but still just school. I'll be fine. Maybe better. You know…than I was."

Dad eyes me. He doesn't believe me, but he's going to pretend he does.

I clear my throat. "You could have let me drive myself."

"What if you didn't get a pass? Or couldn't find a spot? Best to figure out the lay of the land…"

"The lay of the land" is one of the phrases Dad uses when he's worried. To be honest, I'm worried myself.

It's been ten years since my One power — going weightless — showed up. Seven years since Mom and Dad started to worry in whispered voices that I'd never get a Second, like the other kids. Only one year since I'd pretty masterfully failed at Superior High. One year since we all knew I would always float instead of fly — knew I would only ever be a One.

I was worried sophomore year at Superior would suck anyway, what with the fliers and the speeders and the teleporters rubbing their superpowers in my face just by being there. This way, maybe it doesn't have to.

"Did your hair for the first day, Merry Berry?" Dad flips an end of my hair with his finger. He's lucky I'm feeling slightly optimistic this morning, or I might mess his up right back. It looks flawless for work at the Hub, as usual.

I don't answer.

"Well," he says, "you look beautiful."

I humor him with a shake of my head and a smile.

All my features are slight, like my stature: a pixie nose, near-translucent skin with not even a freckle to decorate my cheeks, sparse eyebrows.

But my hair is the worst. The longer I let it grow, the more it tapers from thick brunette into dull, baby-fine ends, so I keep it short, at my shoulders. At least it waves instead of lying stick-straight. It's as wispy as the clouds on a clear day.

"I know Mom gave you a new lock. Did you clear out your smartcuff from last year?"

I roll my eyes and push up my sleeve to show him that, yes, the three-inch-wide, flexible tablet that holds all the information I need to get through the day (besides acting as a phone, GPS, and universal ID) has been wiped clean of all the stuff I needed at Superior. I don't tell him that I spent days hacking it to change the ID status from "Merrin Grey: One" to "Merrin Grey: Normal."

I pop the handle open and crack the door before we're even fully stopped. The football field, which peeks out from behind the school, has a fresh frame of bright white lines and a state-of-the-art looking scoreboard. I imagine the classrooms and locker rooms feature an according disparity. Great.

"Three-thirty, Dad. Okay?" I scoot myself out of the seat and onto the sidewalk. I let the door fall shut before he can answer. Not because I'm trying to be rude, but because I think if I hear Dad's voice now, I might cry and mess up the first mascara I've worn for about 10 months.

I'm not really upset about transferring from Superior High to Nelson.

I'm not. I'm not.

No one really says it out loud, but everyone knows Supers and Normals hate each other — too much decades-old bad blood. Supers say the Normals were jealous of them, and that's what caused tensions in the first place. Normals say they didn't know anything about Supers or whether they could be trusted.

I can see that. The way the Supers treated me — a sad, powerless kid — at SHS, I figure maybe the Supers scared the crap out of Normals sixty years ago. Super-strength or teleporting or being able to shoot fire could be terrifying if it was used as a threat.

Being a One is the worst — we're caught exactly in between Super and Normal, between stuck-up and terrified. Supers assume we're jealous, and Normals assume we're full of ourselves.

But here, I'm the new kid. No one knows anything about me. And no one has to. I take a deep breath through my nose, trying to ease the pit in my stomach.

I'm feeling a little too light this morning.

The wind feels like it might blow me away today. My loose, tissue-thin shirt hangs off my bony shoulders, blows against the curve of my back, and I know that everyone can tell how thin I am in the tank top underneath. My cuffed denim shorts go down to my knees, and because Mom picked them up in the girl's department, they fit snugly to my legs. That's fine since I learned that baggy pants only made me look ridiculous and even tinier.

I look down at the ground and take a deep breath. *Heavy. Be heavy.* My eye catches the one thing that can make me smile: my blue plaid Chucks. My brothers, Michael and Max, gave them to me for my sixteenth birthday last month. They thought I would like them, and they were absolutely right. Awesome kids, no matter how jealous I am of their insanely rare water-walking skills.

With any luck, this year will just be the boring prelude to where I really belong: occupying one of the spots in the Biotech Hub's summer internship program. I can do anything if it leads to that. I breathe deeply, hoping the air pressure in my lungs will make me heavier, and take my first steps toward a normal year at Nelson High.

I'm guessing there are 300 students in the whole school, which means everyone here knows everyone else. I let out a slow sigh of relief when I realize none of the students milling through the halls look at me. Either no one notices me, or no one cares. Or, since it's the first day and I'm new, I'll pass for a freshman.

I find the administrative office easily enough. I have to pound on the ancient touchscreen installed there to get my schedule, and when I finally manage to download it onto my cuff, it takes another torturous several minutes of waiting for the map of the school to appear. Through the thick, translucent office wall, something catches my eye. A tall, middle-aged man with glasses and black hair slicked back from his forehead pushes out the door. I swear the faint scent of licorice wafts out after him. He looks just like my organic chemistry professor from Superior High.

Maybe not everything about Normal High will be awful and unfamiliar after all.

I wave my wrist under the ID scanner in a variety of positions, but it just won't register. It's all I can do not to growl at it. Finally, it beeps its recognition, and I push out through the door as the stilted robotic voice croaks, "Good morning, sophomore Merrin Grey."

The hallway teems with students, but I think I see him. Yes. The black hair and those thick-rimmed glasses. That's got to be him. He's talking to a petite woman in a navy suit at the end of the hallway, leaning close to her ear, his eyes darting around at the students. They both nod at each other and start to walk down the hall, away from me. She motions toward a door.

As I get closer, I see the placard next to it reads "Principal Lee." I push through the crowd, but just as they reach the door, some clumsy kid rams into my shoulder, spinning me around. I don't even care enough to be embarrassed or yell at the jerk because, when I look up, the door's closing behind them.

I pinch my lips together, cursing under my breath. Mr. Hoffman is the one who came and dragged me out of the first horrific day of freshman biology, gave me a test, checked it over in about three minutes, and walked me to his class full of AP organic chemistry seniors without another word. While the other freshmen were trying to impress each other with their superpowers, I was staying behind in his classroom while he graded assignments, building models and generally kicking Orgo's ass. By the end of the year, I was working from a college textbook.

Mr. Hoffman's the one who made me think I could score a spot in the Biotech Hub's summer internship. Only five kids get to go every year, and I don't think a One has ever landed a chance.

I slump against one of the walls and check my schedule on my cuff. Nothing with Hoffman. I'm sure that, whatever he's teaching, it's so high level I'll have to get notes from Mom and Dad and a meeting with the principal just to get me a seat in the class. That is, if I actually did see him. I can't imagine why he would actually leave the state-of-the-art Superior classrooms to come teach at this dump.

I pass my locker, number 5637, noting its location. I have nothing to put in it yet and don't feel like programming the new print-scanning lock Mom slipped in my bag, so I don't even stop.

My first class is History: Modern American. I sigh with relief. At Superior High, freshmen take this class, so I should've already learned all this stuff. When I click through my reader to find the textbook, though, it's not *AMERICA: PATHWAYS TO PROGRESS*, the one we used last year. Instead, it's *AMERICAN HERITAGE AND YOU.*

There's no teacher's desk at the front of this classroom. When one of the few adults I've seen walks into the classroom, plugs a cartridge into a port on the back wall, and a 3-D projector displays a life-sized image of a teacher at the front of the room, I almost cry with disappointment.

This year, the weird projected holo-teacher says, we'll be focusing on American history post-Uranium Wars, but that she wants to go through a brief summary of that thirty-year period before we begin.

"Seventy-five years ago, foreign missiles suddenly and deliberately attacked a transport of uranium cores being transported to safe storage in the American desert, triggering the Uranium World Wars. The leakage into Lake Michigan made thousands sick, killing some and fundamentally altering the genetic structures of thousands of others.

"Many of these individuals developed extraordinary powers: for

example, super-speed or -strength, control of natural forces, teleportation, or telekinesis. Twenty years later, a diabolical group of five of these mutants, all leaders in their communities, formed a plan to assassinate the President of the United States and overthrow the government. Thankfully, it was stopped before damage was done.

"Never had our nation experienced such a threat from within our own borders.

"Most of the mutant population, some 30,000 strong, was concentrated around the Great Lakes. Even after the investigations and trials in the aftermath of said threat, we knew that some among them were potentially dangerous. Though most were loyal Americans, no one knew what would happen among this concentrated population if the new leaders' efforts congealed into a full-fledged revolution.

"Military authorities therefore determined that all of them would have to move. Tens of thousands of men, women, and children, all affected by supernatural abilities caused by the uranium contamination decades earlier, were removed from their homes to communities in established, out-of-the-way places. Of course, the government helped in any cases of financial hardship and — once the families had reached their destinations — provided housing and plenty of healthful nourishment for all.

"The mutated citizens wanted to go to work developing their abilities for the betterment of society. Many were allowed to do so in areas away from our main government and weapons stores and under appropriate safeguards, with the condition that they would work together with the existing United States government for the welfare of all United States citizens."

After every sentence this non-teacher speaks, my mouth drops open just a little farther. This is not the history they taught us at Superior.

Of course, they taught us about the Uranium Wars and the attempted government takeover. But the story of the camps sounded totally different at Superior.

Notices were posted. All mutated persons and their families were required to register. The evacuation was not cheerful. Stones were thrown, and jeers were screamed. It was out of fear, they taught us at Superior. Of course the Normals feared the Supers. But this twisting of history was inexcusable.

The lecture doesn't include video footage of the internment camps' shoddy housing or the mothers clutching their crying babies while they waited for the food trucks. It doesn't show the Supers waiting in long lines to see doctors they didn't trust or the makeshift schoolrooms full of dirty-looking kids in clothes that didn't fit quite right.

The holo-teacher directs us to the touchscreens in our desktops to answer some multiple choice questions about the lecture. I force my brain to go numb as I answer them the way I know the textbook wants us to.

I don't know exactly what this means for the next three years I'm supposed to spend here at Nelson High, but after hearing this lecture, I know I can't spend my life among Normals. No way.

I've got to get that internship.

By the time I've sat through calculus, bio, and English, I'm feeling grateful for the remote-lecturing holo-teachers — it means there's no one to ask me to stand at the front of the classroom and introduce myself. That is, until I realize that people are going to start asking me who I am to my face.

I have no idea what to expect from these Normal kids. Will

they suspect that I'm not like them? Can they see that I can float if I want to?

I manage to keep my head down all the way to my locker. All I want is to get there to ditch my sweatshirt, retreat to the girl's room — if I can figure out where it is — lock myself in a stall for a few minutes, and take a deep breath for the first time since I got here.

And maybe eat my lunch in there. Just for today.

I wiggle the handle of my locker, but it won't open. I bend down to take a look at it. No jerk's poured superglue in there or anything.

Before I know it, I'm shaking the stupid locker handle so hard that it's making a racket, and a few people standing near me look over and cock their heads. When I almost whack my own face with my struggling hand, I give up, resting my head against the cool, solid metal for a second, breathing in through my nose.

I am seriously losing it. Over a locker.

Half a second later, a shoulder taller than my head pushes into the metal door, and a large hand with long, thin fingers jiggles the handle side-to-side a couple of times and wrenches it up, letting the locker pop open.

I feel the warmth of his nearness against my cheek, countering the chill of the locker, like a shock on my skin.

The guy clears his throat, and says quietly, "They're tricky."

I barely glance at him before I look down at the floor, but I do catch that he has blond hair and glasses.

"You new here?"

Before I can answer, some guy halfway down the hall hollers, "E! Coming?"

The guy at my locker — "E" — gives his head half a shake, smiles a little, then turns to walk away.

And now everyone's staring at me. Great.

As soon as I find my way to the bathroom, I place both hands on the rim of one of the sinks, steadying myself there. After a few seconds, I splash my face with water and reach over to the soap dispenser. Everything about this place feels dirty.

As I'm lathering my hands, I notice the logo on the soap dispenser. Hub Technology — it appears on every product they make. It's four arcs, one for each Hub, intersecting in the shape of a circle. Someone has crossed out the "Hub" in "Hub Technology" and written "Freak" next to it.

Suddenly I can't get enough air into my lungs. I duck into a stall, sit on the toilet, bury my face in my hands, and take one, two deep breaths.

I hope with everything in me that all the other kids actually eat in the cafeteria.

Find out more about One at www.leighannkopans.com

Proof

21348008R00209

Made in the USA
Charleston, SC
14 August 2013